NATURAL SELECTION

NATURAL SELECTION

Dave Freedman

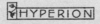

New York

Library of Congress Cataloging-in-Publication Data

Freedman, Dave
  Natural selection / by Dave Freedman.—1st ed.
    p.   cm.
  ISBN 1-4013-0209-2
    1. California—Fiction.   I. Title.

  PS3606.R4383N38 2006
  813'.6—dc22   2005057429

Hyperion books are available for special promotions, premiums, or corporate training. For details contact Michael Rentas, Assistant Director, Inventory Operations, Hyperion, 77 West 66th Street, 12th floor, New York, New York 10023, or call 212-456-0133.

FIRST U.S. MASS MARKET EDITION

Mass Market ISBN-10: 0-7868-9392-3
ISBN-13: 978-07868-9392-8

10 9 8 7 6 5 4 3 2 1

for PB

NATURAL
SELECTION

PROLOGUE

MONSTERS AREN'T real. . . . *Are they?*

Outer space. Toxic radiation disasters. Mad scientists' labs. These are the places monsters come from. Or so we've been told . . .

But aren't dinosaurs, crocodiles, lions, and sharks really monsters? Of course they are. And they come from right here on earth, and evolution made every single one of them.

So could evolution make *another monster*? *Today?*

It might be difficult for some to picture. Evolution is arguably the most powerful force in the earth's history, but paradoxically, it is also irrelevant to daily human life. Although the expression *survival of the fittest* is still used colloquially, the literal meaning no longer applies. For the human species, *real* life-and-death struggles, where the strong survive while the weak perish, have long since vanished.

This is not so in nature. Nature is an entirely different world, where there are no easy meals. When an animal in the wild is hungry, it must find, catch, and kill its prey, or risk dying itself. This harsh and brutal reality plays out daily, and evolutionary adaptations are a natural result. In just the past hundred years, literally thousands of such adaptations have been recorded: house finches in the Galápagos growing longer beaks, army ants in Brazil doubling their body weights, blind gourami fish adapting "feeler fins" in place of eyes, just to name a few.

But these are all examples of *minor* evolutionary change. What about major change? Or even spectacular change? Will we ever see a true "evolutionary leap," the equivalent of, say, the very first amphibian to crawl out of the ocean or the first tiny dinosaur to fly like a bird?

We will indeed. Only this time, the evolving species won't be a salamander or a bird. It will be a predator. In fact, it will be a phenomenally dangerous predator unlike any ever known. Previously, the species' entire existence was confined to the one place on earth still inaccessible by humans. But now a cataclysmic series of events is under way. One that will force the species out of its world and into ours for a violent first encounter.

The adaptive process is gradual and only a single animal, or perhaps a small cluster, will initially make the transition. Others might follow, but in the short term, human society will barely be affected.

Soon a small group of men and women will come face-to-face with a living nightmare. And then, even the skeptics among them will realize not only that monsters are real, but that evolution has just made the most horrifying one of them all.

PART I

CHAPTER 1

CHAD THOMPKINS took a breath of the fresh sea air. Oh yeah, he thought, this is why I became a lawyer—to buy myself this kind of freedom. He took another breath and let it out, long and slow. Chad was thirty-two and had just purchased a new forty-foot cabin cruiser. Along with his wife; his pal, Dave Pelligro; and Dave's new girlfriend, he was cruising out to Clarita Island, off the coast of Los Angeles, on this sunny June day. They were forty-five minutes into the one-hour trip from Newport Beach. The sea was fairly flat, tiny waves here and there, and they'd arrive soon. They had already passed the better-known Catalina Island, and Chad could see their destination in the distance. The plan was to work on their tans, then settle down for some lunch, though Chad was getting a little hungry already.

"Get me a sandwich, will you, Gabby?"

On a molded seat, his wife gave Chad an angry *I'm not your maid* look. But she tossed him a Saran-wrapped turkey and mayo anyway. "Here you are, Your Majesty."

He chuckled. "Thanks, Gab."

"Nice, huh?" Dave Pelligro said to his date, Theresa Landers.

In a tight sky-blue top, white shorts, and too much makeup, Theresa surveyed the water. "Beautiful." She turned to her host. "Thanks for having us, Chad."

"Glad you guys could make it. I'm sure I would have been bored if it were just me and Gabby out here."

Theresa shook her head. She didn't like Chad much. He was an arrogant preppy in a red polo who didn't wear sunglasses. But it was his boat, and she'd never "lunched" off Clarita Island before. She looked forward to getting there.

WITH THE exception of a small tourist area with restaurants, docks, and a beachside bar, the bulk of Clarita Island was undeveloped, overrun by trees and thick shrubbery. Clarita's western shore, mostly jagged black rocks, was downright desolate. Miles away from the clattering human noise of the island's eastern side, it was barren of people, the only sounds from the wind and tiny breaking waves.

Gliding on a current of air, a seagull appeared from behind the trees. A couple hundred feet high, the bird flew over the dark ocean and looked down, scanning for fish.

It saw absolutely nothing.

And yet something was there. The bird had missed them. They were perfectly still, just below the surface, watching it.

The gull spotted something and dove down. It plunged quickly, but then, just yards from the water, veered off. It had seen a strand of kelp, long and greenish brown, and mistaken it for a fish. Carried by momentum, the tiny flier ripped across the water, unknowingly passing a single pair of black eyes. Then it passed a second pair. Then a hundred. But still, nothing moved. The eyes simply shifted as the little feathered body tore past. They were all watching it.

CHAD THOMPKINS cut the gas, and the boat came to a bobbing stop. They were a few hundred yards from Clarita's main docks, where the mammoth Clarita ferry had just deposited the latest batch of tourists, mostly families with obnoxious kids. To the right of the docks, Chad eyed a beach slightly larger than a Wal-Mart aisle, jam-packed with out-of-shape sun worshipers. He found it unappetizing, to say the least. "You guys don't want to stop here, do you?"

Gabby, Dave, and Theresa all shook their heads.

Chad nodded. "My thoughts exactly." The lawyer hated crowds. As he started up the boat, he looked forward to the solitude of Clarita's always-deserted western shore.

THERE WERE more of them. Another hundred had crept up from below, joining the ones that were already studying the seagull. They still didn't move. They just watched the bird glide above the waterline.

Then their eyes shifted. From behind the trees, two dozen more gulls flew out over the water, also scanning for fish.

Looking down, the birds saw nothing but empty seas.

Then one of the creatures below them moved. From ten feet down, it swam toward the surface, a winged ray, flapping much like the birds themselves. A second creature rose, then a third. Then a hundred.

They ascended quickly all at once, shot clear out of the ocean, their bodies flapping frantically in the air.

There were so many that they were difficult to make out precisely. They were thick little animals, larger than the gulls, jet-black on their tops, gleaming white on their undersides. In the air, their wings moved much faster than in the water, their flapping rapid and uncoordinated. They rose to various heights, none more than ten feet, then belly flopped right back in. Then they leaped out again. Then again and again and again.

As the gulls watched them, their tiny hearts were beating faster than normal. They were birds and had bird brains, but on an instinctive level what they were seeing made them nervous. The strange creatures from the sea were trying to fly.

"WHERE THE hell is it?"

Chad Thompkins had been to Clarita's western tip before, but he still didn't see the familiar rock outcropping.

Dave Pelligro smiled at his date. "We'll get there soon."

Theresa nodded, eyeing the tree-lined shore. "I'm not in a rush."

But Dave *was* in a rush, or at least his stomach was. Gabby had made some special salami, ham, and cheese sandwiches just for him, and he couldn't wait to devour them. He squinted behind his ninety-dollar sunglasses, trying to see the western tip. "I think I see it." It was just off the black rocks, right near the pack of seagulls.

But then Dave saw something else. Something leaped out of the ocean then flopped right back in. A single animal. He squinted anew. What the hell was that? A jumping fish? He walked to the bow and pulled off his shades. Only birds were there now. He decided not to mention it.

As they motored closer, Gabby eyed the seagulls herself. "Keep away from those birds, Chad. We don't want them pestering us."

"Yeah, I wish I had a gun." And the pseudoyachtsman meant this; the damn birds were in the exact spot in which he wanted to anchor. But as they rumbled closer, the birds scattered, and Chad didn't consider why. "Hey, Dave, get the anchor."

"OH MAN, I'm stuffed."

They'd just finished lunch, and Dave Pelligro was proud of how much he'd eaten. Standing next to Chad, he glanced at Gabby and Theresa, in bikinis now and stretched out on lounge chairs in the back of the boat. "I could go for a little sun myself."

Chad nodded. "Go ahead. I'll be there in a sec." He wasn't in the mood to tan yet. As Dave joined the women, Chad leaned over the guardrail and stared at the sea. It felt good to get away from the office. He blew out a deep breath and watched the tiny breaking waves. He didn't notice the wind pick up.

THE WINGED creature was fifteen feet below the boat, its horned head pointed straight up. Its eyes were wide open, but it didn't see Chad. It didn't even see the boat. It was blind. A mutant gene had led to the deficiency, just as it occasionally did in humans.

The creature was by itself now, every one of its brethren long gone, many thousands of feet away. This one hadn't leaped from the sea earlier because it hadn't been able to. With all the churning caused by the others, it had become disoriented and literally couldn't figure out which way was up. But it had a sense of direction now. It could feel the wind.

It began to rise. Slowly at first. Then much faster.

I HOPE the wind dies down, Chad thought, eyeing the ripples as a gust blew his collar back. He suddenly squinted. What is that? It was something ten feet down. He leaned over the guardrail to get a better look.

It looked like a pair of beer bottles. Litterbugs, he thought. But then he saw the bottles were rising. Rather fast. Wait, they weren't bottles at all. Jesus Christ, they were eyes!

He jolted away frantically.

Noticing, Gabby rose from her chair. "What's wrong, honey?"

Dave stood. "You OK, Chad?"

Chad backed away as fast as he could when suddenly a thick winged ray shot out of the sea. It simultaneously caught the wind, then, out of control, blew straight toward him.

Trying to get away from it, Chad backed up faster but tripped and fell.

The thing rushed closer.

He tried to get up but couldn't.

It was going to land on him. . . .

And then it did. Catching his arm and the deck.

"Jesus!" He yanked his arm away but quickly realized he was all right. Breathing in gasps, he just watched it.

They were all watching it.

CHAPTER 2

AVE PELLIGRO thought it was a cool-looking creature, its entire body—horned head, torso, and wings—a single, seamless aerodynamic form. Flat on the white fiberglass deck, it looked like one of those black army planes he'd seen pictures of. What were they called again, stealth bombers? This thing was a miniature version, albeit with horns the size of shot glasses sticking out of its head. It had the rough dimensions of a fat Sunday paper, nearly as thick in its middle, its longest side across the wings, which tapered to cardboard thickness at their tips.

It didn't move. It simply lay on the textured white fiberglass.

Dave had never seen anything like it. "What the hell is it?"

Chad rubbed some slime off his arm. "Who cares what it is? Just throw it off my boat."

"I'm not picking that thing up."

They all slowly circled it, maybe ten feet away. Gabby stepped closer, peering down. It was a tough-looking little thing, muscular and solidly built, maybe twenty pounds. She surveyed its entire body when she noticed its eyes. They were the size of golf balls, cold and black, lodged in deep sockets at the base of the horns. They were horrifying eyes.

How come it's not moving? she wondered. Was it dead? She leaned in even closer and studied the skin. It was jet-black and slick, like wet vinyl. "It's pretty cool-looking, isn't it?"

Then she heard something. It was making a noise of some kind, and she tilted her head curiously. *"What's that sound?"*

Chad felt nervous. His wife's face was getting close to it and he gently tugged her arm. "Just get away from it, Gabby."

Dave suddenly leaned down. "I think I hear it too." He stepped closer, listening. The creature was emitting a wheezing sound, labored but slow and steady, apparently coming from underneath it. Dave dropped into a push-up position and watched it from another angle. The little form was gently rising and falling. He studied it for several moments then stood, visibly stunned. "Jesus Christ."

Chad turned, annoyed. "What?"

"I'm not sure but it looks like . . . It's breathing."

"It's not dead. Why shouldn't it be breathing?"

Dave gave his friend a you're-a-moron glare. "Because fish don't breathe air, Chad."

"Maybe it's still removing oxygen from the water in its gills."

Dave turned to Theresa, surprised by the sophistication of her comment. "What?"

Theresa inched toward it. She'd been watching the creature more closely than anyone. "I think it's some sort of ray."

Theresa was the youngster on the boat, her college days only a few years behind her. A University of Southern California grad, she'd once taken a course called Introduction to Oceanography and Ichthyology. Oceanography referred to the ocean's physical geography; ichthyology, to the study of fish. The creature on the white fiberglass was definitely some sort of ray, Theresa knew. Rays were cousins of sharks. Most rays were docile except electric rays and stingrays. But Theresa was certain this animal was neither of those. She didn't see a barbed tail. Many rays looked like disks or tiny flying saucers, with varying degrees of thickness. They varied tremendously in size. Some were huge, literally as big as small planes, others smaller than a human hand.

I've got a pretty good memory, Theresa thought, congratulating herself. She didn't recognize this particular ray, but there were tons of different species. This one was certainly thick. Her eyes settled on the horns. Unlike those on a kid's Halloween devil costume, these horns didn't stick up and out of the flattish head. Rather, they were parallel to it, flat against the boat deck and part of the body's same seamless form. The horns looked familiar, but Theresa couldn't say why. She again noticed that the creature didn't have a tail, so it definitely wasn't a stingray. How harmful could it be?

"Why don't we just toss it back in?"

Chad nearly laughed. "Be my guest."

Theresa shrugged. "I don't think there's much to worry about."

Dave and Gabby shared a look. Yes, Theresa was a crazy woman.

"Most rays are docile," the crazy woman said. "I'm sure it will be fine." She circled behind it. Then reached toward its back.

Dave watched her warily. "You sure you wanna be doing that?"

Her hands moved closer. "We'll find out. . . ." Her fingernails were about to touch it.

Suddenly it spun around and its jaws snapped open and instantly thundered closed.

"Jesus!" Dave yelled.

"Oh my God." Theresa couldn't believe it. The animal had moved so quickly! *Voom!* She didn't know rays could move that fast. It was perfectly still now, and she focused on its mouth. She hadn't noticed the mouth earlier. Its opening was a slit the size of a stapler, massive in proportion to the body. And its bite hadn't only been vicious but powerful. Theresa hadn't noticed any teeth—she remembered that most rays didn't even have teeth. But even without them, its bite had been so strong it could have broken her fingers.

Gabby stared at her hand. "Are you all right?"

Theresa checked that all five fingers were in fact still there. "Yeah, I'm fine."

Suddenly the creature leaped up into the air.

"Oh my God!" Gabby slammed back into the railing, nearly falling overboard.

But the animal simply fell back onto the deck, landing with a wet thud.

On its back now, its underside was even whiter than the fiberglass.

Dave Pelligro studied it anew. The mouth's slit looked very large indeed, maybe larger than a stapler. And the stomach was slowly moving up and down, in harmony with the wheezing sound. The damn thing looks like it's breathing to me, Pelligro thought.

The creature suddenly leaped up again. It nimbly flipped in the air, landed rightside up, then once again, didn't move.

Dave, Theresa, and Gabby just stared at it, anxious to see what it would do next.

Chad had another reaction. "That's it, I'm killing this damn thing. . . ." He walked to the bow to find something to whack it with. But then he paused. What's it doing now?

The little animal was rapidly flapping its wings, whacking them hard on the deck like a loud jackhammer.

Dave just watched it, amazed. Jesus, the damn thing's trying to fly. And failing miserably. It showed no sign of lifting off.

The animal seemed to realize the same thing and abruptly stopped.

It's been out of the water at least five, maybe ten minutes, Theresa Landers thought. How can it survive that? And how did it move its wings so quickly? Theresa had seen rays swim before, and they always moved very slowly, like birds in slo-mo. She supposed, however, that when their wings were only pushing against air, they could move much faster.

The animal moved again—sort of. The muscles on the left side of its back suddenly seemed to rapidly flex, and Theresa watched them. Wow. She'd never seen muscles move like that, almost like superfast rippling waves. Boy, were they fast! Then the muscles on the left side stopped and the ones on the right began. The process repeated itself. Theresa just watched, fascinated.

Then, very quickly, the muscles froze and the body's front half lifted off the deck until the horned head was completely vertical. Then the animal effectively stood there, about a foot tall, its front half in the air, its back half flat on the white fiberglass.

It looked quite menacing and Theresa got the hell away from it.

But the ray didn't budge. It simply remained where it was, like an upright seal or a stiff jack-in-the-box. Looking at it, Theresa remembered that many ray species didn't have spines. Their entire bodies were made of cartilage that made them extremely flexible. A stiff jack-in-the-box indeed.

The wind started gusting, and the horned head slowly turned.

What's it doing? Theresa thought. She wasn't sure but it looked like . . . Did it sense the wind?

The shifting head froze, and then it happened.

In a surprisingly fluid series of motions, the creature leaped off the deck diagonally, pumped its wings, and, with a touch of luck in the timing, caught the wind and . . . flew. Flapping frantically and lacking body control, it headed straight for the guardrail, smacked into it, and tumbled into the sea.

Everyone rushed over to try to see it.

But there was only dark water. The animal was gone.

Suddenly Dave squinted. Did he see a second one? No, he didn't think so. He slowly looked up at Theresa, astonished by what had just happened. "Do you believe what we just saw?"

Theresa didn't answer. She just gazed at the water.

But Dave was dumbfounded. *"That thing flew, for Christ's sake!"*

Theresa turned to him, visibly stunned. "It did. It really did."

"Wow," Gabby said simply.

Chad marched to the head of his vessel. "Yeah, really incredible. A jumping fish, up in the air for a whole second. You guys call Jacques Cousteau; I'm out of here."

As Chad turned on the engine, Theresa wondered if she actually *should* call Jacques Cousteau. Or at least the closest thing to him. Eighteen months earlier, she'd visited a brand-new manta-ray aquarium in San Diego. The visit had been a big disappointment—there hadn't even been any mantas—but if the place was still in business, she wondered if she should discuss the afternoon's events with someone there. She decided on the spot. She'd go. Theresa loved puzzles, and she wanted an answer to this one right away.

What the hell had they just seen?

CHAPTER 3

"**S**O IS what I saw of interest, Mr. Ackerman?"

Harry Ackerman, fifty-two and rail thin, looked up from a note-filled legal pad and focused on Theresa Landers, sitting on the other side of a small brown wood desk. Theresa had come to this massive complex of aquariums, once known as Manta World, to describe the ray she'd seen off Clarita Island to whoever would listen. A bored UC San Diego girl, chomping on bubble gum and obviously working a summer job, had started writing down Theresa's statement when Ackerman had overheard and taken over.

Ackerman was practiced at taking statements and questioning people. He hadn't interrupted her. He'd simply let her talk and written down every single thing she'd said. He dismissed the crazy parts, about the flying and possible breathing, as exaggeration. People regularly exaggerated when they retold a story they were excited about.

Ackerman was actually excited himself—though he didn't look it. Harry Ackerman rarely looked excited about anything; it just wasn't in his character. With the exception of an antique Patek Philippe watch with lots of Roman numerals and a $62,000 price tag, he didn't look like a multimillionaire either.

He'd started to take her statement because he'd been bored. Theresa was an attractive young woman in a too-tight all-white outfit and too much makeup. But looks aside, Ackerman had just assumed she was another loony. They regularly came into most marine facilities claiming they'd seen this fish fly, that fish breathe, or that sea monster playing cards. The statements were always outlandish and very comical. And that was why Ackerman had spoken with her. He'd been reading debt covenants, trying to find loopholes that could allow him to desert Manta World's lenders legally, when he'd decided he'd needed a laugh. Theresa had indeed given him one, at least with the flying and breathing parts. But then a funny thing had happened. As she'd continued, she'd started to make sense. Ackerman was no expert, but the animal she described in vivid detail sounded like it might somehow be . . . significant.

"It most certainly is of interest, Theresa. I have some questions if you don't mind."

Theresa nodded. She wasn't sure what she thought of Harry Ackerman. He sounded nice; it wasn't that. It wasn't his attire either. Khakis and a button-down; who could argue with that? His eyes had something to do with it. They were cold eyes, dead too—even when he was silently laughing at her. He hadn't laughed out loud, of course, but Theresa knew he'd found her amusing. Given what she'd told him, she hardly blamed him. But he wasn't laughing now, not even silently—Theresa could tell. Something she'd said had caught his interest. She thought he was way too corporate to be a marine biologist, yet he seemed to know his stuff.

"Ask away."

"You said it was black on its top and white on the bottom?"

"That's right."

"Pure jet-black and pure milky white—you're sure?"

Theresa thought for a moment. "Yes."

"No shades of brown or gray?"

"No, none."

"No stripes or dots or other discolorations?"

"No, nothing like that."

She didn't change her story, Ackerman thought. He'd asked her the same questions several times, and she'd come back with identical answers. She had a good memory and wasn't making this up. Exaggeration perhaps, but not outright fantasy. What had she seen out there? The coloring she'd described was classic manta ray—numerous physical traits were also—but several details didn't fit. She'd said the animal didn't have a tail, and mantas almost always had tails. Many other physical characteristics didn't jibe either.

Harry Ackerman stroked his cleanly shaven chin. He didn't like mysteries. He preferred things to fit into neat, clearly defined packages. Frustrated, he glanced down at something.

What's he looking at? Theresa wondered. She could see it was something beneath the desk; it looked like—

"Are you a marine biologist, Mr. Ackerman?"

He glanced up, and the eyes seemed to chill further. "I'm a lawyer by training actually. Now—"

"A lawyer? How did you get into this?"

"I'm on the board." This was sort of true.

Theresa nodded and looked around. They were seated in Manta World's massive east wing. She couldn't believe the size of the place, with towering ceilings and wide spaces that made a shopping mall look small. Except for the two of them and the bored college girl gabbing on the phone at another small desk, the place was empty. There wasn't even a sign out front anymore. There certainly weren't any manta rays. Theresa stared at the biggest fish tank she'd ever seen in her life. It was literally the length of a football field and the height of a three-story building, filled with turquoise water and nothing else.

"They all died."

She turned. "Excuse me?"

"The mantas. They all died. We don't know why, we just couldn't keep them alive."

"Oh." Theresa stared at the tank anew. "I'm so sorry."

"It's still very sad."

And Harry Ackerman meant that. He wasn't on Manta World's board; he *was* the board. Ackerman was a patent lawyer by training, but at the height of the late-nineties dot-com boom, he'd done what others had. He wrote a business plan on a cocktail napkin, created an Internet company, and took it public. The goal had been to create a legal marketplace, an online subscription service that lawyers across the country could use to share information on cases. The company IPO'd for $1.8 billion, and while it went bankrupt just nine months later, the investment bankers had their fees, and Ackerman had obscene amounts of money, $500 million after taxes. Rather than buy a pro basketball team or sailing crew, he invested his money, and not necessarily wisely. He put massive chunks into a handful of the era's other hopeful high-tech ventures, including a fiber-optic company, as well as Manta World. None had done well.

But besides money, what Ackerman also craved was respect from a group of people who didn't dole it out easily. Despite his success, none of the real players at the dozen charitable foundations and golf clubs that he and his wife had joined would give him the time of day. This elite group of entrepreneurs, real-estate moguls, entertainment CEOs, and hedge-fund managers hardly spoke to him. In their eyes, Harry Ackerman was nothing more than another dot-com idiot who'd gotten lucky. They were always polite but brief in that typical CEO style Ackerman despised. The message was clear: he could join all the charities and golf clubs he wanted, but he wasn't in *their club*.

Ackerman longed for the day when he would be, when he and his wife would casually stroll into a thousand-dollar-a-plate black-tie charity ball, and heads would quietly turn. Isn't that Harry Ackerman? Then all the fancy types would jockey to meet *him* for a change—to ask him to dinner or discuss investments and his favorite flavor of ice cream.

The Manta World project had been a disaster from the get-go. Five years old and counting, it was almost dead, even though Ackerman still had a handful of marine biologists under contract. They were on the ocean in tropical Mexico now, still with the nominal goal of trying to make it all work. Ackerman had been in salvage mode for months, but maybe, just maybe, this woman could help take things in another direction. But he had to be sure. "You said it didn't have a tail."

"Correct."

"No tail of any kind, not even a little stump?"

"No, nothing."

Ackerman nodded. Still sticking to her story.

"And it wasn't more than a foot across the wings?"

She nodded.

"You're sure? It wasn't, say, three or four feet?"

"No. I remember it distinctly—it was as wide as a phone book is long."

Again, exactly what she'd said before. "And you said it was . . . stocky?"

"Very—muscular, too."

"Hmm."

Something else that didn't fit. Mantas could be called stocky, but only when they'd grown into adults. When they were immature, they were extremely thin, almost wispy, certainly not stocky and muscular. It didn't fit.

Theresa watched Ackerman closely. For the first time, he looked downright puzzled. Without a trace of embarrassment, he removed what he'd been surreptitiously studying earlier: a large coffee-table book, *Circumtropical Rays of the World*. He opened it on the table, and Theresa watched as he flipped colorful, glossy pages, settling on a spread about mantas. Theresa noticed a photo of a manta with a scuba diver, and her eyes bulged slightly. That thing's enormous! The size of an airplane! Boy, did they get big!

Ackerman turned to her. "You said its eyes were large?"

"Very."

"How big were they?"

"The size of golf balls."

"Golf balls?" He stared at the pictures again. "And it had horns sticking out of its head?"

"Yes."

"Hmm." Ackerman didn't know rays like the biologists who worked for him, but he'd still learned a great deal about them in the past years. The horned head was a very distinctive feature; very few ray species had it, only two that Ackerman knew of. They were the two he'd kept going back to, the manta and the mobula ray. But the large eyes were something else that indicated that the ray had been neither of those. Ackerman shook his head. What had she seen? He flipped another page, focusing on a marble ray. Marbles were round, unmistakably so, but she'd said this animal was shaped like a stealth bomber, the classic manta shape. He flipped again. Not a stingray either. All stingers had clearly defined spines with tails that were impossible to miss.

He shook his head. That left only one other possibility. A new species. What if she'd actually seen a new species out there?

"Thank you for coming in, Theresa."

"Oh." Theresa hesitated then uncrossed her legs. She'd been dismissed. She stood.

Embarrassed by his bad manners, Ackerman stood as well. "Sorry. What I meant is I really appreciate this. It could be useful. We'll see." He smiled warmly and shook her hand.

"My pleasure."

Ackerman picked up the phone. He wanted an expert opinion. Now. As he dialed, Theresa pretended to look for something in her pocketbook. She watched as he tapped out a very long series of digits. She heard a jolt of static and guessed it was an overseas connection. "Hi, Monique? It's Harry Ackerman calling for Jason. . . . Oh, someone just came in who may have seen a new species. Can I speak with him, please?"

As Theresa left, she wondered who Jason was. Perhaps a marine biologist? As she entered Manta World's massive empty parking lot, she realized she'd forgotten to mention the animal's very odd muscle movements. She wouldn't bother now. She got in her car and drove off.

Moments later, Ackerman hung up the phone and was quietly thrilled. One of the world's premiere experts on rays had just said something fantastic: he had no idea what the woman had seen.

Well, they were going to find out. Ackerman picked up the phone again. "Get me a car. Now."

CHAPTER 4

"**W**HAT'S HE doing here?"

Lisa Barton wiped a strand of dark hair away from her binoculars.

It was another gorgeous, sunny day here in the middle of the tropical ocean. Alone at the front of a white fiberglass yacht, Lisa had been sunning herself on a lounge chair when she heard the boat engine in the distance. She was a very pretty twenty-nine, with a young face, big brown eyes, and soft white skin that never darkened thanks to heavy use of number thirty lotion. People often said she looked like something out of an animated film, the damsel in distress who's rescued by the hero. Lisa Barton was anything but a damsel in distress. Her opinions were strong and, when necessary, so was her mouth. She was also a top oceanic nutrition specialist.

She held her hair back, peering through the binoculars. Yes, it was Harry Ackerman, her boss's boss and the man who was paying them. Why was he here? Ackerman was a businessman and never showed up to chitchat. They were in the Sea of Cortés on the Gulf of California in tropical Mexico. Ackerman's yacht cut out, and Lisa guessed he'd stopped to take in the scenery or something else.

In a bikini, she put on a bright green T-shirt and khaki shorts and realized both were wrinkled. Son of a bitch! Lisa loved clothes and was sick of living like a vagabond. She hadn't signed up for this. Manta World was supposed to have been a land-based job. No ocean work— none. But things hadn't gone according to plan, the aquarium had been a disaster, and now the six of them—four men and two women— were virtually living on the water, either in the five tiny bedrooms below or at junky seaside motels that went for thirty-nine dollars a night with continental breakfast included.

Their boat, the *Expedition*, actually wasn't half bad. White fiberglass with lacquered wood accents and a rough-hewn teak deck, the ninety-foot yacht had been converted into a floating research facility. With generous amounts of space in the front and rear decks, it featured a tiny living room; an even tinier galley; three bathrooms like those on United Airlines coach class; and a satellite for TV, phone, and data transmissions.

They'd been out here for eighteen months. For eighteen months, they'd done nothing but try to determine why the manta rays had died in their specially designed San Diego aquarium. They'd considered everything—food, water temperature, salinity, amounts of natural and artificial light. They couldn't figure it out. It had been a frustrating, unsolvable mystery, and everyone except Jason Aldridge, their leader, had accepted that.

Still, frustrations aside, at least they had jobs, and Lisa had grown accustomed to the relative lack of outside intervention. She was focused on her core research now and didn't like surprises. She slipped on some leather flip-flops and wondered again: Why's Ackerman here? She turned to two men at the very back of the boat, a good distance away, so—

"Darryl! Craig! You guys know what Ackerman's doing here?!"

"What?! Just a second, Soccer Mom!"

Lisa shook her head. *Soccer Mom.* This had come from Darryl Hollis, what he swore she'd become if she ever got off the boat and actually met anyone. Lisa liked Darryl, but she didn't care for what he was doing at the moment: shooting at skeet again. God, she hated that. Darryl and Craig were always very careful with their weapons, but it still made Lisa nervous to see arrows and bullets flying off the back of the boat. But what else were they going to do? They were as bored as she was. Finding little use for their advanced degrees, they had to do something, and needlepoint wasn't an option. The two of them, as well as Darryl's wife, Monique, were former ROTC members who'd met during active duty as they learned to fly Sikorsky helicopters and fire rifles. The guys weren't "regular army" at all, more fun-loving, likable partyers. Darryl was tall, preppy, and black, with a powerful, athletic frame. Craig was a slovenly white guy with a beer gut who rarely did his laundry in the stacked machines below deck. They got along famously.

As Lisa walked closer, Craig shook his head at a jammed skeet machine.

Darryl just smiled at her, his customary big, toothy grin on full display. "I told ya I'll never make any bad calls on your little ones, right?"

Lisa paused. "I don't have any little ones, Darryl."

"You will one day, and if I'm a ref, no bad calls for the Barton kids."

"Barton? So these kids will have *my* last name?"

A nod. "As will your husband."

Craig looked up, annoyed. "Wait a second. I'm pretty traditional about that kind of thing. Lisa, we're gonna have to talk about that before the wedding."

Lisa chuckled. Craig Summers had been lusting after her for a year.

"Even if your kids go against the Hollis kids," Darryl continued, "I'll still treat 'em right."

Lisa paused. *"The Hollis kids?* So you and Monique are expecting now?"

"Planning, Lisa. The great ones always plan." He looked down at Craig. "How's it going with that, Sloppy Joe?"

In jungle-green cargo shorts and a stained white undershirt, Craig whacked the skeet machine. "Fantastic."

Lisa put the binoculars back to her face. "You guys don't know why Ackerman's here?"

"Got it!" Craig said suddenly.

"Hold on, Lisa." Darryl grabbed his hunting bow off the deck, and Lisa put down the binoculars to watch. As much as weapons frightened her, she found Darryl's archery skills fascinating. She eyed his bow. It wasn't some skimpy thing, but a formidable piece of equipment, nearly as thick as a baseball bat at its center, made of shiny, hard cherrywood, and four feet long fully strung. Darryl put the whole thing over his big shoulder. Darryl was one-eighth American Indian. As a kid, he'd spent eleven summers on his grandfather's Indian reservation, owned by the Limble tribe of Hoke County, North Carolina, and was very experienced at hunting with a bow and arrow. Before she'd met Darryl, Lisa had thought of bows and arrows as archaic, almost cute devices. But when Darryl described one of his hunts, she realized there was nothing cute about seeing a twenty-eight-inch, hundred-and-fifty-mile-per-hour speeding projectile plunge into a stampeding wild boar's chest. Bows and arrows were serious weapons, Lisa now knew. With characteristic cockiness, Darryl had assured her they were more dangerous than guns and carried far more foot-pounds of kinetic energy than bullets did. Why were guns so popular? Because any idiot could fire them. Craig Summers could fire a gun.

"OK, gimme some skimmers, Craig."

"Yes, your lordship." Craig put the machine on a sidewall and angled it out to sea.

Darryl shook his head at Lisa. "So hard to find good help these days."

Craig looked up angrily. "Ready?"

Darryl was still facing Lisa. "Yep."

Whoosh! A skeet rocketed away above the ocean. Then: *Whoosh! Whoosh!* Two more.

In a fluid series of motions, Darryl turned and fired three arrows. *Voom! Voom! Voom!* In rapid succession, they sped away at truly frightening speeds. *Crack!* One skeet down. *Crack!* A second. *Crack!* A third.

"Jesus," Lisa said quietly, watching white ceramic pieces scatter over the turquoise sea.

Darryl nodded coolly. "Don't mess with the Big Dog."

"I won't. So you guys don't know why Ackerman's here?"

The two men shrugged.

"Maybe to follow up on that talk he had with Jason earlier."

They turned. It was Monique Hollis, Darryl's catwalk-pretty wife, up from below deck in cropped khaki pants and a navy polo. Monique was in her early thirties, exceedingly bright, tall, elegant, and with an easygoing down-home attitude that made her impossible to hate despite her looks.

Lisa nodded. "What was that about anyway?"

Monique shrugged. "Somebody came in saying they might have seen a new species."

"Really?" Normally, Lisa wouldn't have cared about a new species sighting, but strange things were happening in the world's oceans. The plankton supply had been behaving particularly oddly, and Lisa and her colleagues in the oceanic nutrition community had no idea why. Plankton were tiny, even microscopic, plant and animal organisms that drifted near the ocean's surface in large masses. With a PhD in oceanic nutrition from UCLA, Lisa Barton had dedicated a large part of her life to studying the stuff. During the past weeks, with the aid of the *Expedition*'s onboard Plankton Measuring System, she'd seen levels drop alarmingly. Typically, plankton masses congregated around thermoclines, zones of abrupt temperature change between overlying warmer waters and colder, deeper waters. But recently, a number of thermoclines Lisa had personally sampled indicated levels 62 percent below normal. In addition, measures of turbidity, conductivity, temperature, and photosynthetic radiation were all way off.

In the vast, interconnected ecosystems of the oceans, plankton were at the very bottom of the food chain. Problems with them usually led to problems elsewhere. Lisa didn't know if it was related or not, but she'd recently read reports about several of the Gulf's medium-depth species—the Sargassum triggerfish, medium-bill wall fish, among others—migrating to considerably shallower waters. Then, six months ago, the government's annual midocean survey had reported that for reasons unknown, there had been a significant depletion in the Gulf's midocean plant life, especially crinoids, a type of starfish, and gorgonians, a type of coral.

Something significant was going on in the ocean. It had affected many animals, and Lisa wondered if it would affect more. She paused. Or had it done that *already*? She suddenly turned to Monique.

"What new species?"

CHAPTER 5

MONIQUE HOLLIS cleared her throat. "It was sighted off L.A., I think."

"What was it?"

"I only heard bits and pieces. I think it had something to do with a flying fish."

"Oh." Lisa rolled her eyes. "One of those." Then she considered the possibility more seriously. "A real flying fish or just something that leaped out?"

"This woman thought a real flying fish."

"In the *Northern Pacific Ocean*?"

There were fifty known species of "real flying fish," part of the Exocoetidae family, and almost all of them were found in the tropics, a number in Barbados. Exocoetidae were basically regular-looking fish with oversize pectoral fins that could spread out and be used like wings. Lisa recalled that several species of squirrels, lizards, and snakes flew by the same principles. Typically, these fish glided just above the water's surface for a few hundred feet, usually to escape predators. But Exocoetidae were nowhere near the Northern Pacific Ocean.

Lisa's eyes narrowed. "Did this woman identify the species?"

"I think she said it was some sort of ray."

"A ray? Really?" Rays had nothing to do with the Exocoetidae family. "Well, what did Jason say?"

"What could he say? He was polite to Ackerman, but you know Jason."

Lisa shook her head. Yes, she knew Jason. "Why would Ackerman care about something like that anyway?"

"I guess if he really thinks it's a new species, he might want us to go look for it. We're doing next to nothing down here, and we're still under contract after all."

Lisa shook her head. She hoped Ackerman didn't make them go off on some wild-goose chase. "It was probably just a little bat ray that wanted to get some air."

Darryl shrugged. "Who cares what it was."

Craig looked up at the blazing sun. "Agreed."

"Then again," Darryl added enthusiastically, "if Ackerman paid us more, I'd love to go look for a new species."

Monique eyed her husband sadly. "He won't be paying us more money, Darryl."

"Yeah." Darryl suddenly looked morose. "I guess not."

All soccer-mom jokes aside, the Hollises wanted to start having kids in the next couple of years, and the topic of money was a sore one. Children were expensive.

Seeing how down they suddenly looked, Craig gently turned to them. "Take it easy, guys."

Darryl and Monique nodded, almost obediently.

Lisa smiled to herself. The Hollises and Craig Summers were an odd, yet strangely copasetic triumvirate. Lisa admired their loyalty and often wished she had something like it.

She looked down at the turquoise water, wondering where Jason was. "Jason's been down there a long time. Do you think . . ."

She suddenly spotted something enormous and black rising fast from the depths. She backed up nervously. . . . It continued to rise, ten feet from the surface, turned, and flapped away. She breathed again. Just a manta ray. A diver rose up right after it and climbed quickly onto the boat.

Standing in fins, Jason Aldridge was five-ten with intense eyes and dark hair. He was male ambition in a wet suit, no interest in firing weapons, working on his tan, or anything else. A lean thirty-four, he was a single-minded workaholic, the type who liked to be busy every minute of every day and got antsy when he wasn't. He was also more than a little depressed, but that wasn't easily detected.

No one turned when a second diver with a yellow underwater camera draped around his neck popped up. A chunkier thirty-four, his name was Phil Martino. He climbed up happily and grabbed a towel to dry his curly dark hair. "Hey guys."

There was no response. With the exception of Jason, no one liked Phil Martino. He was the only one of the six who didn't have a PhD in ichthyology—though it wasn't intellectual snobbery that made him unpopular. It was more that he served no purpose at all. As Darryl once put it, he was always "just hovering around, an all-around annoying dude." Phil's connection to the group was Jason. The two had met during an introductory marine-bio class at UCSD. While Phil later flunked out of that class, he and Jason never lost touch. Since college, Phil had held many jobs, including one as a professional photographer. So at Jason's urging, Ackerman hired him to document the original manta aquarium's progress pictorially. Phil Martino had been with the team ever since.

Lisa turned to Jason, seated on the deck now. "FYI, Ackerman's here, Jason."

He didn't seem to hear her. He angrily yanked off his fins. "I thought you were coming down to take that jellyfish sample."

"Oh," Lisa paused. "I was, but then I saw Ackerman."

"You should have come down before that."

"Whatever."

He stood. "No, not whatever, Lisa. You don't tan well anyway, and we needed a sample."

She faced him fully, not backing down. "Yeah, why'd we need that again?"

"Because the only thing these mantas seem to be eating lately are jellyfish."

"Yeah, so?"

"So if we determine jellies are safe to eat out here, they could be safe in the aquarium and—"

"And . . . *what*? We can restock and try to make it all work one more time?"

He looked at her blankly. "Yeah."

"You actually believe Ackerman will pay for that at this stage?"

"If we give him something promising . . . yes, I do."

She shook her head. "We have five months left on our contracts, Jason, and then *we are gone*—do you understand that? *Gone.*"

"You don't know that, nobody knows that."

"*Everybody* knows that except you. If the job market weren't so awful, we'd have new jobs already."

He hesitated, glancing at the others. "You've been looking?"

She paused. "*I* have. I can't speak for anybody else."

"Then that's your business. It doesn't mean Manta World can't work."

"You're not being realistic."

"I don't see it that way."

"It doesn't matter how *you* see it, it's how Ackerman sees it."

"Well, I still think—"

"Jason, Manta World is *over*! Don't you get that? Over!"

He hesitated, glancing at the others. They looked away, and he wondered if they agreed with Lisa. He didn't care. "We still have a job to do, and taking food samples is a critical part of that."

"*You* could have done it if it was so important."

"You're the nutrition expert, Lisa!"

"And you're the one who's always looking over my shoulder!"

"Because you don't do your job! And even when you do, it's for your own personal agenda, not the team's!"

Now it was Lisa's turn to glance at the rest of the crew. Jason's "personal agenda" comment had struck a nerve. But Lisa could play rough too. "You look over my shoulder because you're a control freak who can't trust anyone to do anything."

"I like to make sure things are done correctly." Jason's voice was tight.

Lisa just shook her head. Everyone on the boat thought Jason was a control freak. He constantly checked and rechecked their work on everything. But Lisa did feel a little guilty. Jason wasn't a bad guy, and taking jellyfish samples was indeed part of her job description.

"I'll take a sample after Ackerman leaves, OK?"

"Don't bother, they're all gone now."

She was shocked. "*All* the jellyfish are gone?"

"Those mantas were hungry down there."

Wow. A day earlier, Lisa had seen literally *tens of thousands of jellies*, normally enough to feed a small herd of mantas for a week.

He eyed her curiously. "What do you make of that?"

"Like you said, they must have been hungry."

"You think it's related to the low plankton levels?"

Darryl turned suddenly. "I thought levels had gone back up."

Lisa shook her head. "No, that was very brief. They've actually gotten worse. Are the mantas still jumping out more than usual, Jason?"

A sober nod. "A lot more, actually."

"Does that . . . concern you at all?"

"I wouldn't say it concerns me exactly, but it is kind of . . ."

"Strange?"

"Yeah, strange."

Many ray species, especially mantas, regularly leap out of the sea, and even Jason, who despite his recent failures was still considered a top-ten expert on the great creatures, didn't know why. There were theories of course: to rid themselves of parasites, to evade predators, even just to have fun. Regardless, they had been leaping out much more frequently than usual. Within just the past two months, the Gulf's mantas had been seen heaving their four-thousand-pound winged bodies out of the sea up to seven times per *day*, considerably more than the typical three times per week.

More strangeness in the world's oceans, Lisa thought. Then she heard the sound of a motor in the distance and put the binoculars back to her face. "Five minutes until Ackerman."

Craig licked his lips lecherously. "Watch for bags of money falling off the side of his boat."

The others chuckled, but Jason turned urgently to Phil. "Borrow your laptop real quick?"

"Note time? Sure."

As Phil trotted downstairs, Lisa rolled her eyes. Jason had been using Phil's laptop every day for months to record his notes. Taking notes was indeed an important part of a marine biologist's job, but as with everything else he did, Jason was beyond thorough; he was obsessive. Phil handed him a sleek black IBM, the only computer on board configured to the *Expedition*'s satellite data link, and still in his wet suit, Jason began to type.

Minutes later a massive hundred-and-thirty-foot yacht motored closer at the pace of a snail. In khaki shorts and a $250 silk golf shirt, Harry Ackerman stood atop the towering helm. "Ahoy, everybody!"

They put on their best happy faces. "Ahoy, Harry!"

"Hey, Mr. Ackerman!" Phil yelled cheerily.

"Tie this, please." Ackerman hopped on board, handing Phil a braided white nylon rope. "And hold this for me too." It was a worn leather day planner. "Hey, Monique."

"Hey, Mr. Ackerman, how are you?" Monique wondered why he was holding a yellow legal pad.

"I'm fine, thanks." Ackerman had always liked Monique Hollis. She had such an easygoing nature. Lisa Barton was also quite attractive but considerably rougher around the edges. The man's expressionless gaze swept past Darryl and Craig, then settled on Jason.

"Harry, we weren't expecting you."

"Hey, Jason."

They shook hands, and Ackerman noticed Phil's laptop on a seat. Ackerman smiled to himself. Jason was no doubt typing his notes again, before he'd even changed out of his wet suit. Ackerman loved Jason's obsessive side, such a hard worker. Though Jason certainly wouldn't love the reason that Ackerman was here.

"I want to discuss that sighting near Clarita further. Have you had any thoughts on that?"

Jason didn't answer at first. His eyes simply shifted. But he looked like he had quite a few thoughts indeed.

CHAPTER 6

JASON ALDRIDGE didn't change gears easily. He was great at focusing, at working on *one subject*, but change had always been problematic. The five-year quest to make Manta World a reality had been his life, and the notion of ending it in failure wasn't even conceivable. So he simply didn't respond to Harry Ackerman's question. He was a smart, intense guy, but the implications of the answer were beyond his comprehension.

Ackerman cleared his throat. "I said, I'd like to discuss the sighting near Clarita Island. What are your thoughts?"

The question hung in the heated, tropical air for a second time. Lisa Barton, Phil Martino, and the Hollis-Hollis-Summers triumvirate all waited. Jason just stood in his wet suit, eyeing the empty plain of blue water, his intense eyes shifting slightly. "I'm still processing it."

Ackerman grinned. "Still processing it, huh? That sounds like double-talk to me." He turned to Phil Martino. "You agree, Phil?"

"I sure do, Mr. Ackerman."

Ackerman smiled wider. Phil Martino reminded him of a new puppy, the dumbest one in the litter. Darryl and Craig shook their heads in disbelief, and Ackerman continued. "Come on, work with me here, Jason. You're an expert, and I'm trying to understand this. What do you think of the idea of a new species of ray?"

Jason looked him in the eye, respectful but not afraid. While his workaholic tendencies hadn't given him success or riches, they had given him confidence. He feared no one. "I don't think much of it."

Ackerman nodded. He'd always liked Jason's directness and total lack of fear. Sure, there were those who said he was an unambiguous failure after the aquarium debacle, but Ackerman had always thought the guy had balls. At the moment, he didn't care.

"Correct me if I'm wrong, but you and I went over this ray's description in great detail, and you said you didn't recognize it. Is that still the case?" Ackerman held up his yellow pad. "Because I have my notes right here if you want to go over them."

"That's OK."

Jason didn't need notes. He remembered the ray's description well, if only because it wasn't familiar: stealth-shaped and very thick, black on one side and white on the other, with large black eyes, a huge mouth, and horns on the mouth's sides. And aggressive behavior. Apparently, the ray had snapped at someone.

Jason doubted it was a new species, and yet if the description was accurate, he didn't know what known species it belonged to. Ackerman had correctly nixed several candidates, and Jason later eliminated half a dozen more, the *Raja binoculata* and the *Torpedo californica* among others. There were additional possibilities, but they were all remote.

"You think it could have just been a newborn manta, Jason?" Craig Summers asked.

"Near Clarita? Highly unlikely."

Jason turned to the water. But it was strange, wasn't it? Because what had been described—the horned head, the wide mouth, the black top and white bottom—were all classic signs of the manta ray. But not only were mantas much thinner, they were also tropical and lived in warm locales near the equator. Sure, they migrated to cooler waters in the summer, and a wayward manta from Mexico could easily have strayed into Southern California waters. But only if it had been an adult. A newborn never would have strayed that far. Unless—he turned to Darryl and Monique.

"Any way a pregnant adult would have migrated up from Mexico?"

Darryl readjusted his polo's collar. "To spawn in Clarita?"

"Yeah."

"By itself?"

Jason shrugged. "I guess so."

"Highly unlikely."

Jason nodded. "Monique?"

"A pregnant animal migrating *that far* from familiar waters to spawn? No way."

"What about a *group* of pregnant mantas, then? Could they have migrated up together?"

Monique raised an eyebrow. "It's technically possible, but I doubt it."

So did Jason. While mantas regularly spawned in groups, he'd never heard of them doing so in strange locales. He pulled his dark hair back with one hand. What had that woman seen off Clarita Island? He looked out over the water again. If the physical description was accurate, perhaps it was a new species. But so what? What the hell did a new species have to do with his manta rays?

Ackerman stared at him coldly. "So could it have been a new species?"

"Possibly."

"Does *possibly* mean likely?"

A glimmer of anger flashed in Jason's eyes. He had work to do here. They still had to find a group of mantas capable of surviving in the aquarium—find them, transport them to San Diego, get the aquarium prepared, then perform countless other tasks that could easily take five months. He didn't have time for this.

"Jason, does *possibly* mean likely?"

"*Possibly* means possibly."

"Well, that's enough for me. I think you should go to Clarita and find out for sure if it's new or not."

"What? Why?"

"Because we need to do *something*, we need to make some kind of progress here."

"We *are* making progress, Harry."

"Not the way I define it."

"How do you define it?"

The eyes turned colder. "In dollars and cents. *I've lost millions on this, do you understand that?* This entire project was a disaster from the get-go."

"Harry, we can still fill that aquarium with manta rays. I promise we can do it."

"No, we can't."

"I'm telling you, I really think we—"

"I've been patient; you know I've been very patient."

"And we appreciate that, but if you'd just let us—"

"Jason, Manta World is over." This was said matter-of-factly and without emotion. "I'm not capable of financing it any further and . . . that's it. You know this isn't what I wanted."

Jason didn't move. Under the beating sun, he suddenly felt light-headed in his wet suit, like he'd fall off the boat. He became aware of his feet on the teak and steadied himself on a guardrail.

"I see," he managed to say. He couldn't believe it. He was numb.

Lisa sighed inwardly. She felt bad for Jason, though she wasn't entirely sympathetic. It would always be painful for a guy with his driven personality to adapt to change. Not only was it impossible for him to trust anyone to do his or her job, he also couldn't see when something just wasn't working. He didn't have an off switch. But even Jason couldn't ignore this. The plug had just been pulled, and it was time for the man who had once been called "the next Jacques Cousteau" to finally move on.

Lisa shook her head. The next Jacques Cousteau. She'd first heard the nickname before she even met Jason, six years before, when *Ichthyology Journal* had run a cover story on him in an entire issue dedicated to mantas. In an article filled with glossy pictures, the magazine had chronicled everything, from his typical boyish obsession with the great fish, to his PhD in ichthyology at UCSD, to his then ranking as the number one manta ray expert in the world. The whole thing generated an incredible amount of hype and put Jason's professional expectations through the roof. Then Ackerman had come calling.

The original idea for the aquarium had actually been Ackerman's. A lawyer who suddenly had obscene piles of money after his IPO, Ackerman hired a consulting firm that determined that a new manta aquarium in San Diego could *triple* another famous water park's already booming attendance. The primary reason for such a prediction: nothing like it existed anywhere in the world. While existing marine facilities had exhibits featuring smaller ray species, none was anywhere near the spectacle that a warehouse-size aquarium filled with creatures as big as planes promised to be. Kids loved mantas, absolutely loved them, and across the globe, their parents said they'd pay handsomely for the privilege of seeing them. The consultants determined that if the "right aquarium" were constructed, it could become an attraction on a global scale. Big enough to give Ackerman the respect he so craved. And big enough to put him in *the billionaires' club*.

A manta aquarium had made sense for its research potential too. Ichthyologists, and all animal researchers, tried to analyze their subject in their natural habitats whenever possible, but the reality was that studying large, wild creatures swimming freely in the open ocean was extremely difficult. By comparison, in captivity, animals could be studied extensively and around the clock. Indeed, most of what was known about dolphins—the most analyzed ocean-dwelling species on earth—had been learned from studying specimens in captivity. That had been the aquarium's precise research objective: to allow Jason Aldridge and others to analyze manta rays as thoroughly as dolphins had been.

Construction of the aquarium, which Jason himself had designed, had been completed in two years. Financial pro formas predicted the $95 million cost would be paid off in eighteen months. On every front, hopes had been sky-high for the aquarium's opening. It never happened. The opening was delayed, rescheduled four times, then scrapped entirely. For more than three years, it had been one disaster after another. And through everything, including his own fall from grace, Jason had been nothing but optimistic, a fighter with a fantastic attitude who never gave up.

The biggest problem had been the mantas themselves. For reasons unknown, they simply wouldn't stay alive. Forty-seven died throughout a thirty-two-month period, and neither Jason nor any of the experts hired to support him could determine why. Anything and everything was done to save them. Nothing worked.

Finally, Ackerman decided that Jason, then barely ranked in the top ten in his field, and the few members of the team who still had contracts should get back to working with mantas in the wild, nominally with the goal of still trying to make the aquarium work. They'd been in tropical Mexico ever since.

Ackerman shrugged. "Anyway, it's done. Unless something else comes up, we're turning the aquarium into a home for killer whales."

Jason glanced at Lisa, swallowing an entire humble pie. "I see."

"And I certainly don't want to go this way, but I've already checked with my lawyers, and I have the legal right to terminate your contracts right now. Or you can investigate this. My hope is the latter might lead to something significant."

Jason eyed the grooves in the teak deck. He couldn't believe it. It was over. Just like that, a glass of ice water to the face. He'd just wasted five entire years of his life. He could hardly think. But he somehow managed to consider what Ackerman was proposing. A stockier version of a manta with large eyes? Possibly a new species? So what. Jason hadn't tested the job market in years, but he wondered if UCSD had any new research grants. Or maybe another university. He wasn't wasting more time on Ackerman's wild-goose chase.

He looked out at the ocean, the tropical blue plain. He'd miss it. Then he noticed Monique. She looked . . . different, not laid-back at all. She had tears in her eyes, a dab of black mascara dripping onto her shirt's collar, and was clutching her husband's hand tightly. Son of a bitch! Money had never been Jason's primary motivation, but his coworkers . . . They had bills to pay, rent checks and lease payments for apartments and cars they never used. And the Hollises wanted to start a family soon. While the concept of family was foreign to Jason— he didn't even have a girlfriend—Monique and Darryl were very much planners, and they'd been socking away large portions of every direct deposit to provide for their unborn kids. They were highly educated, both with PhDs in oceanic migration from USC, but if Lisa was right . . . if the job market really was that tough, and they *both* suddenly lost their jobs . . .

Darryl smirked at Craig. "Are there any American unemployment offices in Baja?"

Craig started to return the crack when Monique glared at him through wet eyes. He shut up. So did Darryl.

Jason exhaled. He wanted *nothing* to do with this new project, not a goddamn thing. But the Hollises were his friends. . . . "Monique, what do you want to do here?"

"Oh." Monique wiped her eyes and gathered herself. "Excuse me. Well, I'll do whatever you want, Jason, you know that. But if Mr. Ackerman thinks we should look for this new species near Clarita, than I think we should seriously consider it."

"Me too." This had come from Craig now, with as stern a look on his face as Jason had ever seen, a look that said, *Don't fuck my friends.* Then Craig's cell started ringing, and he answered.

Jason turned. "You too, Darryl?"

"Yeah." Darryl's face was blank, his normal joviality gone.

"Lisa?"

"Definitely."

Ackerman eyed the happy puppy. "How about you, Phil?"

"Absolutely, Mr. Ackerman, I'd love to."

They all turned to Jason.

And Jason felt like screaming. One dull pain was about to be replaced by another. He nodded, his face as blank as a cement wall. "We'll get started right away."

Just then, Craig hung up and Jason immediately noticed that he looked a little stunned. "What is it, Craig?"

"There was another sighting off Clarita Island."

"Of what?"

"Little rays trying to fly. *Thousands* of them."

CHAPTER 7

*T*HOUSANDS?"

Summers nodded. "Some Santa Cruz colleagues of mine are doing a project up there, testing crustacean breeding habits. An elderly couple from Europe said that's what they saw."

Jason narrowed his eyes. "They said they were *flying*?"

"Trying to. Leaping from the sea anyway."

Jason paused. This sounded like another version of the phenomenon he'd seen right here in Mexico. "What did they look like?"

"They just said small rays. It was from a distance with binoculars."

"Can we talk to them?"

"They left today, and my friends didn't get their names."

Lisa shrugged. "It was probably just a bunch of the same bat rays."

It had to be, Jason thought. Though he'd never heard of that many bat rays leaping from the sea. *Thousands?*

"Whatever they were, this sounds promising." Ackerman turned. "So you'll get started right away, Jason?"

The blank stare returned. "Of course."

"Excellent." Ackerman wondered if it was just bat rays up there. But if it was something else . . . Financing the discovery of a new species could be significant. As trophies went, it could be sophisticated, too, considerably more so than, say, winning the America's Cup and dumping overpriced champagne into the sea with bought-and-paid-for professional sailors. The backer of a new species discovery. That had panache. "Hopefully, it will be a new species. We'll see. Phil, give me a hand, please?" A minute later, the rich man was gone.

"Damn it." Phil Martino still had the leather day planner in his hands. "Jason, he forgot this."

Jason nodded distantly. "Hold on to it. Darryl, you and Monique chart the course to Clarita. We'll go when it's dark. . . ." He turned to go below deck but—

"Sorry I lost my cool there, Coach." Monique hugged him. "I know this is the last thing you wanted. I'm very grateful, Jason."

"No problem. I'm sorry we had to go through it." He broke the hug. "Take it easy, OK?"

As he started to go below deck, Darryl slapped him on the back. "Future generations of Hollises thank you too."

The couple chuckled, but as Jason went downstairs he was unable to focus on their relief. What he'd been dreaming of every waking moment for the past five years was suddenly over. Justify the failure with a philosophy, he told himself. Something like "it wasn't meant to be" or "things happen for a reason." He felt like crying. Was this happening for a reason? Maybe there really was a new species out there, maybe even a significant one. Yeah, right. He went below deck and disappeared.

"YOU GUYS chart the damn course yet?" As the dipping yellow sun neared the horizon Craig Summers was anxious to get going.

Seated on a molded seat, Monique looked up from a map, dumbfounded. Charting a course the old-fashioned way would take all of ten minutes, but the Hollises had waited since Jason had said they'd travel at night, when people could sleep. Still, Monique couldn't believe Craig had the stones to pester them while he did absolutely nothing. "Just about, Craig. Why don't you just take it easy and get another beer."

Craig drained the can of Bud in his hand, missing every trace of sarcasm. "Good idea. Want one, Darryl?"

"Yeah, I—"

"No, he doesn't." Monique turned pleasantly. "Do you, my loving husband?"

Darryl hesitated. "No, dear, I don't. I like being stressed out. Craig, I'll just have a mineral water, please."

Craig chuckled. Thank God I'm not married. Wives, even cool ones like Monique, told you what to drink, what to wear . . . Marriage could wait—maybe forever. He started going down the steps when he noticed Lisa, seated near Phil and writing notes on a little yellow spiral pad.

"You only drink red wine, right, Lisa?"

She looked up. "You know, I could actually go for a beer. Thanks, Craig."

She returned to her writing, but Craig didn't budge. Wasn't beer too pedestrian for Lisa Barton? "You feeling OK?"

She continued writing. "Sure, fine!"

Craig didn't move. He knew Lisa well. She was pissed off about something, and if the reason was what he thought, she had real gall. "Are you OK about going up to California? I mean, you can do all of the *personal research* you want up there too, right?"

She shot him an angry look. "Yeah, I guess so. And what's wrong with *personal research* anyway, Craig? I mean, give me a break. All day long, you and Darryl drink and shoot skeet, Monique reads books, Jason lives in his fantasyland, Phil shoots pictures, and I work. So *I'm* shirking *my* responsibilities?"

Craig glanced at the crushed Budweiser can in his hand. "Barton, you make a salient point. I'll get you that beer. . . ."

"No thanks, Craig. I don't want one."

"Oh." Craig turned in mock surprise to Phil Martino. "Phil, I didn't see you there. You don't want one? OK." He shook his head at Lisa—who cared about Phil Martino? Then he glanced down at Lisa's notebook and couldn't help but notice the word *GDV-4* in big underlined letters. "You've been reading up on my favorite virus, Lisa?"

"Actually, I've been wondering if it might be causing the reduced plankton levels."

Summers eyed her dubiously. GDV-4 was an infectious oceanic disease, the fourth strain of the gray distemper virus. "No chance. GDV-4 only infects large, fully grown fish and mammals, the highest levels of the food chain. It would never infect plankton."

"You sure? 'Cause we were wondering the same thing."

Craig turned. This had come from Darryl, who was standing with Monique.

Then, from another direction, someone else said, "So was I. You sure it's not possible?"

Summers turned once more, to Jason, now at the foot of the stairs in red dive shorts and sandals. "What is this? A frickin' ambush? Absolutely not. GDV-4 has not infected the plankton supply."

"Are you sure?" Lisa persisted.

"Who are you talking to here, Lisa? Of course I'm sure. That virus has never been found anywhere outside the Atlantic Ocean. It's nowhere near here, and even if by some fantastic event it was, it would never go as low down on the food chain as your beloved plankton."

"Have there been any updates on it? Anything about it spreading?"

"It hasn't spread at all. In fact, it's disappeared again. They can't find it anywhere, not even in the Atlantic."

"Are you still testing for it here?"

"Three times a week. I do more than just drink and shoot skeet, you know."

"You do?"

Summers didn't smile. He looked her dead in the eyes. "Look, I have no scientific basis for thinking GDV-4 is even within a thousand miles of here."

Lisa nodded. Despite his stained undershirt and beer belly, Craig could be convincing when he wanted to.

Jason walked up the stairs. "GDV-4's strictly a surface virus, correct?"

"Every known case of it has been."

"And it infects only fully grown fish and mammals?"

"Correct."

"But that doesn't mean it couldn't be in deeper waters, does it? Or further down the food chain?"

"Jason, please don't second-guess me on this."

"I'm not second-guessing you, Craig. I'm just saying, viruses *can mutate,* can't they?"

"Of course viruses can mutate. And sure, one day, this virus could o lower down the food chain, turn up in the Pacific, find its way into deeper waters, whatever. Look, it's a tricky virus."

Jason nodded. A tricky virus indeed.

It wasn't known to the public at large, but the fourth strain of the gray distemper virus was a distant relative of the canine distemper virus found in dogs and infamous within the oceanic community. Originally dubbed *gray* due to its initial discovery in beached gray whales in northern France seven years prior, GDV-4 had recently become a much more serious problem, earning the nickname "AIDS of the sea" because of the devastation it wrought on its victims. Degrees of concern varied greatly among scientists, from the doomsayers who claimed it was within twenty years of destroying all ocean-based marine life to the vast majority who were only moderately concerned. The reality was that GDV-4 had only a microscopic presence in just one of the world's major oceans, the Atlantic, and even there, the vast bulk of marine life was totally unaffected. It wasn't even a blip on the commercial fishing industry's radar screen. Craig Summers, with a PhD in oceanic viruses from UC Santa Cruz, shared the majority opinion. He thought GDV-4 might very well peter out, and possibly soon.

But others worried about what would happen if it didn't peter out. What if it spread and made further inroads into the Atlantic? Or the Indian? Or if it found its way into the massive Pacific? What other species would it affect then?

Craig shot them all dirty looks. "I'll let you know what else I hear."

Monique nodded. Lisa was right. It was more strangeness in the oceans. Maybe all of it—the virus, low plankton levels, strange migrations—were somehow related. "Who knows; maybe there really a new species near Clarita."

They all considered the possibilities when Phil Martino, who'd simply been listening, cleared his throat. "Excuse me, guys. I'm gonna go download my pictures now."

No one said anything. The triumvirate and Lisa didn't care what Phil Martino did: download his pictures or jump off the boat.

Jason nodded agreeably. "OK, Phil. Sounds good."

As Phil bounded below deck, Darryl turned. "We worked out the route, Jason. Ready when you are."

Jason eyed the sky, the night almost upon them. They were actually leaving. He hoped they'd determine quickly that the sighted animal was not a new species. Then he could get on with his life. "Let's do it."

THE TRIP to Clarita Island took two days. While Jason licked his wounds and tried to get his head screwed back on, the others did what they always had—a minimum amount of work and a lot of relaxing. Lisa lay in the sun, Monique read a bad book, and Darryl and Craig drank and shot skeet. Phil and Jason talked about the old times at UCSD and also about Phil's problematic love life. Phil's girlfriend had recently broken up with him, and he needed to figure out why. Jason helped him realize it was for two reasons: Phil's unrelenting travel schedule and also his general flakiness.

Jason didn't have girlfriend problems because there hadn't been any girlfriends, not for years. For Jason, the cliché was true: if you don't believe in yourself, you can't get someone else to believe in you either. As great a fighter as he was, the reality was that the constant failures related to Manta World *had affected him*. In fact, they'd quietly crushed his soul. He hadn't believed in himself for some time. Like everyone, Jason wanted a wife and family one day, but not tomorrow. For the moment at least, he was better off alone.

They made great time, moving past Baja into the waters off San Diego, then Orange County, then Clarita Island. No one except Darryl was paying particular attention when they passed Clarita's main docks. His eyes narrowed when the *Expedition* motored toward a familiar rock outcropping on the island's isolated western shore. He didn't know why, but he sensed something was there.

"We're here."

CHAPTER 8

LISA BARTON watched as Jason stared down at the dark, rolling waters. No, they weren't in tropical Mexico anymore. It was an hour before sunset, and they'd anchored off Clarita. All of them except Darryl Hollis were suited up in full-length black neoprene wet suits. In yellow mesh shorts and a black tank top, Darryl would stand watch on the boat while everyone else scanned below. They quickly went over the predive checklist, confirming that regulators, dive lights, and all of the other equipment were working. They were about to jump in when Monique noticed a seagull plunging into the sea. "I wonder how the fishing is today." Then the bird popped up, devouring a struggling silver snack. "Looks like it's pretty good."

THEY DESCENDED slowly, feeling the water's chill around their bodies. Good visibility, Phil thought, pausing to check the camera strap round his neck.

Farther below, Jason surveyed. With the aid of dive maps, he'd chosen this exact spot carefully. Though Darryl and Monique had plotted the route to get here, Jason wouldn't trust them with choosing the exact area in which to dive; it was too delicate. They were very close to deep waters here, unreachable not only by scuba but by almost anything—or at least by anything man-made. The area directly

below, however, was only a hundred and fifty feet deep. It looked like
an underwater quarry of sorts, a massive brown boulder the size of a
ten-story office building, off to the right. Jason followed Monique and
Craig toward it.

As Monique swam along the huge rock, it seemed to grow in size,
becoming a small mountain. Then, as she passed a few foot-long
kelp strands, she realized there was a second mountain, about ten
feet to the left, that created a narrow canyon. She turned on her
flashlight and swam right into it, shadows engulfing her. Eyeing the
dark sandy bottom far below, she wondered if there were any secrets
there. Then she saw movement out of the corner of her eye. She
froze. Adjacent to a deep horizontal crevice, she realized something
was inside it. Jason swam up next to her, and they shined their light
in. It was a small school of cod, about thirty of them, the light
streaming past their dark green bodies. Another midsea species.
Neither asked the question audibly, but Jason and Monique both
wondered why the cod were all the way up here. Phil swam next to
them and snapped a picture. They dove farther. Three stories from
the bottom, the walls abruptly widened, and they fanned out. Reaching the sand, they flipped over, entering an area the size of a living
room, the walls mottled brown rock.

To her right, Monique noticed a gap at the bottom of the wall. She
knelt, illuminating the sand within, and it was obvious: the sand had
been disturbed by something. Not by water currents—there were no
sweeping patterns—but by an animal of some kind. She lay down to
get a better look. Farther in, the sand looked even more disturbed.
She tried to wedge herself in, but her tank caught. She pushed her
hand toward the area. She could almost reach it. . . .

She stopped. Was something still there? She pulled her hand
away. No, she didn't think so. She noticed Lisa kneeling at another
gap and swam over. Lisa was eyeing a piece of kelp, just floating in
the gap. Through their masks, the women shared a look. Kelp was a
surface seaweed. Even if there had been nearby forests, which there
weren't, it was unusual to see it in water this deep. Had something
brought it here? Monique grabbed the strand and studied it. She
saw nothing special and let it go. Instantly, Jason swam up, grabbed
it, and took a look for himself. Monique and Lisa shook their heads.

On the far wall, Phil laughed heartily inside his mask. Good old trusting Jason.

As they ascended out of the canyon for the first time, they noticed the terrain to their left. The sun had shifted, and the area was much more fully lit than it had been a moment ago. Jason spotted something on the sand that he'd missed earlier. A small pool of darkness, a mini–oil slick, probably from a local fisherman illegally dumping. Then he noticed that something was *in* the pool. He drifted downward. It was a marking of some kind. He kicked toward it. It was an imprint. He kicked closer still. An enormous imprint, fourteen feet across the wings and twelve feet long. As the others joined him, he shook his head inside his mask. How do you like that?

WHY'S HE holding that harpoon? Jason was immediately nervous as he popped out of the water. And why does he have that look on his face? Jason had never seen Darryl Hollis with such a look. But Darryl just scanned the dark seas, not even acknowledging him. "How's it going, Jason?"

Does he have peripheral vision I'm not aware of? "Hey, Darryl. You OK?"

"Fine. See anything good?"

Jason removed his mask. "Yeah. What's with the harpoon?"

Darryl finally looked down. "I guess sunsets just make me nervous."

Jason turned. A sunset indeed. The sky was gorgeous, a vast tapestry of lavender, pink, and ruby red. Jason loved Southern California's sunsets and knew from personal experience that they were some of the most stunning in the world.

Monique popped out and smiled, as relaxed as ever. "Hey, Husband."

"Get out of the water, Monique."

"What's your problem? Nice to see you, too."

Darryl turned to her directly. "Monique, get out of the water."

She was about to tell Darryl to shut his smug mouth when she noticed his harpoon. Darryl Hollis never played games with his weapons. She got out of the water.

"What's up, Big Dog?" Craig smacked Darryl's back later on deck. "Something big and bad out here?"

Darryl hesitated. He didn't know why, but he suddenly felt like an idiot. He scanned the dark seas anew, little waves breaking here and there. They seemed to be laughing at him now.

"Nothing big and bad here except me, brother."

Craig glanced at Monique. They'd both seen Darryl become alarmed before, more times than they cared to remember, in dangerous war-torn deserts, soft-sand Caribbean vacations, scuba diving, sometimes just when it was dark out and the crickets were chirping. There were occasionally good reasons for it, but very often there weren't.

"How do you think that kelp got all the way down there, Monique?"

Monique turned to Jason. "You know, I don't know. Darryl, we saw some kelp almost two hundred feet down. And a manta imprint in an oil slick."

"You sure that was from a manta?" Jason said.

"Can we discuss this later, Jason?" Craig toweled off his head. "I mean we're done for the day, right?"

Jason turned irritably. "Yeah, Craig, sure."

Summers walked toward the bridge.

"Note time, Jason?"

"Oh." Jason turned to Phil Martino, standing there with his open laptop out. "Yeah. Thanks, Phil." He took it.

As Phil walked off, Jason realized that except for his notes, they were indeed "done for the day." He stared at the sunset again. Jason had never been able to stop and smell the roses, but savoring a sunset was another story. The sky was stunning. Then he noticed Darryl, staring at the water with the same strange look in his eyes. Jason had always respected Darryl's Indian heritage and suspected it gave him an unusual intuition into the ways of nature. He was a levelheaded guy to boot, so if he sensed something, Jason wondered what it could be. Maybe a shark?

But then Darryl shook his head. He was imagining things. Craig and Monique were drinking Coronas now, and he joined them. So did Lisa and Phil.

Still in his wet suit, Jason put the laptop on his knees and began typing. He'd seen more than he realized down there and he noted all of it: the school of cod, kelp, mini-oil slick, imprint. The imprint.

As he tapped away, Jason kept going back to it. What sort of animal had made it? A manta? Or something else? Then Craig started the boat, and Jason eyed the sunset a last time. It was still gorgeous.

AS THE *Expedition* motored toward the land, Jason had no idea that they were being watched.

CHAPTER 9

THEY FELT the boat's vibrations.

They were more than four miles away, but they felt them and quite clearly. Thirty-five hundred feet down, a level considered deep by human standards, they lay perfectly still. Earlier, one of them had mistakenly ventured into much shallower waters and settled in an oil slick. But they were all together now. They were spread out across the ocean floor. They were unseen. There was no light here. Not now, not ever. It had been filtered out many thousands of feet above.

They were enormous creatures, and they were comfortable here. They knew the darkness intimately. And yet they might be the last of their kind who did; their much smaller brethren were spending increasing amounts of time in another place. The tiny animals were swimming toward it now. These larger creatures could see them, though not with their eyes.

THE SMALLER animals rose slowly and in far greater numbers than before. Tens of thousands of the little winged bodies ascended, flapping steadily. The water was still pitch-black, but the light, they knew, was coming. At least for some. When they reached the five-hundred-foot mark, half dropped off. At two hundred feet, as the water became a dark gray, another large group fell back. At one hundred feet, the first faint traces of the sunset appeared, and another group stopped. But several thousand continued, and this was more than double the number that had ventured to this point earlier.

The blind one was no longer with them. After tumbling off the boat, the little creature had rejoined its herd below. It hadn't been welcomed back. It was savagely killed, crushed inside one of the larger animal's mouth. More than once, it had scared off prey with its careless behavior. It would never do so again. Neither would the others that had been seen leaping from the sea. They too were gone.

The small animals continued rising. When they were just ten feet below the surface, a beautiful watery sunset shone into their black eyes. They didn't see it. They simply swam straight up, moving faster.

First, one shot out of the water. Then another. Then all.

In the air, their wings suddenly moved much faster. They flapped rapidly, frantically, doing anything and everything to fly. None succeeded. Their bodies flailed, knocked into one another, and fell right back in.

They flew out again, over and over. After fifteen minutes, some began to improve. Rather than leap straight up, one group began angling out diagonally, then flapping. Another group didn't flap at all, but simply glided, successfully when they caught a strong wind just the right way. No two animals were exactly the same. They all tried something different. As the last shades of color fell from the sky, their awkwardly moving silhouettes were all that could be seen against the horizon. One after another, they rose from the sea, flew as best as they could, then fell back in and tried again.

Then they detected movement far below. It was their much larger relatives, not going to the surface, but somewhere else. These animals would follow them, but when they were ready. As the skies turned black, they continued to practice.

CHAPTER 10

"**W**E COULD be onto a new species here."

Near Clarita's main docks, they were at a tavern, in a huge wood booth next to a mounted TV with a Dodgers game on. Everyone was dressed casually, eating burgers and club sandwiches. No one responded to Jason at first. Darryl and Craig had just finished their mug beers and were trying to flag down a waitress. Lisa was doodling on one of those place mats for kids. Phil Martino looked visibly famished and was simply devouring his burger. Monique was the only one listening. "I agree, Jason. I think it could be something new."

"You do?" Craig turned irritably. "How does some manta imprint in an oil slick add up to a new species?"

"You don't know that imprint was from a manta, Craig."

"What else would it be from?"

"How about a bigger version of what that woman saw? She saw a newborn; then an adult made the imprint. And what she saw was no manta—not with that description."

Summers wiped some ketchup on the thigh of his jeans. "Then maybe she described it incorrectly, Monique. Or maybe what she saw and what made the imprint were unrelated species."

Lisa nodded. "A manta made the imprint, then separately some bat rays flopped out of the water."

Chewing his burger, Phil turned to Jason with a raised eyebrow. "That's an interesting point, no?"

Jason pushed away the remains of his club sandwich. "No. Two different species coincidentally shaped identically in the same part of the Pacific at the same time? They had to be the same species. You ask me, that could be something new."

Phil turned, still chewing. "What do you think about *that*, Craig?"

Summers shook his head. With his curly brown locks and cud-chewing demeanor, Phil Martino wasn't just a moron but a gutless jellyfish who'd go any way the wind blew. "I think a shoal of mantas spawned up here, then some playful newborns flopped out of the water. That's a simple explanation."

"Except it doesn't make sense," Darryl said.

Summers turned. "Why not?"

"Because massive manta shoals don't migrate to unfamiliar waters to spawn."

"Is that really so unprecedented? You and Monique have *never* heard of that happening?"

"I haven't." Darryl turned. "Monique?"

"Actually . . . Remember that shoal in Australia, Darryl? Migrated all the way from the Great Barrier Reef down to Melbourne? Nearly half of those were pregnant females."

"Oh, right . . . I do remember that."

Craig nodded snidely. "Mystery solved. A strange off-season migration. Although . . ." He eyed Jason. "Why would one settle in an oil slick?"

Jason shook his head. "I was wondering about that too."

"That's it." Darryl abruptly stood. "Our waitress must have been abducted by aliens. Who wants a beer?"

Craig raised a hand.

"I already had you, ya lush. Anybody else?" Phil held his hand up, and Darryl nodded reluctantly. "That's it?" He walked off.

"So is there a way we can actually find these things?" Phil asked.

Everyone shrugged.

Except Jason. "There's absolutely a way."

"How?"

Jason stood. "Let me tell you."

CHAPTER 11

"WITH KELP."

No one responded for a moment, and Jason's words just hung over the table.

Then Phil's face crinkled into confusion. "With *kelp*?"

Jason nodded. "Monique, are you still going to check that strand with a scope?"

Monique Hollis shook her head, annoyed. Yes, she intended to check the kelp strand. But she didn't need Jason to remind her about it *again*. It was the third time he'd brought it up. Though the idea did have merit. If something had indeed brought the kelp to where they'd found it, a microscope could reveal bite marks or other slight indentations not visible to the naked eye. "Yes, Jason, I was planning on it."

But Phil still didn't understand. "So . . . is kelp something we can track?"

"It depends on the situation." Monique turned to Darryl as he returned with three golden beers in mugs. "Can we track kelp?"

Darryl put the beers down. "It depends on the situation."

Tracking doesn't involve following animals per se but a line of bread crumbs related to them. It's grueling work. A tracker sometimes has to search an entire coastline's worth of ocean to find what he's looking for. Other times, a trail can be downright easy to follow. There are no absolute answers.

But Jason thought they could track kelp. From a hook on the wall, he removed his navy sweat jacket, then from a Ziploc produced a long kelp strand.

"Oh, how sweet. You got Lisa a present," Summers cooed.

They all laughed, and Lisa blushed slightly.

Jason stood over the table. "I think we're onto a new species here." He admired the long piece of seaweed. "And I think this is going to help us find it."

"HARRY, IT'S Jason Aldridge."

Outside the tavern by himself, Jason ignored the view of the distant moonlit ocean as he spoke into his little gray cell phone.

"Jason, you sound excited." At a massive cherrywood desk in his twenty-five-thousand-square-foot La Jolla mansion, Harry Ackerman laid down a quarterly financial statement that had put him in a sour mood.

"I *am* excited, Harry. I don't want to overstate this, but we may—*may*—be onto a new species here."

"Is that right?" A faint smile appeared. "When might you be able to say definitively?"

"Well, that's tough to say. If it is a new species, they don't just sit in the ocean waiting for you. A month, a year, who knows."

"Very interesting. I think we should check it out and see. Now, your current contracts finish in what, five months?"

"About that."

"I tell you what. I'll write new ones for an extra year, so if it does turn out to be something new, you'll have more than enough time to locate it."

"That would be great, Harry."

Ackerman pushed away the financials and began dreaming: Harry Ackerman, business pioneer *and* naturalist. "And just so everyone has the proper incentive . . . I'll give twenty percent raises effective immediately." He grabbed a black Montblanc pen and made a note on a sticky. "Tell the others that will start with their next direct deposits."

Jason paused. There was a rare hunger in Ackerman's voice. "I'll pass it on, Harry."

"Good. By the way, are you still taking your daily notes?"

"Absolutely."

"Would you mind if I take a look at them as you go along on this?"

"Take a look at them?"

"If you don't mind, just to keep me abreast. I'm just very interested, and I thought it might be . . . an efficient way to keep me up on the status."

Jason paused. He didn't think he was comfortable with that. "Is there another way we can do it, Harry? Maybe just updates on the phone? It's just that those are my personal notes; they're very informal, and I don't know if I'm comfortable with—"

"Of course. Oral updates will be fine."

"Are you sure?"

"Absolutely. Now that I think about it, that will be easier than trying to read all the scientific jargon anyway. . . . One other thing. I think I left my day planner with Phil Martino. Did he mention that?"

"Sorry. Yes, he did. We're FedExing it to you tomorrow."

"Don't bother. You need your new contracts anyway so I'll just come to Clarita myself. Can we meet, say, first thing in the A.M. at the docks?"

"I'll look forward to it." Jason grabbed the door. "OK, Harry, so I'll talk to you—"

"Jason, I actually need a few of my numbers now. Can you get Phil for me?"

Seconds later, as Phil walked off with the cell phone, Jason stood over the booth and told the others about the new arrangement. Quietly excited, Darryl's eyes began to dance. "You said an extra year *and* a twenty percent raise?"

"The raise is effective immediately. Then, if it does turn out to be a new species, the extra year kicks in, so we'll have plenty of time to find it."

Darryl glanced at his wife. Her eyes were a little wet. Raises *and* an extra year! The Hollises' unborn children's savings accounts had just grown a little larger.

They ditched the boat for the evening. The Clarita Lodge went for forty-nine dollars per room per night and had free cable and a grungy swimming pool. The next morning they had breakfast and met Ackerman on Clarita's empty docks at seven. Aboard the *Expedition*, Ackerman presented them with six twenty-page contracts on nice linen paper that were promptly signed, dated, and initialed. Then Ackerman retrieved his day planner and got off the boat. As the *Expedition* pulled out, she scanned the massive ocean. The sea was so vast, so mysterious. What were they going to find out there?

CHAPTER 12

SEARCHING FOR kelp, the Hollises led a series of methodical forays off of Clarita's perimeter waters. Scanning with binoculars from the boat was always an option, but more often than not they had to put on their wet suits, dive in, and search for strands with their naked eyes. It was painstaking work, but Darryl and Craig's wisecracks, combined with a minimal amount of second-guessing from Jason, made it go quickly.

For the first week, they searched due west, the second week due south, and the third week due east. They found nothing. But when they searched due north, their luck changed. Darryl turned up several strands less than two miles from the island. It was hard to believe, but this discovery had taken a month. It was the nature of tracking, and Jason told the restless Ackerman to be patient. As July began, they continued pushing north and, less than half a mile later, found another strand. Then they found hundreds, an unambiguous trail. With no forests in the vicinity, no one needed an ichthyology degree to see what was happening: something was moving north just twenty miles off the Southern California coastline and leaving kelp strands in its wake.

Jason's mind was constantly working. Whether they were tracking mantas or something else, after one month's time, the little animals wouldn't be so little anymore. They probably weighed ninety pounds or more and had to be gorging themselves on plankton. But then, to Jason's surprise, Lisa Barton said plankton supplies here were also very low. So what were the rays eating? Jason documented everything on Phil's laptop.

On a gorgeous sunny day in August, Craig was stretched out on a cheapo plastic lawn chair nibbling at a turkey, lettuce, and mayo when Darryl walked up. "Long day, Craig?"

"Oh yeah, I'm exhausted."

Darryl stared at his portly friend, noticing that his back and forearms were a painful-looking medium-rare shade of pink. "What the hell are you exhausted from?"

Craig wiped some mayo on his trunks. "Thinking about the big-picture issues."

Darryl chuckled. "Big-picture issues."

"Seriously." The others came around, and Craig looked at all of them. "Here's a big-picture issue for all of us. Why kelp?"

Darryl shook his head, annoyed. "What are you talking about, Burn Victim?"

"It's a simple question. Why kelp? Whatever we're trailing, why the hell are they leaving kelp behind?"

Darryl shrugged. So did Monique and Lisa.

Craig turned. "Jason, you suggested tracking the stuff in the first place. Did you have a reason?"

"I still do. I think they're teething on it."

"*Teething* on it?"

"Newborn mantas, especially in the Bahamas and Caribbean, teethe on baby starfish. As we all know, there aren't many starfish in the northern hemisphere of the Pacific Ocean, but there's kelp everywhere. I think these rays are teething on it."

"Hmm." Impressed, Craig sat up fully on the lawn chair.

"Interesting idea, Jason." Lisa was impressed too. Like Craig, she'd been dubious about the whole new-species idea from the get-go, but the trail they'd been following was no mirage, and this was a very logical explanation.

Craig shrugged. "It still doesn't mean it's a new species."

Jason turned on a dime. "Want to bet?"

Everyone paused. Were they hearing things? Jason Aldridge never bet on anything.

Summers hesitated nervously. "Ah, I don't want to take your money, Jason."

Jason removed three bills, smacked them onto Craig's chair, and extended his hand. "Fifty bucks says that kelp trail goes north for at least another week."

Craig just eyed the hand. He clearly didn't want to, but . . . "Done."

They shook, and one week later, Summers handed over two stained twenties and a ten he had to borrow from Darryl. Jason wouldn't accept a check. They'd found a sporadic trail of kelp strands floating at or near the surface and followed it for seven solid days. As they did, the markings on the strands began to change, unmistakably so. The kelp was becoming shredded, torn, and, increasingly, filled with visible indentations. There was no doubt that something was chewing on it.

They continued moving north.

It was a cloudy mid-August day, and they were thirty-five miles north of Long Beach, the sky filled with big white clouds that blocked out the sun. Darryl narrowed his eyes behind a pair of binoculars. Was that another strand? His eyelids felt heavy, and he couldn't say for sure. He pointed.

"Craig, go that way, please."

Summers motored the boat due east, toward the shoreline. They'd been heading northeast for more than a week. While they'd started twenty miles from the coast, they were now just five. From the boat, Darryl reached down and plucked out another dripping strand. He began studying it when from behind him Phil Martino snapped a picture. Darryl felt like cracking him. As busy as he and Monique had been, Phil's picture-taking had been incessant. How many photos could he take of frickin' seaweed? Darryl's eyes were so tired he couldn't tell if there were markings on the strand or not. He held out the strand to Monique: "May I?" Jason grabbed it first.

Monique shook her head, but Lisa was oblivious, just staring out at the empty ocean. There were much more important things to worry about now than kelp. *Real problems* were mounting in the Pacific Ocean.

Just as in tropical Mexico, the plankton levels here were alarmingly low, particularly around the thermoclines, where they were nearly 75 percent below normal.

Lisa was beginning to suspect that something "of scale" might be going on. She had no idea what, and neither did Craig Summers. Spurred on by Lisa's constant needling, Craig had increased the frequency of his GDV-4 testing, but just as in Mexico, he found no trace of the virus. What was going on with the ocean's plankton levels? Summers had no idea either.

As their trek continued, Jason had many other unanswered questions. *Why* was this alleged new species migrating north? Why suddenly closer to shore? And what were they eating? If the newborns had normal growth rates, Jason figured they could easily grow to weigh a hundred and fifty pounds or more. Perhaps they were great scavengers, adept at finding what little plankton was out there. The *Expedition* continued following the trail.

As AUGUST continued, they moved closer still to the shoreline and right up the Southern California coast, past Los Angeles, Oxnard, Ventura, and into the waters just north of Santa Barbara. Along the way, Darryl and Monique battled through many roadblocks, primarily strong surface currents. Currents could easily destroy a trail and send individual strands in every direction. Staying close was the only guarantee of not losing it, and that was exactly what the couple had done. With Jason second-guessing their every move, they worked hard for a solid month, all day every day, searching relentlessly. Darryl didn't shoot at a single skeet, and Monique didn't glance at a book or magazine.

Lisa found Monique's work ethic incredible. Prior to this, she'd never seen Monique do anything other than stroll around in flip-flops, drink Diet Cokes, and read. While Lisa was well aware of Monique's military background, she'd just never pictured her getting her beautiful fingernails dirty. But every day Monique Hollis came up winded in her wet suit. She'd worked tirelessly, and without complaint. Like Lisa, she was tougher than she looked.

Into September, the *Expedition* proceeded north, to Pismo Beach, San Luis Obispo, and San Simeon. Jason continued to be relentless with his note taking, even starting an outline for a formal report.

Though he remained frustrated with how little the others cared about proper documentation. Darryl and Craig literally hadn't written down their findings on anything, and Monique and Lisa's notes, usually in little colored spiral notebooks, were often illegible.

On another gorgeous September day, mid-seventies without a cloud in the sky, Phil headed to the bow of the boat with his cell phone open. "It's Mr. Ackerman, Jason."

"Hi, Harry." The conversation was brief. Ackerman wanted to know if it was a new species or not. "We still can't say definitively," Jason said. "All we can do is keep following the trail."

They did. But as they continued north they had no idea that someone else's trail was about to come to a violent end.

CHAPTER 13

SETH GETTY was forty-five, about thirty pounds overweight, and recently divorced. He lived in a pathetic one-bedroom apartment on the outskirts of the massive Los Padres National Forest, halfway between Los Angeles and San Francisco, and spent his personal time watching awful sitcoms on television. Heading out to sea, he was by himself. His partner had called in sick today, so he'd decided to do the job alone. Why not? The sun was out, the water was fairly flat, and it would literally be a ten-minute task. Getty's occupation was fiber-optic maintenance and repair. Normally, this required inspecting his phone company's central hub, a massive warehouse filled with routers and telcom switches, but twice a month Getty and his partner had to spot-check their portion of the company's deep-sea fiber-optic cable. Invariably the cable was functioning properly, but the job was to make certain.

Getty was in the company boat, two miles offshore and in no rush to reach his destination. It was beautiful out today. No people, no other boats. Just a ton of kelp strands in the water. Looking forward Getty eyed a few hundred gliding seagulls. A football field away, the birds darted above the ocean, and Seth was pleased to see them. He'd brought along a loaf of Wonder Bread after all. He suddenly squinted. What was that? Directly beneath the birds, two smallish black shapes flew out of the sea then fell right back in. Getty stared at the spot, but as he motored closer, whatever it was didn't reappear. He cut the engine and threw bread all over the large gray deck. Like vultures, the birds immediately descended, hopping everywhere to eat as much as they could. There were so many they took up the entire deck, but Getty didn't mind. He squeezed into a too-small black wet suit and reminded himself to go on a diet.

As he jumped into the sea, the birds continued to eat.

GETTY DOVE to two hundred feet, carefully checked the cable's current readings, and began to ascend. When he was a hundred feet from the surface, however, he noticed a moving black shape to his right. He froze. He couldn't make it out at all—visibility was very poor—but whatever it was, he thought it was swimming toward him. He glanced up and, far above the surface, thought he saw the gulls gliding in the sun. He turned back. The black shape was much closer now. Then he noticed movement from another direction. There was a second black shape also swimming toward him. Then he noticed a third. Then a fourth. Then hundreds. They were coming from all sides.

Suddenly Seth Getty was terrified. He started to swim up. But then he froze again. Now they were coming from above, too.

"WHAT MISSING repairman?" Jason asked.

On the back of the *Expedition*, Craig shrugged. "The coast guard just sent out an all-points. Some guy doing maintenance on a fiber-optic cable. Apparently he just disappeared, right around here."

"Where was he exactly?"

"About ten miles north, off Los Padres."

Jason paused. "That's right where the kelp trail's leading. . . . I wonder if maybe—" He stopped talking.

"What? You think the rays have something do with it?"

A smile. "Of course not." That was ridiculous, not even within the realm of possibility. "But whatever got this guy . . . I wonder if maybe it could get them, too."

"Come on, Jason. He probably just drowned, then got carried away by the currents."

But in the *exact location* they'd tracked the rays to? "Let's get up there and check it out."

THEY DID but found nothing unusual—just more kelp. They continued north, and by late September were easing into the waters off Carmel, then Pebble Beach and Monterey. This was a truly gorgeous part of California, with stunning vistas and jagged rock cliffs everywhere. No one noticed the scenery.

The plankton supply had continued to decrease, and Lisa Barton was still baffled. Her onboard Plankton Measuring System only gave her "what" without the "why." To get real answers, she needed the kind of equipment found only in the most sophisticated marine labs in the country. One morning she called the prestigious Okezie Marine Center, near Washington State University, then FedExed them a plankton sample in seawater. They got back to her in less than a week, on a sweltering-hot day.

"Lisa, an e-mail came for you."

She turned to Phil Martino. Since Phil's computer was the only one configured to the *Expedition*'s satellite link, he managed all of their incoming e-mails. "From the Okezie Center?"

"Uh, I think so."

"Fantastic. Can I see it, Phil?" She started to go below deck, but he stopped her.

"I printed it out for you already. Here . . ."

He handed her ten stapled sheets.

She eyed the cover page, then her eyes suddenly widened. "Holy Mother of God."

CHAPTER 14

LISA DIDN'T move. She just stood in the hot sun, reading the pages slowly and carefully. It wasn't light material, the report's title "Mechanisms for Planktonic Deterrence Based on North Pacific Samples." She suddenly looked up. "Phil, where's Jason?"

"Uh . . ."

"He's still in the water with Darryl and Craig." Monique climbed up from the sea in a tight white one-piece, not noticing Phil's drooling over her. "God, it's hot." Then she noticed the papers in Lisa's hand. "What's going on, Lisa?"

"I'm not the only one who noticed that plankton levels are down in the Pacific. There have been reports from New Zealand to Japan, from the southern tip of Chile all the way up to where we are right now."

"Jesus Christ." That covered a huge chunk of the *entire Pacific Ocean.* "Why?"

"No one knows. But the raw data look accurate."

"What are the raw data?"

"Plankton samples from across the Pacific. All with massive amounts of DMSP."

"What's DMSP?"

Lisa turned back to the report again. "Dimethylsulfoniopropionate."

"Oh, sure, that."

Absorbed in the papers, Lisa didn't hear Monique's sarcastic remark. She simply nodded.

"Lisa. What the hell is DMSP?"

"Oh." Lisa looked up. "It's a defensive chemical that plankton releases."

"What do you mean 'defensive'?"

"When plankton thinks it's going to be attacked, it releases it."

"I didn't know plankton was that smart."

"It's very smart. You know what else it does when it thinks an attack's coming?"

"What?"

"It *cuts its own reproduction.*"

Monique was stunned. "So *that's* why levels have been so low. Do they think it's fighting off GDV-4?"

"No. Just like Craig said, there's no evidence of that at all. Actually, I need to talk to Craig. Right now . . ." She quickly grabbed her fins.

DARRYL AND Jason kicked slowly, heads down, their bare backs glistening in the scalding sun. With the aid of Supra 902 magnifying masks, originally manufactured for exclusive use by the navy, they could see all the way to the bottom, a hundred and twenty feet below. Sand, sand, and more sand. There was no kelp anywhere.

Floating lazily on a giant black inner tube, Craig yawned. "God, this is boring."

Just then Darryl and Jason popped up. "Take a break, Darryl?"

"Definitely. We're not getting paid enough for this."

"Really, Jason, we're not."

Darryl turned to the inner tube. "*We're* not?"

"I've been busting my ass too, Darryl."

Darryl looked at Summers blankly. In angular, silver sunglasses that made him look like he was in a techno band, Craig held the look for a moment—then chuckled heartily.

Jason wasn't amused. Visibly frustrated, he scanned the desolate waters. "Those rays *have to* be around here somewhere, right?" Indeed, they weren't in this particular location by accident. The director of the Monterey Aquarium had called them after an oil-rig diver reported seeing a small group of "fairly large birdlike shapes" on the seafloor near one of the rig's massive legs. Jason and company had immediately visited the hulking metal contraption. They found nothing, but clearly whatever had been there was still close—and still migrating north.

Darryl looked up at the sun. "What do you think that rig diver saw, Jason?"

"What do you mean? He saw the rays."

"I know *that*. I mean adults or newborns."

"He said they were 'fairly large,' right, so it couldn't have been adults; he would have called those enormous, bigger than cars."

Darryl nodded. "That's my point. He must have seen the newborns, only now they're small juveniles. These things grow *fast*, don't they?"

"Not as fast as a shrew, but yeah." Some species of shrew ate up to 1.3 times their body weights in a single day. "They could easily weigh two hundred pounds. What I want to know is what the hell have they been eating? If not plankton, what?"

"It's the ocean, Slick, how about fish?"

"Mantas can't catch fish, Darryl. They can't catch anything. They swim too slowly, that's why they just eat masses of floating stuff."

Craig hopped into the water. "What I want to know is why haven't we seen one of these things yet. All this time and we haven't seen *one*."

Darryl dunked his mask. "You think that's so unusual?"

"Yeah. Mantas are friendly, right? They like to show themselves, they like to play. Whatever these things are, they're not doing that. In fact, it seems like they're hiding."

"Under the circumstances, that's natural."

"What circumstances?"

"Doing a migration they've never done before. They're just being cautious. Even humpbacks, when they do a new migration they're much less visible than normal. What I've been wondering is where are these things from? Any thoughts on that, Jason?"

A shrug. "Could be a lot of places. Mexico . . . Costa Rica or Ecuador . . . Hawaii, the Marquesas. Maybe further west like Australia or Malaysia."

"Hey, is that Lisa?" Craig squinted. Someone was swimming toward them from the boat. "Oh man, I hope she's wearing that bikini I like—you know, the tight one with the blue polka dots."

Darryl shook his head. "Give it up, man. She wants nothing to do with you."

"Some smooth lines and a night of drinking could change that."

"You don't have any smooth lines." Darryl turned. "Besides, I think she might dig you, Jason."

"Yeah, right."

"I'm serious. You guys have that love-hate thing going on. I think there might be something there. Shut up, here she comes. . . ."

As she swam up, she immediately smelled a rat. "Boy talk, huh, Darryl?" She shook her head at him as Craig carefully scanned her body, realizing with disappointment that there were no polka dots anywhere on it.

"Craig." She almost caught him looking. "Is there anything new with GDV-4 lately?"

Summers's demeanor changed. "A ton, actually. Hot off the presses. They're beginning full-scale testing for it in the Pacific soon."

Lisa was stunned. "They are? When the hell did that happen?"

"They announced it publicly first thing this morning."

"Who?"

"The Woods Hole Virus Group."

Lisa paused. Did the virus have something to do with the plankton depletion after all? "Are they looking for anything in particular?"

"GDV-4's origins, among other things."

"They're looking for that *in the Pacific*?"

"Evidently, they're not positive it originated in the Atlantic anymore. They're testing at multiple depth levels too."

"I thought it was a confirmed surface virus."

"It was, but evidently they've been reevaluating that, too."

Lisa realized she had work to do. She'd share her findings from the Okezie Center later. "OK, thanks . . ."

As she started to swim back, Darryl wearily put his mask back on. He was still exhausted but wanted to find one kelp strand—just one—to confirm that they were still on track. He ducked his head into the water and suddenly, with fresh eyes, saw something below that he'd missed earlier. It wasn't kelp but a small pile of little white objects, lying right on the dark sand. He pulled his head out.

"Hey, Lisa."

She continued swimming, not hearing him.

"Lisa!"

She turned back. "Yeah."

"Stick around, I might have something for ya. . . ." He inhaled and dove. He kicked very hard, knowing he had to reach the bottom on a single gulp of air. He reached the pile without difficulty, carefully grabbed a handful, then ascended.

At the surface, Jason didn't even let him catch his breath. "What do you have there?"

Darryl removed his mask and handed them to Lisa. "Shark's teeth."

"Yeah?" Jason tried to see them over Lisa's shoulder, but she became annoyed and turned away, blocking his view. She studied the glistening little objects. Were they really shark's teeth? Most sharks went through tens of thousands of teeth during their lifetime, constantly replacing blunt and broken ones, some species as often as every other week. These teeth were the size of human fingertips, and slightly curved, almost like fat, stumpy S-shapes. Lisa wasn't a tooth expert by any means, but as an oceanic nutrition specialist, she'd seen her share of them. She didn't recognize these, but there were tons of shark species. . . .

Darryl didn't recognize them either. "Can I see those again?"

She handed him a few, but he wasn't as careful as he should have been. "Damn, they're sharp!"

They all watched as a few drops of his blood fell into the sea. Jason shook his head.

Maybe they'd been looking for an excuse, but now they *had* to get out of the water. If the shark that had lost its teeth was still around, it would smell the blood.

They swam back immediately.

As Jason cut through the water, he considered the teeth more carefully. Had they really come from a shark? Was it just a coincidence they'd found them in the exact spot they'd tracked the new species to? It had to be. No ray species had teeth like that. Perhaps some sharks were hunting them.

Darryl suddenly stopped swimming and so did Jason—rather nervously. "Something wrong, Darryl?"

Darryl smiled, raising a dripping kelp strand. "We're still on track."

"Good. Let's get back to the boat."

They reached the *Expedition* without incident. On deck, Phil immediately began photographing the teeth. Then Craig started the engine, and they motored away.

As THE *Expedition* disappeared, Darryl Hollis's blood dissipated. Just as they had feared, something *did* smell it. Only it wasn't a shark.

CHAPTER 15

MORE THAN a mile away, the adult rays smelled the blood. Completely unseen in the blackened waters, they were on the move again, swimming north along the ocean's floor. All were alive but not healthy. Several thousand had recently died.

Far above them, just fifty feet below the surface, were their younger brethren, now juveniles. Unlike the adults, these animals had eaten well and their numbers were undimished. The younger animals now averaged two hundred pounds and were formidable, frightening-looking creatures. Blocks of lean, tapered muscle, they were five feet across the wings, four feet long, and as thick as a three-hundred-pound man's stomach at their centers.

They floated listlessly in the sun-dappled waters. Strands of kelp hung from many of their mouths. They'd frozen midchew when they first sensed the boat. The boat was gone now, and nothing else was near. Still, none moved. Their attention had just shifted. Another sense—smell—had alerted them. Now they knew what their much larger brethren below had known moments ago.

There was blood in the water. They dove down and followed the others north.

CHAPTER 16

T HE *EXPEDITION* had docked at a crowded San Francisco marina and the team was waiting for Lisa Barton to return. It would be a while.

The previous day, Lisa had researched the unusual fat S-shaped teeth using the available resources and come up empty. Sharks and anglers had been the most obvious source of the teeth, but Lisa found nothing establishing a direct link between either. Almost every species of shark has teeth that are fundamentally triangular in shape. The teeth can vary in width, some narrow and pointy, others fat and wide, but every single known species, from tigers to hammerheads to great whites to makos, possesses teeth that are in one way or another triangular. Wondering if perhaps an extinct shark species had reappeared, Lisa also checked fossil records. But from sand sharks to cow sharks, among many others, they all possessed the same triangular shape.

Anglers had been the next suspect. Anglers were vicious, roundish fish, about the size of a baby's fist. But across the board, anglers had teeth that were slightly curved, like a tiger's fangs. Nothing like fat, stumpy S-shapes, either.

With nowhere else to go, Lisa thought of Mike Cohen, an old

friend she'd gotten to know at various oceanic nutrition conferences over the years. Cohen was the number three expert in the world on the arcane subject of animal teeth analysis and was based at the biosciences and bioengineering department at UC Berkeley. Starting today, Cohen's department was hosting a weeklong conference at which Cohen himself was a featured speaker, but he'd still agreed to meet with her.

Before she'd left, Jason had insisted on attending the meeting, but in yet another fight, Lisa had flat-out refused. Michael Cohen was *her* contact, and she wouldn't have Jason second-guessing her in front of an important colleague.

Jason had work to do anyway. While the others did chores on the boat, he spent the first part of the morning on Phil's computer in the tiny living room below deck, writing notes and continuing with his outline. He hoped the latter would eventually become the basis for a formal report to the Species Council, the twelve-person committee in Washington, D.C., that determined what was a new species and what was not.

By late morning, thin cumulus clouds had rolled in above the marina, and everyone except Craig was on deck. In loose-fitting black sweats and a white tank top, Jason was tapping away on Phil's laptop when Darryl sat next to him. "Craig still on that phone call?"

"I think so."

"He's been on for more than an hour, you know."

Jason looked up. "I didn't realize that."

A nod. "I wonder what's so damn important."

"Let me tell you, then." Summers walked up on deck, a strange look on his heavily stubbled face: fatigued and concerned, too.

Darryl's eyes narrowed. "What's up, Craig?"

"What's up is we've got a major problem in the Pacific Ocean with GDV-4. Phil, I'm expecting an e-mail on it, about ninety pages. Can you print it for me?"

As Phil trotted off, Jason was mystified. "A major problem with GDV-4 in the *Pacific*?"

"Yeah. And that's not all. I think GDV-4's affecting this species of yours—maybe catastrophically."

"What?"

"Jason, I don't think these rays are from Mexico, Hawaii, the Marquesas, or anywhere else." Craig gave him a measured look. "I don't think they're surface animals at all."

"What the hell are you talking about?" Every known species of manta lives exclusively at or near the surface. "Craig, that's not possib—"

"It is possible. I'll prove it—all of it." He eyed him ominously. "Jason, I think this species of yours is from the depths."

CHAPTER 17

CRAIG EXHALED, gathering his thoughts. Jason, Monique, and Darryl had just fired fifty questions at him and were waiting for answers. Standing in front of the three-person inquisition, he was ready.

"The first thing you should know is that a number of critical beliefs we had about GDV-4 are apparently . . . all wrong."

Jason looked at him blankly. "You're joking."

"This is straight from Tom York, the head of the Woods Hole Oceanic Virus Group and the number one expert on GDV-4 in the world. Turns out his group's been running tests in every major ocean on the globe for more than a year. They officially released their findings two hours ago." Another exhale. "Here's the deal. GDV-4 isn't a surface virus at all. It *spread* to the surface, it was *discovered* at the surface, but it originated in the depths. And we're talking *the real depths.* Ten, twenty, thirty thousand feet down. That's why I think your species is from there, Jason."

Darryl was flabbergasted. "GDV-4 *originated* there?"

"And it's spreading like wildfire. This thing's algae-based, guys."

"Holy cow."

Phil returned, handing Craig ninety sheets of tiny print. "What's the significance of it being algae-based?"

"Phil, algae are near the very bottom of the food chain so a virus that infects algae has the potential to destroy *entire oceans.*" Craig nodded to the others. "It gets worse. They're now saying GDV-4 is considerably more devastating than AIDS. Not only does it attack immune systems, it also causes severe brain damage, destroys the musculoskeletal system, and spreads with extraordinary speed within the body. And it is *everywhere.* York's guys have found it in every ocean on Earth. Lisa was onto something with her plankton findings. Plankton are surface organisms, but somehow they detected GDV-4 rising up from below and adapted preemptively to fight off an attack."

Jason shook his head. "Craig, is York sure about all this? I mean, how could GDV-4 have spread this far this fast? Especially before anybody even knew it?"

"Because viruses can hide, Jason. They can hide for decades."

The public knew nothing about GDV-4 and that wouldn't change anytime soon. It usually happens that way. The bottom line is that major news organizations become interested in viruses only when they caused human deaths, preferably on a large scale. The mad cow virus in Europe, for example, decimated European cattle herds for years but only garnered real attention after *people* began dying from it.

The long and storied history of viruses hiding from the public has been well documented. None is more infamous than AIDS. AIDS didn't become part of the international consciousness until the mideighties but had existed much earlier. And not just in remote jungles in Africa, but in major American cities. In New York, a sailor died in 1959 of what medical records at the time called "complications caused by immune deficiency and pneumonia." Blood samples analyzed decades later tested positive for HIV and AIDS.

Craig continued soberly. "We have unambiguous proof GDV-4's been in the Pacific for a very long time. I assume you've all heard of that terramouth specimen that turned up in 1976?"

It was a famous discovery from back before any of them even knew what marine biology was. In November 1976, a naval research vessel, the AFB-14, was conducting experiments offshore of Oahu, sending probes to the ocean floor fifteen thousand feet below to perform sediment analysis. But when the AFB-14 retrieved the probes, something came up with them and it wasn't sediment. It was the corpse of a giant fish no one had ever seen before: a previously unknown shark species, a strange-looking animal with dark brown skin, a massive mouth, unusually shaped teeth, and a weight of two tons. Dubbed terramouth, it was an astonishing find. It proved what many in the seagoing community had assumed for years: that there were entire species living in the depths that man knew absolutely nothing about. And these weren't small animals, but enormous ones, and they hadn't evolved recently, *but had always been there.* Fossil analysis determined that terramouth had been evolving for as long as some of the oldest sharks. It had been in the depths for more than 450 million years, but before 1976, man had no clue it even existed.

Jason went to the stern, his mind racing. "Are you saying that terramouth died of GDV-4?"

"That's exactly what I'm saying. York personally flew to the National Oceanographic Institute at Waikiki seven weeks ago to check old tissue samples."

"Then that means . . . that virus has been down there for *thirty years*?"

"At least."

"How could that be? If it's been down there that long, how could we not have known? How could the fishing industry not have been affected?"

"Because the fishing industry doesn't fish the depths, Jason. Do you understand how deep we're talking here? Three, five, even six miles down."

"So we're supposed to believe this virus has just stayed down there all this time without climbing to the mid and upper waters?"

"You know how big the damn oceans are, big guy. It would take *decades* even for a fast-moving virus to cover that much ground."

Jason hesitated. The world's oceans were indeed enormous, *triple* the surface area of dry land and that didn't account for depth. The seas were two miles deep on average with many trenches more than six miles down. Craig was right. Even a fast-moving virus could take decades to form a meaningful presence in the higher waters. Until then, it might show itself only in dribs and drabs, which, of course, was exactly what had happened. It explained why GDV-4 had been so challenging to locate up to this point.

Monique turned. "Did York say anything about it going airborne?"

"What?" Darryl eyed his wife. "They're worried about GDV-4 going *airborne*?"

Craig cleared his throat. "They *were*. The Audubon Society's been crowing about some missing seagulls, but those rumors were gibberish. GDV-4 had nothing to do with it. But it has everything to do with these rays of yours, Jason. It's driving them out of the depths, and they're migrating to escape it."

Jason turned to Monique. "Does a migration from the depths make sense here?"

"It makes perfect sense. If there really is serious devastation down there, these rays would have to go into higher waters to find food." She shrugged. "Lack of food is the single biggest reason for off-season migrations."

"A new food source." Jason loved the simplicity of it. "So what was their old food source? I mean plankton doesn't exist down there, right?"

"I couldn't say what exists down there, Jason."

No one could. The depths are an enigma, not just to them but also to human society; the only place on earth that truly is. There is no light at all in the depths, literally none, an entire world bathed in constant darkness. There is also the pressure. Pressure in the depths is so powerful it can literally crush a dump truck. The most sophisticated subs ever made can get nowhere near the depths, barely capable of diving more than nine hundred feet when the world's oceans average more than ten *thousand*. And that's just the average. While unmanned probes can be sent down, the devices are usually ineffective. The reality is that as advanced as human society is, the depths are still a mystery. Like deep space, they totally defy exploration. Man can attempt to visit but only for the briefest of moments, and even then, with very limited access.

Jason shook his head. He had no idea what the rays fed on down there. "But now we know why that one settled in the oil slick near Clarita."

Darryl pivoted. "We do?"

"If Craig's right, it must have been sick, even dying. I could never figure it: Why would a healthy ray lie down in a patch of oil? It wouldn't. But a sick one, one that didn't know where it was or what it was doing . . . Dollars to doughnuts, it was infected with GDV-4. You realize you could be talking about an apocalypse down there, Craig? I mean, if what you're saying is *actually happening*, this virus could be the deep sea's version of an ice age. These rays could be on the verge of extinction."

Monique stepped forward. "Or *adaptation*."

Jason turned. "You think so?"

"Think about how long these things have been down there."

"How long?"

"Rays are cousins of sharks, right? So they could have been there since Pangaea."

Pangaea was an ancient supercontinent, an enormous landmass that preceded the earth's current five-continent formation. Pangaea's breakup 290 million years ago had profound effects on all the earth's species, on land and at sea, placing them in wildly new environments that either killed them off or forced them to adapt. The evolutionary adaptations attributed to Pangaea are nothing short of astonishing: kangaroo rats in the deserts evolving organs to make their own water internally, polar bears in the Arctic evolving skin to endure temperatures below minus-eighty degrees, duck hawks developing wings to fly 175 miles per hour.

"So you're suggesting Pangaea could have split an ancient population of rays?" Jason turned to Monique fully. "While mantas evolved on the surface, this other species evolved in the depths?"

Monique nodded. "Sort of like a . . . deep-sea cousin."

"*Deep-sea cousin.*" Craig smiled. "I like that."

Jason eyed Monique curiously. "So how would this . . . deep-sea cousin have evolved? I guess it's hard to say, isn't it? Since we know so little about life down there."

Monique raised an eyebrow. "We might know how it *didn't evolve*, though."

"How so?"

"Every species of manta we know lives in warm, tranquil seas, and they've all evolved identically. So doesn't it stand to reason that if another group of rays lived in an entirely different environment, they'd have evolved into entirely different animals?"

"You think? How different could they really be, Monique? No matter where they evolved, you're still talking about very large, slow-moving creatures. Wouldn't their size alone limit their abilities to evolve into anything significantly different from the mantas we already know? It's a rougher environment down there, granted, and I suppose they might have adapted—I don't know—some stinging or electrical capabilities to compensate, but I can't imagine anything much more than that."

Monique wasn't so sure. She recalled reading what Darwin had once said on a similar subject. When asked to explain how two genetically related species, the harmless domestic house cat and the vicious African lion, had evolved so differently, the father of evolution had attributed the results to vastly different environments, stating that more rigorous environments will force surviving species to become more rigorous as well.

"Life's a lot tougher down there, Jason. Maybe these animals somehow evolved to deal with that."

Tougher, Jason thought. In the case of the deep-sea cousin to the manta ray, what did tougher mean? But they'd gotten ahead of themselves. They were speculating, perhaps blindly. "We still don't really *know* anything here, do we? I mean despite everything Craig just said, we don't *know* these animals are from the depths; we don't *know* they're a new species. There's really no proof."

Monique looked at him. "Don't forget the teeth Darryl found."

Jason hesitated. *The teeth.* Was there any way the fat, stumpy S-shapes had actually come from the rays? Jason had previously written that off as unrealistic but now . . . "When's Lisa's meeting with that tooth expert?"

Monique checked her watch. "I think it's starting right now."

CHAPTER 18

THE LOBBY of UC Berkeley's new biosciences and bioengineering facility was jam-packed. With a three-day conference just getting under way, more than six hundred well-dressed men and women in their thirties to sixties were smiling, shaking hands, making small talk, and sipping water from Styrofoam cups.

How am I going to find Mike Cohen in this mess? Lisa Barton thought, standing on her tippy toes to see over the morass of people. She glanced down at her own tailored suit, an elegant charcoal-gray number over a sheer white blouse, and smiled. Lisa hadn't dressed up for *anything* in more than a year and appreciated the opportunity to wear something nice. She pushed into the crowd. Catching the occasional elbow and throwing a few herself, she methodically walked the entire room until she saw him, engaged in a low-key conversation. Mike Cohen was forty-five with a full head of curly brown hair, a laser-sharp intellect, and an ensemble that would make any fashion designer vomit: a navy suit made of 100 percent Dacron with a cheap red tie loose at the neck. When his conversation ended, he spotted Lisa and smiled wide.

"Lisa, how are you?"

"Hi, Mike. Nice to see you." They hugged.

"How you been?"

She shrugged. "Honestly, things were slow for some time, but we might be onto something now."

Cohen smiled anew. "You were always a straight shooter, Lisa. If I asked anybody else here that question, they'd say everything's been gangbusters since birth." He glanced at his watch. "I'm sorry, but I have a presentation in fifteen minutes, so maybe we should get to the reason you're here."

"Is there a place we can talk?"

Seconds later, they entered Cohen's office, nondescript and white-walled. He sat behind a metal desk with a faux-wood top. "So what do you got?"

Lisa placed a few of the fat S-shapes on the desk. "These."

Cohen didn't move. He just stared at the teeth, his brown eyes narrowing. Then, without actually touching the teeth, he ducked down to study them from another angle. Then he stood and moved his head all around, assessing them from more angles still, ignoring his dangling tie.

"Where did you get these?"

"The Pacific."

"Where exactly?"

"About twenty miles off Monterey."

"What depth?"

"A little more than a hundred feet."

"Do you know the coordinates?"

"Longitude and latitude? Two of my colleagues might."

"You said on the phone your team's tracking some kind of new species?"

"We think so."

Cohen picked up the phone. "Janet? I have to cancel my presentation. Please apologize and check timetables so we can reschedule."

Lisa was staring at him now. He raised one of the teeth carefully and tapped it with a fingernail. "These didn't come from a shark."

He studied the tooth further, again from multiple angles. "They didn't come from a barracuda, angler, gar, wallfish, parrot fish, or pike. They didn't come from anything I'm familiar with." He stared at them anew. "I've never seen teeth like this in my life."

Lisa was stunned. Had they come from the rays?

"Would you like me to do an analysis on them?"

Lisa could barely contain herself. "Very much so."

Cohen stood, eyeing the glass door that led to his lab. "Back soon. I'll let you know what I find."

CHAPTER 19

MIKE COHEN began speaking before he was even through the door. "I'll start by telling you where else these teeth *didn't* come from. They're certainly not from anything land-based." Teeth from land-based animals vary considerably in shape and size, and included incisors, canines, bicuspids, molars, fangs, and tusks. Teeth from water-based animals, on the other hand, tend to come in just two basic shapes, sharp cutting incisors and crushing molars. "These teeth obviously came from something that lives in the water, but that's the only thing I can say with certainty." He sat behind his desk. "There are a few things I think are highly likely."

Lisa leaned forward. "OK."

"Three comments. One, these are what we call *specialized teeth;* they're designed for a specific purpose, and in this case, that isn't playful nibbling. These teeth are designed to pierce very thick skin and internal organs. I don't want to scare you, Lisa, but they belong to a predator, and an extremely dangerous one at that. Their curved shape is a fascinating adaptation I've never seen before. It would make it very difficult for any prey to wriggle away, especially if the animal has powerful jaws.

"Two, it's highly likely there's a second type of tooth in the mouth these came from. You found canines, which are located in the front and sides of the upper and lower jaws, very possibly in multiple rows. But I'm positive there are molars, too, because when this thing finishes killing whatever it's caught, it's going to need something to chew the meat. I modeled what the mouth might look like. It's speculative, so I'm not sure, but it could even have extra-long incisors, what you'd effectively call fangs. Sort of like a tiger's fangs, except these would be considerably sharper. I expect the total number of teeth in the mouth could easily number in the hundreds."

"Jesus." Lisa leaned back on her chair. She couldn't believe what she was hearing. Cohen knew his stuff, inside out, and yet what he was saying wasn't possible. . . . "Are you sure about all this, Mike?"

Cohen looked at her blankly. "Yeah, I'm positive."

"Sorry, I didn't mean to second-guess you."

"No problem. Last, what you have here are *baby teeth.*"

"Baby teeth?"

"I don't know how big the adult teeth that replace them will grow. It depends on how big the mouth itself grows. But these teeth *will* grow larger, perhaps considerably so." He shrugged. "Anyway, that's all I got."

Lisa's right leg had gone to sleep, but she didn't notice. She just sat there, stunned. *Baby teeth.* This made sense with what they'd found, of course—it fit perfectly with the notion of the newborns teething on kelp while they replaced their baby canines—but there was something very fundamental she didn't understand: How could the rays possibly have canines? Mantas possessed just one type of tooth, huge molars, which they used exclusively for crushing shells. So how could another similar species have *canines*? And if Cohen was right, if the teeth grew proportionally to the size of the mouth, a manta's mouth . . . My God, Lisa thought, trying to picture it. . . . But it wasn't possible. It would mean the rays they'd been tracking were predators. And that simply couldn't be.

The phone rang, and Cohen picked up. "Half an hour? Thanks."

"Sorry I've kept you, Mike."

"Trust me, I'm glad you did." Cohen looked annoyed, though, at something she'd said earlier.

"Mike, I didn't mean to doubt you before. Believe me, I know you know what you're talking about. But the implications of what you're saying . . . I just don't understand them."

This seemed to take the edge off. Cohen shrugged casually. "Well, I'm only looking at teeth here, Lisa. I can't really comment on 'implications.'" His eyes shifted to the door, and she realized she'd been keeping him.

She stood. It was late in the day now, and she suddenly wanted to get going herself. "I'll let you go. Thank you very much." They hugged.

"No problem. I'm glad you came in. I'll assume all of this is strictly confidential unless I hear from you otherwise. In the meantime, if you don't mind, I'll write up a formal report."

"Would you mind e-mailing me a copy?"

A nod. "A draft might even be done later today." They walked to the door.

"Any closing comments?"

"Just a word of advice." He eyed her ominously. "Lisa, if you actually find whatever these teeth came from . . . Be very, very careful with it."

"THAT'S . . . RIDICULOUS."

It was sunset, and Lisa had just returned to the now-quiet San Francisco marina. After her talk with Cohen, she'd been feeling good, anxious to relay to the others what he'd said. In the back of the *Expedition*, she'd done so, methodically and precisely. Then Jason had belted her with the "ridiculous" comment. She didn't respond audibly, but her blood was suddenly boiling. The man had the sensitivity of a stampeding elephant. Lisa didn't care about the others. She was going to have it out right now with Jason Aldridge if he didn't apologize, and fast.

"What do you mean, *ridiculous*?"

"I mean it's too much. It's just not realistic."

"It explains why these rays are surviving despite the plankton depletion. It's because they don't eat plankton. Not with teeth like that."

"That may be, but I'd still like to speak with this Mike Cohen myself."

"Forget it."

"What's the big deal, Lisa? I just want to check what he said."

"*Check what he said?* Why? Because I got it wrong?"

"Of course not. I just want to go over it."

"Absolutely not. I won't have you embarrass me in front of a colleague like that."

"Come on, just give me his number."

"I said no!! Jesus, will you just trust somebody else for a change?!"

This was a neutron bomb. In the silence that followed, everyone looked embarrassed. Darryl, Monique, Craig, and Phil all turned away. Even Jason looked disturbed. Besides Lisa's visible anger, he thought she somehow looked . . . sad.

No one said anything. They all just stood there, stunned.

Then Monique cleared her throat. Whatever the problem was, these two had to work it out by themselves. "Jason, Lisa. Excuse me. The rest of us are going to start dinner downstairs. Guys?"

Darryl turned to follow her, but Phil and Craig didn't budge; they wanted to see a brawl. Then Darryl smacked them, and they all shuffled downstairs.

Alone, Jason and Lisa stood silently. Neither said anything. They noticed a nearby yacht, barbecuers talking quietly over their food. A few seconds ticked past.

"Sorry I upset you," Jason said after a moment.

Lisa shook her head. "Whatever."

"Really, Lisa, I'm sorry. It's just that—" He stopped talking.

"What?"

"Can I just see a few of those teeth?"

"You'll give them back?"

A smile. "Yeah."

She handed him a few, and he raised one, studying it against the sunset. "Baby teeth. It just doesn't make sense that these came from those rays. I mean, you know as well as I do that mantas can't swim nearly fast enough to catch anything. If this species is their deep-sea cousin, why on earth would they need teeth like this? It doesn't add up. You disagree?"

"No, Jason, I don't. I'm as confused by this as you are, but Mike Cohen is an expert in the field, and I'm telling you what he said. I wish you could accept that."

He exhaled. "I can. I'm sorry again."

"He's e-mailing us a written copy of his analysis. It might be on Phil's computer already."

Jason hesitated. "Well, why didn't you tell me that in the first place?"

"Because I talked to the guy. Got the real color, the stuff he might not actually write up. Jason, you've got to learn to trust somebody other than yourself." She exhaled, visibly fatigued. "I'm just so tired of fighting with you. It wears me out."

"You really think we fight a lot?"

"You're joking."

He smiled. "Yeah."

"Look, Jason, the truth is . . . I admire you."

He looked down at the deck. "Sure you do."

"I do, I really do. That whole manta aquarium was such a disaster, such an unmitigated disaster. . . ."

"Thanks for reminding me."

"I didn't mean it like that. It would have destroyed anybody else, absolutely destroyed them—their career, their psyche, everything. But not you, you just kept plugging. Even with Darryl and Craig shooting skeet and drinking, Monique and me doing next to nothing, and Phil doing . . . whatever Phil does . . . You never gave up, not for a second. Anyway, I really think you're impressive."

He looked at her. "Thank you very much."

"And now, finally, you're being rewarded."

"How am I being rewarded exactly?"

"Jason, we are beyond speculation now. We have *physical proof*. These teeth are real, and the number three expert in the world has no idea what they're from. Call Ackerman and tell him. *We are trailing a new species.* You are definitely onto something here."

He was staring at her now. "Yeah, maybe I am."

She stared at him too, if only for a moment. Then thought, God, what am I doing? "Anyway . . . we'll see what happens." She looked at the sky, suddenly aware of how drained she was. "It was a long day. I'm going to change, then help them out with dinner." She turned to go.

"Lisa."

"Yeah?"

"I forgot to mention it . . . you looked really nice today."

She paused. "Thank you."

"I mean it, really nice. Of course my only basis for comparison is Craig."

"Not to mention yourself."

He looked down at his own white tank top. "The pinnacle of haute couture."

She smiled. "Thanks for noticing, Giorgio."

His intense eyes returned. "We *are* onto a new species here, aren't we?"

"We have to be."

She left and he looked up at the sky. Lisa was exactly right. The teeth proved it beyond a shadow of a doubt: they were tracking a new species! He didn't feel different, but he supposed his life had just changed; perhaps all of theirs had. He smiled wide. A new species!

His smile faded. He still didn't understand. How could the manta's deep-sea cousin have teeth like this? He suddenly thought of the repairman who'd gone missing in the waters off Los Padres National Forest. Was there any way the rays had attacked him? But no, that wasn't possible. Like elephants on land, mantas were incapable, literally *physically incapable,* of being anything other than docile. So didn't their deep-sea cousin have to be docile as well? Jason couldn't help but wonder. Because if they actually did have teeth like this, there was no ambiguity at all about what they had to be. Predators. Real, survival-of-the-fittest predators—nothing like manta rays at all. Jason still didn't understand. How on earth could that be true?

PART II

CHAPTER 20

I T WAS quiet at the ocean's surface. With a full moon shining down, the only sounds came from the breaking waves and blowing wind.

Suddenly, a two-hundred-fifty-pound body shot out of the sea, flapping rapidly, clumsily, rising diagonally and throwing torrents of cold water everywhere. Then, feeling a gust of wind, the creature angled its horned head parallel to the ocean and, like a seagull, surged into a wind-assisted glide. It coasted for nearly fifty yards, gradually dipping lower, then nosed horns first into a large breaking wave. Then another body splashed out. Then another. Then fifty more. Within moments, thousands of juveniles were shooting out. Fully exposed, they revealed how much they'd grown, larger animals now, all with fierce builds made of solid muscle.

It was an explosion of activity, each creature doing its best to fly. Many failed, but others succeeded. With ferocious, awkward flapping, several hundred gradually climbed to heights of nearly two hundred feet before coasting back down. Others focused less on distance and more on learning a specific skill: the first thrust from the water, the first flapping motion once they emerged. Some tried to fly with the wind. Others against it. Others waited until there was no wind at all. Some tried to turn in the air. Others simply flew straight. A few tried nose-diving.

Each tried something different. Like a flock of newborn birds, they continued to experiment.

A THIRD of a mile below the surface, the adults lay at the bottom, unseen. There were fewer of them now. Within just the past twenty-four hours, another 1,500 had died. Some from starvation. Others from a virus.

Two had died for another reason entirely. A shark had killed them. A dozen of the creatures had drawn the animal—a nine-hundred-pound hammerhead—into their darkened lair and attacked it. The shark had thrashed violently, biting anything and everything, and gashed two of them. Both rays eventually bled to death, but not until long after the shark itself had been ripped to shreds and eaten alive.

These predators had devoured tens of millions of sharks during their lifetimes. They'd tasted every type imaginable: hammerheads, requiems, carpets, goblins, great whites, and so many more. Each shark species has its own hunting style, and these creatures knew every one.

Some sharks rely strictly on sound or vibrations to hunt. Others rely largely on sight. Some hunt by locating electromagnetic pulses. Some by smell. Some use every one of those senses and more to varying degrees.

Some sharks approach prey quickly. Others are slower and circle around, sometimes for hours.

Some sharks are very finicky eaters and have sensitive noses. Others can't smell at all and will eat anything.

Some sharks are small, not weighing more than twenty pounds. Others are huge, weighing three tons.

The sharks vary greatly, but they share one defining characteristic. They are stupid. They always come when they sense prey. This fatal flaw has caused a number of their species to be hunted to extinction. Like terramouth and megalodon. Man will never find either again because they no longer exist. They've been hunted far too efficiently.

These predators still bait sharks, just as they always have.

One was doing it at the moment.

Unseen in the blackened waters, it floundered frantically twenty feet above the ocean floor, contorting and twisting in every direction. The animal appeared to be distressed and out of control. It was anything but. Every one of its movements had been precisely choreographed, designed to generate vibrations that varied in frequency from ten to eight hundred hertz. The creature didn't understand the concept of frequency bandwidths, per se, but what it did understand was that sharks use their senses to locate wounded fish; and that wounded fish move in a certain way and at a certain frequency. When that movement and its resulting frequency are duplicated precisely, the sharks always come. They swim right in, hungry and ready to eat their prey. Only when it's too late do they discover who the prey really is.

The creature and more than one hundred others like it continued to shake. With vast numbers of other hungry animals lying in wait, the hope was to attract an entire shark school, perhaps numbering in the thousands. Nothing came. Not a school, not a family, not even a lone rogue. The thrashing ray was exhausted. It had been writhing for more than six hours. The sharks had been coming less and less often in recent months, and now they weren't coming at all.

Normally, a shark swimming in the illuminated waters above would detect a large, apparently wounded fish thrashing in the depths. With short, rapid sweeps of its big tail, the shark would dive down to find it. As it descended into the darkened waters, however, its vision would disappear and it would sense several peculiarities. The most prominent was that there'd be no blood. But even without blood, the vibrations would continue, and the tiny-brained hunter would blindly swim closer.

The attack would come in one of two ways.

Sometimes, the shark would realize something was wrong when it was only ten feet away. Suddenly the wounded animal would be perfectly healthy—and swimming right for the shark. The shark wouldn't see it in the darkness, but it would feel its watery wake from its massive pumping wings. Unable to slow down—sharks possess no form of braking mechanism—the shark's momentum would carry it right into the animal, which would simply open its massive dagger-filled mouth and bite down. The bite, which was more powerful than the crushing mechanisms of most garbage trucks, would sever the entire upper third of the shark's body. Then the others would join in.

More commonly, the predator pretending to be wounded would

continue its act until the last possible moment. Sometimes, it would even allow the shark to bite it. The ray knew from experience that the shark's teeth wouldn't pierce its tough armorlike skin, at least not with a single nip. And a single nip would be all it would get. By then, the other creatures the shark had just swum right over would have risen from the bottom. If the shark had been paying attention, it would have known they were coming for it. But the shark never paid attention. Six or more would surround it and tear away pieces of its body, eating it alive. The bloody feast would finish in seconds.

But there were no feasts now. The sharks weren't coming. Nothing was.

The writhing predator froze and floated down, joining the others. They were all still hungry. Unlike the growing juveniles, these animals had spent their entire lives learning how to hunt a certain way, in a certain place. But the juveniles were different. They weren't learning how to bait sharks, read ocean currents, and hide in the depths. They were learning entirely different skills in another place.

No longer could these elder animals stop them by killing them. The younger rays regularly escaped their attacks simply by swimming into the higher waters—and staying there. The juveniles spent very little time in the depths anymore. Even at the moment, they were at the surface, more than a third of a mile away. They were too far to be seen, too far to be heard, but the animals here were watching them.

They were watching something else, too. They'd stopped their migration because of it. Food was coming. The juveniles didn't know it yet, but that would soon change. The adults were incapable of catching what was coming; they were too large, too slow moving, and too far away. But the juveniles were none of those things. Perhaps they'd find a way to eat.

THE SMALLER rays continued shooting out of the sea, zooming everywhere. Then one of them jerked its horned head to the north. Suddenly detecting what the adults had just sensed, it pulled its wings in tight, dove back into the sea, and didn't return. Instantaneously, the others did the same. In less than a second, the entire ocean plane was deserted.

They hung listlessly below the surface, every sensory organ tuning in. They'd just picked up a group of fifty animals, still a great distance away but swimming in their direction.

The juveniles heard them, though not with their ears and not with their lateral lines either. In a technical sense, they didn't "hear" them at all, though hearing was the human sense that most closely approximated what they'd done. They possessed highly specialized organs in their heads known as ampullae of Lorenzini. Like an inner ear, ampullae are composed of delicate jelly-filled pores that provide magnetic detection capabilities. Land-based animals don't have ampullae of Lorenzini, but they are common in creatures of the sea. Mantas have the strongest ampullae of Lorenzini in the known animal kingdom. Those of their unknown cousins were a hundred times stronger.

The rays didn't move. Hanging in the moon-speckled waters, they simply tuned. The prey were still heading toward them. This particular type of prey wasn't part of their regular diet, but the rays could be opportunistic—or at least try to be. The rays had already attempted to hunt this prey on several occasions and failed every time. But they'd learned lessons. They were concerned about the prey's sonars. The juveniles themselves possessed sonar, sound navigation, and radar, but that of the approaching prey was far stronger. In its crudest form, sonar is an echo-location system in which a sound is emitted and its reflection, or echo, is analyzed. The approaching species used sonar by emitting a series of high-frequency clicks, commonly in the 200,000-hertz range. When these "clicks" met a fish, much like an X-ray, they passed through body tissues but reflected back against bone. But unlike the picture from a doctor's office, these particular X-rays provided an intimate view of three entire miles of open ocean.

But still, as strong as the approaching prey's sonars were, the rays' ampullae of Lorenzini were even stronger. Their ampullae had a range of *five* miles and could detect the electrical activity in every one of the approaching animals' muscles: front and rear torsos, necks, fins—even their hearts. Indeed, from five miles away, the juvenile rays had detected the prey's individual heartbeats, more than fifty of them.

The rays knew the prey's sonars would soon pick them up as well, but the prey's sonars could be fooled. If a small pack of rays swam in a very particular way, they could effectively simulate another predator that the prey would attempt to evade. But in evading what they'd think was a single large predator, they'd actually be swimming toward thousands of smaller ones. A group of juveniles began moving.

FIFTY BOTTLENOSE dolphins zoomed out of the sea, their elegant gray bodies glistening in the pale moonlight. The mammals hung in the air for a brief moment, arching slightly, then knifed back in. A few miles offshore and moving at nearly twenty-five miles per hour, the dolphins were in the midst of a southern migration.

At the front of the herd, the leader was much larger than the rest—a twelve-footer weighing nearly 950 pounds. The animal had been studying the ocean ahead since the beginning of their migration, and until this point, its sonar had detected very little, just schools of tiny fish. But suddenly it picked up something else. The reading was foggy and unclear, but somewhere in the distance was a large creature. Made of cartilage, the creature appeared to be a shark, swimming from the west. The leader changed direction slightly, and like a flock of birds, the other dolphins followed.

They swam for nearly half a minute when the leader picked up something else: an unmoving mass spread out over a square mile. Again the reading was unclear, but the leader's sonar indicated it had to be a kelp forest. Dolphins often swim through kelp forests to evade sharks, and this school intended to do the same.

They swam straight for it. What they thought was a kelp forest was a little more than a mile away.

CHAPTER 21

THE DOLPHINS had reacted as hoped.

Most of the rays still didn't move, however. They just floated, luring the mammals closer. They knew that if the dolphins didn't change course soon, their fates would be sealed.

THE DOLPHINS didn't change course. They knew instinctively that something was "off" in the ocean ahead, but they didn't know what. As they knifed in and out of the sea, the leader's sonar continued producing unusual readings. It now indicated the kelp forest ahead might not be kelp after all, but something else, something indeterminate. The big dolphin didn't have time to analyze it. The large cartilaginous creature from the west was still swimming toward them, and now so was a *second* creature, from the east.

To escape both, the dolphins had to swim right into the middle of the forest. Either that or turn around. They didn't turn around.

THE BLACK eyes watched them. A single ray too far from the herd to participate in the hunt floated listlessly just below the surface as the dolphins leaped out. Through the shimmering water, it watched them, a sight to behold, their silhouettes flying through the night air beneath the moon. The predator saw none of their beauty. It saw food.

THE LEADER'S sonar readjusted again. Now there were *four* large cartilaginous animals. One to the east. One to the west. And two directly behind them.

The big mammal now knew that the mass in front of them wasn't kelp at all. But whatever it was, it wasn't exactly in front of them either. Not entirely. Somehow, it had moved and changed shape. It was now on their sides.

And even behind them.

THE RAYS quickened their pace. They had drifted into position earlier to avoid detection, but now they were swimming as fast as they could, approaching from every angle.

THE DOLPHINS halted.

Floating ten feet below the surface, they tuned carefully. Something had surrounded them, apparently a vast group of animals. At first, the dolphins had determined they were sharks, but sharks moved much faster and were shaped differently. These were winged creatures.

The mammals fanned their tails, rising toward the shimmering surface until their heads poked out. They still couldn't see the rays, but their sonars reconfirmed that they were coming. And also that they had teeth. Very large teeth.

Suddenly the dolphins knew what was happening. They were being hunted.

Smart as they are, dolphins are not courageous animals. They scare easily and often lose their ability to behave rationally when threatened. Floating at the surface, a few twitched ever so slightly. Then their twitches grew larger, turning into jerks. Then the jerks turned into full-torso shakes. Then one of them cried, a single high-pitched squeal that echoed over the watery plane. Then a few more cried. Then they all cried. Suddenly the entire herd was shrieking and shaking wildly. The attack hadn't even begun, and the once-graceful, once-intelligent animals were already reduced to a mindless, terrified mass, sheep before the slaughter.

Then a powerful, piercing scream rang out above all the others. It was the leader. Unlike the others, it hadn't moved and hadn't made a sound. Its strong, 950-pound body was still pointed forward, its head out. The others went silent and swam next to it, forming a straight line.

They slowly submerged to ten feet. A hanging wall of gray, they just read the signals surrounding them. They still couldn't see the rays but knew the winged creatures were moving closer. They'd never get close enough.

The gray wall moved. Slowly at first, as the dolphins searched the waters in every direction. They saw no fish of any kind, just twisted shards of moonlight. They picked up speed very quickly and within moments were streaking through the seas.

Continuing, they looked up and, for the first time, saw two of their hunters a pool length away near the surface, winged silhouettes slowly flapping toward them.

The dolphins sped below and past like they weren't there.

The rays froze. The dolphins had panicked earlier and been on the verge of self-destruction. Now they were putting up a fight. And a good one. They just watched as the speeding mammals disappeared.

The dolphins didn't look back. The moon-dappled waters ripped past, and they veered sharply upward. They couldn't see them yet, but their sonars indicated the next group of rays, a dozen, was two pool lengths away. The rolling surface rose up, and they hurtled through it. Bathed in the moonlit air, they breathed in deeply, then knifed back in. A dozen winged silhouettes came into view moments later and the dolphins simply tore through the sea beneath them. As they passed below, one of the dolphins looked up. Their hunters weren't even moving now. The rays' silhouettes were frozen, so still the dolphin instinctively thought they might be dead.

They weren't dead. They were looking right back at it, studying it, studying all of them. Their horned heads turned slightly, watching the gray mammals disappear. The rays were too smart to waste energy chasing prey they knew they couldn't catch, but they instinctively realized there might be another way to catch the dolphins. It was too late for these rays of course but perhaps not for the next group. . . .

THE NEXT group of rays was already within the mammals' view, two dozen of them. Strangely, these rays were swimming *away* from the dolphins, toward the surface.

The dolphins ripped below and past them, already arching up for the next gulp of air.

MANY POOL lengths away, more than a hundred rays were also swimming toward the surface, the water surging past their horned heads. The previous group's timing had been off, but these rays sensed theirs could be perfect.

THE DOLPHINS hurtled through the seas, moving at nearly forty miles per hour now. Their heartbeats had already slowed considerably. The next group of rays was the last major obstacle. If the dolphins could make it past them, they'd soon be free. . . .

THE RAYS swam higher as fast as they could. The dolphins were rapidly coming closer and within seconds would pass directly below this exact spot. The predators pumped hard, the shimmering plane approaching. They pierced it and, spraying water everywhere, rose straight into the night air. Ascending to different heights, they turned back to the sea. The undulating gray bodies were speeding closer, moments away. The rays just had to hang in the air long enough and then . . .

THE DOLPHINS were suddenly confused. The rays had disappeared. Speeding through the moon-dappled waters, the mammals turned in every direction. They couldn't see them anywhere.

THE RAYS were directly above them now. Plunging down, eyes locked. Just like seagulls hunting for fish.

SUDDENLY THE dolphins picked something up. Something *above* the water.

They didn't have time to react.

Suddenly big winged bodies were dropping everywhere. Ten landed in front of the herd, a dozen behind it, and they all missed. But half a second later, another platoon landed, and they were on top of them.

Powerful jaws thundered closed on the dolphins' defenseless bodies, gouging huge chunks from their backs, necks, torsos, and faces. The speeding gray wall disintegrated, shrieking dolphins swimming off in every direction. The mammals thrashed furiously, desperately trying to shake off their attackers. None let go. The rays had wrapped their entire winged bodies around them, and as they were hurtled through the seas their frantically chomping jaws simply tore off more and more meat.

Within minutes, more than half the herd had given up, resigned to death. Others, even though chunks the size of footballs were missing from their sides, tried to swim away in vain. Five dolphins actually shook their attackers off, but soon others leaped on.

Two of the mammals were in such shock they dove toward the depths, not realizing they wouldn't have enough air to get back up. They didn't need it. Bleeding severely as they passed the thousand-foot mark, their muscles suddenly stopped working. They entered complete paralysis and, within seconds, drowned. Their corpses floated for a moment until a dozen of the rays they'd passed earlier began to eat them.

The largest dolphin, the 950-pounder that had been the herd's leader, continued to fight. A few feet below the waterline, it swam as fast as it could, less than five miles per hour now. Seven juvenile rays were tearing away at it, three on its back, two on its stomach, and one each on its face and neck. It swam for another twenty feet, then gave up. It emitted a final cry, a weak gurgling sound, and died. The rays continued to feed on it. They'd removed 350 pounds, and though their stomachs were full, they worked on the 600 pounds that remained.

But suddenly they stopped.

They leaped off the floating piece of meat and swam away.

Something was coming. Something much larger and considerably more dangerous than they were. One of the adults had left its hiding place in the depths and come to steal their spoils. The smaller animals couldn't see it yet, but they sensed it. They had first sensed it rising

twenty minutes earlier but had been so focused on the hunt, they'd ignored it. But the massive animal was too close to be ignored any
longer. They wouldn't challenge it. If it wanted their food, it would
have it—and without a fight. They swam farther from the corpse and
looked down. Never before had the juveniles seen an adult come to
the surface, not once. An adult that would do so had to be on the
verge of starvation. Its massive pumping body slowly appeared below.
The juveniles backed farther away still. They didn't want to be close
to it.

They drifted lower, glancing up at the watery moon. Then the gargantuan form rose up in front of the white orb, its curtain-size wings
slowly flapping. When the animal reached the floating piece of meat,
its purpose was unmistakable. A pair of jaws wide enough to swallow
two men whole stretched open, then thundered closed, severing the
dolphin in half. The jaws quickly chewed and the animal swallowed.

The juveniles didn't move.

Another corpse, an inedible infected one, they had determined, was
floating nearby. The huge creature swam toward it. Again, the jaws
opened and thundered down. But this time, there was no chewing. The
creature sensed what the juveniles had: the meat was infected. It deserted the severed pieces and dove down, descending toward the darkness.

After the great animal was gone, the smaller ones returned to the
surface. As they edged their horns out of the sea, they heard it: faint
high-pitched screams echoing across the watery plane. A few of the
slaughtered dolphins were still alive, hanging on, their cries an offer-
ing of fresh meat to whoever could reach them first. This group wasn't
interested. Their stomachs were filled, and they were too tired to
swim. They wanted to rest before they continued north again. They
slowly descended. Then, floating like a cluster of enormous starfish,
they simply closed their eyes.

The ocean's surface became perfectly quiet. The only sounds were
from the wind and the waves. The cries of the dolphins were no more

CHAPTER 22

T WAS 7:30 A.M. on this day in the first week of October. The sky was a bleak gray, without a trace of sun anywhere. Good fishing weather. Three tuna fisherman, Don Gilroy, Kurt Hicks, and Mark Balson, had been trailing a pack of seven dolphins for an hour and were now in the waters off of Santa Cruz, a few miles north of Monterey. Tuna fisherman regularly followed dolphins to help them locate their catch. Biologists still didn't know why, but dolphins and tuna often swam together, dolphins near the surface, tuna a couple hundred feet below it.

The gods appeared to be smiling on the fisherman this morning because the dolphins abruptly stopped swimming forward and began circling. This was unusual behavior. Normally, dolphins slow gradually as they tire. The men didn't suspect there might be a reason for this. They'd seen relatively few dolphins recently, so now that they'd actually found a small pack, they weren't asking questions.

The fishermen let out a massive weighted seine net. It drifted down to the tuna below, caught them, then began to tighten and ascend. In compliance with the Marine Mammals Protection Act of 1972, the men watched carefully as one by one, all seven of the dolphins leaped over the net and swam away. In less than a minute, the mammals were gone—apparently. The three had to be certain. The Marine Act had a second procedural requirement stipulating that someone had to paddle out in a rowboat and physically check that every dolphin had escaped. Many fishermen regularly ignored this rule, but not Gilroy, Hicks, and Balson.

Balson had gone last time, so Gilroy and Hicks flipped a quarter to see who would go now. Kurt Hicks lost. Paddling out in a tiny rowboat in his overalls, he noticed a single strand of kelp, oddly shredded, but didn't give it much thought. He reached the middle of the net, then rolled into the sea with a mask. Holding it against his face, he scanned for any stray dolphins.

Back on the boat, on a peeling wood plank that doubled as a bench, Balson and Gilroy made small talk.

"So what do you got going this weekend, Gilroy?"

"Ah, nothing much. Watch the baseball game, get drunk with Darlene."

Balson chuckled and glanced toward Hicks. "What's Kurt doing out there anyway?" It normally took all of ten seconds to confirm the dolphins were gone, but it had already been longer than that.

"Ah, who knows, probably playing with himself." Gilroy stood. "Hey! What are you doing out there, Hicks?!"

Kurt Hicks raised his sopping head from the water. "There's something down here! I'm gonna go see what it is!" He put the mask on completely and disappeared.

Gilroy sat. "So, what do you got going this weekend, Balson?"

"Ah, I'll probably watch the ball game myself. Maybe the Giants can win one, huh?"

They continued to chat casually for another minute when Gilroy realized that Kurt Hicks still hadn't come back up. He eyed the empty rowboat nervously. "Think he found a dolphin tangled in the net or something?"

Balson hesitated. "I only counted seven and I thought I saw every one of them swim off."

"Maybe there was an eighth we didn't see." Gilroy checked his watch. "Let's give him another thirty seconds."

Exactly twenty-five seconds later, Kurt Hicks still hadn't come up.

Gilroy stood. "Son of a bitch. Maybe he did get tangled up down there. All right, I'm gonna go get him. . . ." He ripped off his shoes, grabbed a life preserver, stood up on the gunwale, and . . . Kurt Hicks popped up, gasping for air.

Gilroy shook his head. "What the hell were you doing down there, Hicks?!"

Kurt Hicks didn't answer. He frantically swam toward the rowboat.

"Hey, are you all right?!"

Again, Hicks didn't respond. He just swam to the little boat.

Gilroy put binoculars to his face and saw that something was behind Hicks, swimming after him.

Hicks swam as fast as he could—but not fast enough. The thing was getting closer.

He reached the boat and climbed in.

Then Gilroy realized that whatever was behind him wasn't actually swimming. It wasn't even moving. It just seemed to turn over when a wave struck it. But what was it? "What'd you find down there, Kurt?"

Hicks paddled forward as fast as he could, still not answering.

That's when Gilroy realized. It was a dead dolphin.

Gasping for air, Hicks climbed onto the boat and collapsed on the peeling wooden deck.

"We didn't kill that thing, did we?"

"No." Breathing heavily, Kurt Hicks looked up at Gilroy. "But something else sure as hell did. We gotta tell somebody about this." He blew out a deep breath. "Call the Coast Guard."

CHAPTER 23

"*A* NEW species—you're sure that's what it is?"

Jason nodded to his cell phone as he and Craig followed a uniformed coast-guard officer down an ugly, brown-tiled hallway. "Absolutely sure, Harry. The analysis of the teeth confirmed it. It's a new species."

Ackerman's voice remained calm and matter-of-fact. "That's fantastic. As we agreed, you and your team will have another year on your contracts. Do you think you're close to finding it?"

"We're certainly trying to."

"Well . . . *do it*, then."

Jason paused. "I said we're trying, Harry."

An exhale. "Sorry, Jason. I'm dealing with . . . some financial issue with some of my companies. It's been stressful."

"No problem." Jason could picture the man rubbing his forehead in the office of his gigantic mansion. "OK, Harry, so I'll talk to you—"

"I have some other questions, if you don't mind."

Jason followed Craig and the officer into another hallway. "Shoot."

"You said the teeth didn't come from barracudas, anglers, gars, and—what other fish again?"

A pause. "I honestly don't remember." Jason didn't realize he'd mentioned the fish that the teeth *hadn't come from.* "You'd have to ask Lisa for further details on that." He looked up as the officer reached a door. "Harry, I'm sorry, but we're kind of in the middle of something here. Can I get back to you?"

"Oh. Not necessary. But anything you need on this, just let me know."

The line cut out, and Jason hung up. "Sorry about that, Officer Bell."

In a crisp navy uniform that made Jason feel underdressed, Officer Gavin Bell nodded. "No problem." The guy had a crew cut and was the size of an NFL linebacker. "Anyway, here it is."

They entered a windowless white chamber that looked like an examining room in a doctor's office. But the room wasn't a doctor's. It belonged to the Monterey Coast Guard. And the specimen on the silver operating table wasn't a person. It was a dead dolphin the guard had picked up from three fishermen earlier in the day.

It wasn't standard practice for the coast guard to alert ichthyologists of such finds. The day before, Jason and his team had bumped into a coast-guard trawler on the ocean, and the two boats had gotten to talking. Monique explained to the "Coasties," as the officers were known, that they were tracking a new species and Darryl and Craig had invited the men aboard for drinks. As employees of the federal government, the Coasties politely declined this offer, but clearly appreciated the gesture. As it happened, they had a chance to repay it. Earlier in the day, a freshly killed dolphin had turned up in the exact area that Jason and company had tracked their new species to.

"You guys all set in here?"

Jason turned. "We are. Thank you very much, Officer Bell. We owe you one here."

"You don't owe us squat." Bell smiled at Summers, who was wearing khakis four sizes too big for him. "Nobody ever offers us beers."

As the officer left, Jason started thinking about Lisa and didn't know why. It wasn't like him to think about her at all, much less during business. Was their relationship changing? She'd once despised him, but he suddenly couldn't help but wonder if something more amicable might be brewing.

He turned back to the examining table. He was glad she didn't have to see this. "Jesus." What was lying there was truly gruesome: the corpse of a bottlenose dolphin. Jason guessed it had weighed 650 pounds. This was a guess because only the body's top half was there. The lower half had been bitten off. Bitten off clean. No shark had done it. No shark alive possessed a mouth big enough or jaws strong enough to sever a dolphin in half.

Craig shook his head, eyeing the once-lively eyes, now sealed closed in death. He pivoted, leaned into the bloody red stump, and studied what looked like . . . vertical lines, from whatever had severed the body. He tried to count them. This wasn't easy, but there appeared to be a dozen, each as wide as a human hand. They were teeth marks. Made by much larger versions of the fat S-shaped canines they'd found earlier, perhaps the size of champagne bottles. He took a few steps and studied the carcass from another angle. It was covered with smaller bites, gaping red chunks the size of footballs. Craig couldn't believe what he was seeing. This was proof, and it was unambiguous. "My God, Jason, these rays are predators."

Jason felt numb. "So . . . they've been feeding on dolphins all this time?"

"I don't think that's possible."

"Why?"

"You haven't heard what the USDS has been saying?" The USDS is the United States Dolphin Society, a conservation group out of Monterey that monitors the migratory habits of bottlenoses in the Northern Pacific.

"No. What have they been saying?"

"That California's bottlenose population has been swimming south to Brazil and Chile for two years. York says to escape GDV-4. So these rays can't be feeding on dolphins, at least not regularly."

"So what are they eating, then?"

"I have no idea. I'm just wondering why they didn't eat this."

"What do you mean?"

"Why didn't the rays eat this dolphin? They attacked it, they killed it, why didn't they eat it?"

Jason shook his head.

"Wait a second. . . ." Summers's eyes sharpened. "I bet this animal has GDV-4."

"You think?. . . ." Jason picked up a wall phone without a dialing mechanism. "Gavin, did your lab people do any tests on this specimen?" He hung up and Bell instantly brought in a manila file and left.

Summers tore into it and pointed. "Look . . . 'tested positive for GDV-4' . . . 'only recently entered the bloodstream' . . . Sounds like a mild case."

Jason read the words himself. "So they detected *a mild case in a living animal.*"

"And they caught a dolphin. They caught and killed *a frickin' dolphin.* How is that possible?"

Jason looked at the ceiling, clueless. Slow-swimming rays didn't possess the physical equipment to catch speedy dolphins. The land equivalent was like a turtle catching a cheetah. It wasn't possible. And yet it had happened. How? He considered it for several silent moments. And then the answer hit him.

"There's only one way—there's only one possible way."

"What?"

"They must have outsmarted it."

Craig absorbed this. The rays were more than just predators. Somehow they'd outsmarted what many believed to be the most intelligent wild animal on the planet. "How on God's earth did they outsmart a dolphin?"

Jason looked up at the ceiling again. "I know. My God, I think I know."

CHAPTER 24

"**W**E NEED to find a brain, a physical brain."

It was night, and Craig and Jason had just returned to the boat. The Monterey marina was deserted now except for a lone patrolling security guard. Beneath the pale yellow light from the dock's streetlamps, everyone was on the rear deck, dressed casually, seated on the built-ins or freestanding chairs. The others had just finished a dinner of burgers, grilled chicken, and sides.

As Craig went below deck to change out of his khakis, Lisa shook her head at Jason, not getting the logic. "You've seen millions of manta brains, haven't you?"

"*Manta brains,* yes. But these animals are not manta rays, Lisa. They've got to be much smarter than that."

"Meaning they'll have larger brains?"

"I don't know. That's why I want to see one."

Monique nodded. "That's a fascinating idea, Jason. But how would we do it? It's clear now that these rays are hiding, and we haven't even seen one yet."

"Not a *living* one anyway."

A pause. "Are you saying we can find dead one?"

"Yes."

Lisa turned to Jason skeptically. "How the hell are we going to do that?"

As Craig emerged from below deck in a white terry robe, Jason smiled at Lisa Barton, for the first time noticing what she was wearing: tight jeans and a yellow shirt with a lower-than-average neckline. Her head was jutted forward, and the chip on her shoulder was almost as big as the quarter moon hanging over the docks.

"I like that optimistic nature of yours, Lisa. It's kind of sweet."

She reddened slightly, suddenly aware that she was leaning forward. She didn't know why she'd worn her sexy jeans tonight.

Jason smiled, more to himself, happy he could stick her a little. "Tell her how we're going to find a dead one, Craig."

Craig took a step forward. "GDV-4."

She turned. "What?"

"We know GDV-4's been forcing these rays out of the depths, right?"

"Right."

"But it must have killed a bunch of them, too."

"OK, so . . ."

"So maybe we can find a dead one."

"How do you figure that? You know how quickly the ocean's food chain works, Craig. We wouldn't find more than a skeleton."

Normally, when an animal dies at sea, its entire body—skin, muscle, fat, liver, brain, even eyeballs—is eaten and digested with great efficiency. The feast takes place in three phases. First, the largest of the scavengers eats large chunks of meat and muscle. Second, smaller animals eat the bulk of the insides, including the major internal organs. Finally, the vermin, the tiniest of the flesh eaters, pick the bones clean. Nothing is left to waste, and within forty-eight hours, skeletons are all that remains.

Monique's eyes shifted to Craig. "I don't get that logic either."

"Let me explain it, then. This isn't just a normal dead body. If GDV-4 did actually kill it, then nothing will even touch it, much less eat it. The virus would actually serve the beneficial purpose of preserving the body."

Monique smiled. "That's very clever. You think it will work?"

"Jason figures there's gotta be at least one body down there, and I'm inclined to agree."

Darryl turned. "How deep are we talking, Craig?"

"A couple thousand feet."

"A couple *thousand*? How are we gonna get to that? Will Ackerman pay for that?" The cost of renting the necessary equipment could easily be ten times their combined salaries.

"I get the feeling Ackerman's financial situation is getting worse, so I'd prefer not to lean on him here." Jason shrugged. "We might not need to."

"You know someone who's got the equipment?"

"I've got to check. What's up with the kelp trail, Darryl?"

"We can't find it."

The starkness of the answer knocked a blank stare onto Jason's face. "We've got to find it. If we don't . . . we could be in real trouble."

"Then we're in real trouble," Lisa said.

"What? Why do you say that?"

"Because the kelp trail's probably gone, Jason."

"Why would it be gone?"

"Because these rays have got to be finished teething by now."

"Why? Mantas teethe for—"

"We're not dealing with manta rays here; you just said it. These rays are predators, and predators grow teeth much faster."

"How much faster?"

"Typically, with barracudas and sharks, lower-central canines peek out within hours of birth, upper centrals within weeks, first primary molars, maybe two months. I'd say all the primary teeth are generally present within four months tops."

"But these rays have been teething on kelp for almost five."

"Exactly my point. A very long time for a predator. I think the dolphin you and Craig just saw confirmed it: these things have real teeth now; *they've got to be finished teething*." She slumped slightly, waiting for him to rip into her with his second-guessing. Instead, he simply nodded.

Lisa paused, not understanding this reaction. But then she realized: if they wanted to find a brain in the depths, they had to do it fast. Even if a body had been preserved by GDV-4, it wouldn't last down there long. Water currents could destroy it in days. They had to get moving, and Jason didn't have the *time* to second-guess her now.

On cue, his shoe started tapping. "How are we going to track them, then?"

Monique shrugged. "Maybe we can track them directly."

"How, Monique?"

"Darryl, are these things big enough to pick up with sonar?"

A devilish smile. "You know, they might be. We got a bunch of buoys in storage."

Jason raised an eyebrow. "Would that actually work?" The *Expedition*'s sonar buoys had an acoustical range designed to track torpedoes but could also be used to detect whales, dolphins, and other large animals. So why not the rays? The buoys were just like regular buoys except they had sonar microphones on their bottoms with a range of five miles each. With two dozen, more than a hundred square miles of ocean could be covered. They could just toss them in and see what they picked up.

Jason nodded. "It's worth a shot. All right, Monique, tomorrow you and Darryl will throw out buoys, then track from the boat. The rest of us will see if we can find a brain."

Darryl raised a finger. "Jason, if you're planning to use a submersible, you know that requires a special license, right?"

"Oh." Jason paused, looking around the boat. "Does anyone have that license?"

Blank faces looked back at him.

Then Monique turned to Darryl. "*You* have that license, right, my modest husband?"

Darryl smiled, his lovable smugness in plain sight. "Big Dog to the rescue again."

Jason shook his head. "Fine. Darryl comes with us to find the brain, someone else goes with Monique." He glanced at Phil, silent in the corner. "How about Phil?"

"Oh." Darryl hesitated awkwardly. "Uh, well, Monique's worked with Craig for years. Why doesn't he just help her?"

Jason said nothing. He had to play this carefully. On the one hand, he thought this could be a perfect chance for Phil to actually do something useful on the boat. But on the other hand, this job was critically important, and he didn't want Monique Hollis unhappy. "Sure, Phil will come with us and Craig will go with Monique."

Darryl pivoted to Summers. "Test your harpoon gun before you go, Craig. Carefully."

Summers nodded. While Monique could more than handle herself with a rifle, Craig, Darryl, and Jason were the only ones on the boat who'd used harpoon guns before.

"You really know someone who has this diving equipment?" Lisa asked.

Jason popped open his cell. "Let's find out."

"Sɪᴅ, ɪᴛ's Jason Aldridge."

Sid Klepper paused, eyeing the cordless phone in his hand. He couldn't believe it. "Jason Aldridge?! How the hell are you, man?!"

In an enormous living room, Klepper and his business partner, Ross Drummond, were stretched out on a pair of custom-made eight-foot leather couches, their large, shirtless bellies on proud display. The men didn't look it, but they were the multimillionaire owners of Marwood Enterprises, a hugely successful conglomerate of diving businesses. The pair knew Jason from much leaner times, when all three had spent a summer working on the tiny white-sand island of Yap, in Micronesia, when Jason first learned about mantas and Sid and Ross were mere clerks in a local dive store. Drummond and Klepper's lives had changed dramatically since then, but they'd always considered Jason a friend. "What's going on, Jason?!"

Jason smiled quietly at the greeting. Klepper and Drummond had once been friends of his, real ones, and with the exception of Phil Martino, he didn't have many of those anymore. "Let me tell you what's going on, Sid."

When he finished explaining, Klepper didn't hesitate. "Of course you can borrow the equipment. When do you want it?"

"As soon as you can do it, Sid. Sure, I'll hold." Jason literally crossed his fingers. Then he smiled. "Tomorrow would be perfect."

CHAPTER 25

THE NEXT afternoon was a gorgeous mid-October day, perfect for jeans and sweatshirts. While Monique and Craig dropped sonar buoys in strategic locations at sea, Jason, Lisa, Darryl, and Phil were at the busy Monterey docks, waiting to be picked up. Watching one yacht after another enter the marina, Jason anxiously drummed his fingers on a guardrail.

"Excuse me, Jason?"

He turned. Phil Martino was standing there. "Hey, Phil, what's up?"

"Can we talk really quick?" Phil seemed to mean in private, away from Lisa and Darryl.

"Sure." They walked down the dock then stopped. "What's up?"

Phil raised his camera. "I sure take some great pictures, don't I?"

"You really do, Phil. I'm glad we have you."

Phil nodded sadly. A white lie from a friend. "Jason, I don't feel like I'm a part of the team." He rubbed his curly hair and looked out at the fancy boats. "I haven't felt like I'm a part of the team for some time."

"Oh." Jason nodded, quietly disappointed. Phil had been the *Expedition*'s whipping boy for as long as he could remember. Maybe Darryl's outright snub the night before had finally pushed him over the edge. "You're not saying you want to quit, are you?"

"Not at all. I'm just wondering if I can do anything else to con-tribute."

"Hmm." Jason scratched his chin. He had no idea what else Phil Martino could do.

"So I was thinking. Since you and everybody else are so busy, maybe I could transcribe all of your findings, analyses and all that, into the laptop. There's tons of stuff floating around among all of us, and I fig-ure things can get lost or whatever. This way we'd have a written record on a hard drive. What do you think?"

"That's a fantastic idea, Phil."

"Yeah, you like it?"

"I love it. I'll still write up my own stuff, but for the others, it could be very helpful."

Phil chuckled to himself. Of course Jason would still write up his own stuff.

Jason thought there could be other positives. The Species Council was a demanding twelve-person committee with very strict proce-dural requirements that tended to favor analyses written by multiple scientists. Formalizing Craig's findings on GDV-4, Lisa's on plankton, and Darryl and Monique's on migratory habits could be extremely useful in the credibility department. Also, any excuse to have Phil deal directly with the others on a daily basis could have more . . . touchy-feely benefits as well. If his efforts actually made Darryl and Craig's lives easier, maybe they'd finally stop giving him such a hard time.

"Let's discuss this with the others, but I think it's a great idea."

Phil Martino smiled like an encouraged child. "Excellent."

Suddenly Darryl yelled from farther down the dock. "Hey, Jason! Are these your buds?!"

Jason turned as a towering two-hundred-foot research behemoth cum yacht entered the marina. Sid Klepper and Ross Drummond had just arrived.

"HEY, GUYS!" Leading the others, Jason bounded up the stairs of the massive boat toward two men waiting enthusiastically at the top.

"Hey, Jason!"

"Great to see ya, buddy!"

Klepper and Drummond smacked him hard on the back, lost chums reuniting. As Lisa arrived, she smiled at the genuine camaraderie. Drummond and Klepper were a happy pair, with sizable bellies, freewheeling demeanors, and the clothes to match. Klepper wore baggy blue sweats, a V-neck sweatshirt with a gold chain, and fluffy moccasins. Drummond had on a faded long-sleeved T-shirt, jungle-green camouflage pants, and $1.99 flip-flops. Millionaire hippies. After intros to Lisa, Darryl, and Phil, Ross got down to business. "We still going to those same coordinates, Jason?"

"Yep."

Ross walked toward the controls. "Be there in twenty minutes."

"So someone has a submersible license?" Sid Klepper asked.

Darryl raised his hand. "Me."

Sid looked him up and down. "Big dude. You're really gonna have to squeeze in."

"Yeah." Darryl glanced down at his own crotch. "I'm used to that."

Everyone laughed, and Lisa shook her head. Then Darryl's cell started ringing. "Excuse me. Must be one of my groupies." He fumbled to remove the little device from his pocket.

"COME ON, Darryl, pick up."

The *Expedition* very slowly moved north, on autopilot, as Craig eyed what looked like a desktop computer monitor but was actually a sonar analysis station set up on the back wall. On-screen was an interactive computerized map of the twisting coastline: land colored white, and ocean colored blue. In the middle of the blue was a blinking black dot the size of a pencil head that Summers had been staring at for ten minutes. Standing behind him with a cell phone to her ear, Monique was staring at the dot too, wondering where the hell her husband was. *"Come on, Darryl, pick u—"*

"What up, Wife?"

"Darryl, we found the rays immediately, and we're trailing them. Can I talk to Jason?"

"Hold on."

Monique drummed her fingers. She couldn't believe how quickly it had happened. She and Craig had dropped buoys over a wide swath of ocean, hooked up the station, tuned it to the appropriate UHF signal, and crossed their fingers. Almost immediately, the blinking black dot had appeared. Its source was just two miles offshore.

"Still moving north, Monique?" This was Jason's voice.

She looked forward as they approached a yellow triangular buoy bobbing in the sea. "Yeah, Jason, slowly but surely."

"Any chance you'll actually see one?"

"Think we'll see one, Craig?"

Summers shook his head. "No way. They're nearly three miles down."

"Way too deep, Jason."

"Stay on it. Maybe they'll go into shallower waters."

She hung up, and the blinking black dot continued up the coast.

SID KLEPPER turned to Darryl. "Want to see my equipment now?"

The toothy grin flashed. "If it can measure up, bro."

"Come on." In his sweats and fluffy moccasins, Klepper led them along the giant deck, past half a dozen Jet Skis and a massive gray crane, stopping at a tiny yellow sub perched on rudders. The sub was the length of a car but much thinner, almost like a hot dog, the words DEEP DIVER printed on its side. Klepper gently touched it.

"Three of you will go down on this, two inside the sub, one outside it, the latter wearing special equipment and standing on that little deck. You see it?" The deck on the rear of the sub looked like the world's tiniest apartment terrace, a bright red platform with a waist-high railing. "We'll lower you to the bottom with the crane so you won't use the sub's internal engines until you get there. Darryl, as big as you are, whoever goes down with you inside should be physically small, but I'll let you guys decide that. Jason, I assume you'll be the one in the suit?" The "suit" referred to the atmospheric diving suit, a highly specialized piece of equipment with a $2 million price tag.

Eyeing the little red deck, Jason swallowed nervously. "We'll be going, what, more than a third of a mile down?"

Watching him, Lisa suddenly felt bad for Jason, clearly scared as hell, probably like some people felt before getting on an airplane, except much worse. She hardly blamed him. The prospect of being alone in a pressure-filled world that could crush you to death in a millisecond if anything went wrong would make anyone nervous. His eyes were wider than normal, and he kept swallowing. It was the first time Lisa had actually seen Jason Aldridge *scared*. Strangely, she liked it. It made him less of a machine, more human, even attractive. Little things like this had been building for months, and despite her better judgment, Lisa Barton was becoming . . . interested in Jason. She wished he could relax, though. You'll be fine, she thought, you'll be fine.

"You'll be fine," Sid said. "The suit connects directly to the sub's oxygen supply, and you'll have enough for four full hours." He smacked Jason on the back. "So chill out. Darryl, I need to show you a few particulars with the sub. Phil, you wanna come?"

The three men walked off, and Lisa leaned into Jason and whispered, "You *will* be fine."

He nodded, trying to look cool. "I know."

"You want me to go down in the sub?"

He'd just figured Phil would go. "You'd do that?"

"Actually, I think it could be fun."

Oh. Now he wasn't sure why she wanted to go.

"Hey, Jason!"

They turned to Ross Drummond, waving at them from the outdoor flying bridge. "Come over here and talk to me, brother!"

They walked over. "What's going on, Ross?"

"Ah, not a thing. How about you? Seeing anybody these days?"

"Well . . . you know I have serious intimacy issues, right, Ross?"

They all chuckled as Ross noticed that Lisa's wedding finger was ringless. Was something going on with these two?

"Who else is going down in the sub, Jason?" Sid had just returned with Darryl and Phil.

"Lisa."

"What?" Phil looked wounded by this. "But I wanted to go."

Sid shrugged unapologetically. "Then lose the belly, pal."

Jason leaned in and whispered, "Lisa's more appropriate here, Phil." He paused. "They'll be safe, Sid?"

"Safe as a church. Ross and I have personally used this thing thirty times without a problem."

Jason nodded and Lisa glanced at him sweetly. Was he concerned for her safety? Then the boat stopped, and Ross quickly walked toward them. "Enough conversation. We're here."

CHAPTER 26

"YEAH, PHIL. That could actually be helpful."

Phil smiled. He'd just explained his idea of recording every-one's findings in the laptop to Darryl, and to his delight, his crewmate liked it.

"Great. You think Craig and Monique will feel the same way?"

"Definitely. You're helping them out, brother. You're helping us all out."

"Why don't you take this down in the sub, then?" He handed Darryl a mini–tape recorder. "So we'll have a record if you see anything worthwhile."

"How do I look?"

They turned. It was Jason, wearing the atmospheric suit except for the helmet.

Darryl looked him up and down. "Like Neil Armstrong."

Phil snickered. "Or maybe the Pillsbury Doughboy."

The suit indeed looked like something an astronaut would wear. White, with big bubble-shaped body parts. But instead of puffy fibers, it was constructed of a hard magnesium alloy that made it nearly im-possible to walk in.

His junky flip-flops slapping the deck, Ross approached Jason from behind. "Before we get going, I'm just gonna check there aren't any holes or cracks in this thing." This wasn't a joke. At one third of a mile, roughly two thousand feet, a hole the size of a pinprick in the suit would mean certain death. Ross quickly inspected every bulge and seam. "Everything looks fine. Oh, but . . ." He checked the casing around the heels. "Yep, fine." Then he saw Jason's face. The guy looked terrified. "Loosen up. Your friends will be with you every step of the way, and Darryl knows what he's doing. There won't be any problems, I promise."

"Can anything go wrong with the tube?" Lisa asked.

Ross turned to her. The tube was the size of a vacuum cleaner's and screwed into the back of the suit's neck. "No. The tube's reinforced with magnesium alloy and steel. It's been crush-tested to thirty thousand feet. It can't get tangled; it can't implode; it can't explode, either. A shark could bite down on it without making a dent." He got in Jason's face. "You'll be fine. Try to relax and have a good trip down."

Jason nodded tightly. "Let's do this before I chicken out."

Seconds later, he stood on the red platform holding a helmet as Ross screwed a tube into his back.

"How you two doing in here?"

Crammed into a sub the size of a phone booth, Darryl and Lisa looked up as Sid Klepper dropped in two men's ski jackets. "There's no heat in this thing and it can get down to thirty-five degrees on the ocean floor. Sorry they're so big, Lisa, but Ross and I love fried food and hate exercise. I'd put them on now."

They did, and Lisa was indeed swimming in hers.

"Both of you OK?"

They nodded.

"All right, have a good trip." Sid closed the containment door, sealing them in like sardines.

"Jason, I'm gonna lift the sub now." Ross walked over to the crane's controls. "So grab ahold of the railing."

Jason clutched the red terrace's guardrail as best as he could with his clunky hands.

"Got a good grip?"

Jason nodded.

"OK, here we go. . . ." Ross flipped a switch and the crane's electric motor raised the sub straight up into the air, carried it twenty feet away from the boat, then slowly lowered it into the ocean.

Inside, Lisa smiled as sloshing blue seas appeared in front of a viewing pane the size of a big TV. Darryl ignored the view. At the controls, he began fiddling with switches and knobs.

Then a voice sounded from the ceiling. "Darryl, everything OK?"

He flicked a switch. "Fine, Ross. All systems go."

"Lisa, you too?"

"Fine, Ross, thanks." She eyed a monochrome monitor of Jason in the back of the sub, fully submerged now in the sun-dappled seas.

"Jason, everything OK?" Ross asked.

From the back platform he looked up at a watery sun. "Yeah, Ross, fine."

"OK, all of you, listen up. A cable will take you all the way to the bottom then disengage. Once you get down there, you'll have a fully active sub. And Jason, you'll be able to walk around as much as you want. That's it. Any questions or problems?"

No one said anything. Inside the sub and out, they were ready to go.

"All right, I'm gonna cut out. Have a safe trip, guys."

The sub lurched slightly as a big steel cable began turning. Then Darryl Hollis, Jason Aldridge, and Lisa Barton descended toward the darkness.

CHAPTER 27

BUBBLES STREAMING past his helmet, Jason eyed the departing boat's underside. His gaze leveled, and he took in the sun-dappled world surrounding them. The water was bright blue, almost turquoise. He didn't feel nervous anymore. He felt fine, even relaxed. The only sound was from his own machine-assisted breathing. The sea was like a great vacuum, quiet, peaceful, and immense. He stared into its blueness as they descended thirty feet, then fifty, then seventy. Jason had spent a large part of his life in the water, but the ocean still awed him. Inside his helmet, he thought of how foolish the three of them had to look, invading the gargantuan silent world with the aid of their tiny man-made contraptions. As a scientist, Jason had tremendous respect for man's inventions, but there was something about the vastness of the sea that made them seem puny. He often wondered if astronauts felt similarly in space. He'd never be an astronaut, of course, never look down at the earth from a distant, cold, faraway place, but he'd read the accounts of those who had and imagined himself being there. It was strange, but at the moment, he felt like he actually was. The sunlight was disappearing. The water was darkening.

At the three-hundred-foot mark, he descended toward a few thousand cod, their silver bodies swimming effortlessly. He whirred down and past them. Looking beyond his hard white boots, he saw that what had been blue only moments ago was now a chasm of darkness. His gaze leveled. The water in the immediate vicinity was now a grayish shade, similar to early evening on land. He turned back up to the cod, but they were already gone, silently dissolving. He noticed the cable, their lifeline, and remembered the boat at the surface. It, too, was only a memory now.

Inside the sub, Darryl glanced at a depth gauge as they passed five hundred feet. "Keep the lights off, Lisa?"

"Yes."

Darryl flicked a switch. "Keep the lights off, Jason?"

"Definitely."

None of them had actually been this deep before. They wanted to see the darkness, to feel it, to experience it, a silent, watery darkness that didn't exist anywhere else on the planet.

They passed seven hundred feet then eight. And then, very gradually, it became totally black.

Alone on the platform, Jason's eyes were wide open but saw nothing.

"Passing one thousand feet," Darryl's calm voice said inside his helmet.

Jason enjoyed the mystery of being here. Not long ago, the basic laws of marine biology had said no marine life at all existed in the zone they'd just entered. But as everyone now knew, those "laws" had never been laws at all but fundamentally flawed beliefs. Who were we *kidding? We still* don't know anything about life down here. Staring into the pitch darkness, Jason thought of all the species that had only recently been discovered—the red shrimp, gelatinous squid, black fishes, and so many others. But what about those that hadn't been discovered, that were still unknown? Were any of them close?

They passed 1,200 feet then 1,500.

Then the lights came on. Not from the sub but from fish, several thousand light-emitting jellyfish, each a few inches long and shaped like an ice-cream cone. The jellies suddenly surrounded Jason, and he just watched them, lit up in blues, reds, and whites, a platoon of slowly rising champagne corks, climbing straight up into the darkness. Whirring down and past them, he twisted his neck, marveling as their pulsing forms ascended. And then they were gone, fading into the abyss in seconds. It became pure black again.

Jason looked around. "If you guys are ready, I wouldn't mind having my vision back."

"And then there was light," the voice in his helmet said calmly.

Like a spaceship, several dozen headlights illuminated from all angles, and the water became bright blue again. Jason looked around anew. The light had a range of just a few hundred feet. Beyond were vast walls of blackness in every direction.

Darryl focused on a depth gauge. "Passing eighteen hundred feet. Should be touching down soon."

They continued descending, until, two and a half minutes later, at a depth of exactly 2,102 feet, the sub lurched up and they landed on the ocean floor.

JASON SUDDENLY jerked to the left. What was that?

Inside the sub, Lisa jolted toward the same spot. "Did you see that, Darryl?"

"No."

She flicked a switch. "Jason, did you see that?"

"Not well enough to make it out." But he knew where it was, hiding in the darkness just beyond the range of the lights. And then it returned, swimming out of a black wall. A rattail fish, long and snakelike. Not what they'd come for, but it was good to confirm that life was actually here.

Lisa and Darryl watched as the foot-long fish swam right up to their window. It peered in curiously, looking right at Darryl. Lisa smiled. "I think he wants a date, Darryl."

Darryl smirked. "He's not the only one who wants one of those, is he, Soccer Mom?"

"What are you talking about?"

Darryl smiled. "Don't worry. I'm not gonna tell." He flipped a switch. "So, Mr. Aldridge, want to try out your sea legs?"

Jason turned on the platform. Looking very much like Neil Armstrong indeed, he wished he had a waterproofed American flag. "This is one small step for man, one giant leap for mankind."

"Go get 'em, Neil!" Darryl yelled happily inside his helmet.

Lisa watched him on the monitor. Be careful, she thought.

As if testing whether the sand could actually support his weight,

Jason tentatively put one foot down. Then the other. He just stood for a moment, literally getting grounded. Then, for the first time in his life, Jason Aldridge walked on the seafloor. Boots clanking, the oxygen tube growing longer, he ambled to the front of the sub and peered in.

He reminded Darryl and Lisa of the rattail fish a moment ago.

Darryl flicked a switch. "Everything cool?"

"Great. Now let's look around. . . ." He thumped away, noticing a big brown rock the size of a pool table. As he walked closer, he spied a colony of foot-long pogonophora worms, several hundred writhing around on the rock like snakes, apparently feeding on greenish-brown algae. Many weren't moving. He looked up and realized tiny, guppy-size fish were everywhere, floating belly-up. "GDV-4's down here, guys."

His eyes shifted beyond the light, to the darkness, and he wondered if anything else was hiding. Then he noticed movement near his feet. A kelp strand was just floating there. He picked it up. There were no visible bite marks, but the tips were dried out and brittle. It had been on the seafloor for some time. "We're in the right neighborhood."

He flipped on two tiny flashlights embedded in his hands, and a pair of miniature beams illuminated little circles on the sand. "Let's see what's here. . . ." He walked toward the darkness. Then disappeared within it. All that remained was the air tube, slithering on the sand.

"You think he's all right?"

"I'm sure he's fine." Through the viewing glass, Darryl eyed the air tube, taut now and sticking out of the black wall like a knife into cheese. "He's a little stretched, but I'm sure he's fine."

Lisa checked a digital readout on the instrument panel. "It's been nineteen minutes, Darryl."

Darryl gave her a look and flipped a switch. "Jason, you all right out there?"

He waited. Two seconds ticked past, and there was no reply.

"Jason?"

Another two seconds ticked. Still nothing.

"Jason. Do you hear me? Is everything all right?"

"Yeah, guys, fine."

Darryl and Lisa shook their heads.

Surrounded by darkness, Jason looked down at the sand. "Nothing's here, but what we're looking for is close." A massive bird-shaped imprint was at his feet.

"It's very, very close." He scanned the watery blackness. "What do you say we go find it."

CHAPTER 28

"**H**E'S A goddamn machine." Two and a half hours had passed, and Darryl was stunned by Jason's endurance. Sand, sand, and more sand, that was all there was down here. What's the point? Darryl thought. He steered the tiny yellow sub over yet another stretch when Lisa leaned into the mike.

"Jason, you think we should come back and try another time?"

"No, but thanks for the encouragement, Lisa." Little particles flowing past his helmet, Jason shook his head as the dark sand plain continued. The deep-sea desert indeed *appeared* to be endless, but what they were looking for was here. He could sense it. It was close. "Veer to the right a little."

In the sub, Darryl turned to Lisa. "So . . . read any good books lately?"

"Your wife's the reader, Darryl. Hey, you hungry?"

"Always. What do you got?"

From a denim pocketbook, she produced a tiny bag of pretzels. Darryl tore them open and ate a few. "Didn't bring any sleeping pills, did ya?"

"I wish. We could be down here for days, huh?"

"Whatever. So what else is—"

"My God." Jason's stunned voice interrupted them. "They're here. They're really here."

THE SUB hovered to a stop above a deep-sea graveyard of sorts. A fleet of white, winged skeletons, each the size of a small plane, stretched well beyond the range of the lights.

"Jesus." In all his years in the ocean, Darryl Hollis had never seen anything like it. "How many do you think there are?"

Lisa shook her head. "I have no idea. What do you think, Jason?"

Looking down from a height of two stories, Jason shifted his eyes from one enormous skeleton to the next. "Can we get a closer look?"

They touched down on one of the few patches of sand not occupied by a skeleton, and Jason walked toward the closest specimen. Getting closer, he was amazed at how horrifying it looked, just a skeleton, the height of a coffee table at its deepest point.

He turned as a rattail fish swam toward it. Then *through it,* as if it were an underwater jungle gym, dodging in and out of ribs, eye sockets, then teeth. Jason stared at the teeth. My God, look at those things. They were as wide as champagne bottles at their base and as tall as soda cans, the tips as sharp as knife points. Jason tried picturing them in a living animal. . . . Then the fish swam off, and he remembered why they were here. "I don't see any bodies, guys."

In the sub, Darryl surveyed the darkness. "Let's find one."

"MY GOD, how many of these things are there?"

Lisa Barton was astounded. They'd been passing over skeletons for forty minutes and still hadn't seen the end of them. One enormous winged frame after another passed under their cruising machine. She turned. "Any idea, Darryl?"

"One thousand four hundred and twenty-one so far," Jason said from the intercom.

Lisa shook her head. "Big surprise. He's been counting."

Darryl chuckled then pointed at the glass. "Look, Soccer Mom. It's snowing."

"Hey, it really is."

Small white flakes were indeed falling everywhere. "Snowstorms" occurred regularly in the depths, when spawning plants above emitted literally billions of seeds into the water.

Lisa glanced at the monitor. "See the snow, Jason?"

"Unfortunately."

On the platform, he tried to ignore the white stuff flowing past his helmet. He didn't want to lose count of the skeletons—1,422, 1,423, 1,424 . . . He squinted inside his helmet, the snow thickening—1,425, 1,426, 1,427 . . . It thickened further—1,428, 1,429 . . . The sub turned slightly, and the snow blew right into him—1,430, 1,431 . . . The snow began sticking to his face mask. . . . He tried wiping it away, but his hands couldn't do it—1,432 . . . or was that 1,431? . . . 1,432, 1,433, 1,434 . . . The snow fell harder, a driving storm, and the skeletons began to merge—1,434, 1,435 . . . The snow fell harder still. . . . And then he lost count. But not because of the snow.

He'd spotted something lying among a cluster of the skeletons. He squinted as the sub got closer, trying to make it out.

Inside, Darryl squinted too. "Hey, do you see that, Jason? What is that?"

Jason's eyes narrowed. "It's a body, Darryl. We just found a body."

It was much smaller than the skeletons, just five feet across the wings and 250 pounds. A dead juvenile, its body preserved by the same lethal virus that had killed it. With the exception of a few patches of skin chafed away from the wing tips and lower torso, it looked to be in perfect condition. As the sub zoomed closer, Jason focused on its head. A small smile formed on his face. He couldn't wait to get it to the surface and take a look at its brain.

CHAPTER 29

"**M**Y GOD, *will you look at that.*"

With bags under his eyes, Jason stood alone in a small marine lab. Surrounded by wood cabinets and cheap framed pictures of dolphins on the walls, he was astonished at what was before him. He'd expected to see a large brain, of course, but this . . . Sid Klepper and Ross Drummond had set him up here the previous night, in one of Marwood Enterprises' Monterey labs. He hadn't spoken with anyone since. Klepper and Drummond had gone home to sleep, and Darryl, Lisa, and Phil were also snoozing in a few of the back offices. He didn't know where Craig and Monique were—perhaps still on the ocean.

It was nearly 7:15 A.M. Jason had just worked through the night.

Staring into a three-inch-deep water-filled plastic tray, he wasn't tired. Below the waterline was a large, strangely shaped brain that he didn't know what to make of. He'd already packed the body in ice and put it in an industrial freezer in back. The procedure had taken six hours longer than normal because the brain had some unusual spinal-cord connections that had to be carefully severed. He flipped off the tiny recorder Phil had given to Darryl earlier and vowed to write up notes in the laptop.

He stared into the tray again. Jason had done more than his share of manta-ray autopsies—north of a hundred and fifty in ten years— and he'd never seen a brain like it. "My God," he said once more.

Unlike other brains, this one wasn't circular, but rectangular and flat. It looked like a badly infected slab of prime rib, the length of a forearm, the width of a hand, and an inch and a half thick. Jason had worked all night to remove it, but now that he had it, he had no idea what to do next.

"LISA."

She didn't move.

"Lisa." This was followed by a mild poke.

Lisa Barton was asleep in a big leather easy chair she'd snuggled into the previous night.

"Lisa, wake up."

She opened her eyes and smiled. "Hey."

Jason smiled too. She looked at home in her sweatshirt and jeans. He suddenly forgot where he was, forgot everything about the brain. He felt like asking her out to breakfast, just the two of them, something casual. "Hey."

"You look tired."

He nodded, saying nothing.

"What time is it?"

"Seven fifteen."

"In the morning?" She sat up, readjusting clothes. "You've been up all night?"

"I really wanted to get that brain out."

"No one will ever accuse you of not being dedicated, Aldridge. So did you?"

"You've got to see this thing."

"*OH MY God.*"

They both stood over the tray, marveling.

"How big is it?"

"Almost six pounds."

"Jesus!" Lisa knew a human brain weighed three pounds on average.

Jason nodded. "It's *one hundred and ten times* the size of a manta's brain."

"They really did outsmart that dolphin. . . ." She eyed the brain, astonished. "So what do you want to do with this?"

"I guess take it to a neuro expert. I just don't know who."

"Craig might know some people."

"Oh, right." Jason had forgotten that Summers had attended several symposiums on the effects of viruses on animal brains and made his share of contacts in the neurological community. "I'll try Craig on his cell right now. Why don't you wake Darryl and Phil." Lisa walked off, and Jason tried to reach Summers—once, twice, then three times. All were fast busy signals. Then Darryl entered the room and peered into the tray.

"Holy cow."

Phil came in next. "*My God.* I gotta get some pictures of *this*. . . . " Like a kid in a candy store, he ran out for his camera and returned instantly, snapping from every angle.

Darryl was still flabbergasted. "This is real. You actually cut this brain out of that animal?"

"That's ri—"

"Did you get Craig and Monique, Jason?" Lisa asked, entering.

"No. I wonder what they're up to out there."

Lisa walked closer. "Maybe they found something useful too."

"WHAT THE hell is that?"

Monique Hollis was asleep, cuddled in a fleece on one of the *Expedition*'s lounge chairs. As tired as she'd been at 4 A.M. the previous night, she hadn't bothered going below deck. She'd simply dozed off right there at the back of the boat. It was sunrise now, the sky an ugly slate gray. Monique didn't notice. She continued to sleep peacefully.

"What the hell is that?"

Monique's eyes reluctantly creaked open. "Come on, Craig, what the hell is *what*?"

"That." Unshaven and unshowered in an old gray T-shirt, Summers pointed at the monitor. "It's a good problem to have, but now we've got *two* sonar readings."

Monique got up and immediately saw two blinking dots on the

interactive map. The first one—the one they'd been following—was two miles off the coast; the second one, just half a mile off. She stared at the second dot. "Could this be whales?"

"No, the magnitudes aren't nearly big enough."

"Dolphins?"

"Moving much too slowly. It's gotta be the rays, Monique. They must have split up."

She stared at the one closer to shore. "If this one keeps going, it will be out of range soon."

"Exactly why I woke you. We have to decide which one to follow."

"What are the depths?"

Craig hit a button and two numbers appeared: 17,308 beneath the first dot, but just 100 beneath the second. Monique's eyes widened.

"This one's just a *hundred feet* down?"

Summers nodded. "That's my point. We have a real shot of seeing them. Do you want to change course and follow them instead?"

Monique stared at the second dot. "Definitely."

Craig went to the controls, and Monique grabbed her phone. "I'll update Jason." But there was no signal. She turned back to the monitor curiously. Why was the second group of rays only a hundred feet down? The boat changed direction, and she supposed they'd find out.

JASON SHOOK his head. Another fast busy. "I need those damn neuro names from Craig."

Darryl turned away from the brain. "Why?"

"To decide who to show this thing to."

"Met some of those brain mavens myself, you know."

"You did?"

"Yeah, went to a conference with Craig. Lemme tell you, they're a hoity-toity group."

"We need to get someone's opinion on this, Darryl."

"You know who Bandar Vishakeratne is?"

"Oh, right." Jason hadn't heard the name recently, but Bandar Vishakeratne was the world's premiere brain expert. A decade earlier he'd been named a runner-up for the Nobel Prize and more recently the chief of Princeton University's brand-new neurosciences facility. "Sure, everyone knows who he is."

Darryl raised an eyebrow. "Don't be too impressed. All his brilliance aside, he's a cocky bastard." Darryl stared into the tray again, newly amazed. "But he'd lick the soles of your shoes to get a look at this."

"Should I call him?"

"He wouldn't talk to you."

"No?"

"A guy like that? Without a referral, no way. And even if he did, he wouldn't believe what you have here. Not without seeing it himself. I suppose you could schedule an appointment."

"A guy like that must have a busy schedule."

"You'd wait months. Seeing him immediately would require being . . . aggressive."

"What do you mean? How aggressive?"

Darryl rubbed his chin, thinking out the nitty-gritty. "I'd say pack-this-brain-up-right-now, buy-a-plane-ticket, and show-up-on-his-doorstep aggressive."

"You think that will work?"

Darryl looked into the tray again. "In a heartbeat."

"Then . . . you guys will get back on the trail without me?"

"I think we can handle it, Jason."

Lisa shook her head, annoyed. "Either that, or *I'll* take this brain to be analyzed."

Jason looked nervous. "I don't want you doing that."

Lisa nodded angrily. "I know you don't. So you'll just have to trust us not to screw up without you."

"Lisa, it's not that I don't trust you."

"Do you want us to do it or not?" Lisa didn't want to hear it now. "Because if I were you, I'd be *curious as hell* to know what this brain means."

Jason turned back to it. "You're right." He checked his watch, wondering how quickly he could get a car to San Francisco airport. It turned out to be ten minutes. Monterey had a lot of taxis. He didn't even pack a toothbrush.

CHAPTER 30

"I CAN'T believe it. We lost *both of them*." Craig eyed the lifeless interactive map furiously, about to blow a gasket. "Son of a bitch!"

He and Monique had left the sea for only a moment. Just to pick up Darryl, Lisa, and Phil at the Half Moon Bay docks, thirty miles south of San Francisco. But when they'd returned, *both signals* had vanished. There were no blinking dots anywhere.

At the *Expedition*'s bow with Lisa, Monique heaved another buoy into the sea, valiantly trying to find the rays again.

Lisa shook her head. She had her own problems. They'd left the lab so quickly they'd forgotten the body Jason had cut the brain out of, leaving it in the freezer. And since Jason's friends, Klepper and Drummond, had left town on business, the corpse could only be retrieved in a few days, no doubt rock solid and far less suitable for autopsy.

Craig calmed down, trying to think out what had happened. They were a mile offshore now, in the exact spot where the signal had been only twenty minutes before. "Where the hell did they go?"

Darryl scanned the dark water. "Maybe they didn't go anywhere. Maybe they just stopped." If anything simply stopped moving, especially on the seafloor, sonar would have great difficulty picking it up.

Craig shook his head. That didn't make sense. The rays were in the middle of a migration, so why stop? "Wait a second . . . what if . . ." He tapped a button and the map became three-dimensional, land still in white, water still in blue, but now, within the water, a vast deep-sea mountain range in gray. "Son of a bitch."

Darryl raised an eyebrow. "Well, that changes things, doesn't it?"

"You think they're swimming the canyons?"

"It would explain where they went."

If the rays swam the canyons, sonar would struggle to detect them. And these mountains were enormous, half a mile high and buried in three-mile-deep water—basically sonar's worst nightmare. With this particular topography, the echo-location system's clicks would simply reflect off the mountains and not detect anything else.

Craig stared at the gray. "So *both* groups must be in there. You know, I don't get why there are two separate groups anyway."

"Are you sure they're really 'separate'?" Monique asked, approaching with Lisa.

"What do you mean, Monique?"

Monique walked closer. "I mean there are clearly two groups migrating, but it seems like they're moving more . . . in conjunction with each other, same direction and pace but at different depths and distances from the shoreline."

"Whatever. They split up and that seems odd. Have you ever seen a migration like that before?"

"I haven't. Have you, Darryl?"

"Never."

Craig nodded. "So why did they split, then?"

The Hollises shrugged.

Lisa had no idea either and she wondered what Jason would think. It was strange not having him on the boat. She hoped he was learning something useful from the brain expert in Princeton, New Jersey, whose name she couldn't pronounce.

BANDAR VISHAKERATNE, or "Veesh" to his friends, hailed from Sri Lanka and was a classic rags-to-riches story. A decade earlier he'd been an unknown doctor toiling in the neurology department of a poorly funded public hospital in New Delhi when a paper he'd submitted a year prior to the International Federation of Neurosurgeons was judged to possess "unparalleled knowledge of the inner workings of the animal brain." Entitled "Synapse Multiplication of Visual Cortexes in African Lions," the paper was subsequently disseminated to everyone in the worldwide neurology community. Global recognition followed. Within six months, the man was a runner-up for the Nobel Prize. Twelve months after that, an offer was extended to become the chairman of Princeton University's then-new neurosciences department, and with great fanfare, Vishakeratne took the job. While his salary and other compensation were never publicly disclosed, it was widely rumored that Princeton, whose endowment was larger than many small countries' treasuries, had given him a total pay package rivaling those of America's best-paid professional athletes. Bandar Vishakeratne had been sitting pretty ever since.

"Jason *who*? What kind of stupid name is *Jason* anyway? Get rid of him."

"Dr. Vishakeratne, he's the one I told you about." Andrea, Vishakeratne's thirty-year-old assistant, shuffled into the room, speaking in a New York accent that contrasted humorously with her boss's Indian accent. "Remember he called earlier? From California? Well, he's here now, waiting outside actually, and he'd very much like to speak with you." After reaching San Francisco airport in record time, Jason had taken the next plane to Newark, and a fast taxi straight to Princeton.

"Tell him to get the fuck away. I'm busy here, for Christ's sake."

Andrea suppressed a smile. Vishakeratne was famous for his bad temper and filthy mouth, characteristics not highlighted in Princeton's 250th anniversary fund-raising pamphlets. Seated in a massive, elegant office the likes of which most academics only dreamed of, the sixty-one-year-old pointed to a few stapled sheets in her hand.

"What the hell is that?"

"A confidentiality agreement." Andrea meekly handed him the sheets. Darryl had recommended that Jason make him sign one; the doctor was rumored to be quite a shark and having some legal protection couldn't hurt.

"A confidentiality agreement! This crazy bastard from California not only wants to meet with me unannounced, he wants me to sign a confidentiality agreement!" The doctor laughed heartily, genuinely amused. "He should be castrated! What a crackpot!"

"I don't think he's a crackpot, Doctor."

"No, of course you don't." He tore through the sheets. "What's he promising here? That the moon is made of cheese? That the earth's crust is composed entirely of low-fat yogurt?" He threw the confidentiality agreement on the floor. "All Californians are crackpots. Maybe he arrived early for Halloween. Now just get rid of—"

Jason entered the room. He'd been listening at the door and just couldn't take it anymore. His eyes were lasers as he carried a medium-size white cooler with a red top. He didn't have time to screw around.

"Dr. Vishakeratne, my name is Jason Aldridge. I'm sorry to barge in on you like this, but I have something here that just can't wait. I know you'll be very interested to see it, but I need you to sign that confidentiality agreement first." He walked closer and placed the cooler on the large desk.

The doctor hadn't heard a word. He was terrified, stock-still in his leather chair, worried that the man who'd just entered his office was some sort of terrorist, and that his cooler held a bomb. Vishakeratne was far from paranoid; in the country he came from, suicide bombers were not uncommon. A colleague had recently been killed by just such a person, and Vishakeratne himself received three death threats a year. Maybe someone was finally following up. Despite his horror, he stayed cool.

"Call security," he said quietly to his assistant. Then he didn't move, tried not to even breathe. The cooler was three feet from his face.

Unaware of the man's concerns, Jason leaned forward and pulled off the top. Vishakeratne jolted backward, nearly falling off his chair.

Jason was astonished. "What are you doing? Doctor, I'm not a mad bomber. I have something here *you want to see, believe me.* Just take a peek, and if it doesn't interest you, I'll leave." He held up the red top harmlessly. "Fair enough?"

Vishakeratne breathed easier. Nothing had exploded, and the white man didn't look or sound like a suicide bomber. He was wearing khakis and a light blue, button-down shirt, purchased at a men's clothing store at the San Francisco airport. Vishakeratne's curiosity was suddenly piqued. If this intense-looking fellow had really come all the way from California, what had he brought with him? The scientist slid toward his desk and peered into the cooler.

"Sweet mother of Buddha," the chairman of Princeton's neuro-science department said.

"Doctor, I need you to sign that confidentiality agreement."

Vishakeratne didn't respond. He simply gazed into the cooler.

"Doctor?"

He still didn't respond.

Jason put the top back on and suddenly had Vishakeratne's attention. The doctor looked up at him quizzically. "Yes?"

"The confidentiality agreement?"

"Oh." Now Vishakeratne couldn't move fast enough. He fumbled at his shirt pocket, searching for a pen. He couldn't find one. He patted down his jacket. Nothing there either. He ripped open a drawer and rooted around inside, pulling out a Bic. He literally ran to pick up the now partially torn confidentiality agreement off the carpeted floor. Not bothering to read it, he scribbled his signature and the day's date four times. He gave it to Jason then placed a hand on the cooler's top.

"May I?"

Jason eyed him evenly, even more anxious than he to learn about the fantastic brain.

"Please."

CHAPTER 31

IT'S REAL all right. The number one brain expert in the world had just finished prodding and probing the strange brain with his bare hands. It wasn't a fake. The bloody brain was real!

"Where did you get this?"

Jason explained.

"I see. And why are you showing it to me, Mr. . . . . ?"

"Aldridge. Jason Aldridge. I want you to analyze it. Tell me what you make of it."

"In exchange for what?" Excited as he was, Vishakeratne was still a businessman—and Jason knew that.

"An exclusive. You can analyze this brain from top to bottom and publicly release your findings before anybody else even knows it exists." Jason knew it had to be the best offer the great man had ever received.

But Bandar Vishakeratne barely blinked. He'd recently entered a Thursday-night poker game with a group of engineering professors and had become quite adept at hiding his emotions. He simply stared into the cooler. Then, in a low, quiet voice, he said, "That's a fair offer. You'd better let me get to work now."

"SON OF a bitch . . ." Craig Summers looked up from the interactive map. "We just got a signal, guys!"

The others ran over; Darryl arrived first. "Where?"

"North of San Francisco, right off Point Reyes."

A whistle. "All the way up there without us detecting them." Point Reyes was sixty miles north of their current location in Half Moon Bay.

Craig nodded. "That's what swimming the canyons will do."

"You think they're doing that intentionally? To evade detection?"

"Ah, I can't imagine."

"Excuse me, is that depth right?" Monique pointed at the monitor.

Craig's eyes bulged. "Jesus, they're *at* the surface. And . . ." He leaned in. "Look how close to shore they are. Christ, they're almost *on the beach.*"

Monique nodded. "Craig, we better get up there. Right now."

Summers literally ran to the bridge and suddenly they were flying up the coast. No one said the words—they could barely hear themselves think over the wind—but they all wondered the same thing: Why were the rays suddenly so close to shore?

"NOTHING HERE." It was ninety minutes later, and Darryl shook his head. "Not a damn thing."

They'd made fantastic time, passing El Granada, Daly City, and Muir Woods at record speed. As the boat's engine took a needed break, they bobbed just twenty yards offshore of a desolate Point Reyes beach.

"This is where the signal came from?" Monique asked, scanning the shoreline with binoculars.

Craig nodded. "To the inch."

Darryl put down a harpoon gun he'd been holding just in case. "Well, I don't see a damn thing."

"Wait a second. . . ." Monique suddenly pointed. "Look at *that.*"

They all turned toward the beach.

"Goddamn," Darryl said.

Phil almost whistled. "Wow."

Craig just shook his head. "That's why they were so close to shore."

Lisa's eyes narrowed. "Let's get over there. Carefully." She reached for her cell. "And I'm calling Jason. . . ." Whatever the Princeton brain expert was telling him, she knew he'd want to hear what they'd just found immediately. She just hoped his phone was on.

CHAPTER 32

BANDAR VISHAKERATNE put down his pencil and rose from a stool. The preliminary analysis was complete. The scientist had just worked nonstop for an entire day, literally twenty-five hours straight, not taking any breaks, not even a visit to the snack machine down the hall for junk food. He was exhausted. He grabbed his blazer, yawned twice, and entered a tastefully appointed hallway.

Seated on a wooden chair embossed with the black-and-orange Princeton University seal was Jason Aldridge. He was wide-awake, eyeing his cell phone and realizing he had messages. He put the tiny contraption away when he saw that the doctor had returned. "So, Dr. Vishakeratne, what did you find?"

Veesh-ah-ker-aht-nee. The neurologist had noted it earlier. Most people butchered his name with shocking regularity, but this American took tremendous care to pronounce it correctly. The linguistic touch didn't make him Albert Einstein, of course, but it demonstrated respect as well an attention to detail that the doctor rarely found in anyone except himself. Vishakeratne decided on the spot that he liked Jason Aldridge. He gestured courteously.

"Please, come into my office. Let me share my analysis with you."

They sat on two small leather couches on either side of a fancy glass table. Vishakeratne went over "general brain preliminaries" first. The human brain weighed 1,400 grams, about 3 pounds, and possessed a large cerebral cortex, or upper brain. Despite man's apparent "brain superiority," three—and now four—animals existed in nature that actually had brains that were heavier than man's. The sperm whale's weighed 20 pounds, the elephant's 13, the bottlenose dolphin's 3.75, and now the new animal's, 5.81 pounds. Yes, brains varied in size just as any other organ did; just as someone might have longer legs, they might also have a larger brain. The heaviest human brain ever recorded weighed 4 pounds, a full pound heavier than the average.

Large nonhuman brains didn't demonstrate nearly as much intelligence as they should have. Unlike man, other big-brained animals didn't appear to use their brains, which led to the obvious question of why they had evolved to such great size in the first place. Vishakeratne had been one of the first to suggest the presence of an "animal intelligence" that humans simply couldn't appreciate. Dolphin and whale brains, he postulated, were dedicated to support awesome sensory perceptions, such as sonar, rather than the communication and reasoning skills that human brains were largely limited to. Just as a brain that supported communication and reasoning skills had been critical to man's survival, so had the dolphin's and whale's brain been critical to theirs.

The preliminaries continued when the eminent scientist noticed that Jason's eyes were glazed over. It was as though the young ichthyologist was being polite but had heard it all before. He had. On the flight from San Francisco to Newark, Jason had read or skimmed every available piece of information on the findings of Bandar Vishakeratne. Not normally one to waste people's time, the doctor switched gears immediately.

"Obviously, you're here to discuss the brain you brought with you. Let's do that."

He pressed a button. Instantaneously, Andrea entered the large office, carrying the brain in a deep-rimmed white plastic tray, submerged in a few inches of water. She placed it on the glass table, careful not to drip, then left the office.

Vishakeratne began. "A number of items strike me as most unusual with this brain. The first, clearly, is its weight. Second is its shape. It's most . . . strange. In fact, I've never seen anything like it. Before this, every brain I've seen has been rounded, perhaps elliptical, cylindrical, or oblong, but essentially rounded. But this"——he gestured to the lumpy gray matter on the tray—"as we can see, is flat. . . ." His voice trailed off and he became quiet.

Jason studied the man. The skin above his forehead was crinkled. His eyes looked strained. "This brain didn't evolve into this particular shape by accident. It happened *for a reason*. My preliminary judgment is that this is a highly specialized brain. A highly *focused* brain."

Jason leaned forward. "Focused on what?"

Vishakeratne looked him in the eye, ominously so. "On hunting, Jason."

CHAPTER 33

"**O**N HUNTING?"

"You said earlier this animal is a predator, and my analysis bloody well supports that. And not just any predator. A highly, highly efficient one. Almost too efficient, I'd daresay. This brain is capable of supporting sensory perceptions unlike anything I've seen before. Now, I haven't determined which senses—sight, smell, hearing, various magnetic sensory abilities—are the strongest yet, but my guess is that they're all are very strong on an absolute basis. Perhaps even unparalleled."

"Unparalleled senses." Jesus, Jason thought.

In rapid succession, Vishakeratne pointed to a series of bulging lobes on the soaking brain. "As you can see, all of this brain's sensory cortexes—acoustical, visual, auditory—are very large; huge, in fact." He pointed at one particularly large bulge. "This is its electrical cortex, the largest I've seen by far. Jason, the sensory capabilities of this brain are arguably *too strong*. No capable predator would need a brain like this. But"—he raised his index finger—"an *incapable* predator very well might. You said these rays are physically underqualified to be predators, but this brain, just like the human brain, would allow them to overcompensate for that."

"So it evolved out of need, just like any other organ."

"Of course just like any other organ." It never ceased to amaze the neurologist. Everyone always assumed the brain was different from other organs, that it hadn't evolved at all, but had simply appeared inside everyone's skull by magic. "I assure you, Jason, despite its complexity, this brain evolved just like the giraffe's neck."

The giraffe's neck was a famous example of how the evolutionary process worked. Due to its simplicity, it was frequently used to demonstrate the critical concept of *variation*. Variation was the fundamental building block that allowed the entire adaptive process to occur. Every body part and organ of every species—from the neck of the giraffe to the brain of man—had evolved as a result of *prolonged variation over time*. Giraffes were the example often used to describe this.

Thirty-five million years ago, giraffes were much smaller animals, resembling Great Danes, their necks just a few inches long. But just like any animal, prehistoric giraffes were all *slightly different* from one another. They varied in height, weight, fur color, and in literally billions of other ways, including neck length. In a litter of ten prehistoric baby giraffes, the typical animal's neck might have been three inches long. But a few might have had necks that were just an inch or two, while a few others had necks that were four or five inches.

And what would it have mattered? Depending on the circumstances, a slightly longer neck might have given a prehistoric giraffe an advantage, a disadvantage, or simply had no effect at all in its quest to survive. But as it turned out, a longer neck provided a distinct advantage. Thirty-five million years ago, the land was filled with hungry herbivores, plant eaters, who fought hard to eat every plant as quickly as it grew. But some greenery—the upper leaves of the tallest trees—was simply too high to reach. But not for the longer-necked giraffes. These animals were able to reach previously unreachable leaves. As a result, they ate and prospered, while the short-necked members of their species starved and died off. The lucky survivors mated with one another and, in doing so, passed on their "long-neck" genes to the next generation. So what could have been a "mutant" long-neck gene instead became standard for the entire species. With a continued shortage of easily accessible greenery, the giraffes that had long necks continued to have an advantage. So over the years, as they survived and mated, the long-neck genes were repeatedly "selected," and eventually, the entire giraffe species evolved into its current, modern form.

The same basic process had led to the evolution of every organ in every animal ever known. While the variations among ancestral giraffe populations resulted in the selection of long necks, similar variations among other species in other environments led to completely different adaptations: the tiger's fanged mouth, the elephant's long trunk, the cougar's powerful legs. They'd all evolved out of necessity, to help a given species survive in its particular environment, and each variation demonstrated the unambiguous power of natural selection.

Jason stuck his index finger into the tray and ran it along the brain's eighteen-inch-long surface.

"So why did this brain evolve flat?"

"Good question. The short answer is to make these rays of yours hard to kill."

"A flat brain makes them hard to kill?"

"Yes," the doctor said matter-of-factly, leaning back on his sofa. "That's a pro. But there are cons. The major one is that the brain itself is less efficient than it would be if it were rounded. You see, with a flat brain, there are fewer synapses"—connections—"between brain cells, which makes the brain work harder to process the same amount of information."

The human brain contained 14 billion cells and trillions of connecting synapses. A spherical shape was the most efficient at supporting such a complex network because it allowed multiple connections.

"I'm not saying this animal is stupid, mind you. No, far from it. Not with a brain this big. Even flat, this animal is still very smart. It's just not as smart as it could be."

"Thank God for that." Jason was beginning to wonder if he actually wanted to find one of the rays alive. "And what makes it hard to kill?"

"Three factors. First, the cerebral cortex is spread over a large surface area and is far less susceptible to damage than normal. Second, like the brains of many predators, the pain center here is tiny; actually this one borders on nonexistent." The pain center is what informs an animal when it is hurt, and in effect, tells it to slow down and take care of itself. "Humans have very large pain centers. If we get the slightest pinprick, we know something's wrong. But this animal effectively doesn't feel pain at all and it won't slow down for anything. It will literally do whatever comes naturally to it right up until it dies. And in the case of a predator, that means hunting.

"Third, this brain has what I call *spread sensory systems*. Spread sensory systems exist to a limited extent in all brains, but they are here in abundance."

"Spread sensory systems." Jason had never heard the term before.

"Yes. I suppose you could think of them as the neurological equivalent of emergency generators. They provide the brain with a series of 'support cells' that effectively act as *backups* for every function in the body. It is these backups that make this animal hard to kill. All brains, this one included, have specialized cortexes—motor, visual, auditory, et cetera, et cetera. These cortexes act as control centers for particular body functions. So normally, when a given cortex is damaged, the body function it supports ceases operating and the whole body dies.

"For example, if a person were shot in the head, and the breathing cortex was damaged, all the body's respiratory functions would immediately stop—even if the respiratory organs themselves were entirely functional. And even if the breathing cortex weren't damaged, if the bullet entered here"—he pointed at a spot on his own head—"it would rip through the left and right frontal lobes, the parietal, the occipital, the temporal regions; it would rip through bloody everything, and do critical damage to other important cortexes. By the time it was done, the heart, the immune system, and every other function the body needed to live would instantaneously stop and the body would die."

Jason nodded. "OK."

"But"—Vishakeratne held up a finger—"with a brain that has spread sensory systems *and* is flat, a single bullet would not irreparably damage any individual control center. The destruction would be far, far less."

Jason's brow crinkled up tensely—he couldn't believe what he was hearing. "How much less? How many 'backups' are there?" Two or three, he imagined.

"Oh, I don't know exactly." The neurologist huffed. "I'd imagine . . . thousands."

"*Thousands?* Are you saying it would take thousands of bullets to kill one of these animals?"

"No, I'm not saying that."

"What are you saying?"

"Look." Veesh shaped his fingers into a gun and aimed the "barrel" at the brain in the tray. "I'm saying if I placed a gun right here and fired, this animal wouldn't die. A small part of one cortex would be slightly damaged, but the bulk of the brain, and the bulk of the animal's body functions, would continue to operate normally. I doubt if it would even be seriously wounded."

Jason almost laughed. "Are you saying it's indestructible? That it can take an infinite number of bullets?"

"No, of course not. I have no idea how many bullets it could take, just that it would be more than a few. Surviving a bullet to the head isn't nearly as uncommon as you might think. I've seen Tanzanian bobcats take four or five and survive."

Decades earlier, Vishakeratne had performed an extensive twenty-two-week study on the famously bullet-tolerant predators. In a well-known report, he linked their phenomenal ability to survive "severe head and brain injuries caused by gunshots" to what he dubbed "unusually shaped cerebral cortexes that have a tendency to be flat."

"Something else is significant here. This is a mature brain."

"As opposed to immature?"

"Precisely. A brain's maturity refers to its evolutionary age. And this brain has been around for a very long time. Humans actually have an immature brain, only four million years old, which, compared with the developmental period of other large brains—the dolphin's, whale's—is shorter than a twenty-four-hour flu."

Vishakeratne carefully lifted the entire brain out of the water with his bare hands, little drops falling onto the glass. "You see, there are no cavity suppressions here."

Unlike mature brains, immature brains show evidence of having been compressed, as if they'd been squeezed into a container too small for them. Cavity suppressions, which are small dents in a brain's surface, appear when a brain literally outgrows the skull it is encased in. The human brain, for example, has evolved so quickly that it often folds on top of itself and actually appears squashed when it is removed from a skull.

The scientist returned the gray mass to the water. "This is a very mature brain, and that fact is not trivial. It indicates these rays have been fully functional predators for much longer *than man has even been alive.* I know you must be very anxious to find one of these animals, and I wish you luck in doing that, but I can't emphasize this point enough. *These rays know how to hunt; they know how to kill.* Believe me, in any confrontation, they'll know more about you than you know about them. So if you do find one, you should be *very, very* careful with it."

Andrea's voice rang out from an intercom. "Dr. Vishakeratne, your staff meeting is in fifteen minutes."

"Oh." The man checked a $6,000 Rolex. Fifteen minutes indeed. Despite his stature, Vishakeratne insisted on attending monthly staff meetings. "You're going to have to excuse me now." He stood. "But stay on top of this, and please keep me abreast of what happens."

Jason quickly rose from his sofa. "I will. If it's not too much trouble, would you mind e-mailing me your findings?" He handed him his card.

"Of course. I should have something very quickly. In the interim, I won't breathe a word of this to anyone." He eyed Jason anew, his dark eyes dancing slightly. "I must say, I'm glad you had the balls to bust into my office! You're an impressive, focused young man. It was a pleasure meeting you."

Jason literally turned red at the compliment. He thought it ridiculously flattering, especially considering the source. But Bandar Vishakeratne prided himself on character analysis. He had already decided that Jason Aldridge was a lot like he had been many years ago—dedicated, smart, and hungry. The Princeton man knew well what it was to sacrifice, to work long, hard, lonely hours, to toil away in utter obscurity, to be nearly destitute but still focused. Indeed, Vishakeratne thought he might be seeing a humbler, younger version of himself. And like all great men, by making such a comparison, he was paying Jason Aldridge the greatest compliment of all.

Jason almost bowed. "It was an honor meeting you. Thank you very much, Dr. Vishakeratne."

"Of course. By the way, from now on, I'd prefer it if you'd address me as Veesh."

It was an honor bestowed upon few people.

"Thank you very much again, Veesh." They shook firmly and Jason walked out the door.

Rushing around the exterior office, Andrea looked up immediately. "Jason, a Lisa Barton called for you." She quickly grabbed some papers off her desk and went to the door as Veesh followed. "You can use my phone. Have a good trip back to California." They were gone.

Jason dialed, and there was an immediate pickup.

"Jason?"

"Hi, Lisa. What's up?"

"Jesus, it took you long enough to call back. I've been trying to reach you for half a day."

"Give me a break. I've been busy here." He paused. "Is something wrong?"

"Another juvenile turned up."

"Really? That's fantastic. I still have to finish the autopsy on the first one, but we'll have two now."

Lisa didn't bother mentioning that the first one was still inaccessible in a freezer. Perhaps it didn't matter now. "This one's not ready for an autopsy yet."

"What?" He suddenly felt light-headed. "Are you saying you found *a live one*?"

"We found a live one."

"You're being *extremely careful* with it, right?"

"Very, but we don't need to be. It's in pretty bad shape."

He looked at the phone. "Lisa, please be very, very careful with it."

"You don't understand; it's not doing well. I don't think we have anything to worry about."

"Please be careful. Tell everyone to be careful."

An annoyed exhale. They *had been* careful—extremely. At all times, the triumvirate had had at least two rifles pointed at the animal's head. "OK."

"I just don't want you to get hurt, all right?"

"All right," she said more softly.

"Where are you keeping it?"

"In a cage."

Jason gave the phone a look. *In a cage?* "You mean in a tank."

"No, *I mean in a cage*. We didn't find this animal in the water, Jason. We found it on a beach north of San Francisco. By the time we got to it, it had been there for more than thirty-seven minutes."

"Lisa, you're not making sense. If it was on the sand for that long, then how could it still be alive?"

"Because it's breathing air."

"What?"

"I can't explain it and I'm not attempting to. But the live ray. That we have here. Right now. Is breathing. I'm looking right at it, and it's *breathing air*."

Literally speechless, he didn't respond.

Lisa continued. "Whatever we might have thought earlier, that woman off Clarita didn't imagine or exaggerate anything. What she said she saw that day *actually happened*. This animal is as real as the nose on my face, and it's breathing air."

Jason suddenly felt as if he were out of his body. "You said it's in bad shape?"

"Worse than bad. I think it's dying. If you want to see it alive, you'd better get back here fast."

He didn't say another word. He simply hung up the phone. As he rushed out of the office, he tried to understand. How on earth could it possibly be breathing air?

CHAPTER 34

THE CREATURE was looking right at him. The moment Jason walked into the room, its eyes were watching him. It couldn't see him—the room was pitch-black—but a host of other sensory organs told it he was there.

"Here, let me get the lights."

Lisa squeezed past him in the dark. Perhaps it was inadvertent, but they rubbed against each other. She flipped a switch, and five banks of fluorescents flickered, then illuminated. Jason abruptly forgot why he was here, noticing what she was wearing: a low-cut white top with preppy but tight checked lime-green pants. His brain shifted back to business when Darryl and the others entered. USC's Northern California research facility was in Point Reyes, forty miles north of San Francisco. Harry Klepper and Ross Drummond had a relationship with the staffers who ran it and before going out of town had arranged for Jason's team to have access. The lab was the size of a middle-school lunchroom, completely unfurnished except for granite counters, glass cabinets, and wood stools. Jason didn't notice the periphery. The cage, plopped in the middle of the vast room, was as tall as he was and as wide as a station wagon. Darryl Hollis had borrowed it from a local zoo.

Walking quickly toward it, Jason realized the animal lying behind the bars was staring at him. Immediately—and quite unconsciously—he froze. He was afraid of it. After everything Vishakeratne had told him, how could he not be? It wasn't the creature's brain that made him nervous, however. It was its eyes. They were slightly bigger than golf balls, cold and black, and staring right at him. They were terrifying eyes. He'd never felt an animal look at him like that before.

He averted his gaze and walked closer, taking in the rest of it. It was a very thick ray, much thicker than a manta, three feet at its center. Five feet across the wings and four feet long, it was very muscular, very solidly built, a dangerous, dangerous-looking creature. He guessed its weight at 250 pounds.

He scanned the head area. The closed mouth was the size of a snow shovel, with horns like stumpy soda cans sticking out on either side.

He heard something. A wheezing sound. The animal was actually breathing air, its body gently rising and falling.

He inched closer, the eyes following him through the bars. The sound was coming from underneath it. But then he heard a *second* wheezing sound, from a small hole the size of a quarter on the top of the horned head. "It's breathing through its spiracle?"

Summers nodded. "We think so."

Normally, a manta used its spiracle to take in water, from which it then removed oxygen.

Jason crouched. "And it evolved lungs?"

"More likely *lung* singular." Monique knelt next to him. "We think it's a modern version of the lungfish."

"So . . . it adapted an air bladder?"

"It must have."

Most fish possess air bladders. Similar to a scuba diver's inflatable vest, an air bladder controls buoyancy by varying the amount of air in the fish's body, causing it to sink or float. But some species—the African lungfish, the walking catfish, the snakehead fish, among others—have adapted their air bladders into lungs that allow them to breathe air on land.

Jason shook his head, mystified. "When did this species ever have access to land?"

Every known water-based species that has evolved lungs has done so only after extensive time away from the water. The lungfish, for example, adapted a lung after the lakes where it normally lived dried up and it was forced to live on mud. But these rays were from the depths and had never been anywhere near land. Until the past months, their entire known evolutionary history had been on the ocean floor. How could they possibly have evolved a lung down there?

Monique stood. "You ever heard of Fritz Bedecker, Jason?"

"That German ichthyologist with all the crazy theories?"

"We think one of them might not have been so crazy."

"What are you talking about?"

"Did you know he had a theory about underwater air geysers in the depths?"

Jason paused. "No, I didn't."

Monique explained. Bedecker, a German ichthyologist and oceanographer—as well as a raging alcoholic—had come out with a series of controversial theories during his heyday in 1899. The most inflammatory of these was that prehistoric amphibians had evolved lungs not as a result of spending increasing amounts of time on land but rather *in the depths of the ocean.* The deep sea, Bedecker had argued, was composed of a worldwide network of what he called "underwater air geysers." It was these air geysers, not the land, that had led to the evolution of the amphibian's lung. It was only *after* the lung had fully evolved in the water that the very first amphibian crawled onto the land.

In 1899 the notion of deep sea air geysers was considered utterly ridiculous. But late in the twentieth century, that perception changed dramatically with the famous 1977 discovery in the Galápagos islands of a sea vent emitting pure hydrogen-sulfide gas. While hydrogen-sulfide geysers were very different from air geysers, the realization that gas vents of any kind were present in the depths was shocking, and caused many geologists to wonder aloud if somehow air geysers might, in fact, exist as well. To date, an actual deep-sea air geyser still hadn't been discovered, but in 1992, the theory achieved global credibility when world-renowned Harvard geologist Milton Thornberg said that air geysers not only could exist in the depths, but also that *they had to.*

Thornberg's reasoning could not have been more simple. It is a known fact that 49 percent of the earth's crust is made of solidified oxygen. With a nine-thousand-degree molten core beneath it, it is perfectly reasonable that the solid oxygen could be superheated, turned into liquid, then gas, and be emitted straight into the depths of the ocean, much like an underwater volcano. Thornberg further explained that the reason these underwater air geysers have never been discovered is that they move around. Created by a volatile molten core that is constantly bubbling and changing, they are never in the same place for more than weeks at a time. And since they are also several miles below the surface, in blackened waters with crushing pressures, they are literally impossible to locate. But air geysers are absolutely real, Thornberg assured the world. And if so, Bedecker was right. The lungfish had evolved naturally as a result—and so could other species.

Jason turned. "Where exactly did you find this animal?"

"Just north of Point Reyes." Craig approached the cage. "One hundred and fifty feet from the waterline."

"*One hundred and fifty feet?* So . . . it washed up on the beach?"

"We don't think so. We checked. The tide hasn't come that far up in six months."

"Then . . . it crawled?"

Lisa shook her head. "No. We studied the sand, Jason, we studied it very closely for almost an hour. There were no marks of any kind."

Jason glanced at Phil, rapidly typing this into his laptop, then turned back to Lisa and Craig. "What are you saying? How did it get there?"

It was then that he noticed a dozen thick textbooks on the counter near Phil. The one on top was titled *The New Physics of Animal Flight*.

Craig looked him in the eye. "We think it flew."

CHAPTER 35

JASON WAS silent. Craig Summers was serious. They were all looking at him, and they were all serious. Phil was still frantically typing, the tapping keys the only sound in the lab.

"How could it possibly have flown onto a beach, Craig? This animal must weigh two hundred and fifty pounds. The existing theories of aerodyn—"

"The existing theories of aerodynamics don't apply here, Jason."

A glance at the textbooks. "What do you mean?"

"I mean there have been some dramatic new findings about animal flight in the past five years." Craig had minored in fluid dynamics at UCSD and was very familiar with the physicists behind these analyses, highly regarded names like Michael Fink, Gloria Rimmelstob, Karl Heinz VonKroyter, and Phillip Goldfarb. They were all brilliant, aggressive scientists who were constantly pushing the limitations of accepted theories and regarded as the Einsteins of their time.

"What did they find exactly?"

"Are you familiar with all those flying animals that every aerodynamic theory said couldn't even get into the air?"

"You mean bumblebees and all that?" According to established theories of aerodynamics, bumblebees, as well as several species of hummingbird and turkey, could not fly.

"No. Not bumblebees, not modern animal flight. We're talking about prehistoric animal flight, Jason. Have you heard of Quetzateryx?"

"No."

"It's some dinosaur whose fossils turned up at the very top of a mountain range in Colorado in 1981. There's unambiguous proof it flew there. For years the experts couldn't figure out how, but they were only working with conventional aerodynamic theory."

"Are you talking about that tiny flying dinosaur that evolved into a bird?"

"No, that's Archaeopteryx. That weighed just a pound or two. This is Quetzateryx. It weighed six thousand pounds."

"Six *thousand*? And it flew?"

Summers nodded. "A true flying reptile." It was a distant cousin of the much better known Quetzalcoatlus, first discovered in Texas in the 1970s.

"But how could it have—"

"Because it flew by an entirely different set of principles than any other animal we've ever known. This thing was nothing like modern birds, Jason. Different bones, musculature, wing structure—different everything. Have you heard of Gloria Rimmelstob? She's a fluid-dynamics superstar out of Hamburg University." Craig pointed to the pile of texts. "Three of her *entire books* are dedicated to something called 'the new energy-to-lift ratios of muscles.'"

Jason glanced at the texts. "They explain how this Quetza . . ."

"Quetzateryx."

". . . how Quetzateryx flew?"

"In more detail than I could come close to understanding, but yes. Muscle strength is a big part of it."

"Muscle strength."

"Correct. For years, just one major theory explained animal flight, and it only covered physically light animals like birds that fly by manipulating their feathers. But these scientists collectively constructed a second theory for much heavier animals that didn't have feathers and flew by manipulating specialized flying muscles."

"What are those exactly?"

"They're called 'rippling muscles' and they're on the top and bottom of an animal's wings. They say if they're manipulated in just the right way, they can create lift with an efficiency nobody previously thought possible."

"How do these . . . rippling muscles work?"

"According to Rimmelstob—and I guess VonKroyter and Fink did research on this too—in a way not covered by Bernoulli's theorem."

"Which is . . ."

"Lift is created when a fixed wing, any wing—a plane's, bird's, whatever—passes through the air. Wings are shaped with a curved top but a flat bottom. So when air passes around them, the air that goes over the top has to move faster than the air that passes under the bottom so both airstreams reach the other side at the same time. The increase in air velocity on the top creates a decrease in pressure, which creates lift, which in turn makes the wing rise. That's how most things fly. Fair enough?"

"Sure."

"Now, rippling muscles work by a very different concept. When rippling muscles tense, or fire, they almost undulate, sort of like a dolphin's body undulates when it swims. So when the muscles at the top of a wing *undulate in the same direction as the air*, they increase the air's velocity, and that creates greater lift."

"OK."

"And when a separate set of rippling muscles at the *bottom* of the wing undulate in the *opposite* direction, they *decrease* the air's velocity there. So this creates an even greater difference between the two airspeeds. One moving much faster than normal on the top, the other moving much slower than normal on the bottom. Collectively, that creates *significantly* greater lift. Fink conducted some lab tests in wind tunnels in Geneva last year that concluded the difference is *exponential*."

"Holy cow."

"You have no idea. It can increase lift by a factor of *five hundred times,* maybe more. Rippling muscles are how Quetzateryx flew, Jason." He pointed to what was in the cage. "And they're how this animal flew, too."

Jason eyed the creature behind the bars, scanning its back, wondering if he could actually . . . *Jesus, I see them. There they are.* They were clearly visible beneath the leathery black skin: a million different little muscles, each an inch or so wide, stretching from the head down to the tapered backside. He actually saw them rippling ever so slightly when the animal breathed. He'd never seen muscles move like that in his life.

Craig shrugged. "But obviously, the reality's different from the theory."

"What do you mean?"

"I mean rippling muscles may work well in theory, but the reality—for this animal at least—is that they didn't work well enough."

Jason noticed the animal was staring at his feet now, and was clearly in very bad shape, sickly, and breathing heavily. He tapped his hand against the bar, trying to get its attention, but it didn't move. "Has its condition worsened?"

Lisa looked down at it. "We just hoped it would stay alive until you came back."

"Should we try putting it in the water?"

"We already did." With the help of a boat crane, they'd lowered the entire cage into the sea. "It almost drowned."

"It did?"

"You know how quickly gills dry up."

"Right." Gills become unusable in a day. "What about food? Have you tried feeding it?"

Lisa shook her head. "Everything. It won't eat. It won't eat a damn thing."

Jason began pacing. "Well . . . we're going to test it anyway. . . . Vision. Hearing. Smell. Radar. Sonar. Magnetic abilities . . . I want to test this animal for everything."

Not hearing him, Lisa suddenly crouched next to the cage.

"And these rippling muscles. We've got to find out how they fire, determine their strength. And its breathing, and . . ."

"We're not testing for anything, Jason."

He turned to Lisa. "What? Why not?"

"Because I think it just died."

"No . . ." He crouched down. Behind the bars, the animal's eyes were closed, and its body wasn't rising and falling anymore. "Son of a bitch," he said quietly. "Son of a bitch." No one else spoke. The only sound was from Phil Martino's rapidly tapping keys.

Then Jason cleared his throat. "Let's start the autopsy. Right away."

CHAPTER 36

F OR THE next few moments, no one said a word. They simply
stared at the dead creature in the cage. As Monique studied it
through the bars, she reconsidered the events of the past twenty-
four hours. This animal is going to be *huge,* she thought. Much bigger
than a new species. A species, the most basic of animal classifications,
was defined as a group of physically and genetically similar animals. Related species composed a genus, related genera made up a family, and
related families constituted an order. She eyed the dead predator. The
key to animal classifications was that they were somehow related. But
was anything—*anything at all*—truly "related" to this animal? Mantas
were, of course, but that was a distant link from the days of Pangaea.
In their current form, mantas were entirely different from this animal
and lacked everything that made it so fantastic—the large predatory
brain and the ability to think, breathe air, possibly fly. Was there anything else, *any order* of animal ever, now or in the past, that could be
classified with it? She couldn't think of one.

"Come on!" Jason pulled hard on the cage door, straining to get
it open.

Darryl looked down to him. "Want a hand with that?"

"I can get it." He yanked even harder, giving it everything he had.

"See, Darryl." Lisa patted Jason's back playfully. "He can't even rely on someone to open a cage."

Darryl watched Lisa's hand closely. She wasn't patting Jason's back the way he would have. It was much more gentle, intimate even. Then Lisa saw him looking and removed her hand. Is something brewing between them? Darryl wondered.

The door popped open, and Jason looked up at her. "See?" He opened it fully. Then he just stood there. He didn't enter the cage, didn't even move. He just looked at the animal. There were no bars between them now and he wondered if it was really dead. He ducked his head slightly, stepping onto the metal.

"Be careful." Lisa suddenly felt very nervous.

He took another step and entered the cage fully. The predator was just a few feet away now. He leaned down to touch it. His hand moved closer. Then closer still. Then suddenly jolted back.

"Oh my God!" Lisa stammered.

Jason exhaled. The creature hadn't moved. "Sorry—nerves." He touched the skin. The animal didn't budge. It was dead. "Phil, Darryl, Craig—can you give me a hand with this?"

THE RAY was belly-up on a pair of pushed-together operating tables. Its wings drooped lifelessly over the tables' sides, its middle so thick it almost looked like an inverted sea turtle.

As Phil jumped to and fro snapping pictures, Lisa touched the white skin. It was thick and leathery. Fantastically so, perhaps tougher than rhino skin.

Sweating from having just helped to lift it, Craig crouched beneath the tables and looked up at the horned head. Jesus, that's a big mouth. Wide enough to swallow a physics text whole. He put his hands on the jaws and tried to pull it open. It didn't budge. He pulled as hard as he could. Nothing. He pulled again, really straining. Not a damn thing. Annoyed, he looked up at Darryl. "Gimme a hand?"

Darryl joined him, and together they yanked.

It still didn't budge, and Darryl paused. "Back away a sec. Let the Big Dog try solo."

"Be my guest." Craig got up, and Darryl carefully positioned his hands. Lisa watched as he pulled as hard as he could, forearms strain-ing mightily. The mouth slowly opened. Holy cow. Propped open, it reminded Lisa of those shark jaws from museums, except consider-ably more frightening. Look at those teeth.

The fat S-shapes were as wide as shot glasses at their base, with dagger-sharp tips, and too numerous to count. They were the teeth of a child's nightmare.

Summers eyed some pus oozing out of a closed eyelid. "This ani-mal died of GDV-4."

Phil paused from his pictures. "You sure?"

Craig almost laughed. "Yeah, Phil. I'm sure."

Phil got back to snapping. "Don't forget the recorder, Jason."

Jason turned it on, snapped on some surgical gloves, then turned to Lisa. "Want to assist?"

"Oh, sure. Uh . . ." She quickly rooted around a cabinet for a lab coat. Putting it on, she didn't notice Jason's disappointment when her hips disappeared behind the white fabric.

Then Jason forgot about her hips. He grabbed a small cutting knife. Then he began to cut.

"ONE LUNG."

Four separate flaps of white leathery skin were peeled back; in the middle of them, a very large lung, pink and healthy.

"Just like the lungfish," Monique said in quiet amazement.

Jason turned to Lisa. "Now check the stomach?"

"Definitely."

He started the next incision.

IT HOVERED just below the surface, a three-hundred-pound juvenile.

Perfectly still, its eyes shifted, watching as a seagull plunged into the water ten feet away.

The bird knifed in, grabbed a minnow, and returned to the surface. It quickly gobbled its food, then just floated there.

THOUSANDS OF other rays also watched the bird. None moved.

This one was the closest. Very, very slowly, it swam toward it.

JASON STUCK a gloved hand into the cut-open underbelly. "*Why would they fly?*"

Lisa turned. "*Why?*"

"Yeah, *why?* What's the reason?"

THE JUVENILE swam closer, propelling itself ever so gently.

BOBBING, THE seagull glanced up at the gray sky. Then back to the sea. But there were no fish there, just empty, dark waters.

MONIQUE TURNED. "They'd fly for the same reason they left the depths. To find food."

Jason reached into the belly up to his forearm and rooted around. "What food is in the air?"

Monique didn't answer. She just watched as a strange look formed on his face. "What do you have there?"

"I don't know." But it didn't feel like a fish.

THE GULL turned back to the water again. All it saw was its own rippling reflection, but still no fish. It looked up, noticing a dozen other gulls gliding nearby. It turned back to the water. Now, just beneath its reflection, were two large black eyes, staring at it coldly.

The gull flew away as fast as it could.

Then there was a frantic splashing behind it . . . and the sound of wings beating. The bird didn't look back.

"*IT'S A seagull.*"

Jason washed it off in the sink and held it up for all to see: a dripping-wet, crushed, feathered body. No one said anything. They just stared at the bird.

As Phil snapped a picture, Jason put it on the counter. Then he reached into the stomach again.

THE CREATURE thundered out of the sea, flapping violently, water shooting everywhere. It rose fast on the diagonal, its eyes locked on the prey ahead.

The gull flew very fast . . . but not fast enough.

The predator picked up speed, the mouth opening, the fat S-shapes zooming in.

The bird crowed loudly, desperately. Then it went silent.

"ANOTHER ONE." Jason rinsed off a second gull, then reached back into the stomach. He removed a third one. Then a fourth and fifth.

"Jesus," Craig said quietly.

Jason began removing crushed birds by the handful. When he finished there were fifty-six in total.

Darryl just stared at them, in five neat rows on the counter. "They're *feeding* on them. My God, they're *flying* to eat."

Craig paused. "We don't know that."

"We found this animal a hundred and fifty feet from the shoreline, and now its stomach is filled with seagulls. Do the math, Craig."

Summers stayed calm, analytical. "This ray could have caught every one of those birds when they bobbed on the ocean. We don't know it flew, Hoss."

Lisa's cell phone rang. She checked the ID and picked up. "Lisa Barton . . . Is that right? Hold on." She glanced up. "Is there a fax here?"

Monique pointed. "The other room."

Lisa walked off, and Jason turned back to the cut-open ray. "These animals are certainly *trying* to fly—right?"

"The *juveniles* are," Monique said. "The juveniles alone."

"But not the adults?"

"No."

"Why not?"

"Think about what you saw on your deep dive, Jason."

"What do you mean?"

"More than a thousand skeletons, and every single one of them was an adult. It's plain as day. The adults aren't adapting. GDV-4 wiped out their old food source, they can't find a new one, and now they're dying because of it. But the juveniles . . . they're swimming into higher waters, hunting new prey, maybe even flying. They are doing absolutely everything they can to eat. They *are* adapting. Or at least trying to."

Darryl shook his head. "So . . . why wouldn't the adults do the same thing?"

"Maybe they can't. The adults have spent their entire lives, their entire evolutionary history, in one place, learning one way to feed, one way to live. Suddenly their food disappears and they just have too much . . . inertia holding them back to do anything different."

"But the juveniles don't have that problem?"

"No. At least not to the same degree. They're brand new to the world. They have much less holding them back."

"Are *all* the juveniles are learning to fly, then?"

Monique paused. "I don't know if it's supposed to work that way."

"If *what's* supposed to work that way?"

"Adaptation. I don't think they all adapt at the same rate. When species change environments, they say it's very gradual. And individual. When ancestral penguins deserted the air for the sea, it didn't happen en masse. Two hundred thousand penguins didn't just wake up one day and decide to jump into the water. But *one* penguin probably did. It went in before all the others. Then, whether it took days, months, or millions of years, at some point, another one followed. Then forty more followed, then a thousand, until eventually, the entire penguin species was swimming. According to the science books, the same phenomenon played out repeatedly over geological time. There was one Archaeopteryx that flew before all the others, one amphibian that crawled, one whale that swam. Maybe there will be one ray that flies. Every species has its pioneers."

"And its martyrs," Jason said gravely.

Monique stared down at the cut-open ray, a strange look in her eyes. "So what? If there are martyrs, Jason, so be it. They died for a worthy cause. Everyone's always said mantas were an evolutionary mistake, that they swim just like birds fly and never should have evolved in the water in the first place. Maybe this creature is nature's first shot at correcting that. I mean, do you realize what we have here? This animal, this species, is literally evolutionary history in the making." She touched the dead ray, newly amazed.

"Charles Darwin himself dreamed of seeing something like this. When we talk about all the species that evolved in this planet's history—the amphibians, birds, mammals, man himself—they were all just tiny pieces of evolution, incremental improvements along the way. But this ray—this ray *is evolution*. It's not just a new species, a new genus, even a new family. There has never been anything like this animal *ever*. It's a *new order*." She looked at all of them, her eyes blazing. "We just discovered a new order."

"So how are we going to find them again?" Phil said.

Monique shook her head. "I don't know."

The room was silent. Neither did anyone else.

"I know."

They all turned. It was Lisa. She was staring at a fistful of fax pages.

CHAPTER 37

"**W**HAT IS that?"

Holding the papers, Lisa reentered the lab. "A report from the Audubon Society. A report about *seagulls going missing up and down the California coast.* I called the Audubon people a while ago, when I thought GDV-4 might have gone airborne, but clearly something else is happening to the gulls. . . ." She eyed the papers. "It's like a plague moving up the coast, and it's followed the rays' migration *exactly,* from Clarita Island right up to here in Point Reyes. They're feeding on the seagulls en masse."

Jason drummed his fingers. "The Audubon people don't think it's anything else?"

"They have no idea what it is."

"It's the rays." Darryl eyed the crushed birds. "I'm telling you, they've got to be flying."

Jason could almost dream it. "Maybe they really are."

"You don't actually believe that, do you?" This was from a calm, rational voice behind them.

They all turned. It was Harry Ackerman, near the entrance, in a surprisingly cheap-looking gray suit, with a laptop slung over his shoulder.

"Harry, what a surprise." Jason walked over to him.

"Nice to see you, Jason. My assistant mentioned you were up here." They shook hands.

"What brings you to the neighborhood?"

"Actually, I've had more . . . challenges with my businesses. So I scheduled meetings in San Francisco and the Valley to raise capital."

"I'm sorry to hear that."

"It's nothing dire—I assure you." The voice was as cool as ever. "I thought I'd stop by. Oh, excuse me. . . ." He grabbed his laptop just before it fell from his shoulder.

"You should be careful with that, Mr. Ackerman," Phil warned.

"Is that new, Harry?" Jason tried to see the machine. "I'm tired of borrowing Phil's all the time, so I've been thinking about buying one myself. What kind is that?"

"Toshiba. I don't know computers at all, but I was told this is a good one."

Phil nodded. "Are you backing it up, Mr. Ackerman?"

"On rewritable CDs." Ackerman said the words almost officially, as if it was his first time using them in a sentence. Then he noticed the cut-up ray and forgot about the computer. "This is nothing short of a miracle, a true evolutionary miracle." He thought of how much it would impress the bigwigs on the black-tie charity circuit—a prize so vastly superior to the traditional trophies of success that it would smack the smug looks off their faces faster than they could cash out a stock option. But only if they actually knew about it. Ackerman was tired of the project being sidetracked by what he regarded as unrealistic scientific speculation. "Tell me, Jason, do you think this animal actually flying is realistic?"

"We don't know, Harry. There's evidence it might have flown, so—"

"*Evidence?* You consider crawling a few feet from shore and eating some birds as they float on the ocean *evidence* of flying?"

Exactly what I said, Summers thought.

Jason gave Ackerman a look. "It's just a possibility at this stage."

Ackerman chuckled. "Who knows? Maybe they really will fly. In twenty million years. Right, Phil?"

Phil Martino suddenly laughed so hard he could barely speak. Watching him, Lisa and the triumvirate were genuinely amused. But

Jason looked like he was going to blow a gasket. Phil was laughing in his face, and in front of the boss.

Ackerman discreetly leaned into Phil's ear. "OK, calm down."

"Oh." Suddenly aware of Jason's anger, Phil shut up. "Sorry, Jason. I don't know why I found that so funny."

Jason relaxed. "Yeah, sure, Phil. No problem." It was forgotten.

"Either way," Ackerman continued, "your progress has been spectacular. All of you. I just wanted to see this specimen in person and say good luck." He quickly shook everyone's hand, checked to make sure his laptop was still slung over his shoulder, then went outside to a waiting limo.

Through a filthy window, Monique watched as the car pulled away. "So what's next?"

Whether it was the result of being the butt of Ackerman's joke or not, Jason suddenly looked extra motivated. "What's next is we're going to find another one of these things. . . ." He started pacing. "We'll set up more sonar. And radar, too. We have the equipment, so we'll put it onshore in case another tries flying to land. And we'll track the seagulls. These rays will have massive appetites, could put on two hundred pounds a week, so we'll follow the birds." He continued to pace. "Lisa, you said some gulls went missing right here in Point Reyes?"

"Yes, but there's another data point here I didn't see before. . . ." She was looking at the report's last page, at something handwritten and initialed on the very bottom. "Apparently some more birds went missing just"—she checked her watch—"two hours ago."

Jason halted. "Two *hours*? Where?"

"Bodega Bay." It was the sight of a well-known Hitchcock movie, thirty-odd miles north of their current position.

"Let's get up there." Jason glared at all of them. "We're gonna find another one of these things. Whether it flies in twenty million years or tomorrow."

"NOTHING HERE."

They were a mile offshore of an ugly Bodega Bay beach of mud and rock. They'd set up sonar buoys at sea, tripod-mounted radar guns on land, and kept their eyes open.

Two monitors were set up on the *Expedition's* back wall, and Craig shook his head at them. "What do you want to do, Jason?"

Jason scanned the ugly terrain, the pathetic little trees behind the beach, the tiny breaking waves. "The rays were just here . . . they couldn't have gone far." He looked around some more. "We'll wait."

THEY DID wait. One week, then five. There was no sign of the rays.

It was a cold, drizzling December night, and they were half a mile off a desolate Schooner Gulch state beach. In gray gym shorts and grungy flip-flops, Craig was crouched beneath a blue tarp covering the monitors. There were still no readings of any kind. "They've gotta still be swimming the canyons."

Behind him in a hooded yellow slicker, Lisa looked around. "How big do you think they are now, Jason?"

"Big. Fifteen hundred pounds, maybe eight feet across the wings."

Summers stood. "I wonder if they're still trying to fly."

"According to the Audubon reports, they are." Lisa had been reading them regularly. Seagulls had continued to disappear in vast quantities right up to their current location.

"Lisa, those birds could be missing for other reasons entirely."

"Like what?"

"Like . . . maybe GDV-4 really did go airborne. Or maybe some other virus. It just doesn't make sense that animals *that big* would still be feeding on seagulls."

"It makes perfect sense." Monique walked forward in her own slicker.

"How do you figure?"

"Because adapting to hunt yet *another* type of prey is hard as hell. Now that these rays have learned to successfully hunt seagulls, they'll feed on them for as long as they possibly can. If they're putting on as much weight as Jason thinks, they must have enormous appetites. They can't afford to experiment right now."

Lisa eyed the desolate seascape. "So where are they, then? If they're still eating seagulls, how are we not picking them up?" She eyed the monitors. "Is this equipment still working, Craig?"

"It's working fine. But it's not infallible. Sonar and radar signals don't cut through land, so if the rays are only coming up where there's a bend in the coastline or where we don't have a buoy or tripod . . . we wouldn't pick them up and—" His phone started ringing and he checked the ID. "York. Excuse me."

As Craig went below deck, Lisa shook her head. "But how are they consistently finding the *exact locations* where we can't detect them? Dumb luck?"

"I don't think it's luck at all." Monique scanned the dark waters suspiciously. "They've got to be evading us intentionally."

"How the hell are they doing that?"

"The same way they caught the dolphin, Lisa. Only now they're using those senses defensively."

"What does that mean?"

"You don't think these things *know* something's in the ocean tracking them?"

The idea took Lisa aback. "I couldn't say for sure."

"They know, and they're outsmarting us. They've *been outsmarting* us from the get-go."

"So where does that leave us?"

"We've got to outsmart them for a change. I just don't know how."

Neither did anyone else. They were all silent. Until Summers returned.

"Any idea how we can find these rays, Craig?" Jason asked.

Summers looked astounded by his own answer. "Actually . . . yes. I know where they're going. I know where they've *been going* this entire time. They have a destination; they've been migrating to it all along."

"What is it?"

Craig looked up at the rainy sky. "I've got a map downstairs. Let me show you."

CHAPTER 38

THEY'D LOST thousands of pounds of weight and become emaciated skeletons on the verge of death. They lay flat on the dark sand four miles below the surface, their thick leathery skins too big for their bodies, excess folds everywhere, the result of having eaten nothing.

They were the only members of the older generation still alive. Within just the past hour, thousands more had simply closed their eyes and died right here. The move north would continue. It had to. But only when they had the strength to lift themselves up off the seafloor.

The young adults, they knew, were at the surface again. Their elders tried tuning to them, but they couldn't. Their sensory organs weren't functioning properly. For these members of the species, the darkness was dark now. They saw nothing.

FOUR MILES above, under the drizzling night sky, the rays shot out of the sea, flapping and gliding in every direction.

They were a hundred yards off of a desolate, evergreen-lined shore. While this part of the coastline looked just like any other, not special in any way, it was very special indeed. The rays *knew* it was safe here. During their migration, they'd repeatedly detected sonars in the ocean, not from whales, and not from dolphins, either, but from something, and always pointed toward them. As predators, the rays instinctively understood that they were being tracked. Over and over, they had evaded the strange signals with little effort at all: simply by swimming the canyons, then returning to the surface after a bend in the shoreline. They'd just done it again. No sonar, including their own, could pass through land.

The juveniles were now young adults. Fully exposed in the drizzling night air, they revealed how much they'd grown. They were now enormous 1,500-pound creatures, eight feet across the wings and six feet lengthwise, with deep muscular middles, huge mouths, and pupilless, jet-black eyes the size of squash balls.

An enormous fleet of out-of-control airborne bumper cars, they zoomed everywhere. The differences in flying abilities were dramatic now. While no two animals flew exactly the same way—there were literally millions of subtle, often imperceptible differences—four broad skill levels existed.

The first group comprised those creatures whose increase in body weight had caused great problems. While these animals still thundered out of the ocean successfully, they never climbed higher than fifteen feet. As they'd grown larger, they could no longer properly control their rippling muscles to achieve true lift. Catching unsuspecting gulls bobbing on the seas was easy, but that was all.

The second group flew considerably better. By mimicking a seagull's diagonal liftoff exactly, they ascended just like one, picking up speed horizontally and gradually climbing. But unable to manipulate their rippling muscles for the subtle changes in air density, this group tended to experience lift problems above fifty feet. Discontinuities in the airflow resulted and consistently caused crashing falls.

The third group was more advanced, capable of performing many of the basic flying motions successfully: liftoff, flapping, gliding, turning, and dipping. More sophisticated maneuvers like soaring, diving, and flying across wind currents were beyond their skills, but they continued to practice and improve.

The fourth group, composed of just four dozen animals, had successfully learned virtually every type of movement there was: flapping, gliding, turning, diving, soaring, angling, flying into currents, with currents, across currents, and skid landing. While not yet graceful, every movement was consistently achievable.

With one exception. Hovering. Even the most talented of this group couldn't master it. Every time they attempted to hover, beating their wings superfast above the water's surface, they lost control and fell in with awkward crashes. The four dozen animals continued to practice, however. They were particularly conservative, even for their species, and knew they weren't ready for the land.

Suddenly they detected movement far below the surface. It was the adults, resuming their quest.

These animals would follow, but not yet. As the drizzle turned into a full rain, they zoomed in every direction. As close as they now were to the looming forest, they were instinctively tuning toward it. Earlier in their development, their sensory organs hadn't functioned properly in the air, but as they'd grown, their organs had matured and adjusted to the new medium. As a result, the prey from the land was calling them. Softly but very persistent. They'd detected only tiny traces earlier, but now they knew with absolute certainty. Vast amounts of food existed on the land.

Long ago, one of them had attempted to find that food. A single juvenile ray had flown inland but not made it past a hundred and fifty feet. It had long since died.

The others were more cautious, however. Some were so cautious they'd never be ready for such a journey. But others might. The land possessed a variety of different signals, almost all of them unknown. One signal was familiar, however. From a particular type of prey these rays had tasted once before, a species that had been easy to hunt in the water and perhaps would be easy to hunt on the land as well. They continued to practice.

CHAPTER 39

"**W**HAT THE hell is that?"

It was still raining and dark, but Darryl had spotted something in the distance. It was silhouetted against the dreary night sky. Something large, dark, and flying. He squinted. "Oh." An airplane.

Monique shook her head. "Let's get downstairs and see what Craig has to say."

They joined the others in the galley. Around a little white table next to the fridge, Summers was already speaking. "They've been migrating to it from day one. It's an island in the depths."

"An *island?*" Jason had no idea what this meant.

"Correct. One spot, one relatively small area. Filled with every type of sea life imaginable and apparently without a trace of GDV-4." He pointed to an open map on the table. "It's four miles down and surrounded by mountains that York thinks have effectively blocked out the virus."

Jason leaned into the map. "Where is it exactly?"

"Off the coast of Eureka. About fifty square miles. If the rays actually get there, they'll find all the food they need."

Darryl nodded. "So how far do they have to go?"

"At the current pace, they're days away at least. Jason, we can beat them up there and set up the equipment."

"Then let's do that. Right now."

BY THE next afternoon they'd finished. Sonar buoys covered the deep-sea island from the water and radar guns, staked into nearby shorelines, covered the land.

Darryl Hollis didn't think any of the equipment would help with their task. In a sweat-soaked red polo at the stern, he shook his head at the closest buoy. "Four miles down and surrounded by mountains? Sonar's not gonna pick up a damn thing down there, Craig."

Summers eyed the dotless crisscrossing gray formations on the sonar monitor. "We still gotta try. We might get something."

Jason was suddenly depressed. "Why would we? If those rays actually make it into these waters, why would they ever come up again?"

"Because this island might not stay an island for long, Jason. Don't you understand. GDV-4 isn't in these waters *right now*, but that could change."

"When?"

"Who knows. A day, a week, a year."

"Where does that leave us, then? We can't go down there after them, not at these depths. So what do we do here?"

Summers eyed the monitors patiently. "We wait."

THREE DAYS later, the equipment turned up the reading everyone expected. The rays swam right into the virus-free island. But then some of them apparently left it. Over the next weeks, sporadic sonar and radar signals painted an unambiguous case. For reasons unknown, a small number of rays were repeatedly venturing to the surface. They nevertheless remained elusive. Given their extraordinary sensory abilities, their potential to hide in the canyons, and the island's fifty-square-mile size, they were impossible to pin down. They successfully evaded Jason's team for months.

It was near sunset in late April. In the waters offshore of Eureka, with a stunning line of ruby red on the horizon, Darryl shook his head. "I don't get why these things are still coming to the surface at all. They've got all the food they need down there, they're not feeding on gulls anymore"—Audubon reports indicated the birds had returned to the coastline en masse—"so why are they still coming up? It doesn't make sense."

"Yes it does," Monique said. "They're not coming up for food, Darryl. At this stage, I think it's much more complicated than that."

"How so?"

"I think some of these rays spent so much time at the surface they might be . . . linked to it in a way."

"*Linked* to it?" Darryl knew that Monique had been spending a great deal of time with her old evolution texts lately. Apparently, she'd learned some things. "How do you mean?"

"Maybe *accustomed* is a better way to put it. Their muscles, their brains—everything about them is accustomed to the surface now. So they can't just desert it. At least not entirely. Despite the food below, I think certain physical and even physiological changes might have occurred that will make disappearing down there an impossibility."

"You almost make it sound like an addiction."

"In a lot of ways, I think it is. For some of them anyway. They may have spent so much time up here that they can't just quit it cold turkey."

"How big do you figure these things are now?" Summers asked.

"Full-size adults. Fourteen feet across the wings, twelve feet long, four thousand pounds. Hang-glider size."

"You been keeping Mr. Ackerman up on all of this, Jason?" Phil asked.

"I've left messages, Phil. I think he's got other things on his mind right now."

"Like what?"

"His businesses. They're doing worse, and I don't know how his capital raising's been going."

Phil nodded and went below deck. Darryl turned back to Jason. "*Four thousand* pounds?"

"If not more."

"My God. Can you imagine seeing one of those things *actually* flying on land?"

"It could happen, Darryl." Monique cleared her throat. "It really could. And much sooner than twenty million years. Maybe sooner than any of us could fathom."

"Let's say it did." Jason noticed a glowing full moon was overhead now. "Where would they go, Monique?"

"Around here . . ." In the pale white light Monique looked around, noticing the trees onshore. These particular trees weren't ordinary trees but coastal redwoods, towering evergreens the height of office buildings that stretched as far as the eye could see in every direction. Monique knew that in their current location they were very close to several redwood parks: Redwood National Park, other private parks, and the biggest park of them all, Leonard State Park, a truly gargantuan forest that stretched right up to the Oregon border, nearly a hundred miles away. "I don't know where they'd go, Jason. All I know is this area makes me nervous."

"Why?"

"Because there aren't any beaches here."

"So . . . ?"

"So if another one of those things really did come to the land . . ." She looked around some more. "We'd have a hell of a time finding it."

"Monique." Phil Martino peered up the stairs from below deck. "FYI, I'm printing a really big e-mail that just came in for you."

"Who's it from?"

"A . . . professor, uh . . ."

She looked stunned. "Professor Benton Davis?"

"Yeah."

"Son of a bitch, he got back to me."

Jason turned. "Who's Professor Benton Davis?"

She went to the stairs. "An evolutionary historian, the author of one of my textbooks . . ."

"Why'd you contact him?"

"If one of these things really does try going to the land, he can help us determine exactly where. . . ." She rushed below deck. "Where's that e-mail, Phil?"

CHAPTER 40

THEY'D LEARNED to hover.

With the full moon lighting up the ocean plain, the four dozen most talented fliers continued to practice. Visible in silhouette, they were hang-glider size indeed, with mouths the size of a sports car's front end and eyes as big as baseballs. A recent growth spurt of a thousand pounds had added powerful lean muscle to their wings and undersides, their rippling muscles now vastly faster and stronger.

Thousands of other animals hung just beneath the ocean's surface. They were resting. They'd practiced flying for hours, but fatigue had set in and forced them to stop. They simply watched as the others darted in and out of the moonlight above.

The experts consistently moved with grace now. No frantic flapping, no violent splashes. Body movements were controlled, precise. Discontinuities in the airflow still occurred, but they were far less common, and even when they did happen; the resulting turbulence no longer sent them crashing into the ocean. The four dozen creatures had learned to regain continuity, to fly through turbulence just like an airplane or a bird. Wind wasn't a problem either. By manipulating their flying muscles in literally thousands of subtle yet significant ways, they'd learned to use the wind to their advantage, to manage it, to massage it.

After months of practice, hovering, too, had become more than doable. Like the rest of the movements, it was almost *natural* now.

Almost. With the full moon shining down, the four dozen predators continued to practice. There were different types of hovering, and several focused on the most basic, hovering in the stationary position, beating their wings in rapid smooth movements and holding steady. Others hovered while simultaneously moving forward. Others still hovered straight up, rising like helicopters, then descended the same way. Half a dozen worked on arcing motions, rising up, moving forward, then descending again. A few dive-bombed, then came to gentle hovering stops just above the water. They all practiced something, over and over again.

All of them wanted to stop, however, to submerge and join their brethren in the water. None dared. Earlier, one had tried, and the one that had become their leader savagely killed it. They continued to practice.

As they did, those beneath the waves just watched them soaring like great, watery seagulls beneath the rippling moon. Then a mass of clouds drifted in front of the orb and threw the submerged creatures into darkness. Still none moved. They simply continued to watch. Even as everything faded to black.

CHAPTER 41

"**I**s MONIQUE still reading that e-mail?"

It was night on the *Expedition*'s stern. Craig, Darryl, and Phil were crouched at the back wall, eyeing the monitors. Lisa was jotting something in her notebook. So no one answered Jason as he looked up from the laptop. "Darryl? Is Monique still reading that e-mail?"

"Oh." Darryl thought about it. "She must be." When he'd gone down earlier, she hadn't even looked at him, just read page after page of information. "Hey, turn that up a little, will ya, Sloppy Joe?"

"You like this, Big Dog?" Craig increased the volume on his enormous boom box, playing a soulful female singer.

"Love it."

Jason put the laptop down. "I like it, too."

Craig was surprised. "Seriously?"

"Seriously." Jason had just finished typing his notes for the Species Council report and, despite his curiosity about what Monique had found, actually felt like relaxing a little. He looked up at the sky. It was gorgeous, no clouds and a trillion stars.

"Jason."

"Yeah."

It was Darryl, at the stairs with Craig and Phil. "Phil's gonna show us a new video game. Wanna come?"

"Oh, thanks, but I'm not really into video games, guys."

They disappeared, and Jason looked back up at the sky. It was just stunning. He exhaled and tapped his feet to the music, wondering who the singer was. Then he noticed Lisa, still jotting in her notebook, and saw her feet were also tapping. He realized the two of them were alone.

"Nice night, huh?" She was looking up now too.

"Beautiful."

She turned back to her notebook. And right there, Jason summoned up the courage to do something he'd been thinking about for quite a while. "Lisa."

"Yeah."

"Would you like to dance?"

She paused when Darryl and the guys started coming back up, but Darryl overheard and turned them around.

"I'd love to dance."

They went to the middle of the deck.

Lisa raised an eyebrow when he put an arm around her waist.

"You probably had no idea I was such a smooth lothario," he joked.

She laughed, maybe too hard, and he immediately felt self-conscious. "Or maybe you just thought I was some controlling, insecure marine biologist."

She smiled. "You guessed it."

"So the music's pretty good, huh?"

"Changing the subject?"

"Not at all. What do you want to talk about?"

"Why you're so controlling, of course." She was still smiling. "Seriously, why do you micromanage everything, Jason? Why can't you trust anybody?"

"Maybe I'm just wired that way."

"I don't buy that. It's more than that."

He looked around, at the gorgeous sky, the moon. "Come on, I thought we could try to relax here."

"I didn't think you could ever relax."

"This isn't helping."

"Why can't you trust anyone?"

He turned to the glistening ocean. "I've honestly never thought about it."

"Tell me." She gently turned his chin. "Please."

He looked at her. "Maybe it started with all the Manta World problems."

"OK."

He looked at the stars. "You've got to understand, Lisa, people I'd known for years, people I'd trusted . . . They all suddenly stopped calling. Meetings got canceled, my tables at conferences ended up empty. . . ." He looked her in the eye. "They abandoned me and they never came back." He shrugged. "After a while, you start to lose trust in people."

"I see." This was a real answer, and she almost hadn't been expecting it. "I'm very sorry."

"To be honest, for a long time, I felt *you* were letting me down too. You were so totally focused on your own research. Often at the expense of what the rest of us were trying to accomplish. I think I really resented that. It might be why we fought so much."

She swallowed this bitter pill silently. "Do you still feel like that?"

He paused. "I haven't felt that way for a while. About you, about anyone on the boat. It's really been a great turnaround."

"Then how come you still can't trust us?"

"I can trust you."

"No, you can't."

"Really, I—"

"Good things happen when you trust us, Jason. Look at what happened when you went to Princeton to talk to that Ban . . . Bar . . . Bardan . . ."

"Bandar Vishakeratne."

"Look at what we did, what we found while you were away with him."

"That's because I trusted you. You just proved it."

"You didn't trust anybody, Jason You left because you had to. It's not the same thing."

He smiled. "It isn't?"

"Jesus Christ, no, it isn—"

"You're very pretty, Lisa. I don't think I've ever told you that, but I've noticed. I've noticed every single day. Wrinkled clothes or not, you are beautiful."

She hesitated. "Changing the subject again?"

They kept dancing, maybe a little closer.

"Thank you," she said quietly.

"Thank *you*. I'll think about what you said."

As they continued he held her tighter . . . and it felt a little strange. On the one hand, physically holding Lisa Barton after all this time was odd, definitely odd, but on the other hand, it was also natural.

It was the same for Lisa, strange but natural, too.

The song ended, and they heard something. . . . It was the guys, starting up the stairs. Darryl poked his head up meekly, as if asking if it was OK to return. Jason waved him forward.

They walked up, and the grin on Phil's face was bigger than the boat. "So what's goin' on, guys?"

Lisa was casual. "Just giving Jason some dance lessons. He only stepped on my feet three times."

Craig nodded, not missing a beat. "The over-under was four."

Darryl smiled softly. Before they'd left Baja, he never would have guessed it. Lisa and Jason. Seeing them together made him think of families, kids, and life beyond the *Expedition*. The Hollises had been discussing those subjects a great deal recently. Issues like which towns had the best public nursery schools and day cares, the possibility of buying a place, which banks offered the cheapest mortgages. It all depended on Monique getting pregnant, of course, but they hoped that would happen in the near future.

Just then Monique appeared on deck. Right away, Darryl saw she wasn't in a romantic mood. She held a map of Northern California and a printout of the massive e-mail she'd been reading.

Jason couldn't help but notice how serious she looked. "What's up, Monique?"

"Every species that ever transitioned from one environment to another did it through a *conduit*. A specific place where the species was physically comfortable. The very first penguin left the air for the sea via a particular hole in an iceberg. The very first whales entered the ocean by way of a submerged tunnel. Archaeopteryxes, crocodiles, dolphins—every species that's ever changed environments did it via their own special conduit. These rays are looking for theirs."

Jason eyed the map. "Can we figure out where that is?"

"I already did."

CHAPTER 42

"**T**HIS IS where the virus-free island is. . . ."

In the living room below deck, Monique pointed to an open map on the table. "And this . . . is Redwood Inlet."

On the map, it was a wide spoke of blue, flowing from deep in the green forest right into the ocean.

"It's nearly a quarter of a mile wide and the perfect conduit to the land. It could give the rays direct access without ever having to leave the water."

Jason eyed the spoke dubiously. "*If they actually use it.* No one *knows* this 'conduit' theory actually played out, right, Monique? And even if it did, who's to say it will happen *here?*"

"Agreed, this is guesswork, but it's extremely educated guesswork. And common sense, too. Jason, if these animals actually want to explore the land, they'll want to be as physically comfortable as possible. What better place than an inland river?"

"Wouldn't the freshwater bother them?"

"It might, but nothing's perfect."

Jason paused, his eyes drifting farther north on the map. "Are there other 'conduits' we should consider? . . . Like these mountains further north."

"Maybe." Monique eyed the spoke. "But I think this creek's a great start."

"What do you want to do exactly?"

Monique paused, thinking it out. "Wire it. Sonar buoys in the water, radar guns on land. Get prepared in case they actually do go there."

Jason nodded. "Let's do it."

Seconds later, they were on deck, about to head to the creek, when Lisa leaned into Jason and whispered, "See what happens when you trust people."

Jason just smiled as the boat lurched forward.

"JASON, YOU got a second?!"

The *Expedition* was really moving now, violent wind rushing past even faster than the redwoods onshore.

Jason turned. "Sure, Phil, what's up!"

"Can we go below deck?!"

They did, and it was much quieter. "I just wanted to see if the additional work I've been doing has been helpful."

"Oh, very much so, Phil. I really appreciate it and think everyone else does too."

"Excellent. Because I was wondering if I might become an official researcher like they are. On your reports and all that."

"Oh." Coincidentally, Jason had just written a cover page for his Species Council report, listing everyone except Phil as core researchers. "Mind if I ask you something, then?"

"Sure."

"Don't take this the wrong way, but are you actually doing any research?"

"Well, I'm typing and analyzing everybody els—"

"But are you actually doing any research yourself?"

"Well . . . no."

Jason nodded. "Phil, you are doing a fantastic job, believe me. . . ."

"But . . ."

"But . . . you don't have an ichthyology degree. Unfortunately, education makes a difference in this field, and all of us need that degree to make more . . . meaningful contributions. You know how hard I worked to get my degree, and believe me, Darryl, Monique, Craig, and Lisa worked hard as hell to get theirs, too. Would it be fair to them to just give you, or anyone, the same credit without having done all that work?"

Phil looked up at the ceiling. "I take your point."

"Do you think it's reasonable?"

"I guess so."

"Phil, the last thing I want is for you to think I don't appreciate everything you're doing. I do. Your work is going to be invaluable in preparing my final report on this."

Phil nodded sadly. "Thanks, Jason. I appreciate that. Maybe I was getting a little ahead of myself."

"We OK, then?"

"Yeah. Thanks, buddy."

Jason patted him on the back, and they joined the others on deck.

They continued for miles, passing evergreens, evergreens, and more evergreens. Then, rounding a bend in the coastline, they saw it under the moon's white gaze: a perfectly flat, quarter-mile-wide creek flowing right into the sea. They slowed down and Jason turned.

"Turn on the spotlight, will you, Craig?"

A big headlight went on, and Jason immediately noticed a wood sign staked into some tall, drooping grass. Painted yellow letters said RED-WOOD INLET. He stared at it for a moment and noticed Darryl, arms crossed and eyeing the creek suspiciously. "You buy this conduit theory, Darryl? You actually think they'd swim inland?"

Darryl didn't answer at first. He simply studied the landscape. The flat moonlit water, the trees, how isolated it all was . . . This place felt right. "Yeah, Jason. I think they might."

"Craig, let's anchor." Jason didn't even want to wait till morning. "I want to wire this thing right now."

LATER THAT night, they finished. Two yellow sonar buoys were bobbing in the ocean near the creek and two white radar guns were staked into its grassy banks.

They awoke at seven the next morning. With the others up on deck, Jason and Lisa bumped into each other in the galley, and he quickly kissed her on the cheek. He seemed embarrassed by it; she thought it was adorable. When they arrived on deck, Craig immediately looked up from his monitors.

"Still aren't any readings here, Jason. What do you want to do?"

Jason turned to Monique. "Did you say there are other creeks we should also wire?"

"A little further south."

"There's your answer, Craig."

Summers rose from the equipment. "I'll turn us around, then."

As the *Expedition* began moving, they motored away with confidence. If anything entered Redwood Inlet, they'd know it—and right away.

THOUGH NO one considered one additional possibility: What if something had entered Redwood Inlet *already*?

CHAPTER 43

A s THE boat's vibrations disappeared, the four dozen predators didn't move. They were perfectly still at the bottom of the muddy creek. Several hundred yards from the ocean, they hadn't moved for two full days. They were physically uncomfortable here. The seafloor felt different. So did the water itself.

They were strategically positioned behind a bend in the creek. Here, they couldn't detect the two floating devices with their sonars, just as the devices couldn't detect them. Their ampullae of Lorenzini had no such problems, however.

The predators weren't focused on the unseen equipment at the moment. They couldn't focus on anything other than the smell. The smell was from the ocean, farther south and very deep, but potent nevertheless. It was the smell of blood. Far away, there was a fantastic amount of it, so much that every single animal here was salivating.

THE SLAUGHTER of the great whites was complete. There was still enough blood to fill several Olympic-size swimming pools, but the meat was long since gone. The sharks, like the rays themselves, had been very hungry, and that hunger had been used against them. A school of more than eight hundred had been lured here, nearly four miles below the surface. Then they were ripped to pieces and devoured. Three dozen of the sharks had actually escaped, but then the smell of their very own blood had lured them back. Then they, too, had been eaten alive.

Thousands of predators rested on the ocean floor, unseen. Most were of the younger generation. Their experiences at the surface were only a memory now, as was their migration. They had no plans to move. They'd found the place they'd been searching for.

IN THE creek, one predator rose up and flapped toward the ocean. Then a second animal followed. Then a third and fourth. Then all except one. The smell of blood was too much to take. Against the leader, which didn't budge, they moved en masse, their winged bodies flapping slowly in the darkened water, heading toward the bend and the two hanging devices beyond it.

But then they stopped. The leader had just made a sound. A strange sound not designed to be heard in water. They all had the larynxes to produce the sound, but only the leader had learned how to do so while airborne. In the air, the sound would have been described as a roar, a rather terrifying one, but here, submerged and far less menacing, it was closer to a waterlogged truck horn. The others had blinked anyway.

The leader rose, lifting its great body from the mud. The four dozen animals obediently turned away from the ocean and joined it anew.

Unseen in the blackened freshwaters, they flapped inland. Most were tentative at best. Their instincts were in a dramatic state of flux, and they were physically and physiologically uncomfortable with what they were doing.

The leader moved with purpose. Its instincts alone had been irreversibly altered. Even with the vast amounts of shark blood still in the depths, it no longer felt like it belonged there. The animal veered upward. It didn't know where it was going exactly, but it knew one fact with absolutely certainty. The light was coming.

It would never see the blackened depths of the sea again.

CHAPTER 44

"FINISHED." CRAIG Summers nodded to himself. The fourth and final creek was wired. Sonar in the water, radar on land.

Darryl Hollis doubted if it would turn up anything, however. This creek and the two others they'd just wired possessed relatively undesirable topographies: not straight but curved, narrower, and with considerably rougher waters. Redwood Inlet still felt right.

It was early afternoon. Sweating in dappled sunlight, broken up by an onshore redwood, Craig knelt, checking the monitors. With a tiny joystick, he scanned the creeks one by one, scrolling up the coast. "Nothing . . . Nothing anywhere . . ."

Behind him, Jason turned to Monique. "You really think this conduit theory plays out?"

"I think it's our best shot."

"What do we do now?"

"Wait."

Jason paused. He hated waiting, despised it; it made his skin crawl. But then he glanced at Lisa. One look said it. This is what it means to trust someone. "OK. We wait."

———

THE BLACK eyes held still. Through the rippling water, the great staff of wood seemed to be almost moving, but the brain behind the eyes understood this was an illusion. The eyes shifted, moving up along the shaft, branchless for several hundred feet until a crown formed, topped off by a massive evergreen treetop.

The eyes shifted, scanning the rest of the terrain. The predator couldn't see the prey under the early-afternoon clouds, but it knew it was out there, scattered for miles.

The hulking forms next to it sensed nothing. They didn't even know there were trees. In a place they'd never been before, they were still uncomfortable. The water still didn't feel right on their thick skin.

The leader's eyes shifted as a seagull appeared.

Hundreds of feet above Redwood Inlet, the bird glided lazily, looking right back at it, looking at all of them. They were a sight to behold, four dozen living hang gliders, perfectly still just beneath the creek's flat surface.

Comfortable here as the leader was, it knew instinctively that this was not the place. Not for its brethren anyway. They wouldn't join it. Not here.

It turned, swimming back toward the ocean, and the others eagerly followed.

They swam for nearly an hour, a squadron of colossal, slow-moving bats.

As they neared the sea, they paused. The devices floating just beyond the bend were still emitting their powerful signals.

They swam forward, and two triangular shapes came into view, bobbing at the surface. The rays moved below and past them, entered the ocean, then hugged the jagged coastline until, again, the powerful signals disappeared. Then they continued north. This was not the place.

"SON OF a bitch. We just got a reading."

The others dashed toward Craig.

Jason arrived first. "Where?"

Somewhat mystified, Summers pointed. "That first inlet."

"Let's get up there, Craig. Now."

Summers marched to the controls. As the boat started moving, Jason turned to Monique. "Maybe your conduit theory isn't so theoretical after all."

Monique just eyed the blinking dot on the interactive map. "We'll see." Then they really started moving.

CHAPTER 45

A HEARTBEAT.

The rays had been swimming alongside the towering mountain range for hours. Looming right over the sea, the mountains were black with silver flecks, had no vegetation at all, and were several thousand feet high. They were also dotted with caves. The creatures had passed hundreds of such caves, most of them small and well above the waterline.

This cave was different. First was its size. It was massive, ten stories high, four lanes wide, and with a huge rock lip opening right into the ocean. But size alone wasn't the reason they'd halted there. It was what this cave had *inside it*. A heartbeat.

The creatures were ten feet below the surface, perfectly still.

Except for the leader, they were still uncomfortable and knew instinctively that they didn't need to be here. There was food in the depths.

Still, they had detected the heartbeat, and now their predatory brains were curious. What did it belong to? The frequency was totally foreign.

They didn't move. Minutes passed. Then hours.

The others gradually lost interest, but the leader remained focused. Its eyes didn't leave the cave. As time passed, it began to find the space almost instinctively inviting. The towering hole was enormous, big enough to hold its own body, and totally devoid of light, just like the depths.

It suddenly refocused. They all did.

There was a light padding noise. Footsteps. Something was walking out of the cave.

The creatures descended deeper into the dark water, instantly becoming invisible.

Then an animal appeared, a shimmering vision beneath a bleak sky: a small figure covered with thick brown fur, a large, almost triangular head, and ambling forward on four legs. It was a bear cub, not more than a hundred pounds.

The creatures watched it coldly.

The cub wandered out of the enormous space and, for no apparent reason, rolled over and pawed at the air. Then it righted itself and hoofed to the very edge of the rocky lip. Apparently overheated, it playfully dipped a paw into the lightly breaking waves. It seemed fascinated by the moving water.

The leader moved toward it—very slowly.

The others didn't budge. They focused on the cub.

The bear didn't notice the dark shape appear directly below it. Then it saw something huge and black rising incredibly fast. It didn't have time to react.

With a powerful thrust, the ray thundered out with lightning quickness. The great mouth snapped open, then slammed closed, catching the bear. As the giant body landed on the rock, smacking loudly, the bear screamed briefly then went silent. There was a sickly crunching sound, then the mouth opened and the lifeless little form spilled out. The creature quickly ate some of the meat and fur, then, with a violent head twist, flung what remained into the water, so the others could get a taste.

But they weren't there now. They were already hundreds of feet beneath the surface, on their way to more than twenty thousand. Their wings pumped quickly, propelling them downward. Their heartbeats had been beating faster for days, but now they were slowing. The darkness was returning. They were going home.

The predator remained on the rock plateau. It would not follow them. Instinctively, it felt it wasn't meant to follow at all but to do something else entirely.

Flat on the rock, its massive form rose and fell unevenly. It was experiencing breathing problems, its lung not yet fully adapted to the air. The baseball-size eyes shifted, studying the surroundings: seagulls gliding overhead, a dozen crabs bathing in little puddles on the lip, the desolate mountains.

Like a beached big-bellied airplane, it simply laid still and breathed. It wasn't ready.

CHAPTER 46

"*J*ASON, ARE *you all right?!*"

In full scuba gear, their leader had just flung himself from the water, gasping for air.

Jason was too winded to answer her, but Monique saw from the boat that he was OK. He just needed to catch his breath. She eyed the dark water nervously. But where were Darryl and Craig? Armed with harpoon guns, they'd joined Jason to check the waters near Redwood Inlet for any sign of the rays.

Lisa sprinted up from below deck, her eyes wide. "My God, is he OK?"

"He just needs to catch his breath; he's fine."

Phil trotted out, visibly confused. "What the hell happened?"

Monique shook her head. "I don't know."

Darryl and Craig popped up, ripped off their masks, and swam toward Jason. Before they could even ask, he said through gasps that he was fine.

Craig gently put a hand on his shoulder. "What happened?"

He finally caught his breath. "I don't know. You saw me; I was a hundred and eighty feet down, and somehow I had an empty tank."

Craig looked up at the boat, eyeing Monique, Lisa, and Phil. "I checked that tank myself."

Jason shook his head. "I'm fine; forget it. You guys see anything down there?"

Neither said anything. They wanted to be sure he was really all right.

"Guys, I'm fine. Did you see any sign of the rays?"

They shook their heads.

"I wonder where they went."

Craig looked around. "Maybe inland. Maybe further north. Who knows?"

Jason certainly didn't. The blinking black dot had only appeared on the interactive map for seconds and disappeared. "What do you think, Darryl?"

Darryl slowly turned to the inlet then stared at it. "I think this inlet's a perfect conduit, we just got a reading here, and we shouldn't overcomplicate this."

"Meaning . . ." Jason eyed the flat water mass himself. "You want to check it out?"

"Yeah."

"Let's do it, then."

Minutes later, the *Expedition* motored into Redwood Inlet.

As Lisa looked up at the looming trees, she couldn't believe it. They were actually looking for the new species inland. She turned when Darryl came up from below deck—carrying something she hadn't seen in some time. A rifle. Lisa's stomach turned. She didn't think Darryl had taken the weapon out to shoot at skeet.

REDWOOD INLET went on and on. After forty minutes, they still couldn't see the end of it.

For reasons they couldn't articulate, everyone was amazed by their new surroundings. It was just so quiet here, just table-flat water, towering redwoods, and silence. No one spoke. Even Phil wasn't typing. They all just studied the strange landscape.

Looking up, Darryl Hollis couldn't get over the trees. Darryl had spent a great deal of his life in the woods and he'd never seen anything like them. Where Darryl was from, most trees were fifty, maybe eighty feet tall. Redwoods were absolutely massive by comparison, the height of thirty-five-story office buildings and as wide around as small water towers. He eyed a huge specimen growing right on the side of the bank. Moving his eyes up along the great shaft, he saw it was a perfectly clean piece of timber, literally not a single branch until twenty-five stories, where the crown began to grow.

Sequoia sempervirens. That was the official term for coastal red-woods. Darryl had read it in a book once and for some reason the name had stayed with him. But books didn't begin to do these natural skyscrapers justice. Many were more than two thousand years old, he knew, literally old enough to have seen Jesus. Alive now, yet alive when Jesus had been.

Call your congressman, Darryl thought morosely, keep the damn logging companies away from these things. Only two hundred years ago, more than two million acres of the great old-growth trees had grown in this part of the country. Now 95 percent of them were gone. What had literally taken two thousand years to grow, an electric chain saw had cut down in twenty minutes.

"Look at that." Craig pointed as an elk calf trotted from the forest's shadows and began drinking from the creek. They all just watched it. With dark hair on its front half, lighter hair in back, the calf was three feet tall and thirty-five pounds.

Monique smiled cutely. "Isn't he adorable, Darryl?"

Darryl rolled his eyes. He was a trained hunter and had never seen any animal as "adorable." But Monique loved little furry things. They seemed to go well with babies.

Jason eyed the drinking calf with surprising dispassion. Nature was a dangerous place, and he tried to picture what one of the rays would see looking up at the animal from the water. There was only one possibility. Food.

In a sparkling new white undershirt, Craig read his mind. "You think one of those rays would try to eat it?"

Jason started to answer when he noticed Lisa, standing by herself at the front of the boat. He joined her. "Hey."

"Hi." Hair in a ponytail, she looked unsettled, even nervous.

"You OK?"

She didn't answer.

He put a hand on her shoulder. "What's wrong?"

She eyed the calf, almost angrily. "What's wrong is I saw Darryl take out his rifle before. What's wrong is this is getting frightening."

"We'll be fine."

"You don't know we'll be fine at all. If we actually find one of these things . . ." She just shook her head.

"Can we stay rational about this and *see* what we find, not decide it beforehand."

She said nothing.

"Lisa, *we* will be fine. *You and I* will be fine."

"You and I?"

He leaned into her, looked her right in the eye. "I'm not gonna let a goddam thing happen to you, all right? I swear it on a stack of Bibles."

She saw the fire in his eyes, the fire normally reserved for his work alone. Now it was focused *on her*. She kissed him on the cheek.

"You feel better?"

"Did you just promise to be my guardian angel, Jason?"

"I guess I did."

"Then I feel better. For a few minutes anyway."

He smiled, and they joined the others. "What do you want to do now, Jason?" Craig said immediately.

Jason studied the landscape. "Look around. The water, the riverbank, everything."

They searched as much as they could right up until it got dark. They found nothing. Rather than navigate the creek at night, they tied the *Expedition* to the inlet's only dock and slept on flat water for a change.

The next morning they returned to the ocean. A few hundred yards north of the inlet, everyone studied the rocky shore's sloshing white water with binoculars.

Jason shook his head. "I don't see anything."

"Me neither." Craig pivoted. "How 'bout you, Phil?"

"No, nothing."

Jason gave Phil a dirty look. Phil had become increasingly short with him as of late, and Jason knew why. Clearly, Phil felt he deserved to be an official researcher after all. Jason no longer had the time or patience to deal with this issue. He'd treated Phil fairly, honestly, and as a responsible adult. Phil was still his friend, but if he wanted to act like a petulant child, so be it. No one else even noticed the subtle change in behavior. The bottom line was that Phil continued to work hard documenting the group's findings and that was what mattered most.

Jason turned. "You see anything, Lisa?"

"I'm not sure, but"—she paused, readjusting the focus knob—"I think I do. . . ."

"What is it?"

"I'm not sure. I can't make it out exactly." She paused. This was a classic moment for Jason's second-guessing. "You want to take a look?"

"No, that's all right."

She paused. "You don't want to see for yourself?"

"I doubt I'd make it out any better than you. Where is it exactly?"

"On those rocks jutting out of the water. Over there." Maybe I really got through to him, she thought.

"Want to check it out, take a closer look?"

"Yeah."

They paddled to shore in a twelve-person rubber raft, tied it up, and stomped through white water. Shin-deep, Lisa led the way, her head slowly turning. "It was right around here. . . ." She pointed. "There."

Jason saw it right away. Caught on a big black rock, a skeleton of some kind.

They waded toward it, and Lisa wondered if it was another dead dolphin. But as they got closer, she saw it was something else entirely.

Craig's eyes narrowed. "What is that?"

Lisa struggled to lift it out of the sea, a heavy bone-white skeleton. Clearly not a fish but a land-based animal of some kind. Bigger than a dog, with four legs, a large triangular head, and thick bones.

"It's a bear cub," Darryl said quietly.

Craig eyed it closely. "God, I think you're right. So . . ." He looked around. "Where'd it come from?"

Jason glanced up the coast. "With the currents, who knows." Currents were deceptively powerful and could carry inanimate objects for miles in just half a day.

"What the hell are those?" Lisa said suddenly.

Jason sloshed up next to her. "What?"

She pointed to the top of the skull. "Those."

She was shaking slightly, so he took the skeleton from her. There were two huge holes in the top of the skull. "My God. I think they're . . . teeth marks."

Craig leaned in. "Holy cow, *they are*. So . . . one of those rays killed a *bear*?"

"A bear *cub*," Darryl said precisely.

"But a bear."

Phil looked around. "So where'd it come from?" He scanned the landscape, the towering redwoods, the black rocks, the coast farther north. "I mean did this thing fall into the ocean and get attacked?"

No one answered. They all told themselves that must have been what happened.

Lisa continued to shake. Jason didn't know whether it was from the cold water or something else. He put an arm around her, but she just continued, and he noticed her face was tight. He wished he could say something to calm her down, but he wasn't sure that was possible.

Darryl just eyed the holes in the top of the skull. "Jason, I think we better teach you . . ." He glanced at Lisa and Phil. "I think we better teach all of you . . . how to fire a rifle."

Jason scanned the wild, desolate terrain. "I think you're right."

CHAPTER 47

THE PREDATOR hadn't moved. Flat on the plateau in front of the cave, its colossal frame gently rose and fell. It was breathing evenly now, its large lung fully adapted to the air.

Its eyes shifted, calmly studying the giant dark space before it. The animal was ready.

It started flapping, smacking its wings loudly and ferociously against the rock. It didn't lift off. It barely budged.

It ceased all movement.

Then the muscles on the left side of its back began rippling very fast. They continued for several seconds, then froze, and those on the right began. Then they stopped and the left started. Then the right. Then both sides froze, and very quickly, the front half of the great body coiled off the rock. When the massive head was completely vertical, the hulking form went still. The animal didn't move. It effectively stood there, more than six feet tall, its back half flat on the rock, its front steady in the air.

From the new vantage point, it studied its surroundings anew, little puddles on the plateau, two dozen wriggling crabs, the spray of seawater from the breaking waves behind it, the mountains, and the sky.

The wind started gusting and the head turned slightly, sensing it.

Then, in a fluid series of motions, the creature bodily threw itself into the air, simultaneously flapped its wings and, like a seagull, rose on the diagonal. Pumping hard, it surged straight for the vast cave opening, then banked and veered over the ocean. It rose to one hundred feet then began testing itself: flapping, gliding, speeding up, slowing down, rising, diving, and hovering. Every movement was smooth and graceful. Like breathing air, they were all effortless now.

The creature veered into a wide, sweeping circle and focused on the cave. Then it dove toward it.

The air whipped past and the space rapidly grew larger. Surging closer, the animal felt a tinge of cold air. Then it arched lower and rocketed right in.

The tunnel seemed to go on forever, an abysmal shaft of dank black rock, small stagnant puddles on the floor. The great body hurtled through, the sounds of the ocean quickly fading. Then the creature began pumping, its wings blowing away one puddle after another. The puddles were growing smaller. The light was disappearing. . . .

The predator didn't know the significance of what it was doing. It didn't know it was about to become the first animal to permanently leave the sea since the amphibians 300 million years before. It only knew there was food on the land.

It rocketed forward and disappeared within the lightless cavern.

PART III

CHAPTER 48

THIS CAVE was smaller than its oceanside counterpart, eight stories high and three car lanes wide. At the very top of the mountain range, it offered a towering view. A field of gently flowing cornstalks was below; miles beyond that, the looming redwood forest.

It was midmorning, and there was no sun. Near the cave's entrance, the creature was sprawled out on the dank stone, still moist from the previous night, its thick hull rising and falling as it breathed. Submerged in shadows, the animal blended seamlessly into the black rock and was very hard to see. It had long since made its way to this side of the mountain, the land side.

It was an ugly, cloudy day, and its eyes were pointed at the sky. Though the predator wasn't looking at the sky, nor at the clouds. It was studying the light. It had just brightened, if only slightly. Human eyes, which took in one-five-hundredth the amount of visual information, never would have detected it. It was another shade of gray, one of more than four hundred the creature had seen in just the past hour.

It didn't move. As the day continued, the sun gradually peeked through the clouds, reached a maximum height, then began to dip. A sunset followed, then disappeared. The night came, the moon rose, and still, the animal remained still. The moon fell, the muted light of day arrived, the sun rose again, and the process repeated itself. When the sunrise returned once more, the study of light was complete. It was time to sleep. Though not here.

Seconds later, the predator zoomed through the maze of blackened tunnels behind it, cold air whisking past its large horned head. It saw nothing yet sensed everything. It continued for several seconds when it entered a towering, unseen central cavern. It pumped its wings hard, rising several hundred feet, then glided down in wide, sweeping circles. Ten feet from the dank rock floor, it simply stopped flapping and landed with a loud, echoing thwack. Then it closed its eyes and slept.

FOURTEEN HOURS later the creature awoke. It was pitch-black here, yet the animal *knew* it was light outside. Its study guaranteed it. Hungry, it flew to the nearby carcass of a bear it had killed, the mother of the cub. It feasted savagely, tearing off ragged bloody chunks of fur-covered meat, then chewing. When its stomach was full, it flew back to the cave mouth and landed with a thump that kicked up surprising amounts of black dust. As the dust settled around and on top of it, it didn't move. It focused on the distant redwood forest, knowing prey was there. It wanted to hunt badly but knew it could not. The sun was in the sky. It just had to wait for it to disappear.

CHAPTER 49

TRY THIS one, Jason."

Craig handed him a Winchester Game 94 rifle.

Under fading bleak skies, they were half a mile offshore of Redwood Inlet. They'd been practicing shooting for hours, aiming at a huge floating target Craig had set up in the ocean. The size of a Las Vegas roulette wheel with big white and blue rings and a faded red bull's-eye, the target sat on its own little raft, weighted heavily so it bobbed as little as possible when a wave struck.

Jason nodded, taking the rifle. The previous one, Craig's old Mossberg RM-7, had been surprisingly heavy; but this one, he felt right away, was much lighter.

"Load it, aim, then fire. Phil, when he's done you'll go." Craig turned to Monique. "Lisa still doesn't want to shoot?"

"That's why she's at the front of the boat by herself, Craig. All right, I'm gonna go hang with Darryl. Let me know if you need a hand with this." She went below deck.

"OK, get to it, Jason."

Jason aimed carefully, waited as a big wave splashed the target, and . . . *Bang!* The rifle kicked back with a violent jerk, and he missed completely.

Craig shook his head. "Pay attention, and watch the recoil. This is a lighter gun. Hold it firmly but not too tight."

"OK." Jason drew the rifle close, eased down on the trigger again and . . . *Bang!*

Craig nodded. "Three rings from the bull's-eye. Not bad at all. OK, Phil, now you."

"Oh, sure." Phil pivoted and inadvertently pointed his rifle right at Craig when . . . *Bang!*

"Jesus Christ!" Craig felt a bullet whistle past his ear. He grabbed the firearm away furiously. "You could have fucking killed me, Phil!"

"My God, I am so sorry. Are you all right?"

Jason put his arm on Craig's shoulder. "Are you OK?"

Summers exhaled, feeling around his ear. "Yeah. I guess I'm fine."

"I'm so sorry." Phil was devastated. "You know that was an accident."

Craig chuckled. "Yeah, no harm, no foul. You spend so much time on your laptop, maybe you should shoot that instead."

Jason smiled, but Phil didn't seem to find this remark amusing.

"All right." Craig returned the rifle. "Try again. *Carefully.*"

Phil held the rifle out in front of him, eyeing the target.

"Aim."

"I am."

"Watch for the recoil."

"Uh-huh."

Craig shrugged. Phil Martino wasn't listening and it showed. He was holding the rifle too tightly, not looking down the line of the barrel, and, worst of all, not easing down on the trigger. Craig could already tell he was going to jolt it down like a kid on a pinball machine. "Fire whenever." *Bang!* As expected, the bullet didn't even come close to the target. Craig just shook his head. How had Phil Martino even learned to type? He glanced up at the sky. It was starting to get dark. "All right, guys. I think that's it for the day."

Jason handed over his firearm. "Thanks again, Craig."

Phil just put his on the deck. "I've got some work to do. No more jokes about shooting my laptop, Summers. Your notes are on there too."

He went below deck, and Craig stared after him blankly. "Is he kidding?"

Jason just shook his head. Somehow he didn't think Phil Martino was kidding at all.

"What's going on, fellas?"

It was Darryl, up from below deck in a bright orange Izod and green pants, looking like a guy off a Hamptons polo field except for the big bow over his shoulder. "Big Dog's been getting rusty." He held up three arrows. "Just gonna fire a few for fun."

Before Jason even realized . . . *Voom! Voom! Voom!* The arrows rocketed through the darkening air. . . . One after another they ripped into the dead center of the target, the last splintering into the first. Darryl shrugged. "Not as rusty as I thought." He started to smile, but then he glanced at the nearby creek and suddenly looked unsettled, even disturbed.   \

"Grab a beer, Big Dog?" Craig asked, not noticing his friend's change in demeanor. \

"Definitely." Darryl turned. "Jason?"

Jason eyed someone at the front of the boat. "Uh, maybe in a little bit, guys." Darryl and Craig disappeared below deck, and Jason walked toward Lisa. She immediately glared at him.

"What did I do?" he said as if wrongly accused.

She glanced around, checking to see that nobody else was on deck. "Guns scare me, Jason. They scare the hell out of me. My God, look at what almost happened to Craig."

"That was an accident."

"It's always an accident with those damn things!"

He wanted to stay calm. "Guns scare me, too, Lisa. But if we actually find what we're looking for . . . we've got to be cautious, right?"

"I'm not touching a damn rifle, you got it?"

His cell started ringing, and he saw it was Ackerman. He didn't pick up. "Lisa, in this situation, it might be more dangerous *not knowing* how to shoot than—"

"Jason, *I am a biologist.* Do you understand that? And if *any* situation arises where we need to use guns, I am gone, get it? *Gone.*" She gave the ringing phone a dirty look and stormed away.

Jason picked up. "Hi, Harry . . . yes, I know; this area has horrible service. . . . How are you?"

The voice on the other end was cold, matter-of-fact. "Honestly, there have been some more . . . financial challenges with my companies."

"Really?"

"Plus, I gave personal guarantees on a few bank loans."

Personal guarantees? Jason had heard the term before but didn't know what it meant. "What is a personal guarantee anyway?"

"To put this in perspective for you, Jason, the bank is trying to take my house." Harry's tone remained matter-of-fact.

"I had no idea, Harry. Are you going to be all—"

"I'll be fine. I can't seem to raise capital from the VCs, but I have a new plan to harvest an existing asset to cover our liquidity needs."

"So . . ." Jason didn't know what any of that meant. "You're all right, then?"

"Fine. What's the latest on your new species?"

Jason explained, and when he finished, Ackerman's retort was direct.

"So you think this bear-cub skeleton further suggests these animals could have flown? I guess a bear is a land-based animal, but don't they swim once in a while? I don't know, Jason—to be candid . . . flying monsters . . . I just don't see it."

"I'm not saying I see it either, Harry. I just want to keep following the trail."

A chuckle. "That sounds reasonable. Keep me abreast; we'll see what happens."

Jason hung up and went below deck looking for Lisa. Then he noticed Phil's open door and remembered he still had to type up his notes. In sweats, Phil was stretched out on his single bed, going through pictures on his digital camera.

"Mind if I type up the day's notes, Phil?"

A blank look. "Sure; computer's over there."

Jason went to the desk. The laptop was in screen-saver mode, and he smiled wide at what he saw. "What the hell is this?"

Pleased by the reaction, Phil looked up. "You like it?"

"Very cool." Jason leaned in. It was an animated simulation. A massive winged creature flying toward a redwood forest from the ocean.

Flapping in slow, mechanized movements, the animal looked shockingly real. It almost appeared to be flying right off the screen.

"How'd you do this?"

Phil smirked cunningly. "That's my secret, pal."

"Pretty damn frightening."

"It would make a great video game, wouldn't it?"

Jason stared again. "It really would."

Phil went back to his camera. "Maybe I'll work on that next."

Jason smiled. Phil Martino was into his own thing, wasn't he? And clearly still angry that Jason hadn't made him a researcher on his report to the Species Council. Was that why he'd snipped at Craig earlier? Jason decided he didn't care. He typed his notes then joined the triumvirate and Lisa in the galley when Lisa surreptitiously slipped past him.

"You got a sec?"

He followed her up on deck and . . . was amazed to see a full moon. The sky had been completely socked in with clouds only half an hour ago. The weather patterns in Northern California were bizarre.

"You want to howl at the moon or talk to me?"

He turned. "Can we do both?"

She smiled. "Maybe later."

"I didn't mean to scare you with the rifle stuff."

"I know. And I shouldn't have jumped down your throat like that. Guns just really scare me."

"I got that. Like I said, they scare me, too."

"But I was thinking. . . . If you really think I should learn how to fire one . . . I will."

"I don't want you to do it if you're not comfortable with it."

"I'm not comfortable with it!" She exhaled. "Sorry." Then added softly, "But maybe it is . . . prudent."

"That's how I meant it, to be prudent."

"All right, I'm gonna help with dinner."

She disappeared, and he looked up at the moon once more, then at the dimly lit redwoods. With Phil's computer simulation fresh in his mind, he tried imagining one of the creatures flying among the trees and to his surprise, the vision came quickly. Just like the simulation, it was incredibly lifelike.

"You look like I feel." Darryl Hollis walked up on deck.

"What's up, Darryl?"

Darryl eyed the distant creek, glistening in the moonlight. "That bear-cub skeleton's stayed with me, Jason—makes me nervous. Makes me wonder if maybe one of those rays really would come to land."

"What are you getting at?"

"We should double-check the creek. Make damn sure no people are on it."

"We already did that, and we didn't see a soul. Monique thinks there could be a better conduit further up the coast anyway."

Darryl gave him a stern look. "We should check it again, Jason."

There was something ominous in his tone. "OK, we'll check it again." Jason paused, looking up at the moon. "You don't think anyone would go near that creek at night, do you?"

"Nah, the park doesn't have overnight campgrounds, and it's probably closed anyway. I just want to be conservative." But just as he said the words, Darryl Hollis reconsidered. *Would* anyone go out at night? But no, that was ridiculous. Who on earth would do that?

CHAPTER 50

WAYNE ABBOTT was a big guy, six-three and a rock-hard 235 pounds. A former tight end for UCLA, Wayne had been out of school for a little more than a year and liked to stay in shape. He had big strong thighs from squatting up to four hundred pounds, a ripped, muscular chest from benching nearly as much, and healthy lungs from runs like this one. Wayne hadn't made the cut in the NFL and didn't have a job, so he lived with his mother in a desolate area near the outskirts of Leonard State Park. The park was closed for maintenance and almost entirely empty, but Wayne didn't care. He snuck in regularly. The paths here were nice and flat. After two hundred push-ups and four hundred sit-ups, he ran them almost every night.

Screw the NFL, Wayne thought, pumped up and running hard, thinking about what awesome shape he was in. Wearing sky-blue UCLA mesh shorts and a white T-shirt drenched with sweat, he was two miles into a seven-mile run. Redwood Inlet Trail was his favorite, a runner's dream: perfectly flat, as wide as a two-lane road, and topped with black soil that was easy on the knees but still allowed good traction. The scenery was great too. Wayne had already passed the prettiest part, the creek itself, but here, much deeper in the forest, wasn't bad either. There were towering redwoods everywhere, as far as the eye could see.

Wayne glanced at a little green metal sign staked in along the side, a trail marker that told him he'd run two and a half miles. He was feeling good and had a good sweat going. Wayne liked it when he sweated. It made him feel like he was working hard, like he was young and strong. And like he would live forever.

THE PREDATOR surged out of the towering mountaintop cave. Easing into the moonlit air, it surveyed the surroundings. To the west, the sea, quietly rumbling, a place it no longer belonged. To the south and north, more mountains. And farther inland, the cornstalk field, blowing slightly in the wind, with the redwood forest beyond.

As the creature banked into a wide, sweeping glide, it focused on the trees, their silhouettes looming in the pale white light. Then it dove toward them.

Rocketing through the air, momentum carried it to the end of the mountain range in seconds. It banked, smashing a patch of stalks, then sped toward the forest. Moonlight guided the way when the white orb was blocked out, and the forest rushed up. . . .

The animal hurtled in, and suddenly shadowy redwoods were everywhere. Speeding like a flying freight train, it banked sharply, nearly crashing into a grove of two dozen trees growing much too close together to squeeze through. It began tuning its sonar, only now it was radar, the echo-location organs seamlessly adapting to the air. Navigating with great precision, it immediately located clearings that could accommodate its massive form. Tearing through the trees, it focused on one particularly large one, studying everything about it: the deeply grooved bark, the perfectly straight, branchless trunk, the crown, the powerful evergreen scent. It ripped past it and continued.

Then, for no reason at all, the creature made a sound. It was the same sound it had once made at sea, only now it was considerably more chilling, a deep, bass rumble, rolling over itself like an idling cruise-ship engine. It continued for a moment, then stopped.

The predator flew on in utter silence, its eyes studying leafy ferns, rhododendrons, flowers, and evergreen after evergreen. Then it began flapping, first rising gradually, then very sharply. Climbing to just below the treetops, it leveled off and began tuning for prey.

Suddenly its head jerked downward. Several hundred feet below was a foraging raccoon, sluffing among the ferns. Its black eyes studied the rodent briefly, then the animal flew forward. Up ahead, through the trees, was a very large clearing. . . . Hurtling into it, the creature looked down, and its own speeding reflection looked right back at it. It was flying over a familiar creek. The reflection disappeared and it entered the forest on the other side.

That's when it picked him up. Wayne Abbott was more than five miles away, and he hadn't been seen, smelled, or heard. His heartbeat had been detected. The predator locked onto it and flew forward.

SPEEDING THROUGH the shadows, Wayne Abbott sprinted toward a small footbridge. Wearing size thirteen New Balance sneakers that sprayed black dirt behind him, he focused on the bridge's wooden lip. He'd tripped over it once before and wanted to be careful. . . .

He took the entire structure in three big strides. On the soil again, he eased into a jog, just as the moon came into view over his right shoulder.

THE CREATURE turned. For a moment, it had lost the signal. But then it heard the pounding on the bridge, a very distinctive sound. The resulting directional change was slight, but significant. The range was narrowing.

WAYNE SUDDENLY felt bored. The sprint to the bridge was the last big test of the jog. He still had a few miles to go, but the rest was routine. He looked up. Damn, those are some big trees. Wayne was a physically large man and not accustomed to feeling small. But every time he jogged through a redwood forest, he felt tiny. Minuscule even. Like an ant next to a blade of a grass.

IT SMELLED him. His sweat. Speeding hundreds of feet above the forest floor, the predator continued, the tiny nostrils on its underbelly pulsing. Suddenly a narrow tract of straight, treeless land appeared. A trail. The same trail Wayne Abbott was jogging on. The great body sped into it.

WAYNE STARTED picking up the pace.

———

SUDDENLY A massive shadow sped past the green metal sign. . . . Then the footbridge . . .

ARMS PUMPING, legs kicking, Wayne didn't notice the moon. It was directly behind him now, casting a halo on his bobbing head. He also didn't notice the squirrel. In front of a huge fallen redwood on the side of the trail, the furry rodent stood on its haunches. If Wayne had seen it, he would have thought it looked scared. He also would have thought it was looking right at him.

It wasn't. It was looking *above* him. At the gargantuan gliding form near the treetops.

WAYNE'S SENSES were poor. The predator saw that immediately. He didn't seem to hear, smell, or otherwise detect anything. His eyesight was weak as well. He'd run right past a host of birds, squirrels, and raccoons without so much as a head turn.

THE FOREST became quiet. The birds stopped chirping, the squirrels disappeared, even the wind seemed to die. Nothing stirred. Except Wayne Abbott. In his light blue shorts and soaked T-shirt, he bounded down the trail.

SUDDENLY AND silently, the shadow rushed toward his back. . . .

WAYNE SUDDENLY stopped dead in his tracks. He didn't know why, but he thought something was behind him. He spun around.

Nothing was there, just an empty path, towering redwoods, and the moon.

He chuckled, a deep manly laugh. Wayne was a tough guy and had never been afraid of the dark. That was why he ran at night—because he was tough. Calm the hell down, he ordered himself. He started jogging again.

The shadow returned immediately, speeding toward him. . . .

Wayne ran forward, growing nervous, though he didn't know why.

THE SHADOW rushed closer, a hundred feet away, then fifty, ten . . . then it froze a yard from Wayne's back.

A CURIOUS look formed on Wayne's face. He heard something. A flapping sound. It was coming from behind him, and he knew he wasn't imagining it.

He turned around.

THE CREATURE was just hovering there, flapping like an enormous seagull, ten feet above the trail and staring right at him.

Strangely, Wayne Abbott's sweating, chiseled face was a perfect blank. He literally didn't believe what was in front of him. The animal was the coolest thing he'd ever seen, the size and shape of a hang glider, only alive, flapping very rapidly. His first thought, which lasted for three confused seconds, was that he was the victim of a practical joke. That somehow his football buddies from L.A. were playing a gag on him.

But what he was seeing couldn't possibly be a gag. He calmly surveyed the massive form. The milky-white underside. The nearly five-foot-thick torso. The fast-pumping wings. The enormous head. The partially open mouth—he'd never seen a mouth that large in his life. The enormous puffs of breath coming from it and condensing in the cold air. The horns, bigger than his biceps and jutting from the head. And the eyes—the coldest, blackest, most deadly calm eyes Wayne Abbott had ever seen.

"Jesus Christ," he said in a surprisingly clear, unpanicked voice.

He still didn't know if the animal was real.

Then, real or not, it moved. Like an enormous bat, it pumped its wings and passed directly over Wayne's head. He didn't flinch. He simply stared up at it, scanning its rippling milky-white underside as it blotted out the moon, its backdraft blowing back his hair. Then it dipped lower and faced him, now hovering on the other side of the trail.

Why'd it do that? Wayne wondered. Why did it move?

It still hadn't occurred to him that his life was in danger. But then he noticed the eyes again. Black. Enormous. And staring at him with chilling intention. Suddenly something clicked. "Oh my God," Wayne said quietly.

The predator made a sound then, a rumble, deep and chilling. Then a series of rumbles, rolling on top of one another.

Wayne stepped backward. He'd never heard such sounds coming from an animal before. They reminded him of something from a church organ.

Suddenly the rumbles erupted into a shattering roar.

Wayne fell on his back, shocked by the power of it. And the mouth producing it . . . It was wide open now, big enough to swallow two of him and filled with rows and rows of curvy teeth as fat as his forearms.

He just watched the ferocious gaping form . . . the mouth, the teeth, the breath condensing in the air.

He got up.

It was like a switch. The mouth closed and the roaring ceased.

Suddenly it was silent, the only sound from the steadily flapping wings.

Nothing else moved.

Then the eyes shifted and looked directly into Wayne's. They almost seemed to be asking him a question. Don't you know what's happening here?

And suddenly Wayne did. Then he did what he'd been doing all night. He ran.

As HE sprinted into the forest, Wayne's once-even breathing and smooth strides deserted him, replaced by wild, desperate motions. He had no idea where he was going, he simply had to get away. He stomped over everything, soil, fern patches, fallen redwoods, a field of tiny white flowers, a trickling stream. After ten minutes, he realized he was alone. Gasping for air, he leaned against an enormous, moss-covered tree.

"My God, what the hell was th—" He held his breath. Was it up there? With shafts of moonlight shining into his eyes, he scanned the forest canopy above, his head quickly turning.

No, nothing was there, just trees and broken moonlight. He breathed again. He had to find his way back to the trail. He knew the way, he was sure of it. . . .

Ten minutes later, he was lost.

Trying to get his bearings, he entered a small clearing. His head turning in every direction, he didn't notice the moonlight directly above him disappear.

But then he sensed it. He looked up and saw the animal in silhouette, a massive gliding form near the treetops. He could actually feel its eyes watching him. He didn't think. He just ran.

The silhouette suddenly changed shape. The wings pulled tight, and the creature dropped like a stone.

Speeding toward the moon-speckled soil, the great body banked and hurtled toward Wayne's back.

He didn't turn around. He just ran as hard as he could, chest heaving, legs pumping. He picked up speed rapidly, sneakers rising and falling, rising and falling, when suddenly . . . the sneakers didn't come back down. Like a feather in the breeze, they were swept up and away.

"Jesus Christ," Wayne said, as if startled.

He realized he was inside the creature's mouth, wedged in its teeth.

"Jesus Christ!" His scream was suddenly guttural and desperate.

He tried moving his arms, his legs, but everything was pinned.

"Come on." He strained his powerful upper body, trying to twist free but not moving a millimeter. *"Come on!"*

The animal rose quickly, the cries growing louder and more desperate. Then there was a sickly crunching sound and Wayne Abbott went silent.

The creature burst through the canopy and emerged into the moonlit sky. Without the screaming, it was much quieter now, the only sounds from the wind and distant ocean.

Physically exhausted, the predator found a place to store its dangling kill, then ascended back into the night air. It would return here very soon; but for the moment, it was finished. It focused on the mountains in the distance and flew toward them. It gradually grew smaller . . . until it blended into the black rock and disappeared. All that remained were the moon and the gently blowing wind.

CHAPTER 51

THE RIVERBANK felt different today. Darryl Hollis didn't know why exactly, but there was no mistaking it. Last time it had been peaceful and calm here, but now . . .

The sun was already quite high. They'd docked, and the six of them were walking on the creek's north side. In jeans and a red-and-blue checked shirt, Darryl felt his rifle's heft, glad he had it. Craig was carrying as well.

Stomping over tall grass, Darryl suddenly turned to the woods. "What is that?"

Before anyone could answer, he walked in. "Oh." It was a campground: a dozen wood picnic tables, steel trash drums, barbecue pits, Porta Pottis . . . But no people, not even rangers, like a summer camp without the campers. *Was* the park closed? Beyond the campground, he noticed a wide walking trail. He glanced at it for a curious moment, then joined the others. As they continued up the embankment, Darryl didn't know why, but he felt even more nervous.

THE RANGER station was miles away and nearly empty. In pressed khaki pants, matching long-sleeved shirt, and a hard-rimmed hat, fortysomething Ranger Allen Meyer was seated at a steel desk that looked like it belonged in a DMV. With darting, beady blue eyes, Meyer was an uptight guy by nature, and this phone call was making him even more so.

His calmer blond wife, Laura, also a ranger and wearing an identical outfit, was at another desk, watching their eleven-month-old, Samuel. The baby was swinging happily in his favorite chair, a battery-operated portable with a blue seat covered with tiny bears. Laura smiled at the baby's outfit. She especially loved the navy sweater with the little sailboat on the chest. Allen had barely noticed it. Whoever he was on the phone with was making him even more agitated than normal. The two rangers had been doing paperwork all morning, and it was now early afternoon. Time to go. They'd been just about to do that when the phone rang.

"Mrs. Abbott, I'm a ranger here. My wife and I were just about to leave ourselves, so believe me, the park is closed. Right, for prescribed burns . . . Of course they're controlled by experts. . . . No, just scheduling difficulties . . . Huh? . . . No, no one. Literally, just my wife and me and our baby. We're the only ones in the entire park . . . What? Honestly, I'm amazed your call went through at all. The co-location switch has been having problems for a week. . . . That's right, cell calls too, once they hit the ground from the towers. I know we should get it fixed; it's on the list . . . Sorry? . . ." Allen Meyer suddenly gave his wife a deadly serious look. "What do you mean your son didn't come home last night?"

He paused. "He was jogging in the park? At night? . . . He snuck in?"

"THAT'S WHY there's no one here."

Well off the embankment and draped in shadows, Phil Martino photographed a yellow diamond-shaped sign: PARK CLOSED FOR PRE-SCRIBED BURNS.

"Didn't you used to do prescribed burns, Phil?"

Phil glanced back at Jason. "Good memory, genius."

What the hell's your problem? Jason thought. He knew that "assistant fire ranger" in Lake Arrowhead near L.A. had been one of the many jobs Phil Martino had held during his hopscotch career. If Jason's memory served, Phil had actually stuck to that one for some time and even gotten good at it. Jason didn't know what a prescribed burn was exactly, but he thought it had something to do with intentionally starting small fires so a major one didn't burn later.

Without another word between them, the two men returned to the sunny riverbank and joined the others. Jason caught up with Darryl and right away saw he was extremely ill at ease.

"What's wrong?"

Darryl didn't answer at first. He glanced at Lisa, trailing them by just ten or twenty feet. He didn't want to frighten her unnecessarily. "Walk with me, and I'll tell you."

"HE PROBABLY just twisted an ankle, honey."

Allen Meyer had just hung up the phone. He wasn't sure what could have happened to the woman's son. "You think so?"

Laura Meyer nodded confidently. "Jogging at night? He probably didn't see something, stepped wrong, and twisted it really bad."

"Well, we got to find him. Forget clearing out of here, Laura; we got to find him right now." Tense, Allen glanced out a tiny window. "There's probably not more than four hours of light left out there."

Laura was perfectly calm. "No problem. We'll search the appropriate trails, find this guy, and just leave a little later than we thought."

Allen rapidly opened a park map. They talked it over, quickly decided where the jogger must have entered the park, then divvied up trails to search. As Allen went outside, Laura put Samuel in a chest Snugli, grabbed his chair, joined her husband, and headed toward a massive parking lot within the trees.

"Taking the chair?"

"Just in case, Allen. You know how crabby he can get." Samuel was prone to screaming fits, and the swinging chair could calm him down like nothing else.

"You're still charging your walkie-talkie?"

She nodded. "It's in the truck." Neither bothered mentioning cell phones. Even under normal circumstances, coverage here was spotty, but with the recent problems with the co-location switch, fewer than one in ten calls went through.

As they entered the parking lot, they passed a pair of helicopters, one enormous, one small, gifts to the park after the Gulf War to assist in fighting forest fires. They passed their own jam-packed Honda Civic and walked toward a pair of ancient white Chevy Blazer SUVs with green park emblems on every door.

Laura strapped Samuel into the back of one, confirmed the walkie-talkie was still charging, then waved to her husband and drove off.

Allen Meyer turned in the opposite direction on a double-yellow-lined road, then sped away amid the trees. *Where the hell's that jogger?*

THE GREAT body twitched. Once, then again and again.

Unseen in the depths of the blackened central cavern, the predator was asleep. Its entire body, from the tips of its horns to the end of its torso, twitched repeatedly, an enormous sleeping dog.

In its semiconscious state none of the animal's sensory organs was tuning per se, but just like any animal, it would awaken if it heard, smelled, or otherwise sensed something.

It continued to sleep.

DARRYL WALKED faster. "What's wrong is this trail we're walking on." Earlier, the trail had been in the woods, near a campground, but now it had twisted.

Jason looked down, realizing they weren't walking through untamed tall grass anymore but on tilled black soil. Still, he didn't understand why Darryl was so agitated. "So you're saying . . ."

"This trail's *on the water,* Jason. So *people* could be on the water. And if someone was on this trail at exactly the wrong time . . . I don't know if one of those things would know to distinguish between a person and a bear cub."

Jason scanned ahead with renewed unease. "I get your point."

Darryl tightened the grip on his rifle, and they all walked forward quickly.

CHAPTER 52

LAURA MEYER pulled over. Moving very quickly, she got out, put Samuel in the Snugli, slung his chair over her shoulder, and started walking. When she entered the first trail, she immediately noticed. It was quiet here, more so than normal.

Tough. She walked forward, the only sound from the occasional twig snapping under her boots.

She continued for a few minutes when she heard something off the trail. She froze, staring toward it.

The sound had come from near a huge patch of redwoods. But now there was no movement of kind, no sign of life.

She focused on three massive trunks lined up next to one another. Was something behind them? She stepped off the trail and walked closer. Then . . . A rifle appeared, pointed right at her.

"Oh my God," she stammered.

Standing before her were three very large men in red-and-black checked shirts, hunters.

"Son of a bitch." The one with the rifle looked devastated. "I am so sorry, miss."

Ranger Laura Meyer exhaled. "You scared the hell out of me!"

The guy noticed the baby. "I am very, very sorry."

She gave the guy a filthy look. "We have signs everywhere that the park's closed. I should probably ticket you, you know."

"Ranger, I wouldn't blame you if you did, but is there any way you can let us off this time? We are so sorry; we really are."

Laura looked up at the guy. He was fiftysomething, balding, bearded, and enormous—six-five with a big belly. Went by the name Big Tim. The two other guys were in their early twenties; one, the spitting image of the older one, clearly his son, and the other his son's friend.

"We're good citizens, really. I'm Tim Jameson. This here is my son, Timmy. And this runty guy is Tim's buddy Greg."

Laura chuckled. Greg was six feet and didn't have the belly that father and son had. She looked them up and down. They didn't look like criminals, and she didn't even have her ticket book with her. She considered calling the police, but they were seventy miles away, and with the phone problems . . . She had more important things to worry about.

"How'd you get here?"

"We drove, ma'am." Big Tim waved. "Truck's back there."

"Leave immediately."

"Yes, ma'am; thank you. Have a good night."

As they walked off, Laura considered asking if they'd seen the missing jogger. But no. If they had, they would have mentioned it. They disappeared behind some trees, and it became perfectly silent again. Laura glanced at her baby, then continued down the trail.

On the riverbank, Darryl halted.

So did everyone else—quizzically.

"What is it?" Jason said, looking around.

Darryl stared into the forest, dark and shadowy. "Something's in there."

Craig shook his head. "Gimme a break."

Darryl said nothing. Rifle in hand, he walked to the edge of the trees. Then slowly entered.

"Oh, will ya look at that."

Crammed in next to Timmy and Greg in his red Chevy pickup, Big

Tim shook his head. Right in front of their speeding truck, six deer, one a big-horned buck, dashed across the road, then disappeared into the forest on the other side.

His son turned excitedly. "We gonna go get 'em, Dad?"

"Ah, you heard what that ranger said, Timmy."

"Gimme a break; what's she gonna do? Ticket ya? I thought you were gonna teach me to hunt."

Big Tim shook his head. Something didn't feel right. What was that ranger doing out there anyway?

"Oh come on, Dad!"

Big Tim suddenly jammed on the brakes. "You're right. What's she gonna do?" They parked and quickly got out of the truck. "Come on, boys. Big Tim's gonna show you how to do it right."

ALLEN MEYER saw the footprints immediately. In dark soil in the dead center of the trail. They were widely spaced, clearly from some-one who'd been jogging. He removed his hat and studied one closely. In the middle of it was a fat letter *N*. New Balance running shoes. He removed his walkie-talkie.

"Laura?"

He waited for a moment, but there was only static.

"Laura, you out there? Laura?"

He waited again. Still nothing. His wife was no doubt still charging. He holstered the walkie-talkie and followed the prints.

The trail was eerily quiet, but the prints continued, right down the middle of it. He followed them for a few hundred yards, passing a two-and-a-half-mile marker, a small footbridge, and then . . . The prints went off the trail.

Allen Meyer paused. Was he seeing things?

But no, plain as day, the prints went straight into the woods. His blue eyes began darting. Why the hell would the guy have left the trail? Only one way to find out.

He entered the trees.

IN THE forest, the prints continued . . . past redwoods, fern patches, a field of tiny white flowers, a trickling stream . . . right into the middle of a wide clearing.

And then they stopped. Just disappeared.

The ranger looked around. Where the hell did they go?

Confused, he walked forward. They had to be around here somewhere.

"TOLD YOU there was nothing here. Let's get back to the water."

They were in the woods now, fifty feet from Redwood Inlet.

Listening to his own advice, Craig Summers started to turn. Darryl Hollis didn't move.

Then there was a snapping sound from the direction he was facing. Craig turned back nervously. "What was that?"

No one answered. They just studied the shadowy trunks and ferns, all perfectly silent now.

There was another snap.

Then a man in a tan ranger outfit appeared. "Are any of you Wayne Abbott?"

· Darryl looked at him. "Sorry?"

"Wayne Abbott!" Ranger Allen Meyer was annoyed, realizing these people were wearing jeans and not joggers at all. "The park is closed; you know, you're not supposed to be here."

Jason just stared at the man, a ranger. A ranger looking for someone. "Who's . . . Wayne Abbott?"

"A missing jogger. You didn't see him, did you?"

Jason couldn't believe it. "We haven't seen anybody." Then he noticed Lisa, visibly terrified, her face as tight as a drum. He forgot about the ranger. "Are you OK?"

Lisa didn't answer—just shook her head.

Monique turned. "Hey, girlfriend. You want to go back to the boat?"

"Yeah, I think I do."

"Thank you very much, Monique." Jason patted her on the back.

"No problem; everything's cool." She put her arm over Lisa's shoulder. "Guys, we'll see you back there."

As the women walked off, Allen Meyer was even more annoyed. Who the hell are these people? And how am I going to find this jogger? The park was enormous, more light was disappearing every second, it was just him and his wife and . . . "Damn it!"

Jason turned to him. "Anything we can do to help?"

Meyer didn't respond. He worried he and Laura had miscalculated badly, that the jogger was nowhere near here. Four years ago they'd dealt with a similar situation. A teenager had gotten lost and gone missing for three entire days, finally turning up in the cornfields at the northern tip of the forest. Could the jogger have reached the same spot? Meyer wanted to check that next, but it was getting late, the fields stretched for miles, and there was only one way to search that kind of terrain. He turned to his unwanted guests—

"I don't suppose any of you know how to fly a helicopter."

Darryl and Craig shared a look. "Actually, we both do."

"Seriously?"

"Yeah."

"All right . . . You're going to help me. Right now." He removed his hat and started sprinting. "Come on. . . ."

They all ran after him.

CHAPTER 53

"LAURA, YOU out there? Laura, come in. Laura?"

Allen Meyer drummed his fingers impatiently, waiting for a response.

But the walkie-talkie was silent, nothing but static.

He put it down on his now-moving SUV's dash and turned to Jason, in the passenger seat next to him. "My wife. She must still be charging hers."

So was she outside too? Jason tried to appear casual. "She's also looking for the jogger?"

A nod. "Since it's just the two of us, we had to split up." They pulled into the massive empty parking lot amid the trees. "You guys fly either of those?"

From the backseat, Darryl and Craig peered out at two helicopters, a huge jungle-green, twin-engine Vertol designed to carry thirty men and a smaller bright yellow Sikorsky. Craig nodded. "We fly both."

"Let's get going, then."

Seconds later, the Vertol shot into the sky, Craig at the controls, Darryl at copilot, Jason, the ranger, and Phil on a mounted bench in back. Before Craig could even ask, Meyer pointed. "That way."

———

THE EYES snapped open.

Deep in the central cavern, the creature had just been awakened. Not by a sound nor by a smell. By an electrical signal. An extraordinarily powerful one. The animal tuned in the darkness, trying to locate its source. It quickly realized it was from something *outside* the cave.

It flew toward it.

"DAMN IT! Son of a bitch!"

Darryl and Craig shared a look. Ranger Allen Meyer wasn't built for a crisis. They'd just searched the entire perimeter of cornstalks at the forest's edge and hadn't seen any sign of the jogger. Craig tried to ignore the ranger. It was getting darker every second, and they had to stay cool. "What do we do here, Darryl?"

In the copilot's seat, Darryl raised binoculars to his face. "Take her up slowly. I might be able to see that one trail from here."

The chopper began rising. "See anything?"

Darryl shifted the binoculars. "Veer right a little."

Summers moved the chopper's levers. "This any better?"

"It's fine, but these trees really are—" He stopped talking.

"Really are . . . what?"

Darryl didn't answer. He just stared through the binoculars.

"Darryl?"

Darryl still didn't respond. He just removed the binoculars and looked outside with naked eyes.

Craig turned. "Did you see some—" Then he stopped talking too.

Phil looked out, and his mouth fell open.

Then the ranger looked out. "Oh my God."

What's everyone looking at? Why'd we stop rising? At the far side of the chopper, Jason couldn't see anything. He leaned forward. "Guys, are we—"

Then Jason saw what everyone else did. On top of a massive branch was a body in sky-blue mesh shorts, a white T-shirt, and New Balance sneakers.

They'd found the missing jogger.

CHAPTER 54

NO ONE spoke.

Darryl's eyes darted, trying to make sense of what he was seeing. He didn't believe it. He couldn't believe it. "Something else must have done this."

Craig Summers couldn't even begin to process it. "You want to get the body down?"

Darryl nodded, and before Jason realized, the chopper repositioned, Darryl climbed out on a ladder, and the body was put in back, wrapped in a black fleece blanket.

Still, no one spoke. They were too stunned.

Then Craig turned. "Darryl . . . are Monique and Lisa OK?"

"Son of a bitch." Darryl rapidly removed his cell.

Don't bother, Allen Meyer thought absently. But then he glanced at the branch and remembered his own wife. Where the hell was Laura? He reached for his walkie-talkie. It wasn't there. He frantically squirmed, trying to find it. Where was it?!

"Monique?" Darryl had heard her voice, but the call instantly dropped. "Monique, you there? Son of a bitch . . ." He redialed but got a fast busy. He redialed again. Nothing. He swallowed nervously, looking out at the tree, then turned to Craig. "You think she's OK?"

Summers was ice. "*She is fine, Darryl.* She is on the boat with Lisa."

Darryl swallowed again. "But she doesn't know about this. What if she decided to go for a walk or something?"

"Darryl, *she is on the boat.* She didn't go *anywhere.*"

Darryl hesitated. This was logical and probably true. Then Phil leaned forward, snapping pictures of the bloodied tree branch with boyish enthusiasm. "Boy, these are some amazing shots."

Darryl suddenly wanted to strangle Phil. But then he noticed the ranger. Allen Meyer had found his walkie-talkie—it was on his lap now—but strangely, he wasn't using it. "You OK, Ranger?"

"Yeah, yeah. Sure, sure, fine." It was a rapid-fire reply, clearly meaningless.

Darryl was calm. "Is your wife still checking trails out there?"

Meyer didn't respond.

"Ranger, you really should try her on that walkie-talkie."

But Meyer didn't touch it. It was like he was afraid to. "I haven't been able to get her all day. She's out there with our baby."

Darryl and Jason shared a look. The guy was cracking up. They grabbed for the walkie-talkie at the same time; Darryl got it first.

Jason jutted out his hand. *"Darryl, give me that, please."*

"I can't press a button as well as you?"

"This is important! Give it to me!"

Darryl shoved it at him angrily. "Same old Jason."

Jason didn't care about hurt feelings now. "What's your wife's name, Ranger?"

Eyes wet, Meyer turned. "Laura."

Jason pressed the walkie-talkie's talk button. "Laura, are you out there?"

He waited for a moment. One second ticked past, then another. There was no response.

"Laura, I'm with your husband. Please pick up."

He waited again. Just the same soft hissing.

Craig shook his head, eyeing the bloody tree branch. "We better find her. We better find her right now." He turned back to Jason. "Unless you want to fly the damn helicopter, too."

Jason was momentarily silent, upset at the situation—and maybe at himself, too. "Let's just find her, Craig." He eyed the ever-darkening skies. "As fast as we can."

As THE men sped off, they didn't know they were being studied.

CHAPTER 55

THE BLACK eyes shifted as the hulking machine shot across the sky then dipped down and disappeared. Then the eyes blinked. The creature had just seen its first helicopter.

From its mountaintop perch, the predator turned back to the tree branch where its kill had been. It knew instinctively what had happened. Its food had been stolen.

It began tuning for other prey, but the interference from the now-unseen helicopter was overpowering. Then the interference cut out and it immediately detected something else. In another part of the forest. Two signals, their frequencies identical to the jogger's. Then, it detected *another* two signals with the same frequency, in another area still.

The predator looked up at the sky. It wasn't as dark as it would have liked, but the prey was out there *now*. It was going to replace its stolen kill immediately.

CHAPTER 56

"LET'S GO, let's go, let's go. . . ."

Craig Summers drummed his fingers impatiently on the chopper's cyclic lever. They'd landed in the parking lot to split up: some to find the ranger's wife and the others to check on Monique and Lisa. Summers was by himself now, watching the others outside. *What are they doing?* He drummed his fingers faster. Craig hadn't been entirely honest with Darryl earlier. He didn't think Monique was fine. Not necessarily. With what they'd just seen, he didn't want to take any chances. It was getting dark fast, and he wanted to go. He pounded his fist. "Come on!"

In the parking lot, Allen Meyer sprinted toward an SUV, Phil stood by himself wondering what was going on, and Jason and Darryl yelled at each other over the thumping noise.

"Just let Phil do it! We need you to come with us, Darryl!"

"Monique's my damn wife, Jason! And *I'm* gonna check she's OK! You know how that is! Not trusting someone else to do something important!"

"Monique is safe on the boat! Sending Phil is just a precau—" He stopped yelling as an SUV sped toward them and slammed to a stop, the ranger at the wheel, tense and ready to get going.

"Damn it, Darryl, this guy's wife is alone in the middle of the forest *with a baby*! We've got to help him! You want me to trust you more; I want you to trust Phil more!"

Darryl couldn't say no to this. He nodded, and Jason ran over to Phil. "We're all set! You sure you're OK doing this, Phil?!"

"I want to get back to my computer anyway!"

Jason paused over the thumping noise, wounded anew. The sad fact was that he wasn't sure *he* trusted Phil Martino anymore. The only reason he knew he'd go back to the boat was because of his goddamn precious laptop. Jason had no idea why he was so obsessed with it, but he didn't care now. "Go, then!"

As Phil climbed into the chopper, Jason realized the SUV's driver's seat was empty now, Allen Meyer in back and waiting to go. "You want to drive, Darryl?!"

"Can you trust me to!"

"I'm sorry, Darryl, all right? I'm sorry! Let's just go!"

Darryl rushed into the driver's seat, Jason into the passenger's, and they sped off.

As the trees started to blur by, Jason put on his seat belt.

CHAPTER 57

"THERE IT is!"

From an open window, Phil pointed to the *Expedition*, docked farther up Redwood Inlet.

Craig rocketed the big bird toward it, reaching it in an instant, then they started to descend. "Open the door, Phil! I'll take care of the ladder!"

Phil swung the door open, stood strong against the rush of wind, and started climbing. He hopped onto the deck just as Monique ran up.

"What's going on, Phil?!"

Phil waved to Craig. "Come on! I'll tell you inside!"

Below deck, Phil walked quickly to his bedroom. He saw it immediately. His laptop was just as he'd left it on the little desk.

"What the hell's happening, Phil?" Monique was behind him. "What are you doing?"

He eyed his machine for a moment and turned, saying nothing.

"Where's Darryl? Where's everybody else?"

"They're . . . outside."

"What are we supposed to do?"

Phil didn't answer for a moment. His mind seemed to be working, almost like he couldn't remember. "You're supposed to meet them at the rangers' station."

"Really?"

As Lisa walked up, Phil nodded. "Right away. You know how to get there?"

LAURA MEYER walked rapidly down the trail. With Samuel and his portable chair in tow, she wondered if her husband had found the jogger. She'd tried him earlier on her now-charged walkie-talkie, but strangely, he hadn't picked up. It wasn't like her super-anal husband not to have his walkie-talkie on. Could he have gone out of range? Earlier, Laura had sworn she'd heard a helicopter and wondered if he'd been inside it. But that was impossible; Allen didn't know how to fly.

The walkie-talkie was off now. It produced tremendous static, which always made Samuel cry. The baby was prickly already, and Laura didn't want to push him over the edge—she just couldn't deal with that right now. On a wide trail surrounded by towering redwoods, she looked up. Probably not more than twenty minutes of light, she thought. Then Samuel made a sound, and she glanced down at him. Son of a bitch. A crabby look. Such looks typically preceded legendary crying fits. "Come on, Samuel; *please* don't be like that."

She couldn't worry about it now. She had to find the jogger. She walked forward tensely.

THE PREDATOR sped into the forest just below the treetops. The animal couldn't smell them yet, but it was locked onto their heartbeats. It banked around a grove of redwoods and hurtled forward.

"YOU THINK you're going a little fast?"

Darryl didn't answer Jason. The SUV was doing ninety, rattling a little, and he was focused on the road. He didn't notice a 25-mph speed-limit sign as they flew past it. A curve was up ahead, a pretty sharp one. He rocketed into it, barely depressing the brakes, and Jason felt a powerful pull toward the trees. He imagined his life ending in a brief violent instant. It didn't happen. The insides of his stomach shifted as they entered a straightaway.

Darryl glanced back at Allen Meyer. "She's gonna be fine, Ranger."

Holding a handle with white knuckles, Meyer nodded but was too afraid to say anything. Then he braced himself. Another bend was up ahead.

"PLEASE BE quiet, Samuel."

Laura halted in the middle of the trail. The kid was screaming his lungs out now. She gently rocked him in the Snugli, trying to quiet him. It was useless. He continued to howl. Growing more tense, Laura pushed forward.

ON A branch three hundred feet high, an owl ate voraciously, tearing chunks of meat from a dead squirrel, when it suddenly stopped.

The pupils of its bright orange eyes widened, and it looked around. Every direction: left, right, down, a hundred and eighty degrees behind it. It saw nothing in the fading light, just redwoods and shrubbery.

Then it looked *up*. Suddenly a speeding white underbelly tore above the treetops then disappeared.

The owl stared after it. Then it returned to its squirrel.

THE SCREAMS from the baby. The predator had heard them. It hurtled closer when the treetops beneath it abruptly parted and a double-yellow-lined road appeared below. As it followed the road, the sounds abruptly grew louder.

Their source was seconds away.

CHAPTER 58

"**S**AMUEL, PLEASE be quiet!"

Speed-walking in the fading light, Laura looked down at the screaming baby. "Please, Samuel, I'm beg—"

She abruptly stopped talking. It had just gotten dark. Suddenly. Almost as if something had blocked out the light from above. Then she heard something from above as well. A rustling or a flapping? She looked up.

"Oh." The fog was rolling in.

Thick, treetop-only fogs were common in coastal redwood forests, often occurring every day. This is a big one, Laura thought. Great. The fog could thicken fast and would shorten her search time even further. Samuel abruptly screamed even louder, and suddenly she couldn't take it anymore. "You want your chair, is that it?"

She set it up on the soil, put him in, and . . . He stopped crying. She shook her head. "It's a miracle."

The baby swung silently.

She waited for a moment and picked him up again. He immediately began crying. She shook her head, put him back in, and again, silence.

She scanned the trail ahead. She was near the end of it and just wanted to finish the last small portion then call it a day. She'd done all she could to find the missing jogger. She looked up. It was incredible, in just seconds the fog had thickened considerably. And it was getting even darker as a result. She had to go *now*.

She glanced at her swinging baby and wondered if for just a moment she could leave him here. But no, that was beyond stupid, especially with the squirrels and other rodents running around. But then she noticed an enormous burned-out redwood on the side of the trail. Inside it was a cave the size of a Porta Potti, and she got an idea. "Samuel, I'm just going to put you in there for *one minute*, OK? *One minute*."

The baby smiled, but Laura didn't. She was nervous as hell about doing this. Did leaving her child alone for a couple of minutes make her a bad mother? Under the circumstances, she didn't think so. . . . She lifted him, chair and all, and put him in the cave. He swung happily, and she quickly knelt to check it was safe. There was a strong charcoal smell from the burned wood, but no spiders, mites, squirrels, raccoons, or anything else. She stood.

"I won't take my eyes off you. I just want to see what's a little further up here."

She walked forward quickly. She didn't notice that the fog had thickened even more.

THE TWO heartbeats were very close now. Following the twisting double-yellow line, the creature rocketed toward them.

But then the animal saw something peculiar. A hanging white mass straight ahead. The great body immediately slowed down and began tuning. Strangely, despite what its eyes saw, the creature's other sensory organs indicated nothing was there.

The animal glided closer and the whiteness leaked toward it . . . then gradually enveloped it. It looked down, but the double-yellow line was gone now. So was the road. Unable to see, the creature instinctively navigated with its radar. It continued for several seconds when it glanced below and saw the line. Saw it *through the fog*. Its powerful eyes had taken just a moment to adjust. Up ahead, it spotted an owl. The little animal was just below the mist, on top of a massive branch jutting out over the road, apparently unaware it was coming. Speeding closer, the creature rumbled, and the owl suddenly looked up, turning in every direction. It couldn't see the creature, it couldn't see through the fog.

The predator sped up. Rushing through the whiteness, it came upon the tattered roof of Laura Meyer's SUV. It slowed slightly. The human heartbeats were just yards away now, but . . . the black eyes focused on the car. The animal immediately dipped down toward it.

CHAPTER 59

"IS THAT your wife's?"

Allen Meyer whipped his head around as they accelerated past a dusty red pickup on the side of the road. "I have no idea whose that is." He turned to Jason. "There shouldn't be anyone else here."

Darryl concentrated on the road ahead. "Forget it then. Let's just find her."

Meyer nodded. As they headed into the next turn, he noticed the speedometer. They were doing ninety-two.

A RACCOON foraging near Laura Meyer's parked SUV abruptly looked up. Suddenly, from deep within the fog, something enormous and black appeared, dropping like an elevator. As the raccoon ran off, the predator hovered out of the whiteness, wings flapping furiously. It descended quickly, then, five feet from the dirt, ceased pumping and landed with a thud on the road and dirt.

It didn't move. A few feet behind the car, it just stared at the machine, the baseball-size eyes shifting, studying everything about it.

Seconds passed. The car didn't move, didn't make a sound.

The engine popped.

Startled, the creature coiled its front half into the air and opened its mouth.

But the car still didn't move.

In the upright position, slightly more than six feet tall, the animal just watched it.

More time passed. The car remained perfectly still.

After a moment, the mouth eased closed. The eyes studied the machine more carefully, looking through the glass . . . at the seats, headrests, steering wheel, and dashboard. They were all frozen, inanimate. The engine popped again. This time, the animal didn't flinch.

The eyes swiveled up to the fog. The two human signals were just beyond the trees. The predator would use the mist to hunt them.

SWINGING IN his little tree cave, Samuel Meyer watched his mother walk down the trail. Then he looked up at the fog as a large dark outline surged past his tree and headed toward Laura's back.

LAURA WALKED forward, the forest as silent as a tomb. Suddenly, she heard a snap.

From above the trail.

She looked up as a branch the size of a pencil fell out of the whiteness.

It bounced on the soil and settled.

Laura stared at it for a long moment. Then looked up again.

Nothing was there, just the shapeless mass of silent white. She wondered if an owl was up there somewhere. They often ate things up on the branches.

She glanced back at Samuel. He looked fine, and she was far enough away from him that she could use the walkie-talkie without him hearing. She turned the device on and—

"Laura, you there? Hello; please come in, Laura. Laura?"

Her husband sounded even more tense than usual. "What is it, Allen?"

"Jesus. Where the hell are you?"

"Where do you think? Searching trails."

"Which trail?"

She continued walking. "Smuggler's Gulch."

"Where in Smuggler's Gulch?"

She eyed a tiny metal sign poking out of the dirt. "The seven-hundred-yard marker."

"Near that burned-out tree?"

She glanced back at Samuel. "Exactly."

"Do me a favor, Laura. Get in the tree."

She halted. "What?"

"I can't get into it now; just do it. We're coming to get you."

"We?"

"Laura, just get in the tree." A pause. "You don't see anything there now, do you?"

She looked around. "No, nothing."

"You sure?"

A quick glance. "Positive."

"All right. I'll see you in a few seconds."

She clipped the walkie-talkie to her belt, then walked quickly toward the tree.

Then she jogged. Why the hell had Allen told her to get *inside* it?

She jogged faster, looking in every direction.

She sprinted. The tree was forty feet away, then thirty. Why did she feel like something was following her? She ran harder, twenty feet away, ten . . .

She suddenly froze. What am I doing? Letting *Allen* freak me out? She ordered herself to get a grip. She calmly walked to the tree and peered in at Samuel. The baby looked fine.

The walkie-talkie sounded again. "Laura? Laura?"

Samuel started scowling, and she jolted to the opposite side of the trail. "Yes, Allen."

"You OK?"

She was annoyed now. "I *said* I'm fine. See you when you get here."

But just as she returned the walkie-talkie to her belt she heard something off the trail. A rustling. She looked out but saw nothing, just silent forest.

She didn't know why, but she wanted to look up. . . . Huh. The fog seemed to be swirling ever so slightly.

Something rustled again. Something behind the trees.

An animal? Her husband was nervous about *something*. If an animal was nearby, she didn't want it getting anywhere near her baby. She considered grabbing Samuel, putting him in the Snugli, but if whatever was out there jumped on her . . . Once, a playful dog had done just that, and Samuel had required stitches. The baby was safe in the cave where he was. She removed a pocketknife and quickly walked toward the trees.

SAMUEL JUST watched as his mother walked out of sight.

Instantaneously, an enormous black shadow descended on top of him. There was a flapping sound, and a powerful breeze blew back his hair.

The child looked up.

Something was there now. Looking right at him.

"COME ON, *come on, come on. . . .* "

Allen Meyer sprinted past trees and ferns, leading the way. They'd just parked and were tearing through the forest, seconds away from his wife, his baby . . .

Following, Darryl and Jason darted their eyes, studying the ominously silent landscape. They had a bad feeling.

CHAPTER 60

CLUTCHING HER pocketknife, Laura Meyer took another step. Whatever she'd heard, it was just around the next redwood, she was sure of it. She'd just scare it off and go back to her child. She held the knife firmly, rounded the tree, and—

"Oh my God, Allen."

It was her husband and two men she didn't recognize.

Winded, Allen froze. "You OK?"

"Fine."

He suddenly looked around. "Where's Samuel?"

"He's . . . in the tree cave."

A stunned pause. "You left him alone?"

"I heard something and—"

Allen Meyer ran toward the trail. They all did.

SAMUEL WAS captivated.

The creature was just hovering there, five feet off the ground, flapping rapidly, staring at him.

Swinging in his little chair, Samuel looked right back at it, drawn to its eyes. The eyes were almost magnetic, pure black and perfectly still. Then, like magic, the eyes moved. They looked to Samuel's left, then his right, then back to his left again.

Then the great body dropped lower and the mouth opened.

In his little chair, Samuel was almost swinging into it.

"SAMUEL!" ALLEN Meyer ran as hard as he could.

THE HEAD jerked. The predator hadn't been paying attention, but someone was coming. . . .

It turned back to the child. Then jolted closer. . . .

Samuel just stared at the approaching teeth, hundreds of them. . . .

He swung away . . . then back again.

His father screamed once more. . . .

The head turned. Then there was a powerful surge of wind. The mouth snapped closed, and the teeth disappeared.

ALLEN MEYER halted. On the opposite side of the trail, Samuel was swinging in the cave, perfectly fine.

As Darryl, Jason, and Laura came around, the ranger plucked his son from the chair. "You OK?"

The kid cooed.

Jason noticed the soil in front of the tree. It almost looked . . . wind-strewn. Just like Samuel Meyer's hair. Jason noticed the child was looking up.

Jason looked up too. But nothing was there now, just thick, white fog.

CHAPTER 61

"SON OF a bitch!"

Laura Meyer couldn't believe it. She pulled her SUV over to the roadside, and her husband and his two guests did the same. Outside, she pointed angrily at the red pickup. "I saw these guys earlier. Three hunters. I told them to leave immediately."

Allen Meyer exhaled. "Oh boy, what a goddamn day." He eyed the silent trees. "OK, I'll go out there and find—"

"I'll do it."

Meyer turned. This had come from the big strong black guy. "No. That's OK."

"You sure? I'm qualified. I'm former U.S. Army and a licensed hunter in four states with firearms and bow and arrow." Darryl opened his wallet to show his credentials.

Meyer studied them and looked up. "I get paid for this, you know."

"It's not about that. You guys have had a tough enough day already." Darryl Hollis eyed the tot in back of the SUV. "When my wife and I have little ones one day, I hope someone helps me out. No big deal."

The Meyers shared a look. What a genuinely touching offer.

"That's very nice of you. If you're sure you want to, we'll leave you a truck to get back. And a walkie-talkie."

Darryl was looking at the fog now. "Sure."

"Darryl, you got a second?" Jason led him a few feet away.

"What's up?"

Jason swallowed nervously. "Be careful, all right?"

"A bear could have killed that jogger."

"You really believe that?"

Darryl looked around. "I don't know. Just trying to come up with other possibilities. See ya soon." He pocketed the walkie-talkie, then walked into the redwoods and disappeared.

HE ALMOST had the shot. Big Tim and his two minions had been tracking the deer for half an hour and were finally within shooting range. After darting everywhere, the deer had stopped to nibble on some ferns. On one knee, Big Tim aimed his rifle at the buck with the crisscrossing horns. It was a big animal, probably 350 pounds. Yes—he almost had the shot.

THE EYES shifted. From Big Tim, to the deer, back to Big Tim again.

Gliding silently in the fog above, the predator watched every movement. It instinctively recognized what was happening: the stealthy behavior, the careful deliberate movements. One species was hunting another. But the creature didn't understand *how*. Its eyes shifted back to Big Tim. Then to the instrument in his hands. He was aiming it at the deer.

ONE EYE open, one eye closed, Big Tim began to ease down on the trigger. If the buck didn't move in the next quarter second, he'd have it. The buck didn't move.

THE CREATURE shivered when the shot rang out.

The predator didn't know how it had happened, but a metal projectile—its ampullae of Lorenzini had picked it up before it even left the rifle barrel—had rocketed out and plunged into the buck's chest. The deer staggered and fell onto the dirt. Its heart beat rapidly for half a minute, then stopped. The eyes calmly watched it die. Then they swiveled back to the rifle.

DARRYL FROZE. He'd heard it quite clearly. A gunshot. He ran toward it.

"GREAT SHOT, Dad!"

Big Tim blew the nuzzle. "Yeah, not bad."

The three men walked toward the dead buck, its horned head twisted on the dirt.

"How we gonna get him back to the truck?" Timmy asked.

"Gotta tie his legs to a stick and carry him back."

"Where we gonna get a stick?"

Big Tim wondered if his son was brain-dead. "We gotta go find one, Timmy. Come on."

THE CREATURE watched them go.

Then it focused on the deer.

IT TOOK a while, but they found a perfect stick, eight feet long and as thick as a baseball bat. They weren't more than ten feet away when they saw what had happened to their prize.

"Jesus Christ! Look at that, Dad!"

"*Son of a bitch.*" Big Tim suddenly clutched his rifle tighter.

The deer was right where they'd left it. But its chest, stomach, and hindquarters weren't there anymore. They were gone, replaced by a single gargantuan bite.

"You think a bear got it, Dad?"

"I don't know." Tim Jameson knew many bear species had huge appetites, but he didn't think any of them—black, brown, grizzly, or Kodiak—had a mouth large enough to take a bite like this one. Staring at the mutilated animal, he rubbed his beard. What the hell had a mouth like that? A goddamn whale? He glanced up at the fog. "Let's get out of here."

"You don't want the deer?"

Big Tim looked around nervously. "Forget the deer, Timmy. Something wants it more than we do. Put the stick down; let's go."

THE THREE men spotted him from a hundred feet.

"Hey, what's that black guy doing out here? I thought the park's closed."

As they walked closer, Big Tim spoke up. "Hey, mister, I don't think you wanna be out here just now."

Darryl Hollis hesitated. "That's what I was coming to tell you."

"Mission accomplished. We're leaving."

They hustled past him, and Darryl didn't follow. Something had scared them. As the men disappeared, he looked up at the fog. It was very quiet here. Darryl had never thought about it before, but as big as redwoods were, he realized, they actually deadened sound, blocked it out. He scanned the area. But it was more than just quiet, wasn't it? There were no animals—none—not even squirrels or birds. He realized he was alone and didn't have a weapon. He looked up at the fog again. Was something up there?

"Darryl, you out there? Darryl?"

He removed the walkie-talkie. "What's up, Jason?" He didn't take his eyes off the fog.

"A lot. Get back here right away. The rangers' station."

CHAPTER 62

"SO YOU'LL take care of whatever's out there?"

Jason nodded to the ranger. "We will." He, Darryl, and Craig didn't like making major decisions without consulting Monique, Lisa, and Phil, but these were extreme circumstances. Allen and Laura Meyer were leaving the park in minutes, so they had to make an immediate decision right here in the rangers' station.

Allen Meyer was tense. He hadn't cleared the proposed plan with park management. He turned to his wife for support, but she looked away. She was beyond tense. A hearse from the closest funeral home, 110 miles away, had just picked up the jogger. It was the first dead body Laura Meyer had seen in her entire life, and she still hadn't recovered. She was seated at a desk hugging their eleven-month-old tightly, the way a mother would after seeing her first dead person. Still, she was a fellow ranger, and Allen Meyer wanted her opinion of this potential arrangement. "What do you think, honey?"

"I think I just want to get out of here."

"Should we let these guys take care of whatever's out there? They say they want to."

"Then let them. I just want to go."

"Well . . . we can't just leave them here."

"We've hired local hunters to kill bobcats and things before. It will be fine."

"I'd have to call Robinson to check it's OK."

"Then call him, for Christ's sake!" Laura exhaled, calming down. "I promise Robinson will OK it. It just means less work for him." Mark Robinson was Leonard State Park's lazy and alcoholic director of operations.

Allen picked up the phone, but there was no dial tone. He turned to Darryl curiously. "A bear must have killed that guy, right?"

"Oh yeah." Darryl didn't know what else to say. Especially since the ranger had already listed "bear attack" as the official cause of death on the certificate with the funeral home.

Still, Allen Meyer had a trillion questions about what they'd seen out there. "You know, there are still a few things I don't unders—"

"Jesus, Allen! Enough! Let's get out of here! Let's get *our baby* out of here! Just call Robinson, clear this, and let's go!"

The ranger shot his wife an angry look. He didn't appreciate being yelled at like this in front of strangers. But then he eyed his son and nodded obediently.

WITH THE parking lot's streetlamps buzzing overhead, Allen Meyer shook hands with Darryl, Jason, and Craig. "Thank you very much for taking care of this. I couldn't get through to our boss, but we have no doubt he'll OK it."

Darryl eyed the two helicopters. "We can use whatever we need?"

"The entire park's at your disposal. Helicopters, rifles, cars, the equipment in the storage shed . . . anything. You have the keys to the cabin?"

Jason held them up.

"Good. And just to be clear, you guys will be alone out here. All the local businesses know the park's closed for the prescribed burns, so they're closed too. There's pretty much no one within a hundred miles of here, and with the phone service . . . you're isolated."

The three men nodded.

"Anyway, good luck."

They shook hands once more; Meyer walked to his Civic, where Laura was already waiting in the passenger seat. As they pulled away,

Darryl noticed little Samuel in the back of the car. The child was waving. Darryl returned the wave. Then the car disappeared. The three men were alone.

"DARRYL?"

They jolted around. It was Monique, walking out of the darkness with Lisa.

"Monique?" Darryl was stunned. "What are you doing here?"

"What do you mean? Phil told us to meet you here. We got lost, so it took a while."

CHAPTER 63

"THEN I guess I misunderstood you, Darryl."

They were standing on the creek's dock under the moonlight.

"How could you *possibly* have misunderstood me, Phil?! The whole point of sending you here was to tell them not to move!"

Jason shook his head in disbelief. "What the hell were you thinking? My God, they could have gotten hurt."

Phil ignored Jason. "I'm telling you, Darryl. *You told me* to do it."

"You're gonna lie right to my damn face? . . ." Darryl lunged for him, but Jason thrust himself in the way.

"*Please* let's not do it this way."

Darryl stepped back. Then slowly exhaled.

"Darryl, I would never, ever, intentionally put Monique and Lisa in harm's way." Phil shook his head, almost as if trying to figure it out himself. "Maybe I got confused. You're right; when I think about it now, it doesn't make sense to send them out there, but that's honestly what I thought you wanted me to do. I thought you were worried and wanted to see her right away." He turned. "Monique, do you actually think I *wanted you to get hurt*?"

Monique was perfectly calm. "No, Phil, I don't. I think we should all take a breather and relax." She patted her husband's back. "Everything's cool, all right?"

Darryl exhaled again. "Yeah, sure."

Monique shoved him. "It was a misunderstanding. Why not shake on it? This bad blood isn't good for anybody."

Phil extended his hand, and Darryl reluctantly shook it. As they did, Craig watched Phil like a hawk. Jason watched Phil, too. Somehow his college friend had gotten even dumber with age. Then Jason turned to someone who mattered. "Lisa, you got a second?"

The two of them walked farther out on the dock. "What's up?"

"Sorry we didn't consult you before we made the . . . arrangement to stay here."

She glanced at the full moon. "I understand, under the circumstances."

He looked at her. "You going to tell me what's wrong, then?"

She continued to look up. "I'm fine."

He gently turned her chin. "Please."

She exhaled. "Something out there *killed someone*, Jason. I still can't fathom that it's what we've been tracking. . . ."

"Neither can I."

"But it's something; it's out there, and—" She stopped talking.

"And . . . what?"

"And I'm scared. I mean, I am really, really scared."

"Do you want to leave?"

"Do *you* want me to leave?"

"Lisa, you're right; you *are* a biologist. You don't need to be here."

"I didn't ask you that." She looked him in the eye. "I asked you if you want me to leave."

"No, I don't."

"Then I don't want to either."

She scanned the dim, dark outline of the forest, a strange look on her face.

"What?"

"Just realizing I haven't learned how to fire a rifle yet."

"We better get on th—" He stopped talking. Something was behind them. Right on the dock. He turned and—

"Sorry to scare you," Darryl said.

Jason chuckled. "No problem. What's up?"

"I know how we're gonna hunt this thing."

"How?"

"We're discussing it right now." Darryl walked back down the dock. "Let's go talk about it."

CHAPTER 64

"**F**IRST WE gotta confirm that what *we think* killed that jogger actually did."

They stood in the tall grass near the dock, the moon's mirror image gently rippling on the water.

"How are we going to do that?" Craig said to Darryl.

"For starters, by checking the base of the tree where the body turned up."

"Why?"

"To see if anything climbed the tree. Maybe something else entirely killed that guy. Maybe a bear or a mountain lion."

"Can they both climb?" Jason asked.

"Mountain lions sure can. They regularly eat their kills in trees."

Craig shook his head irritably. "Gimme a break, Darryl. That jogger was, what—two hundred and twenty-five pounds? Are you saying some puny fifty-pound mountain lion killed him and dragged his corpse *to the top of a redwood tree*?"

"I'm not saying that at all, Sherlock." Darryl knew full well that mountain lions never went after fully grown adult men. "I just think we should be methodical here, cover all the bases. Maybe a bear did it. Some black bears can get up to nine hundred pounds. They're certainly strong enough."

"But they don't attack people, Hoss."

"Not generally, but there are exceptions. This guy was jogging at night? What if he surprised a hungry bear? Or a bear with cubs? Either of those situations could be *lethal*, believe me. And that jogger's body was covered with saliva, remember?"

Before the hearse arrived, Jason and Darryl had checked the corpse for teeth marks. While they didn't find any discernible evidence, the skull had been partially crushed and dried saliva covered much of the body. Both findings were consistent with bear attacks. Bears could easily crush a human skull simply by falling on it with their front paws, and they often licked their kills as a way of marking them.

"It could have been a bear."

Craig shook his head. "I don't buy it."

Darryl shrugged. "Neither do I. That's why I want to see the tree. To be sure."

Jason pivoted. "What would a redwood look like after a bear had climbed up it?"

Near a few huge suitcases they'd lugged off the boat, Phil cleared his throat. "Torn to bits. I know so from my fire-ranger days. Redwoods have very tough inner heartwood, but their bark is incredibly delicate. You'd be amazed—you can flake it off with your bare hands."

Jason stared at the man he no longer trusted. "So you'd know if a bear had climbed up a redwood?"

"In a heartbeat."

"All right. When do you want do this, Darryl?"

"Now."

"Now?" Jason looked around. "At night?"

Darryl removed a map from the back of his khaki shorts. "I know exactly how to get there. And for those of you prone to the jitters . . ." He grabbed a rifle. "Let's go."

MONIQUE COULDN'T believe the size of it. The tree was monstrous, even for a redwood. With a cornfield and the moon behind it, she made it out in silhouette. The tree reminded her of a Manhattan skyscraper, forty stories high, as straight as a steel bar and so big around that a car could drive through it. As she craned her neck up, she literally couldn't see the top of it. "Could a bear actually climb this thing?"

Craig turned on a flashlight. "Let's see."

A small golden circle illuminated and shifted to the tree. The bark was thick, fibrous, and filled with crisscrossing four-inch-deep grooves. Craig scanned the redwood from the roots to several feet above his head. "Not a mark on it." He methodically circled the entire perimeter. Nothing. "This bark hasn't been touched."

Darryl gently rubbed it with his fingers. Just as Phil had said, small pieces of bark flaked off right in his hand. "You'd know if a squirrel climbed this thing." He grabbed Craig's flashlight and studied the tree himself, carefully circling it. "No bear or mountain lion's been anywhere near here." His eyes drifted to the cornstalks . . . then to the dark looming mountains beyond.

Jason noticed him staring. "What's on your mind?"

"Wondering where it is. Where it is right now."

"Maybe back in the ocean." Monique walked out of the shadows behind them. "Or another part of the forest. Or maybe we've got it all wrong, and it's not here at all."

Darryl continued to stare at the mountains. "Let's get our stuff and go to the cabin."

"KNOCK ON WOOD, my financial problems are solved, Jason. I came up with a plan to raise additional capital, and the bank just called to OK it. Right before you called actually."

On his phone in the SUV's passenger seat, Jason nodded. "Must have been a good omen I got through, then, Harry." On the first try no less.

Ackerman hoped so. He'd been working on this plan for months, and now it was finally paying off. If it actually did, he'd soon be able to harvest his reputation as a world-class businessman and naturalist. *Naturalist*. Ackerman just loved the word. While the $2,500-a-head Union Club cancer benefit in New York had already passed, the spring galas for the new cause du jour would soon be sprouting up everywhere, and Ackerman hoped he'd have something substantial to discuss. "What's the latest with our new species?"

As they pulled into the park's massive lit-up parking lot, Jason outlined the day's drama.

When he finished, Ackerman paused. "So let me understand this . . . you think the species you've been trailing might have something to do with this missing jogger?"

Everybody got out of the car. "I know it sounds a little out there, Harry, but we couldn't explain what happened to him and neither could the rangers."

"It does sound a little out there, but you're the guy with your feet on the ground. I'll support whatever you want to do, Jason. Although . . . I wouldn't mind getting some more details on your plans, especially since it's been so hard to talk because of the poor phone service. Can we meet in person?"

"Sure." As the others lugged bags out, Jason followed them toward the cabin. "Will you be in the neighborhood?"

"I'll be in San Francisco soon."

"That's not exactly the neighborhood, Harry."

"Actually, I'll be testing a yacht I've been thinking about buying, and I can take it pretty much anywhere. How about the docks in Eureka? Say four days at . . . three P.M.?"

Jason paused. Eureka? Making that trip from San Francisco would take time, but if Ackerman wanted to do it, Jason could certainly take the *Expedition* to meet him. "Sure, Harry, that would be fine." He followed Craig through a deserted campground to the cabin's porch. "So I'll look forward to seeing y—"

The line cut out.

"Harry? Harry?"

The line was dead. Jason redialed but got nothing. Then he noticed Phil, huffing toward him with a zippered suitcase big enough to clothe a family of four for a month. "Man, does Lisa have a lot of clothes."

Jason chuckled, but Phil was serious. "I really shouldn't be doing this, you know."

"Why not?"

"Because I'm busy, for Christ's sake."

"Gimme a break."

"Whatever. Did I hear you're meeting Ackerman?"

"In four days."

Phil heaved up the suitcase again. "You gonna type up your notes later?"

"If it's all right with you."

"Sure, no problem." Phil lugged the bag onto the porch. Watching him, Jason decided he had to get his own laptop. He didn't want to rely on Phil Martino for anything anymore.

Then Craig huffed closer, straining mightily with another enormous bag. "Man, does Lisa have a lot of clothes." Jason chuckled as Craig put the bag on the porch. Then the two of them returned to the parking lot. Lisa had more clothes. Just before they reached the macadam, however, Craig paused at the storage shed. "I wonder what's in here. . . ."

As he walked in, Jason noticed Darryl, by himself and looking out at the dark forest. "What's up, Darryl?"

"Just realizing how much land's really up here."

"It's not going to be easy to find it, is it?"

"I'm not gonna believe what 'it' is until I see it with my own eyes."

"How are we going to do it?"

"With all this land, I honestly don't know."

"I know," a voice said from behind them.

They turned. It was Craig. "I know *exactly* how we'll find it." He pointed to the shed. "The answer's right in there."

CHAPTER 65

"WHAT'S 'THERMAL imaging equipment,' Craig?" At the shed, Summers had simply said that the shed held thermal imaging equipment and that they'd use it to find the creature but without explaining what the equipment was or how it worked.

Craig didn't answer Jason as the two entered the rangers' cabin. He had something else on his mind. "Look at this place...." To Craig's surprise, it actually looked very nice, almost like a ski lodge: beamed ceilings, an enormous brick fireplace with a raised hearth for sitting, well-worn brown leather couches with matching easy chair.

Lisa exited a hallway. "Five bedrooms are back there. Also a fully stocked fridge and freezer in the kitchen."

Craig noticed a firewood supply big enough to survive a winter in Alaska. Then he peered out a window and surveyed outside. Beyond the covered porch was a campground—a dozen wood tables, steel garbage cans, a swing set—beyond that the storage shed, and farther, the massive parking lot, lit up like a baseball stadium at night.

"Craig, what's thermal imaging equipment?"

"Oh." Summers turned. "I've never worked with it myself, but fire rangers use it to measure heat when they're doing prescribed burns. You're familiar with it, right, Phil?"

Seated on the easy chair, Phil nodded.

Jason remained focused on Craig. "How does it help us here?"

"By letting us see what's out there. Day or night. It works by using differences in temperature gradients to create an image."

"English, Craig."

"Basically, it's night vision. Air is one temperature. Bodies—human, animal, whatever—are another. A thermal camera creates an image by using the difference. It's easy to set up. Basically a camera on a tripod, so we can put it wherever we want. There are twenty cameras in that shed, so if nothing else, we can set some up near the area where we found the body and see if anything returns to the scene of the crime. And since they've got a monitor that reads the signals remotely, we don't even have to leave the cabin. Between that and the radar, we'll get a great look at what's going on out there."

Impressed, Jason turned to Darryl. "What do you think?"

"Not much."

"Really?" Jason shrugged. "It sounds like a good idea to me."

"Then do it." Darryl walked to a window. "It's technology hunting. Scopes, radar, GPS—it's not my thing. I just wasn't raised with all that crap. What are you gonna do when it doesn't turn up anything, Craig?"

Summers quietly seethed. "Shut up, Darryl. You don't know it's not gonna turn up any—"

"For the sake of argument, let's say it doesn't." Darryl said this with utter confidence, like it was as certain as the sun rising. "What are you gonna do, then? Go out there and look for it?"

"Of course. We all will."

"You're gonna lead us, then?"

Craig paused nervously. "What?"

"You heard me. Are you gonna lead us? Are you experienced hunting wild animals? Comfortable tracking, locating, and killing them?"

"Well . . ."

"Because I *am* experienced. I've spent a large part of my life doing it. And I'm not gonna waste our time on some random search."

"What 'random search'? And what do you mean, 'waste our time'? We have all the time in the world."

"Not what I'm talking about. I don't want to burn our energy, blunt the knife before we even get a chance to use it."

"What do you mea—"

"We'll get tired. As simple as that is, it happens all the time. You realize how big this forest is? Try a few hundred square miles, junior. We go out there looking around, we could go *for days* without seeing anything. We wouldn't just get tired; we'd get exhausted. But we'd be out there. Then, when we really needed it . . . We'd get slaughtered. And I'm not jeopardizing my safety, my wife's safety—even your safety, Craig. When I step out to hunt, there's only one way. Guns loaded and ready to kill."

"And I'm going out there to play hopscotch?" Craig shook his head. "Lisa, Jason, Phil. Tomorrow we'll set up the equipment then practice shooting." He gave Darryl a look. "We'll be guns loaded and ready to kill, too. In the meantime"—he sat—"I'm exhausted. Anybody up for a fire?"

Minutes later, they sat in front of a huge blaze with mugs of cocoa. The cocoa was the cheap watery stuff with fake marshmallows, but it still tasted good. They all relaxed. Even Jason. Staring at the flames, he was mesmerized. "I can't remember the last time I was in front of a fire." Neither could anyone else. They all just looked at the fire, drinking their cocoa, and savoring the rare homey feeling they'd all missed for so long.

Darryl was the least relaxed of everyone. He gazed at the flickers of yellow and gold with particular interest, watching as a steady stream of smoke ascended. . . . Carried by convection currents, the smoke rose beyond his sight, into a flue then out the chimney, emerging into the cool night air. There was no wind, so the smoke drifted farther, wafting up along a redwood trunk. It continued straight up, passing the tree's upper branches, then went higher still, and filtered through the evergreen leaves. Continuing, the smoke filtered into the sky then finally went still, taking on an eerie hue from the glowing moon above.

The only sound was from the distant rolling ocean.

But then there was a second sound, a natural sound that merged into the first.

Breathing. Calm, even, and deep. Gliding silently, the winged body blew the smoke away. The animal tilted its head and studied the stream of white drifting up from the chimney below, tuning in to the signals inside. The creature wouldn't attack them. It simply tuned to their heartbeats and listened to them breathe. Then it tilted a wing and glided toward the looming mountains in the distance. It disappeared gradually. The smoke was gone as well. All that remained were the sounds of the ocean and the silent, watching moon.

THE MOON. In the cabin, Darryl stared at it through the window. As the others slept in front of the crackling fire, he couldn't help but wonder. Is something out there? He didn't know if his Indian mysticism was getting the best of him again, but . . . He went to his room and grabbed a rifle, not bothering with the bow and arrow now; he just wanted something quick. Back to the front door, he was careful not to wake anyone but . . .

"What are you doing?" Monique's eyes locked on the rifle.

"I just want to check around a little."

"By yourself? At night?"

"I think something might be out there. I just want to—"

"I don't want you to go, Darryl." Her eyes were wet. "You understand me?"

"I'm just gonna look around; that's it."

She looked like she was going to cry. "*I said* I don't want you to."

"I have to. I need to."

"You do not *need to*. Please don't lie to me about this."

A line had just been crossed. "Have I *ever* lied to you? One time since the night we got married?"

She suddenly looked guilty. "Of course not."

He touched her cheek. "Best night of my life."

She turned away. She didn't want to hear this now.

"Let me go."

"Why? Why do you want to so badly?"

"To look around. That's it. Get a sense of things. Like my grandfather taught me." He glanced at the others, sleeping and lost in their dreams. "OK?"

She didn't want to, but she had to. "Go."

He kissed her on the lips. "I love you. And I promise I'll be fine."

"I love you, too." She couldn't say anything else.

As her husband walked out the door, Monique Hollis wondered if she'd ever see him again.

CHAPTER 66

ON THE porch, broken strands of moonlight shone into Darryl Hollis's eyes. The night air was clean, dark, and cold. He entered the desolate campground slowly, just watching and listening to the sounds of the nearby forest, birds and chipmunks chirping and chittering. He wasn't sure—he was very out of practice—but he didn't think anything dangerous was here now. Though it might have been recently. Holding the rifle loosely, he walked into the trees and didn't turn back, the cabin's diffused golden light slowly disappearing.

The shadows engulfed him. He continued for several minutes until he emerged into a clearing, the top of his head illuminated by a ghostly pale white light. He just stood there breathing, slowly, calmly, deeply. He focused on an enormous tree, a branchless shaft of wood that climbed straight into the sky. A pair of squirrels scampered past, and he followed them with his eyes. Nothing dangerous was here now; he was sure of it. He didn't move. He just stood, watched, and waited.

"MONIQUE?" LISA knocked on the Hollises' bedroom at 7:50 A.M. No one answered, so she pushed it open. "Oh, excuse me."

In black sweats and a gray tank top, Monique was on the floor, covered in sweat and doing rapid push-ups.

Lisa turned to go.

"Stick around," Monique ordered through deep breaths.

Lisa did. She couldn't help but notice the woman's flexing muscles. Boy, she's ripped! And intense. Lisa knew Monique's background, of course—former ROTC and active duty in the army—but in all the time she'd known her, she'd never seen this side of her. She'd always thought of Monique Hollis as tall and elegant yet totally down-to-earth. But watching her now—her eyes. There was no fashion model behind those eyes, no vapid insecurity of any kind. Monique was a different person—tough, even brutal.

She ripped off forty more push-ups and smiled, suddenly her old friendly self again. "Hey, Lisa." She stood. "Didn't mean to scare you; just doing a little morning exercise."

"You been doing this for a while?"

Monique wiped her face with a fluffy white hand towel. "I took a month off actually; just getting back into it." She'd started the previous night, right before Darryl returned to the cabin.

Lisa eyed her muscular arms. "Look at you! You're a total roughneck!"

"Darryl's a lot rougher, believe me."

"How come you're getting back into it now?"

Monique's relaxed demeanor disappeared. "Did you see that jogger?"

Lisa paused. "Of course."

"There's your answer."

Lisa noticed a serrated hunting blade strapped to her calf. "You're not taking any chances, are you?"

"Are you, Lisa?"

Another pause. "I didn't think so. I'm about to do some rifle practice with Craig. What are you up to?"

"Checking the forest with Darryl. Showering now. See you out there."

Lisa walked to the door.

"Oh, and Lisa?"

She turned back. "Yeah."

"Practice hard."

～～～

"Nice shot, Lisa!"

It was just after eleven in the parking lot and they'd been shooting for hours, their targets—empty plastic water jugs—on top of a spindly-legged table.

Jason and Phil had already shot, and Craig thought their progress was respectable. But Lisa's progress was nothing short of stunning. She had taken to shooting like a fish to water. She fired again. *Bam!* One jug down. *Bam!* A second. *Bam!* A third. She was very accurate. And she paid attention. No matter what the directive, she needed to hear it only once. How to hold the rifle. How to load it. How to unload it. How to deal with the recoil.

And her attitude was suddenly fantastic. Craig didn't know what change had taken place in her psyche, but it was sure as hell something. He could see it in her eyes: she knew there was a deadly animal out there, and she had no intention of getting killed by it. With a rifle in her hand, Lisa Barton didn't look like a dark-haired damsel in distress at all. She looked like a killer.

Bam! The last jug flew off the table.

"Excellent, Lisa! OK, that's it for shooting practice, guys. Let's just clean this stuff up, then head out there and set up the equipment."

Jason and Lisa nodded.

"Sorry, but I don't have time to set up equipment, Craig."

Summers turned to Phil Martino. "Excuse me?"

"You heard me."

"What do you mean you don't have time?"

"I've got things to do."

Jason couldn't believe this. "What things, Phil? Typing more notes? Since we've been here, there haven't been any more notes to—"

"I don't have to justify what I do to you, Jason."

Jason was stunned into silence.

Craig wasn't. He threw his hands into the air. "You know what? I don't want you coming. Stay here. Lisa, Jason, come on."

Phil walked back to the cabin, and the other three headed for the storage shed. They were about to enter when Darryl and Monique walked silently out of the woods. They approached quickly, Darryl shaking his head. "It's not out there."

Craig gave him a look. "What do you mean it's not out there?"

"Just what I said."

"With all due respect, Hoss, we'll set up this equipment and see what's really out there."

"Finished."

Craig, Jason, and Lisa were near the edge of the forest, close to the cornfield. Draped in dark shadows, they'd just finished setting up sixteen big white radar guns and twenty even bigger black thermal cameras. Sweating in his undershirt, Craig nodded in satisfaction. If the killer returned to the scene of the crime, they'd see it. Then find it and kill it. He noticed Jason, at the very edge of the forest, and he walked over to him.

"What's up, Jason?"

"Just wondering. If Darryl's right and that thing's not here, where is it?"

Craig glanced at the black mountains in the distance. "Well, Darryl's not right. Now let me show you how this equipment works. Lisa, you too."

They walked toward an enormous duffel bag, on top of it a pair of monitors, one radar, one thermal. Turned on and operating on batteries, the radar's screen was divided into sixteen credit-card-size boxes, each with its own sweeping green line, like miniature spotlights. The thermal's screen was divided into twenty boxes, separate monochrome images of the forest.

"Now this radar is tuned to filter out stationary objects and pick up moving ones, so to show you how it works . . ." Craig turned. "Lisa, can you walk toward one of those radar guns?"

"Sure." As she did, Craig pointed at the screen. "Look what happens, Jason. . . ." Just then, in the bottom-right sweep, a blinking green dot appeared. Craig touched the image, blowing it up to full screen. As Lisa continued walking, the blinking dot moved across the sweep, reached the edge of the screen, then the next sweep popped up and the dot continued. "Get the idea? OK, come on back, Lisa." When she returned, Craig pointed to the thermal monitor. "OK, now this is the thermal. As you can see, everything's in monochrome."

Indeed, all twenty forest images were in blacks, grays, and whites.

"Now, these cameras are tuned to 'white-hot,' and that doesn't refer to my dance moves. It means anything that's physically hotter than the air—you, me, a skunk, a car engine—will appear in white. Just watch this image right here"—he touched it, blowing it up—"then see what happens when I come into the frame. . . ."

As he trotted off, Lisa eyed the image and thought it looked like a twisted Ansel Adams photograph come to life, with a dark gray redwood trunk, lighter gray ferns, black soil, and then . . . Craig Summers. Only it wasn't Craig exactly but a ghostly approximation of him. His face, hands, and visible forearms were all colored in eerie bright white light, his T-shirt a much darker gray. Then the ghost spoke. "Get the idea?" He trotted back. "Anyway, that's it. Let's get out of here. I bet this stuff will turn up something; you watch."

Jason glanced at the distant looming mountains once more. He wondered.

"WHY WOULDN'T it be out there?"

It was late afternoon, pieces of a bright blue sky peeking through the treetops. Craig, Jason, Lisa, and Phil had just returned from another round of shooting practice, and everyone was gathered on the cabin's front porch.

Arms crossed, Darryl turned to Craig. "You haven't spent much time in the woods, have you, my little friend?"

"What's that supposed to mean?"

"It means cameras, radar guns, and tripods aren't exactly part of nature. It means animals see things. Smell things. In some cases, detect things electronically. You think seeing a thermal camera on top of a tripod in the middle of a redwood forest is normal? No way in hell does that stuff pick up what we're looking for. A smart animal wouldn't go anywhere near it. Besides, I don't think we've got the right weather now anyway."

Jason glanced up at the sky. "What do you mean?"

"I mean this thing has powerful instincts to hide. That jogger disappeared at night, and we found his body on a very foggy day. I don't think that was an accident."

"You're saying it will only come out at night or when there's fog?"

"Fog sure would be a great place to hide, don't ya think?"

Jason looked up at the sun, scanning all around it very carefully.

He had to admit there wasn't a cloud up there. And not a trace of fog, either.

THE BLACK eyes didn't move. They were looking at the sun too.

The creature had been watching the sun since the very early morning, when it first appeared on the horizon. Indeed, it had been watching the sun for days. At the mouth of the cave, the predator was completely exposed, but it didn't care. There was nothing here to see it on this lifeless mass of rock, just a few dozen seagulls gliding overhead. It continued to watch the sun.

"LOOK AT how much darker it is. . . ." Jason walked to the edge of the porch and glanced up at the sky. "Getting pretty close to twilight . . ." He eyed the trees beyond the campground. "I wonder if it will come out."

Monique, Lisa, and Phil didn't respond. Darryl shook his head. "I doubt it."

He eyed a pair of playful squirrels near a picnic table. "I don't think that thing's anywhere near here."

"You sure about that?" Someone said from behind them.

They all turned to Craig, entering the porch quickly, with a rifle and a very tense face. "We just got a reading."

Jason looked up at the darkening skies. "Is that right?"

Craig wasn't in the mood for small talk. "Saddle up. I want to end this fast."

CHAPTER 67

"I DON'T care what this damn thing says; it's not out there."

Inside the cabin, the team focused on one of two monitors set up on the hearth, watching as a speeding dot zipped across a radar sweep, reached the edge of the screen, then continued as a second, then third sweep popped up.

Craig shook his head at Darryl. "Something's sure as hell out there. All right. Let's go. Everybody. Guns loaded."

Jason nodded with conviction.

As they walked out the door, the speeding dot suddenly moved even faster.

"ALMOST THERE . . ." Craig walked quickly through the silent forest, leading the others past ferns and trunks. Suddenly he stopped and pointed. "The readings came from those three right there."

The big white radar guns just sat there on their tripods. Jason noticed they weren't pointed up, but parallel to the dirt. Had the creature swooped down?

Suddenly there was a violent rustling—from something behind one of the radar guns, moving very fast.

Craig jerked his rifle toward it. So did everyone else.

The sound rapidly grew louder.

Craig eased down on his trigger. . . . Whatever it was was just about to show itself. . . .

Two tiny fawns, three feet tall and razor thin, bolted out from behind the trees, apparently chasing each other in a playful game. Monique smiled cutely as they started darting in and out of the three tripods.

She lowered her rifle. Craig lowered his, too.

Darryl Hollis just shook his head.

"IT'S NOT out there," Darryl said the next morning.

"It's still not out there," he said again in the afternoon.

"It's just not out there," he said yet again the next day.

Jason couldn't take it anymore. "Are you sure?" he demanded when Darryl repeated the vile phrase again just before sunset.

"Old habits die hard, huh?" Darryl gave him a look. "I'm sure."

Jason wondered if he was right. He had to admit they hadn't seen a single cloud. For days, the skies had been nothing but a pristine crystal blue. Jason shook his head. "Sorry, it's just that I'm seeing Ackerman tomorrow and I was hoping I'd have something more concrete to tell him." But his frustration aside, Jason suspected Darryl's assessment was accurate. Craig's equipment certainly agreed. Over the past few days, the two monitors had revealed nothing but rodents, deer, elk, and an occasional bear. Was it just a coincidence that there hadn't been a trace of fog?

They cooked a dinner of chicken and steaks on the huge industrial gas grill behind the cabin, ate, then made a big blaze in the fireplace. Everyone lounged around the living room, when Jason looked up from the notebook he'd been jotting in.

"Anybody have a Latin dictionary?"

Craig and Darryl looked at him like he was using controlled substances. Monique just laughed. Jason turned to Phil. "Can I borrow your computer later? I'm sure there's some Latin Internet site."

"Sure, but the Net's not working."

"You tried it?"

"Yeah, sending an e-mail. Phones are down too. I think it's all on the same system."

Lisa stood. "Jason?"

"Yeah?"

"Actually, I think I saw a Latin dictionary in a room back here."

"Yeah?"

"I'll show you. . . ." She entered the hallway near the bedrooms, and he followed.

"Where is it?"

She paused then gave him a little look. "Are you busy right now?"

"Sort of. Why?"

"I don't know." She glanced into her bedroom. "It's just . . . I'm not really doing much."

"Oh, well, after I check the dictionary, maybe we can talk about what I should say to Ackerman tomorrow."

"I don't know if I'm in the mood for talking."

"Well, maybe there's a board game we can play or something."

She looked at him. He wasn't getting it. "You've led a sheltered life, haven't you, Mr. Aldridge?"

He paused, glancing into the bedroom. Then he noticed what Lisa was wearing. One sexy outfit. Tight low-rider jeans with a black sequined rock-concert T-shirt. "Lisa, my . . . hard drive hasn't run in a very long time."

She cleared her throat, reddening slightly. "Neither has mine. And just so there are no misunderstandings, I'm not just looking for . . . a quick reboot."

"You think that's what I want?"

"I wouldn't be here embarrassing myself if I thought that."

"You're not embarrassing anybody. You want me to see if I can get some . . . 'material' off of Phil's machine?"

She laughed hard. "You don't need that, do you?"

He gently touched her hand. "Come on." They entered the bedroom and closed the door.

AT SIX thirty the next morning, the others were seated around the living room with bowls of cereal when Jason and Lisa entered. It took one look. Everyone knew they were a couple now. "Good morning," the pair said. "Good morning," the others replied with small smiles on their faces. No one bothered asking how they'd slept.

"It's still not out there," Darryl announced for what felt like the hundredth time.

Jason shook his head. "I've got to take the boat to meet Ackerman anyway."

"You won't miss a thing."

"LOOK AT this damn thing."

Jason shook his head, watching Ackerman's two-hundred-foot behemoth motor up the coast. With shiny white fiberglass, dark tinted glass, and an arsenal of sophisticated antennas on the third deck, the yacht was the size of a small cruise ship. Jason had arrived early at the desolate docks in Eureka and found nothing else here, just a couple dozen seagulls and a lot of rickety wood.

Sporting a silk Hawaiian shirt with little palm trees all over it, Ackerman looked happy to see him, guiding the master yacht closer from a three-story-high flybridge.

"Ahoy, Jason!"

"Ahoy, Harry!"

Ackerman trotted two floors down to the main deck. "Take the line, will you!"

Jason caught a thick braided rope, tied it up, then hopped aboard. On a vast teak deck, he couldn't help but look around. A Jacuzzi whirlpool big enough for twelve caught his eye, gurgling quietly near a huge oak table and an electric barbecue the length of a car.

"Want a tour?"

Jason shook Ackerman's hand. Rich men's toys didn't really interest him. "Can we go over our game plan first?"

Ackerman's eyes suddenly looked particularly icy. "You may not want to do it after that."

"What do you mean?"

A glint of sun caught his eyes, but they didn't blink. "You're fired, Jason. The whole group of you. I'm terminating your contracts, effective immediately."

Jason was speechless. "What are you talking about?"

Ackerman shrugged. From a familiar laptop case slung over his shoulder, he removed a large, unsealed manila envelope. "Your termination letters. Written by my attorney. I assure you everything's in order, but take a look if you have any questions."

Jason stared at the envelope. This was actually happening. "What are you doing?"

Ackerman just looked at him.

"Harry, we're in the middle of real scientific discovery here. Why on earth would you cut that off at the knees?"

"Flying monsters that kill joggers, Jason? That's what you call 'real scientific discovery'? I thought you had more sense than that. Phil Martino has more sense than that."

"We agreed we'd follow the trail and see where it led. You gave us your word."

"I changed my mind."

Jason felt like punching something. "Why?"

"Ultimately, it comes down to dollars and cents."

"But . . . you said you worked out your financial problems."

"I did. Thanks to you."

"What do you mean?"

"I mean I had an unused financial asset I needed to harvest."

Jason paused. *Harvest.* The only person who used that word other than a potato farmer was a businessman. *Harvest,* the polite word for profit.

"What 'financial asset'?"

"Your new species, of course. Turns out it has tremendous value."

"What are you talking about? How—"

"DVDs, Jason. Among other revenue streams. But I've been working on a DVD deal specifically for months. Turns out they're a tremendous business, and not just for the movie studios. Do you realize that the *National Geographic* DVD on volcanoes sold twenty million copies at nineteen ninety-five per? That's four hundred million bucks in revenues, with extremely high margins."

Jason felt sick. "You're saying . . . You're *selling* the species?"

"Effectively. A well-promoted DVD on this animal could easily move thirty million copies. There's also going to be a book deal, a speaking tour, and a TV special with commentary from some Hollywood actor who likes nature. It all starts after I publicly announce the findings to the Species Council."

"What findings? You don't have any findings. And . . . how do you even know about the Species Council?"

"I have all the findings I need." Ackerman looked up as a feather flew onto his shoulder. He brushed it off casually, reminding himself to buy tickets for next month's cancer benefit at the Metropolitan Museum in New York, something to do with newborns infected with HIV. "And all you need to know is that I know all about the Species Council, too."

Jason eyed the gurgling Jacuzzi. He'd never so much as mentioned the twelve-person ruling body in Washington, D.C., to Ackerman. That had been an oversight on his part, but how would Ackerman know about something like that otherwise? And even if he did, the council's requirements for new species determinations were stringent, to say the least. They demanded detailed documentation from multiple accredited scientists and a host of other supporting documents that Ackerman couldn't possibly have. "You can't have any findings."

Ackerman had been looking at a seagull. "And why is that? Because you refused to share your notes with me."

Jason paused. "I told you I wasn't comfortable doing that, and you *said* you were fine with it."

"I wasn't. It doesn't matter now. This is my discovery: I financed it, I researched it, I own it. And if you need to confirm any of that"—he held out a twenty-page stapled contract—"just read the addendum you all signed."

Jason just looked at the papers, not touching them.

Ackerman released them along with the earlier proffered envelope, and Jason watched as they hit the deck, the pages blowing slightly in the breeze. "You don't have a body, either."

"Are you sure?"

A pause. "You have a body? How?"

"You left one behind in your friend's freezer. I took the liberty."

Jason's eyes shifted. "But that's not enough. That's not nearly enough."

"Combined with everything else it is: the expert analyses from the brain maven and all the others, team notes, the pictures . . . I have everything I need."

"How can you possibly have all that?"

Ackerman didn't answer. He just stood calmly on the massive deck. Jason saw he wasn't bluffing. Somehow, he actually had everything he said he did.

Ackerman checked the Roman numerals on his wrist. "It will be satisfying to finally be recognized by the business community for my accomplishments."

"*The business community?* Will the business community even care, Harry? I mean, about you? Don't they pretty much see you as an Internet joke who got lucky?"

The cold eyes blinked. "We'll see. Take me to court if you like. Your employment is terminated. Take your letters, take your addendum. And get off my boat."

A dismissal on top of everything else. Something snapped in Jason then. He stepped toward Ackerman, his face literally an inch from the man's nose. "Now you're being *rude?*"

Ackerman didn't move. Jason suddenly looked frightening, his face a combination of unadulterated fury and calculating composure. "Don't do anything stupid."

Jason grabbed his hand. "Come with us."

Ackerman tried to pull his hand back—but couldn't.

"Learn to fire a rifle, come out in the forest. See for yourself what's out there."

Ackerman tugged his hand but couldn't pull away. "Go to hell."

Jason squeezed very tight. "You're a coward."

"I'm a multimillionaire."

Jason continued to squeeze. "Can't buy pride as easily as a yacht, can you?"

"Save the nobility speeches; they bore me."

Jason squeezed the hand tighter still. "You should pay attention to the nobility speeches."

Ackerman squirmed in pain. "You're hurting my hand."

Jason's eyes bored into him. "You're hurting my feelings." He released the hand.

"You'll be sorry you did that."

Jason went to him menacingly. "No, I won't."

As Ackerman cowered, Jason noticed his laptop. Did his computer have something to do with this? Then he climbed off the massive boat and boarded the *Expedition*. He had to tell the others right away. As the boat pulled out, he looked up at the sky.

Off in the distance, he thought he saw a tiny puff of white. Is that a cloud? If the clouds were rolling in, perhaps the fog wasn't far behind. As he left the dock, he eyed the distant puff once more. He wasn't sure, but he thought it had already moved closer.

THE BLACK eyes didn't move. They were watching the cloud too.

The creature had been watching the cloud for more than an hour, since it first appeared on the horizon. At the mouth of the cave, the winged body was sprawled out on the rock, the back half shaded, the front half exposed in direct sunlight. The animal was uncomfortable with the heat on its thick skin, but it was too preoccupied with the cloud to move. The eyes refocused. The distant spot of white was moving closer.

CHAPTER 68

"LISA." JASON looked around. "Do you know where Darryl and Monique are?"

Jason, Lisa, and Phil were on the edge of the parking lot, submerged in the redwoods' late-day shadows.

"They went to check the forest again. The clouds started coming in, so Darryl said they might be a while. I tried them on the walkie-talkie earlier, but they must be out of range."

Jason nodded. "Has Craig's equipment produced any readings?"

"Not one." She looked around. "Where is Craig anyway?"

"In the cabin, checking on something for me."

She pointed. "Well, here he comes."

"Excuse me. . . ." Jason walked toward Craig, out of earshot from Lisa and Phil. Jason had told Summers alone about Ackerman's betrayal, then asked him to check into something. "You find anything?"

Craig nodded sadly. "I sure did."

"How's it look?"

"Lousy, Jason. It looks lousy."

Jason looked crushed by this. "Really?"

"The evidence is glaring. I'm sorry."

Jason exhaled, his eyes hardening. "All right, let's do this inside. I'll meet you in there."

Craig walked away and Jason returned to Lisa and Phil.

"What's up?" Lisa said, immediately suspicious.

"Harry Ackerman fired me. Fired all of us. He's taking our data and presenting it to the Species Council as his own. Apparently, his businesses need a great deal of capital fast, and he's found a way to profit from our work very handsomely."

"Very bad." Lisa was dumbfounded. "I don't believe it."

Jason nodded, noticing Phil didn't look particularly upset. Nor surprised. Jason's face turned deathly cold. "Let's go inside. I want to discuss this further."

In the living room, the three sat silently when Craig entered—carrying Phil's open laptop.

"Hey, what the hell are you doing with that, Craig?"

Craig ignored Phil Martino, passing the two monitors on the hearth then placed the laptop in front of Jason.

"I *said,* what are you doing with my machine?"

Craig pivoted. "Checking up on you."

Jason turned like a hawk. "You got a problem with that, Phil?"

The look on Jason's face was downright frightening. Phil Martino didn't move, didn't breathe. "Of course not."

Jason faced Lisa. "Before Ackerman could steal our work, he had to get it somehow. So what do we have here, Craig?"

"E-mails. More than five hundred back and forth over the past few months."

Lisa's eyes narrowed. "E-mails between? . . ."

Craig turned. "Phil and Harry Ackerman. Phil's been sending him every stitch of information we have. See, Jason? See these attachments? That's your outline to the Species Council. Draft one, draft two . . . draft eleven. And remember how he volunteered to type all of our notes? . . . There's mine on GDV-4, Monique's on migration, Lisa's on the plankton . . . There are all his pictures . . . Transcripts of our conversations . . . Oh, and these four . . . That's Lisa's e-mail from the Okezie Center . . . Mike Cohen's write-up on the teeth . . . there's York's on GDV-4 . . . and last but not least, Bandar Vishakeratne's on the brain."

"Jesus." Lisa was flabbergasted.

Craig nodded. "Ackerman wasn't kidding. He has *everything*."

Devastated, Jason turned. "My God, Phil, why? Why did you do it?"

Phil's eyes shifted slightly, and he diddled his thumbs together. He said nothing.

"Let me show you why." Craig scrolled down. "See this e-mail he sent to Ackerman with the subject 'salary increase'?"

Jason leaned forward. "Oh my God."

"Ackerman doubled his salary in exchange for his services."

Jason shook his head. "And to think I had problems trusting people." He abruptly turned to Craig and Lisa, like he wondered if they'd been lying to him, too. Was Phil smart enough to do all this by himself?

Reading his mind, Craig gave him a filthy look. "Jesus, Jason, Phil did this by himself."

"Of course he did." Jason was suddenly embarrassed.

Craig just took a deep breath and continued. "Anyway, here's the real kicker. The son of a bitch wanted to be Ackerman's only listed researcher on his report to the Species Council. But then Ackerman refused. Said that since all of us were physically with Phil the entire time, it might allow us to establish that we actually did the work. But you thought of a way around that, didn't you, Phil?"

Phil looked even more nervous. "What are you talking about?"

"You figured if somehow something happened to all of us, you could get that title after all. Without any . . . encumbrances."

"Wait a second." Jason gave Craig a look. "I don't believe that."

Lisa shook her head. "Neither do I. That's ridiculous, Craig."

"You sure? Because I went over some of the 'accidents' we've had lately, and you know what I realized? Phil was involved in every single one of them. Remember when you almost drowned, Jason?"

"Phil had nothing to do with that. He wasn't even in the water with us."

"*He was alone on the boat with your scuba gear.* I personally checked that tank half an hour before we went down. It was filled. Then all of a sudden when you're at a depth of a hundred and eighty feet and it's empty? He almost shot me during rifle practice. And then there was that convenient little . . . miscommunication with Lisa and Monique. No way in hell was *every one of those* a goddamn accident. It stinks, all of it."

Jason turned to Phil. They all did.

Phil looked back at them incredulously. "You gotta be kidding me. Jason, you don't actually believe all that, do you?"

Jason just looked at him, horrified. He couldn't respond.

"Lisa? I'll admit, maybe I got confused, but do you think I'd *intentionally* try to hurt you and Monique?"

Lisa turned. "You don't have any evidence he did this, do you, Craig?"

Phil nodded with angry vigor. "No, he doesn't. Nothing even close to evidence."

"This isn't a goddamn trial, Lisa. He did it; we all know he did it."

"No, *we all* don't. He's a scumbag, Craig, I don't deny that, but a murderer?"

Craig suddenly looked exhausted. "What's it matter anyway? Ackerman's got every stitch of our work, and he's a goddamn lawyer. We're done."

"Maybe we can call our own lawyer." Lisa swallowed. "Especially for Monique and Darryl's sake."

Summers paused. Monique and Darryl. They didn't know about any of this, but *both of their salaries had just disappeared*. What would that do to their family planning? "We *should* call a lawyer. . . ." Craig picked up the phone, but there was no dial tone and he suddenly lost it. "Son of a bitch!" He whipped it against the wall, smashing it to bits. Then he exhaled, calming down. "Lisa, can I borrow your walkie-talkie to call them? I promise not to smash it."

She handed it to him warily.

He pressed the button. "Monique, Darryl. You guys out there? Monique, Darryl, come in."

Monique's voice crackled back immediately. "Hello—can—hear—" It cut out.

Craig pressed the button again. "Monique, you hear me? Monique?"

There was no response.

"Monique? Hello? Can you hear me?"

There was nothing.

"They must be out of range." Craig turned to Jason. "I wonder what they're up to out there."

Jason looked out the window. It was much cloudier now. "Me too."

MONIQUE CLIPPED the walkie-talkie to her belt. "We must be out of range."

Darryl Hollis didn't respond. He just studied the forest, his eyes slowly moving.

The late-afternoon light was dull and faded now, the air cool, almost cold. Little drops of dew were everywhere—on the bark of the redwoods, the leaves of ferns, the dirt—even on Darryl's knuckles. They'd been here for hours.

He watched a squirrel. A moment ago, the rodent had been scampering everywhere looking for food. Now it was frozen, perched on its hind legs and staring into the distance. It looked frightened.

Darryl looked up. Just below the canopy of treetops a very thin, wispy mist appeared. The fog was rolling in.

Darryl turned to his wife and suddenly looked concerned, even frightened. "We gotta be careful. As in 'get scared' careful."

She looked him dead in the eye. "I understand, Darryl."

He kissed her full on the lips.

They didn't say another word. They walked back quickly.

CHAPTER 69

"JASON?"

Alone in his bedroom, Jason turned around. Lisa was at the door. "Hey. Are Darryl and Monique back yet?"

She walked in. "No."

"What's Craig up to?"

"Checking the computer. I guess that co-location switch is in and out, so the server might be back up again." She stared at him, not lovingly. "Craig was right, wasn't he?"

"About what?"

"You thought he helped Phil. You thought *I* helped Phil."

"Lisa, don't be ridicu—"

"I saw it in your face!" She was suddenly teary. "You thought I helped that pig deliberately deceive all of us."

He exhaled. "For just a second, maybe I did." He gently touched her face. "I'm sorry. I didn't mean to doubt you. I know you had nothing to do with it. Not a thing."

"Then why'd you think I did?"

"Lisa, what Phil did . . . I guess it just stirred up all those old insecurities again." He looked her dead in the eye. "Not being able to trust you is my worst nightmare."

She smiled through teary eyes. "Yeah?"

"Yeah."

She hugged him. "Don't do it again."

"Deal." The hug broke. "Did I tell you today's my birthday?"

"No, you didn't."

"Honestly, with everything that's been going on, I forgot about it." He grimaced. "It's been such a great birthday already."

"The day's not over, Jason."

He smiled weakly. "I'm sure something great's on the horizon." He shrugged. "I've never been a huge fan of birthdays anyway."

"Speak for yourself, mister." She smiled wide and smacked him a huge kiss. "Happy birthday!"

He smiled himself—inside more than out. It had been years since someone had wished him a happy birthday and actually meant it. "Thank you, Lisa."

"I would have baked a cake if I'd known."

"I'm sure Darryl and Craig have one in the oven already."

She chuckled.

Then her smile faded, and she went to the window. "Are we still going to get out there and find that thing?"

"I don't know if Darryl and—"

"If it's up to *you*, do we still go out there and find it?"

"Are you OK if we do that?"

"I don't know exactly." She looked outside. "But what Monique said is exactly right: this animal is literally history in the making. How can we not try to find something like that?"

"I had no idea you felt that way. I just assumed—"

"I'm in this for the long haul, Jason."

He held her look. "So am I."

"Yeah?"

"Yeah."

"If that's the case, then you've *got to* start trusting everybody around here. Especially Darryl."

"I do trus—"

"I mean for real, Jason. The stage we're heading into . . . this is going to get dangerous."

"Don't you think I know that?"

She eyed the floor. "I don't want you to take this the wrong way."

"Take what the wrong way?"

"You're not qualified to lead us anymore. *You* are a biologist, too, and what we're about to get into . . . It isn't your area. You're going to have to trust these people. I mean with your life. With our lives. But only if you can. Because if you can't—I mean if you can't really, truly trust them, their judgment, let them make the decisions, not you, then we should walk away from this right now. After everything Phil did, I wouldn't blame you."

"Are you saying you don't think I can trust them? Like I'm literally not capable of it?"

She held his gaze. "You tell me."

"Server connected."

The message had first appeared a few minutes ago, and Craig had been surfing the Internet since.

Ding. The computer toned, indicating an incoming e-mail.

Ding. Another e-mail.

Ding. Another.

Ding. One more.

Craig glanced at the machine. "What's going on here?"

He minimized his Web site and pulled up the e-mail program. *Ding . . . Ding . . . Ding . . . Ding . . . Ding . . . Ding . . .* E-mails were rushing into the in-box, ten, twenty, one hundred . . . and they kept coming, fast. . . . Every one of them was from Harry Ackerman. "What the hell is this?"

Jason entered the living room with Lisa. "What's going on?"

"Looks like Ackerman's machine must have a virus. . . ." The e-mails were rushing in even faster now, hundreds, even thousands of them. "Maybe a really bad one."

Jason walked over and looked down. "Look at the subject on all of them, Craig."

Summers leaned in. Over and over the same e-mail rushed into the in-box.

HAVE VIRUS, REWRITABLE CDS CORRUPTED.
RESEND ALL DATA!!

HAVE VIRUS, REWRITABLE CDS CORRUPTED.
RESEND ALL DATA!!
HAVE VIRUS, REWRITABLE CDS CORRUPTED.
RESEND ALL DATA!!
HAVE VIRUS, REWRITABLE CDS CORRUPTED.
RESEND ALL DATA!!
HAVE VIRUS, REWRITABLE CDS CORRUPTED.
RESEND ALL DATA!!
HAVE VIRUS, REWRITABLE CDS CORRUPTED.
RESEND ALL DATA!!
HAVE VIRUS, REWRITABLE CDS CORRUPTED.
RESEND ALL DATA!!

"Jesus," Craig said. Jason simply continued to stare. "Corruped CDs? "That actually happens?"

Summers nodded. "It's happened to me. More than once. Plus, there are these new sleeper viruses that hide on a computer's hard drive. The user doesn't even know they're there, but every time he saves data to a CD, the virus is passed on so the CD's corrupted the next time he uses it. My God . . . Do you realize . . . ? Ackerman could have lost *everything*. . . ." Craig spun around. "Phil, is your cell phone on?"

"I don't know, uh . . ."

"Can I see it? Now?"

Phil fumbled through his pockets and handed it over.

Jason's eyes narrowed. "What are you doing, Craig?"

Summers turned on the phone and put it on the table. "If Ackerman really did lose all of his data, he'd be panicking right now, doing anything to get in touch with Phil and—"

The phone started ringing.

Jason peered at the ID. "Son of a bitch . . . It's him."

They all watched the phone. It rang and rang. After a moment, it stopped. Then immediately started again.

Craig turned. "He's got nothing, Jason. I can smell it; he doesn't have a damn thing."

"He's got a body."

"A body you cut the brain out of."

A pause. "That's true. And I really had to slice and dice it. And then it was frozen for a long time. In that condition . . . that body wouldn't be enough for the Species Council. Not nearly enough." Jason glanced at the in-box, still dinging. "My God. You're right. He doesn't have anything."

Craig suddenly started. "Did you hear something?"

"No, nothing . . ."

They all spun around. . . .

Darryl and Monique were standing there. Somehow they'd snuck in without anyone hearing. It was odd, but Jason thought they somehow looked . . . different, both wearing all-khaki outfits, with long-sleeved shirts that had big orange patches on the right shoulders. They looked like real hunters on a safari, something out of a magazine. But there was something else different about them, Jason noticed. It was their faces. Tense yet calm. Scared yet confident. Jason had never seen such faces before in his life. "What's up, Darryl?"

"It's out there."

CHAPTER 70

"**F**IRED? *EFFECTIVE immediately?*" Darryl sank into a couch and his shoulders slumped.

"What are you doing, Darryl?" Jason hadn't expected this reaction.

"So we're not getting paid anymore?"

"Well . . . no."

"I'm out."

"What? You can't be *out*. You're the only experienced hunter here. Plus"—Jason glanced at Lisa—"*you're* going to be in charge from now on. Not me. Everything's going to be your call."

"Well, *my call* is I'm not hunting anything."

"Why are y—"

"You think I'm gonna *risk my life*—risk my *wife's life*—and do it for free?"

"So the money made you do it? Is that how it is, Darryl?"

"That's exactly how it is. Sorry to disappoint you, Jason, but babies cost money. Food costs money. Clothes, cribs, strained peas, new homes . . . it all costs lots and lots of money!"

Jason started pacing. "Let's talk about money, then. Do you realize that if what we think is out there *actually is*, we'll get more money than God."

"Sure we will."

"Darryl, *we will*. Book deals, paid appearances, the DVD series . . . Everything Ackerman planned to do and more. If money's your objective, you will have it."

Darryl shook his head morosely. He didn't buy it.

"He's right, Darryl."

Darryl Hollis slowly turned to his wife. "Seriously?"

"I never thought about it but the financial rewards of something like this . . . they'll be gargantuan. The six of us right here in this room could be millionaires overnight."

"But don't do this for the money." Jason looked around the room. "Not one of us should do it for that."

Darryl shook his head cynically. "Then why the hell should we do it? To feel good about ourselves?"

"To feel great about ourselves, Darryl. Like Monique said, we are on the verge of discovering a new order here. Something that's never existed in the known history of this planet. The natural selection process literally coming to life in front of our eyes. Forget money, forget Ackerman, forget all the sacrifices we've made. This is something that could put our names in the history books."

"Or get us killed," Lisa said soberly.

Darryl didn't seem to hear that. He turned to his wife proudly. "I always wanted to be in the history books."

Monique smiled, seeing her husband like this. "Me too, Darryl. Me too."

"Are you in?" Jason asked.

The couple shared a look. Yes, they were in. But then Darryl turned to Craig. "But only if you are, brother. If not . . ." He eyed his wife.

"We walk away right now," Monique finished.

Craig nodded at that, quietly touched. "I'm in."

Lisa nodded. "Me too."

"Me too, guys."

They all turned to Phil Martino.

"If you'll have me."

Craig shook his head. "Absolutely not."

"We should let him come."

Craig turned to Jason. "*What?* You're actually gonna stick up for this scumbag after everything he did?"

"No, Craig. I'll never stick up for him again." This seemed to wound Phil, and Jason continued, calmly venomous. "I'm thinking about the alternatives, like what he'd do if he *didn't* come with us . . . where he'd go, who he might find a way to talk to. This way, we can keep an eye on him."

The room was silent. This made sense. No one trusted Phil Martino anymore.

Craig still had concerns. "He could literally shoot someone in the back."

Jason looked Phil in the eye. "If he tries, I swear to God, I'll shoot him first."

"You will, huh?" Darryl walked over to the window. "If we do this, am I really in charge, Jason? Or was that just BS?"

Jason glanced at Lisa. "No; you're really in charge."

"Then that's not how we're gonna do it. Nobody's gonna shoot anybody in the back. This thing out there is *dangerous*, I'm talking kill-us-in-a-heartbeat dangerous, and we're gonna have to rely on each other—I mean like brothers—to hunt it. So I don't even want jokes about shooting each other. You got it, Jason?"

"I got it. Are you saying we're taking him, then?"

Darryl turned to Phil. "You pull anything, anything at all, I swear to God I'll take care of you myself."

Phil swallowed nervously. This had come from someone the size of a professional athlete who was an expert with weapons. He turned. "Jason, I'll do my best to help. I promise."

Jason couldn't even look at Phil Martino anymore.

Darryl nodded. "You're in, Phil. We're all in. When we get out there, we're literally gonna have to watch one another's backs. Jason, no second-guessing me. None. That could get somebody killed. You do that just one time, I swear to God I am out."

"Understood."

Craig noticed the lifeless monitors on the hearth. "Hoss, are you really sure this thing's out there? Because this equipment's been—"

"Craig." Darryl calmly cut him off, the same look in his eye he'd had in the forest with Monique earlier.

"Yeah."

"It's time to get scared, brother."

"Yeah?"

"Yeah."

Craig slowly stood. And right away, Jason noticed a change in him. His normally sloppy posture was replaced by a ramrod spine, his sometimes glazed eyes suddenly as intense as Jason had ever seen them. Craig Summers even seemed taller. What the hell was "get scared"?

"What's 'get scared'?" Lisa asked.

Darryl turned. "An expression from our army days. What our platoon said to each other so nobody got sloppy, did something to get killed. Just stupid army stuff, Soccer Mom."

Craig hadn't reacted like it was "stupid army stuff." Lisa watched as he walked over to Darryl and gave him a quick little hug. "Thanks, man. Be safe. You too, Monique."

The three smacked one another on the back, and Jason just watched. He didn't know if he'd ever appreciate it at the same level, but this was what it was to rely on someone. *It's out there.*

Craig abruptly turned to a monitor. "Did you see that?" He touched the screen and . . . A dot moved fantastically fast across a pair of green sweeps then disappeared.

Jason leaned down. "Where is that exactly?"

Craig glanced at a map. "The edge of the forest. Whatever it is, it's moving toward us."

Darryl didn't care. "Let's get the stuff. . . ."

Monique and Craig nodded, and the triumvirate bustled into the hallway, grabbed multiple black duffels, then went to the porch. Craig removed four walkie-talkies and shoved them toward Jason, Lisa, Phil, and Monique. "Just in case we get split up. There are only four, so Darryl and I will have to yell. Turn them on and test them."

As Jason took his, he noticed Darryl, facing the redwoods, his index finger tapping rapidly against his thigh. Jason stared at the finger. *It's out there.*

The tapping finger froze and Darryl, faced all of them. "We really gonna do this?"

There were nods all around.

Darryl liked what he saw. Everyone had on their game faces, not cocky clichéd versions, but real ones, scared and tense. "All right. Let's saddle up."

As Jason grabbed his rifle, Lisa leaned into him and whispered, "I told you the day wasn't over. Happy birthday, Jason."

He smiled a small smile. Happy birthday indeed.

CHAPTER 71

"**Y**OU'RE ACTUALLY hunting with that?"

Despite Darryl Hollis's proficiency with a bow and arrow, Jason couldn't believe he actually hunted with them. Shooting at skeet was one thing, but hunting, especially for what they thought was out there . . .

Suddenly an arrow rocketed through the air violently. Before Jason knew what had happened, it rushed past his nose and plunged into a steel trash drum behind him. He didn't have time to react, much less be frightened. He turned to the drum.

"Jesus." The arrow hadn't just pierced the steel, it had ripped a tearing hole through its front *and* back sides, then settled on the dirt.

Darryl gave him a look. "You think it will do, brother?"

Jason looked at the drum. "Yeah."

"Enough small talk. Let's get to it."

Everyone started moving. To blend in with the forest, they were all wearing the same all-khaki outfits—shirt, pants, and work boots. Like pros, Jason, Phil, and Lisa loaded and locked their rifles. Craig and Monique did the same.

Darryl's process was slightly more complicated. From a duffel filled with racks of standard twenty-eight-inch aluminum arrows, he removed four dozen projectiles. Rather than carry his arrows in a cumbersome holder, Darryl wore a specially designed, formfitting vest made of thin down. The garment's key feature was a rear pouch the size of a wastepaper basket, its bottom lined with nonadhesive clay that arrowheads could be jabbed into to prevent movement.

As Darryl finished loading up, Monique and Craig carefully checked the rookies' work, making sure safeties were on and that everything else looked right.

Then Monique smacked a magazine into her own weapon. "Ready, Darryl?"

Darryl Hollis didn't respond at first. He turned to the trees. He didn't know what they were looking for exactly. He refused to believe it was the new order until he saw it with his own two eyes. But whatever it was, he could feel it, he could feel it like a butterfly feels a gentle current of wind. Craig and Monique occasionally made fun of his Indian mysticism, but Darryl Hollis had never found it amusing. It was one of the few things he didn't have a sense of humor about. They could go to hell if they didn't believe in him. But that was just his ego talking, and he knew it. None of it mattered now. A very dangerous animal was lurking in the redwoods, an animal that had killed someone and would certainly try to kill him, too.

But Darryl Hollis had no plans on dying. He gave the looming trees a dirty, almost sneering, look. He hadn't been on a real hunt in years, but all the feelings were rushing back now. Wild animals were dangerous. The notion of "kill or be killed" was a joke for humans, but for animals it was a part of daily life. You had to remember that when you hunted them. But there were no doubts in Darryl's mind. As sure as the sun rose in the morning, whatever the unseen animal was, he was going to kill it. He turned to his wife, and their eyes locked. The look they shared was not one of love. It was a look that said, *Get your fucking game face on and be careful.* He eyed Lisa and Craig the same way. He gave special glares to Jason and Phil. No petty garbage, not an ounce. There were nods all around. Then Darryl turned back to the trees. "Yeah, Monique. We're ready."

No WIND at all. That was good. Darryl Hollis wouldn't have to worry about being upwind of whatever was out there. But it was bad, too.

Without wind, there'd be pure silence. The team would be easy to hear and would have to move especially quietly.

As the six of them walked into the woods, Jason noticed Monique and Craig, their eyes moving very slowly, as if they were studying every single pine needle, their heads continually turning—behind, left, right—their rifles always leading the way. Army training, he guessed.

After twenty minutes, Darryl felt a slight temperature drop. He looked up and saw that the fog had thickened. It had gotten quiet, too. No chirping birds. No trickling streams. Nothing. They were getting closer. He glanced behind him. The group's shape was all wrong. That had to change immediately. He halted.

"OK, we're gonna get into a hunting circle now. The idea's that between us, our vision covers three hundred and sixty degrees, so everybody's relying on everybody else. So, Jason, go stand over there and face out. Monique, you go there. Lisa, there. Craig and Phil, right there."

They quickly formed a circle.

"What's critical here is that whatever happens, everyone faces their assigned directions. Phil, you should be facing out."

Phil turned, and as he did, Darryl trotted into a shrub behind him. Then Darryl shook the plant wildly and screamed.

Phil spun around, his eyes on the shrub. It was surprisingly frightening.

Darryl walked out. "Now that's what we *don't* want happening. Remember, look in your assigned direction. Because you might think you see or hear or smell or just sense something, say, over there. . . ." He waved to his left. "But if what you *think* is over there is actually over *here* . . ." He waved to his right. "Wild animals, especially predators, move very fast, and if just one of us is looking the wrong way, it could strike, and kill all of us. Everybody follow?"

They nodded.

Darryl felt for the bow slung over his shoulder, then went to the front of the circle.

"Everybody's whose got 'em, turn on your walkie-talkies, low volume." He walked forward, scanning everywhere. "And keep your eyes open."

~~~~~

DEEPER IN the forest, the hunting circled moved slowly. Only Darryl had noticed it, but the air had continued to chill. And the fog above was thickening. Looking up, Jason saw it rolling into the treetops in delicate waves. It was far too thin to hide in, but perhaps that would change.

Fifteen minutes later the fog had thickened considerably. Again Jason looked up, and this time noticed the faint shape of an owl, silently gliding through it.

Forty minutes later the sky was gone. The treetops were gone. Anything above twenty stories was gone. The great redwood trunks stuck out of the mist like toothpicks in ice cream.

Anything could hide up there now, Jason thought. Then he heard something.

They all heard it. Straight ahead. Something near the ground, rushing through the shrubbery. Jason turned to Darryl, but the man simply walked forward, like he hadn't heard a thing.

There was a loud crashing sound.

Darryl glanced up calmly. "It's a deer."

Craig didn't believe that. The sound was rapidly moving toward them, and from his direction. He aimed his rifle at a mass of shrubs. The sound grew louder. He eased down on the trigger. The sound grew louder still. . . . A deer sprinted out then stopped, its big brown eyes staring right at Craig. He lowered his weapon.

Then the sounds started again—from something *behind* the deer.

Darryl didn't even bother looking this time. "It's a family."

Craig had his doubts, but then eight more deer sprinted past a grove of thick redwood trunks and disappeared.

They continued forward. And Jason looked up at the fog.

ABOVE THE treetops, the late-afternoon sun shone down on a squadron of birds, flying in perfect V-formation and heading toward a fog bank. Without hesitation, the birds flew right into the white mist and the sun disappeared. Enshrouded, the tiny fliers continued for several seconds when they felt the slightest of tremors in the air. Instantaneously, the V rose, and the tremor dissipated. They continued when they felt a second, slightly larger tremor. The squadron rose again, and again the tremor dissipated. Then they felt another tremor, only this time it wasn't a tremor. It was a gargantuan wave. Then a series of gargantuan waves, one crashing on top of the next. Something huge was flying right at them. The birds turned sharply, just as a massive pumping shape sped past below them. It was gone as quickly as it had appeared, and the birds flew on as if nothing had happened.

DARRYL HOLLIS hesitated. Then stopped. Breaking his own rules, he studied the forest behind him, scanning in every direction.

Watching him closely, Jason thought he looked a little miffed.

Then Darryl turned forward and continued walking.

LESS THAN a minute later, Darryl stopped again.

"Something's close . . . I think."

Monique and Craig shared a look. Does Darryl know what he's doing?

Darryl quickly walked forward, and immediately there was a rustling from the forest ahead of him. Like lightning, he removed an arrow, drew it back, then . . . put it back down.

"It's the deer coming back."

An entire family sprinted past and Darryl turned to where they'd come from. "Something scared 'em." It was on the ground, Darryl was sure of it. "Forget the circle. It's over here. . . ."

He trotted toward a huge mass of tightly packed rhododendrons.

Following, Jason glanced up at the fog. Weren't they looking for something in the air? Then, out of the corner of his eye, he saw the rhododendrons shaking, just fifteen feet away from them. His gaze leveled. Could the creature have landed on the ground?

Darryl walked closer. As they approached, the plants slowly stopped. They circled around them and—

Darryl saw it first.

A massive black bear, nearly ten feet tall, standing on its hind legs and unaware they were watching it.

It was just standing there in the middle of a clearing. Then it fell to its front paws and began storming around in circles, striking out at the air for no apparent reason.

Craig held his rifle tightly. "Look at the size of that thing."

Phil shook his head. "So all this time it was just a bear."

Jason nodded. He couldn't believe it. Nothing but a goddamn bear. "How do you like that?"

The bear jerked toward them. Jason had spoken much louder than he'd intended.

Darryl shook his head. "Not smart, Jason."

The bear looked right at them. Then charged.

Darryl didn't have a choice. In an instant, he removed an arrow and aimed it at the rapidly approaching fur-covered chest.

But he didn't shoot.

Craig turned to him anxiously. The bear was really moving fast. "What are you doing?"

Strange thoughts surged through Darryl's head. Something didn't smell right. "What's bothering you?" he whispered as the bear sprinted closer.

Craig's voice rose. "Darryl, what are you doing? *Shoot it.*"

"We're not looking for you, are we?"

The bear stormed closer still.

"Jesus Christ, Darryl, shoot it."

The bear ran hard, just ten feet away, five . . .

Suddenly it stopped dead in its tracks. It glanced at the six of them, then awkwardly turned and lumbered away. Darryl just watched it go. Ornery bears often played their intimidation games, but there was no need to kill them unnecessarily. Only this bear, Darryl could tell, wasn't trying to intimidate anyone. It was just . . . riled. He looked around.

"There's something else here. Get back in the circle."

The bear disappeared, and it was perfectly silent again.

They didn't move. Didn't make a sound.

Darryl studied the forest anew. His eyes passed over everything—redwoods, ferns, rhododendrons, some little white flowers . . . It was so quiet. But he could tell, something was here now, hiding. He gave no more commands. He simply stood where he was, watching and waiting.

Everyone's head slowly turned, left, right, behind, straight ahead.

No one except Jason was looking up. He'd been looking up at the fog for some time and his mouth was now slightly open.

Craig suddenly jerked toward the soil. *"Look at that."*

Everyone turned to it. It was a marking, about an inch deep. Shaped like a massive bird.

Then Darryl noticed Jason. He was still looking up and he had an awfully strange look on his face.

Darryl looked up too. "Jesus bloody Christ."

Then Lisa looked up. Then Craig. Then Monique. Then Phil. No one spoke another word.

Spellbound, they simply stared at something so incredible it had to be a dream. But it wasn't a dream. It was a new reality.

PART IV

CHAPTER 72

THERE IT is, Jason thought; my God, there it is. Not a dream. Not a simulated computer image. A living, breathing, flying animal. A new order of predator. He had known what to expect, of course, roughly what it would look like. But now that he was actually seeing it, it was even more incredible than what he'd imagined.

Lisa and Craig both had small smiles on their faces. The goddamn thing was more fantastic than anything they'd ever seen.

Phil was dumbfounded. He knew as well as anyone that the animal existed, but only theoretically. To actually see it, living, breathing, flying . . . *It was just so real.* Better than a video game, better than a movie.

Darryl Hollis, strangely, felt light-headed, even numb—like he sometimes did after a particularly severe drinking binge with Craig Summers. He had also known what to expect, but now . . . his carefully constructed concept of what it was to hunt had just been walloped by a sledgehammer.

Monique was the only one who was nervous. The goddamn thing was a living nightmare. She had the eerie feeling that it was watching them, studying them, even. She held on to her rifle tightly.

Six pairs of human eyes continued to watch it.

The predator glided silently below the ceiling of fog. Twenty stories high, it dodged in and out of the massive staffs of branchless wood.

As they looked up at it their most prominent view was of its undulating white underbelly. But then the animal veered around a tree and gave an unobstructed view of its pitch-black topside. It was beautiful, even elegant, its torso, wings, and horned head all melding into a single, seamless form. But beauty and elegance aside, there was no hiding that it was a phenomenally dangerous predator.

My God, look at that thing, Darryl thought.

Suddenly and silently, it veered up and disappeared into the thick white fog.

Rapt, the six didn't move. They simply stared at the place where it had just been, waiting for it to return.

And then it did return, flying straight down, its mouth wide open.

Monique braced herself, but the animal didn't attack. Before they could even become alarmed, it veered up and away, gliding just below the ceiling of mist.

"Did you see that mouth?" Craig asked quietly.

It had been wider than two of him. And its teeth . . . He'd only seen them for a moment, but he could have sworn they were as wide as his forearms and numbered in the hundreds, in more rows than he could count.

Darryl Hollis had noticed the teeth too. Darryl Hollis had noticed everything about the animal. But of all its features, one had made the greatest impression by far.

The eyes.

They were goddamn frightening eyes. Not just because they were bigger than baseballs, pupil-less, and in the strangely unnerving color of jet black. But because of what was *behind them*. They were cold, calculating, and, above all, intelligent. An awfully smart animal lurked behind those eyes. Darryl knew its brain weighed six pounds, but now, actually seeing the creature, he would have believed its brain weighed twenty-five pounds. Look at those goddamn eyes.

Then Darry slowly positioned an arrow on his bow and began to point it up.

Out of the corner of his eye, Jason watched him, neither doing nor saying anything, just watching with a combination of horror and fascination—horror at the fact that Darryl's nearly instantaneous reaction upon seeing the phenomenally evolved new order of predator was to kill it—and fascination as to whether or not he'd succeed.

Jason looked up at the animal, wondering if it was as smart as Bandar Vishakeratne had said. *It will know more about you than you do about it.* Was the creature actually capable of recognizing that the bow and arrow were weapons? Or was it totally oblivious—and moments from being killed?

The black orbs watched Darryl closely, focused on his slowly rising arrow. Then they shifted ever so slightly, to the arrow*head.* Then back to Darryl again.

As he continued, Darryl Hollis watched the eyes watch him and felt queasy. Never before had an animal watched him so closely. He actually sensed it wasn't just "watching" him at all but studying him, even trying to understand what he was doing. But it hadn't flown away. It was exposed, and if it continued to glide as it had been, he'd soon have a shot—and an easy one at that. Then the giant eyes shifted, focusing on Jason. That's right, Darryl thought, look at him.

Darryl continued to raise the arrow into position. I got it, he thought, his weapon almost vertical now, a millisecond from firing.

The animal banked, darting behind a grove of redwood staffs.

"Wow," Jason said quietly. That was no accident. The creature had not only figured out what a bow and arrow were, it had *applied the knowledge* and taken cover.

But it hadn't disappeared. Why? Why had it shown itself in the first place? Jason watched as the gliding form darted in and out of the columns of wood, an obstacle course in the air. Mesmerized, he realized the creature wasn't repeating the same flight pattern twice and he tried to guess where it would go next. Left or right? Down or up? It flew straight, gliding into a clearing beneath the fog.

Then he heard it. They all did. Very faintly, a low rumbling noise, like distant thunder.

Craig had never heard an animal make such a sound before. So deep, rolling over itself like an idling truck engine. "What the hell is that?"

Jason looked up at it. "I think it might be . . . a warning."

The sound grew slightly louder, then faded and stopped. The animal pumped its wings and disappeared into the fog.

The six didn't move. They stood perfectly still, staring at the white mist, waiting for it to return. But it didn't return. The trees, the ferns . . . the entire forest was silent. They stood and stood. There was nothing up there now, just fog. The predator was gone.

After ten minutes, Darryl lowered his weapon—cautiously. "I don't like this; something doesn't feel ri—"

And then it happened.

The creature swooped out of the mist and let out a shattering roar. The volume was phenomenal. Craig and Jason literally fell backward. Phil, Monique, and Lisa cowered. Darryl shivered slightly and covered his ears.

Then, like a switch, it stopped. The creature swooped back into the mist and didn't return. The six of them just looked at one another, stunned.

Craig turned to Jason. "A warning, huh?"

"Territoriality," Darryl said.

Jason turned. "Territoriality. My God, you're right."

The animal had just staked its claim.

CHAPTER 73

"How do we know there aren't more of those things out there?"

It was night, and they were seated in the cabin's living room.

"We don't know." Next to Lisa on a couch, Jason shrugged at Darryl. "And now that I think about it, I don't know if we'll ever *know*, not for sure anyway."

Monique turned to her husband. "I seriously doubt if there's more than one of them."

"Why?"

"Because if there were *even two* of those things out there, we'd have a lot more than a single dead jogger on our hands."

Darryl stood. "Well, that's good. Because just killing one isn't gonna be easy."

"Six of us versus one of it?" Craig nodded from the hearth. "I'll bet on us."

Darryl began pacing. "This thing can fly, for Christ's sake. It's gonna be hard as hell to kill."

"I don't think we should kill it at all."

Darryl stopped pacing. "You don't, huh?"

Jason shook his head. "No. At least not yet."

And that was more accurate. The predator had killed a human being, so it had to be killed itself. But as a scientist, Jason wanted to study it as well. He suddenly realized everyone in the room was staring at him like he was crazy. He stood. "Guys, don't you realize what that animal out there means? No one *in the history of mankind* has ever seen anything like it. We can't just go out there and kill it." He scanned the faces. "Can we?"

No one replied; they just sat awkwardly.

Jason focused on Lisa. "Do *you* think we should just go out there and kill it?"

"Honestly, Jason, I do. I understand the argument you're making. I think we all understand that argument. But given what's happened . . ." She paused, thinking it through. "It killed a human being, so *it has to die* too—no question."

"*No question?* I agree it has to die eventually but . . ."

"But what?" Darryl shrugged theatrically. "What do you want to do, Jason? Let it fly around out there? Set up some sort of . . . laboratory and turn Leonard State Park into your own personal 'wild kingdom'?"

Jason didn't answer. It was a good point. He'd agonized over it already. If they actually found one of the predators, how exactly would they study it?

He sat next to Lisa. "We can catch it."

"We can?" Darryl eyed him coldly. "How are *we* gonna do that?"

"We have tranquilizers and things, don't we?" Jason had used tranquilizers only four times. While he'd had problems on every occasion, he assumed someone like Darryl was far more experienced.

But Darryl just shook his head. "No, we don't have 'tranquilizers and things.' At least not on us. Maybe we can call for some, but . . ." He flipped open his cell. "Oh yeah, no phone service at the moment. So we'd have to go get them ourselves. What do ya think that thing would do while we're gone? Wait for us to come back? Or do ya think it might go exploring?"

Jason didn't answer. It was another good point.

"But for the sake of argument, say we can get tranquilizers. You've used them before, right? But you had problems? Well, lemme tell ya, that's because they're dicey. Not just for you. For everybody. Monique and I have used them a fair amount, and there's always this little problem of getting the dosage right."

Jason nodded. He knew this could be very difficult.

Darryl turned to his wife. "Remember Bill Crower, Monique?"

A sad nod. "Of course."

"Old friend of ours who used to do a lot of work in the Bering Sea, with polar bears, penguins, and all that. One day Bill and a colleague had to do some testing on a walrus. So they went into the Arctic Ocean and found one sleeping on an iceberg. Pretty big walrus, too, about five thousand pounds. Now, walruses are generally very heavy sleepers, so they snuck up on it, and it didn't even see them coming. They shot it up and the tranquilizers worked like a charm. Knocked it right out.

"But then it turned out the tranquilizers didn't last as long as they thought. Only they didn't find that out until they were on top of it. Bill took a tusk through the chest, and died right there on that iceberg. His colleague got a crushed spine. So I'm not trying to be dramatic here, but from personal anecdotes like that one, you could say that tranquilizers scare the hell out of me, Jason. In other words, I'm not comfortable using them. Period."

Jason nodded. "I get your point. We have to be careful, but there's still a way, right?"

"It's called trial and error. If you wanna play trial and error with that thing out there, go ahead, but I'm not getting within a million miles of that."

"There's an even bigger problem anyway." Craig turned to Jason. "Even if you could knock it out, what would you do with it when it woke up? You have any thoughts on that?"

Jason exhaled. He'd agonized over this scenario, too. Even if they could catch the creature, what would they do with it then? Put it in a cage? What cage? A cage didn't exist that could contain an animal like that. The notion of constructing one was laughable. It could take months, even years, and would have to be the size of a small city. Where would they keep the animal in the interim? Could they really "keep" an animal like that anywhere?

"It's got to die." Darryl eyed Jason with chilling coldness. "You *know* that, don't you?"

Jason let out a deep breath. "Yeah, I guess I do." So how are we going to study it, then? he thought.

Darryl read his mind. "If you're wondering how we're going to study it, there's only one way. To hunt it. Because while we're hunting it, I guarantee it's gonna be hunting us, too."

Jason eyed Lisa, Darryl nodded. "Like I said, you're in charge."

Darryl scanned the room. "Everybody else on board?"

They all nodded. Then Craig stood. "So what do we want to call this thing anyway?"

Darryl gave him a look. "What do you mean?"

"We discovered this species, Hoss. Now we get to name it. I tried coming up with a few myself but couldn't get anything good. Anyone have any ideas?"

There were shrugs. No one had even considered it.

Craig turned suspiciously to Jason. "Come on, you must have thought of something."

Jason smiled. "It's in the laptop if you want to take a look." The machine was sequestered under lock and key in Craig's room.

Craig exited, returned with the computer, then put it on the table. Jason pulled up the right document, then pushed the laptop away so the others could see. "What do you think? . . ."

Lisa was closest, so she read aloud the title page of Jason's report to the Species Council. "'Dissertation and Analysis, Previously Unknown New Species, Likely New Order, Predatory Cousin of Common *Mantis birostris* . . . Tentatively Named . . .'" She smiled. "Ooh, I like that, Jason. I like that a lot."

Darryl leaned over, trying to see the Latin. "What is it?"

"Demonray," Jason said. *"The Clarita Demonray."*

"Ooh, that is good."

Craig smiled devilishly. "Perfect."

"Yeah, great name." Jason went to the window. "Now we just have to go out there and kill it." Killing had never been Jason's way, of course, but if the rule of the universe was that the fit survived, then so be it. The very first Demonray to reach the land had killed a human being, and now it, too, had to die. Spotting stars through the treetops, Jason realized the fog had disappeared. As his soul darkened a shade, he wondered when it would return. Then he noticed Craig opening a park map suddenly, as if he'd just been struck by a brilliant idea. "What are you doing, Craig?"

Summers barely glanced at him. "I just figured out how we're going to find this thing."

CHAPTER 74

I T WAS a cold night, forty-five degrees, with a glowing half-moon lighting up the forest. A large black bear lumbering on all fours didn't notice the white orb, but the moon was watching it. The moon was watching everything. Nothing could escape its gaze. Floating silently in the blackened skies, neither judging nor sympathizing, neither protecting nor threatening, it simply watched—coldly and without emotion.

THE PREDATOR glided just above the treetops. Already locked onto the bear's signal, it found a hole in the canopy, then dove through it. It leveled off just above the dark soil then, carried by momentum, hurtled forward, the bear's heartbeat and its scent rapidly closing.

THE BEAR halted. It sensed something. It turned left, right, and behind, but all it saw were redwoods, ferns, and broken strands of moonlight. But still, it knew something was near. It reared back on its hind legs, lifting its entire big-bellied body into the air. Nearly ten feet high, it scanned anew, but even from here, saw nothing.

Still, the forest was whispering to the animal. Something was coming.

THE RUSTLING of pine needles, a trickling stream, the creaking trees. The predator ignored every sound except one: the bear's beating heart.

Rushing past redwoods and speckled shafts of moonlight, it saw the fur-covered mammal from several hundred feet. The bear was just standing there.

THE BEAR spotted it zooming closer and immediately roared, producing a sound that normally scared away anything and everything.

The creature flew straight for it. And began making its own sound. A series of low deep rumbles.

Barely hearing them, the bear roared again, louder, convinced its intimidation was working.

The creature's rumbles erupted into a shattering roar so loud that it actually hurt the bear's eardrums.

Confused, the bear instinctively swung its arms. Then, as if struck by a freight train, its nine-hundred-pound frame was suddenly flying backward. It was carried a hundred feet, then slammed violently to the dark soil. It desperately tried to escape but couldn't move.

The winged creature was on top of it, and it was relentless, tearing away at it, large portions of the bear's neck and upper body already gone. The bear's horrific, desperate screams echoed everywhere. To the ferns. To the redwoods. Even into the sky. Cold and knowing, the moon just watched.

ABOVE THE treetops, the Demonray flew toward the ocean. Visible against the moon's whiteness, the top half of the bear carcass dangled from its mouth.

It flew beyond the trees, passed the churning shoreline, and continued out to sea. It found the spot it was looking for, then released the carcass. It watched as the chunk of ragged meat splashed in and submerged. Then it banked and flew back to the land.

CHAPTER 75

"**F**OUR DATA points?" Jason walked toward Craig. "How do you figure four?"

Craig pointed to the map spread out on the living-room table. "One, where the jogger disappeared. Two, where the body was found. Three, where we got the radar readings. And four, where we actually saw it." He drew four big *X*s. "All four are in the same vicinity. Darryl, you talk about territoriality . . . well, this looks like a classic case of it to me."

Darryl shook his head. "This equipment of yours will *not* help us find that thing."

"Why not?"

"Because this animal detects things *electronically*, Craig. It will know that equipment's out there and stay the hell away from it."

"It didn't stay away from it today."

"That had nothing to do with us finding it."

"Of course it did. It confirmed it was out there. It will help us even more going forward." Craig returned to the map. "We should rejigger the equipment to cover as much of this area as we can. That Demon-ray will keep coming back, you watch. Then we'll be able to figure out *exactly* where it is."

Jason studied the four *X*s then turned at Darryl. "It's not a bad idea."

"Maybe theoretically, but Darryl's right, Jason, it will be a waste of time." Lisa eyed the two lifeless monitors on the hearth. "That thing will definitely detect the equipment."

Craig turned angrily. "Says who? Bandar Vishakeratne? What the hell does he know?"

"The number one brain expert in the world? Oh, nothing, Craig, I'm sure."

"Lisa, I'm not questioning the guy's analysis of neurons, but even he doesn't *know* what this Demonray will detect out there. The bottom line is that this animal hasn't stayed away from our equipment yet, and we should use that to our advantage. Jason, we should reconfigure the layout."

"As long as it doesn't interfere with what Darryl wants to do . . . I'm inclined to agree."

Craig nodded. "First thing tomorrow, then."

Jason nodded in kind. "First thing tomorrow."

CHAPTER 76

"THERE THEY are." Lisa pointed as Monique and Darryl emerged from the forest in their all-khaki outfits.

Darryl looked tense. "It's still out there. Let's go. Let's go right no—" He paused when Craig sluffed from the cabin, bleary-eyed and still in his pj's. "Get dressed Craig."

Summers seemed to wake up. "What? Hold on. I wanna reposition the equip—"

"You're not repositioning anything now. That thing's out there and we're going to look for it."

Craig turned angrily. "Christ, Jason, that's not what we agreed to last—"

"Craig, you got up late, and we don't have time now." Jason saw that thin streams of white were already flowing into the treetops. "Reposition it later if you like, but let's go. For now, maybe just grab a radar gun."

Summers did as he was told, and within minutes, everyone was dressed in khaki, armed, and ready to go.

As they started off, Jason looked up again and was amazed. The fog was already very, very thick.

IN A hunting circle fifteen minutes later, they walked slowly, heads pointed up.

The fog was a tomb, no signs of life at all, and Craig wondered if they were wasting their time. "Think it's still up there, Hoss?"

Darryl's head slowly turned. "Don't know for sure. But stay sharp; everybody stay sharp."

An hour later, Craig was exhausted. So were Jason, Lisa, Monique, and Phil. After staring at the white mist for as long as they had, their necks hurt and their vision had blurred.

Darryl Hollis was as alert as ever, studying the fog in every direction, his bow and arrow always at the ready. "This thing is smart. Knew we'd be looking for it." He squinted, trying to see *into* the fog. "If we can't see it, it can't see us, right?"

Jason shook his head. "It might be able to see *through* the fog, Darryl. The visual cortex in that brain wasn't small either."

Monique nodded. "Its eyes evolved in total darkness. It's either blind or has fantastic vision."

Craig scanned the whiteness with his rifle. "No way in hell is it blind." He vividly recalled the way the Demonray's eyes had watched them, studied them. "For all we know it could be up there right now."

Darryl slowly halted. "I think it is."

CHAPTER 77

T HE CREATURE coasted silently, studying the six upturned human faces.

Its eyes moved slowly, patiently, taking in everything about them. Their eyes. Their bodies. Their clothes. And then their weapons.

JASON GLANCED at the rifle in his hands.

"It can detect our guns."

"What?" Darryl had heard him but didn't understand.

"It can detect the metal in these rifles. I don't know if it understands what they're used for, but it knows we're holding them."

Craig removed his radar gun. "You think it can detect this?"

Jason glanced at it. "When you turn it on."

A nod. "All right, I'm going t—"

"Don't bother." Darryl continued to look up. "If it will sense it anyway, what's the point?"

"Because it will confirm if it's really up there."

Darryl's eyes didn't leave the fog. "Believe me, it's up there. You really think it can see us, Jason?"

"Probably."

"It's time for a game of chicken, then."

Jason looked up curiously. "What do you want to do?"

"Aim right at it. If it sees me, it will get the hell out of the way, then reveal where it is." In an instant, Darryl drew an arrow back, and rapidly swept it across the fog. "This thing doesn't have spiritual powers I don't know about, does it?"

"You never know."

"OK, everybody aim at a different patch of fog. Keep your marks twenty feet apart. Now."

A clever strategy, Jason thought. He wondered if it would work.

They aimed at six different patches.

Then waited.

There were no signs of movement, just a silent white mass.

They continued to wait. Nothing happened.

"It could have flown away," Jason whispered.

Darryl continued to stare. "It could have. But I don't think it did. The damn thing's playing chicken all right. On three, everybody fire five shots. Ready? One. Two . . . Three."

Gunfire shattered the silence. Twenty-five bullets and five arrows ripped into the fog bank.

They waited again. But nothing moved.

Craig raised the radar gun. "I'm gonna use this now, OK?"

Darryl exhaled. "Technology hunting" was unnatural, untrustworthy, the opposite of how he'd been taught to hunt. But he couldn't say no here. "Go ahead."

Craig turned on the gun. A sweeping green line appeared on the rear display and then he swept it across the white.

But there was no reading, just an empty sweeping line. "Maybe it's really not up there."

Darryl shook his head. Something didn't feel right. He couldn't say what—but something. "This damn thing is smart. I don't like this." He studied the fog. "Let's go back to the cabin."

The others paused. Go back to the cabin?

"You sure, Darryl?" Jason asked.

"I don't want anyone getting killed out here. Let's go."

But then Darryl Hollis didn't move. A particular patch of fog had caught his eye, and he stared at it.

———

THE BLACK eyes looked right back at him.

The predator wasn't flying anymore. Like cellophane, its entire winged body was wrapped around the trunk of a redwood, gently rising and falling as it breathed.

The eyes suddenly shifted. To something on the dirt. The predator had been so focused on the humans that it hadn't detected it. But something had just moved. The faces turned to it as well.

"HEY, LOOK." Monique saw it first, a mountain-lion cub, the size of a house cat, with little paws and golden fur with dark stripes. The tiny animal had been there all along, but none of them had noticed it. One of its hind legs was caught in a bear trap, and it had just made a sudden and useless attempt to escape.

Darryl shook his head. "Somebody should kill that thing."

Monique gave her husband a filthy look. Then she trotted over to it.

As she did, Jason ran his eyes up and down a few of the redwoods. What if the predator had somehow attached itself to a tree? No one had aimed at a tree; their shots would have missed it, just as Craig's radar gun would have. Jason followed the largest trunk from the ground into the fog. Was the predator smart enough to realize they wouldn't fire at a tree?

"Jason." Darryl was looking at the same spot. "You think?"

"Maybe."

Suddenly there was a hissing scream—from the mountain-lion cub. Monique was crouched over it, yanking hard on the clamps that had ensnared its paw.

Darryl turned angrily. "Not the time for that, Monique! Just shoot the damn thing!"

The clamps snapped open, and Monique was her typical calm self. "No need for that, Husband." She lifted the little animal gently, crying softly now, like a cat that wanted its milk.

"Keep it quiet," Darryl snapped.

Monique walked over. "Shut up, Darryl."

He ignored her and turned back to the tree.

THE BLACK eyes focused on the cub, studying it, analyzing it. Then they returned to Darryl.

One of his arrows was pointing right at it now. Pulled back in the bow and ready to fire.

The Demonray didn't move, didn't breathe.

DARRYL GAZED at the patch of white above the tree trunk. Unsure if the predator was up there or not, he noted how quiet it was. No movement at all. He lowered the bow and turned away.

"Let's get outta here."

Then, without warning, he spun and fired—five times.

Whoosh! Whoosh! Whoosh! Whoosh! Whoosh! The arrows ripped into the fog and plunged into something unseen.

Then nothing. Silence.

No one moved. They just watched and waited.

THE EYES shifted. To an arrow an inch away.

Then they swiveled back to Darryl.

HE STARED right back at the animal, albeit unknowingly. "Let's go back to the cabin."

AS THEY turned to go, the creature didn't move. It just watched them. Then it focused on the bear trap.

CHAPTER 78

"WAIT A second." In the middle of a clearing, Craig paused. "Let's reposition the equipment. Cool, Hoss?"

Darryl Hollis hesitated. He actually felt like using the equipment here might be to their detriment, but—

"What do you say Darryl?" Jason didn't see any reason not to reposition it.

"Sure, whatever."

Craig crinkled open a map. "OK, we need to go . . . this way. . . ." As he and the others walked off, Darryl didn't budge. He looked up and was amazed. In just minutes, the fog had thinned considerably, so much so that he could see. He could make out the upper tree trunks and branches now. But nothing else was up there. He turned and followed the others.

"ALL BETTER now. Thanks a lot, Jason."

Jason smiled. "Looks like the patient's doing fine."

Snuggling on a towel, the mountain-lion cub rubbed its tiny head on Monique's thigh. On the living-room floor, Jason had just assisted Monique in splinting the animal's broken leg. While Jason had held the little creature down, Monique had done the real work, and she'd been impressive. The cub had been in excruciating pain, and when Monique reset the bone, the animal bit her hand, gashing the skin and drawing blood. She'd barely blinked. Monique had simply absorbed the pain and continued. Sometimes Jason forgot, but despite her looks, Monique Hollis was one tough hombre.

"OK, baby; all better." She gently petted the cub, which was purring loudly now.

Watching from the couches, Lisa and Jason thought this was adorable, but Darryl couldn't have cared less. "What are we gonna do to hunt this thing, Jason?"

Jason got up from the floor. "I don't think we can sneak up on it. That might be impossible, literally impossible."

Craig laughed darkly. "Well, that's a problem."

"You know what else is a problem?" Darryl turned. "It might not even hunt on instinct."

"What's that mean?"

"Most predators hunt on instinct, meaning they're not really 'thinking' about what they're doing; they're just sort of going through preprogrammed motions. But what we've got out there *is thinking*. It analyzes what it sees, then adapts to it."

"Maybe we can bait it."

"With what?"

Craig shrugged. "How about Phil?"

Everyone laughed, even Phil Martino.

Darryl wasn't amused. "It will detect steel traps, right, Jason?"

"I think so. Can we hang a net or something?"

"Any nets in that storage shed, Craig?"

"No." Summers eyed the two monitors on the hearth. "I still think this equipment's gonna help pick something up."

Darryl doubted it. "We'll keep hunting it the way we have been."

Craig shook his head. Then he walked to the window and looked out at the moon-dappled landscape. "Anybody ever wonder why this thing came to the land in the first place?"

"We've been over that, Craig." Monique wondered if he had Alzheimer's. "Food."

"No, I mean philosophically."

"Philosophically?" Darryl wondered if he was hearing things. "I didn't realize you knew what *philosophically* meant."

"What do you mean, Craig?" Monique asked seriously.

"I mean, did you ever think this thing might have evolved for a reason?"

"Like what?"

"Like maybe it's nature's way of protecting itself."

"Protecting itself *from what?*"

"From us. You know, Jason, your name choice for this thing is surprisingly apt."

"How so?"

"*Demonray.* Do you realize what the very first 'demons' actually were?"

A pause. "No . . . I don't."

"According to the book of Revelation, the *original demons* were— get this—*expelled from heaven because they wanted to destroy humanity.*"

Everyone paused. This was eerie.

"That's in the Bible?"

"Uh-huh. Kind of ironic, isn't it? Because I'd say if there's anything that could destroy humanity, this species is it."

"*Destroy humanity?*" Darryl rolled his eyes. "When'd you start believing in fairy tales, Peter Pan?"

"It's no fairy tale, Darryl, and the science side is even scarier."

Jason turned. "How so?"

"Why do predators evolve in the first place? To stop existing species from becoming too abundant. So think about the existing species that is the human race. Just eleven thousand years ago there were less than five million people on this planet, but there are six billion today, and that's supposed to go north of ten billion in just a couple of decades. Man's been growing like a weed and nothing. Not a virus. Not another species. *Nothing* has kept that growth in check. Maybe the evolution of this thing is nature's way of doing that."

Darryl wasn't amused anymore. "There's *one* of those things out there, Craig."

"Yeah, right now. But like Monique said, evolution takes place gradually."

"Meaning what? That these things will take over the planet one day?"

"Maybe."

"How long do ya figure, Socrates?"

"I don't know. Maybe twenty million years. Maybe a thousand. Maybe ten."

"Ten?" Monique turned. "Craig, there's no historical precedent for anything like that."

"So what? So you're saying that because it took other species millions of years to make evolutionary leaps, it will take this species the same amount of time?"

"Well . . . yeah."

"That logic doesn't hold, Monique. Just look at man. Man evolved faster than any species in the history of the planet. What it took the others millions of years to do, we did in just ten thousand. So who says this species couldn't evolve even faster than that? I mean, imagine what would happen if there were a million of those things flying around out there."

"*A million?*" Jason thought that was insane. "Craig, that's not possible. That's not even close to possible. There's *one animal* out there right now. How do you get to a million?"

"Jason, you know how big the damn oceans are. Two miles deep on average and almost triple the surface area of land. *Triple.* Do you realize how much space that is? We have *no idea* how many of those things there could be down there."

"It's nowhere near a million."

"No? Do you know what the worldwide shark population is?"

A pause. "No, I don't."

"Fifty *billion.*"

"No way."

A firm nod. "Fifty billion. And if these rays have been around for as long as the sharks have . . . Who knows how many of them there could be."

No one said anything. They just digested the possibilities.

Jason cleared his throat. "So what are you saying here, Craig? That this thing could be our apocalypse?"

"Is it so ridiculous? All the doomsayers always said it would be a virus. Maybe it's this thing instead."

"I think we better just kill the one that's out there now," Phil chipped in from the chair.

Darryl stood. "I'll drink to that. In fact, why doesn't everyone drink to that?" He grabbed a six-pack of Budweiser from the kitchen and returned. "Lord Socrates," he said, tossing Craig his.

Six beers were raised, clanked together, and tipped toward the ceiling. As the amber liquid flowed, the others reluctantly admitted that Craig Summers had raised some fascinating points. What if there really were a million Demonrays? Or just a dozen? Or even two or three?

But they all told themselves that wasn't realistic. For once, Phil Martino was right. They had to kill the one that was out there now.

No ONE slept soundly.

At six the next morning, Jason turned over on his bed when there was a knock on his door.

Craig entered rapidly, fully dressed and tense. "We just got a reading, Jason."

He jolted up. "Where?"

"In the same area it's been returning to. Right where I thought it would be. Let's go."

CHAPTER 79

A BLINKING dot moved quickly across the sweeping green line, disappeared, then continued as the next sweep popped up.

"Where's it going?" Jason said, totally without his bearings.

Summers glanced at a map. "Toward us. Looks like near the first thermal camera . . . We might get a visual here. . . ." Craig bounced to the thermal monitor, enlarging one of the images to full screen. The view was aimed skyward along a redwood trunk: the dark gray trunk, then, above it, a lighter gray forest canopy and bits of sky.

Suddenly, beneath the canopy, a solid white form sped into the frame. It continued for a moment, then banked and flew straight down, heading directly for the camera. It steadily grew larger, then banked again, just above the lens, and sped off and disappeared.

"Where the hell did it go? . . ." Craig checked the other images but didn't see it anywhere. "It's got to be around here somewhere."

Jason just stared at the monitor. "Can you replay that?"

Craig hit a button and replayed it in slo-mo . . . the massive white form eased into the frame . . . continued slowly . . . turned straight down . . . gradually grew larger . . . then very large. . . . Then Craig hit another button, freezing it.

They all stared at the image. It was eerie, the huge eyes, the protruding horns, the open mouth, the teeth . . . all in bright white.

Craig nodded. "Right where I thought it would be. Told you this stuff would help, Hoss."

Darryl just gave the frozen image a dirty look. "Let's see where it is when we get out there."

THE EARLY-MORNING air was crisp and cool. And oddly, without a trace of fog. It was quiet, too. Just two sounds. Their hissing walkie-talkies and little snaps from underneath their boots.

The hunting circle moved slowly. Every head turned, looking high, low, left, right, back, and front.

Jason just looked up, wondering where the fog was.

At the head of the circle, Darryl wondered the same thing. Studying the patches of blue through the canopy, he was growing increasingly uneasy. "I don't think it's up there." He halted. "It wouldn't have anywhere to hide."

Craig nodded. "The readings were from further ahead."

Darryl ignored this, not moving. He didn't think the creature was close.

And yet the forest was so very silent.

THE DEMONRAY banked silently, careful not to make a sound.

It had been waiting for them to stop. Now that they had, it glided *away* from them. Just above the treetops, it tuned in for something else.

After a minute, it detected what it was searching for. It found a hole in the canopy and plunged through it. As it banked over a huge patch of pink flowers, it saw them, nibbling on a fern patch. A family of deer, eight animals covered in soft brown fur, chewing their food unknowingly.

The largest, a three-hundred-pound big-horned buck, saw the creature first, then froze. Simply "not moving" was a well-known tactic deer used to evade detection from predators. The Demonray flew straight for them.

The buck galloped away and the others followed. Within seconds, they were streaking through the trees.

The predator caught up instantly, but did not attack. With the cool morning air surging past its head, it carefully scanned the sprinting animals, first the buck, then the smaller does, then, bringing up the rear, a tiny fawn.

The black eyes locked onto the fawn. The little animal was doing its best to stay up with the herd but wasn't quite able. Its big eyes suddenly went wide when a powerful surge of wind blew through its fur. Then it leaped over a fern patch but didn't come down.

It had been caught by a pair of enormous teeth.

Very much alive, the fawn suddenly began to ascend. As saliva dripped onto its head, it watched as its family ran away below and disappeared. Then it was whisked toward the treetops. . . .

The Demonray continued for a minute when it abruptly banked. Easing into a glide, it surveyed a clearing hundreds of feet below, lined by trunks, rhododendrons, and ferns, and not outwardly special in any way.

Then it released the fawn.

When the tiny animal landed, it tried to run, but couldn't even get up. Its legs weren't working.

The creature watched it coldly, simultaneously tuning to six human heartbeats nearby. Then it banked and flew away.

"THIS IS where we saw it. It was from *that camera*, right there." Craig gestured to a black thermal camera on top of a tripod, pointed up along a redwood trunk.

Phil's eyes darted nervously, scanning the empty forest. "It must have moved, huh?"

Craig raised the radar gun to the sky, and the sweeping green line in back was empty. "I guess so."

"There's not a trace of fog here," Jason observed.

Darryl eyed the camera suspiciously, just sitting there on its tripod. He couldn't make sense of it. "Let's go. Everybody pay attention." He walked forward.

They passed redwoods, ferns, a giant fallen tree, and then they saw it. Darryl first. A fawn in the middle of a clearing. It was just lying on the dirt, a tiny animal, maybe two feet tall and covered in white spots. Darryl couldn't say why exactly, but something didn't smell right about it being there. Plus, it was clearly in pain. He removed an arrow, aimed, and—

"Darryl, please don't."

He hesitated. It was his wife.

"Ahh . . . Jesus Christ, Monique . . ."

"Please, Darryl. *Please.*"

He lowered the weapon, and she trotted toward the fawn.

Jason looked up at the sky, wondering what was going on.

Darryl studied the sky too, eyes darting. "I don't think the damn thing's around here."

Monique crouched next to the fawn and saw it was shivering slightly. "Oh, your leg's broken." She petted its head, trying to calm it down.

Darryl looked around suspiciously. "Think it would try something without the fog, Jason?"

"I don't know." But Jason felt like Darryl did. Something didn't smell right.

Darryl eyed his wife. She'd put her rifle down and was holding the tiny deer in her arms now. "I don't like this. Let's head back. Let's head back right now."

"Wait a second." Craig raised his radar gun. "I got something here."

Phil scanned the sky in every direction. "Where?"

Darryl suddenly pointed. "There."

Instantaneously, an enormous swooping mass fell out of the sky, arching away from them.

Darryl aimed, but the creature was moving much too rapidly, darting behind a grove of trees. But pieces of it were visible. It was within reach. Darryl sprinted after it, Craig, Jason, Phil, and Lisa rapidly following. Flying at head height, the speeding form came into view. Darryl halted and fired twice, but missed. The predator surged away, still within sight.

They ran hard and saw it again. Just above the forest floor, rushing over ferns and rhododendrons . . .

Darryl slowed to shoot, but the animal hurtled past the foliage and the shot was gone.

They ran hard for ten more minutes, the Demonray darting in and out among the trunks. Finally, Darryl had a shot. He dropped to one knee and . . . Jason ran up just as he released. The arrow rocketed away, on a rope, ripping toward the creature. It was the most amazing display of marksmanship Jason had ever seen. He actually felt the arrow tearing through the air. A hit, a hit, a palpable hit.

The creature suddenly banked, and the arrow plunged into a tree, splintering to pieces.

They ran after it. Darryl fired twice more but missed both times. Craig fired three times, all misses.

Suddenly the animal was gone. Disappeared. Darryl froze, looking all around the forest.

Craig ran up, gasping. "Where the hell is it?"

But the forest was silent. Nothing moved.

Jason, Phil, and Lisa ran up.

"How'd we keep up with it for so long?"

Darryl turned to Jason. *"What?"*

"How'd we keep up with it?" Jason tried to catch his breath. "I think it *let us* stay close."

Phil looked around. "Why would it have done that?"

Darryl Hollis suddenly felt ill. "How far did we just run?"

Jason checked his watch; they'd largely sprinted hard for a total of fifteen minutes, so . . . "A mile at least."

Darryl tried to stay calm. "A mile at least. So we're too far to run back now."

"What do you mean?"

"I mean, Monique's not here." Darryl swallowed nervously. "I think that thing isolated us from Monique."

CHAPTER 80

JASON STARED at Darryl. Everyone stared at Darryl.

He methodically exhaled a few times. This was no time to panic. "Can I borrow your walkie-talkie, Lisa?"

She shoved it to him, and he pressed the button. "Monique, you there?"

He waited a moment.

One second ticked past. Then another.

The walkie-talkie was silent, just a light hissing.

"Am I pressing this damn button right?"

Lisa eyed his finger. "Yes."

He pressed it again. "Monique, you there? Monique?"

He waited again.

Again, there was nothing.

He turned to Craig nervously.

Then the walkie-talkie crackled. "Hey, Darryl." She sounded as casual as ever.

Darryl breathed easier. "Are you OK?"

"Fine. You guys ran off, and I couldn't keep up holding this little guy."

Her tone was all wrong. She didn't understand what was happening. "Do you see that thing around there anywhere?"

"No, it's just me and this cute little fawn."

"Forget the goddamn fawn, Monique!" Darryl exhaled, calming down. "I think that thing set you up somehow."

"*Set me up?* It's not even here, Darryl."

Darryl eyed Jason. "Any way this is just a coincidence? That maybe it went somewhere else?"

Jason didn't answer right away. He replayed what had happened. "This is no coincidence. No way. Somehow, it lured us to that area, to *that specific area.* I just don't know h—Craig, those readings we got . . . It *did* detect that equipment. It detected it and used it against us. It *called us to that exact spot.*"

Summers replayed it, too. "Son of a bitch; you might be right. . . . But why? Why *there?*"

Jason went over it again. "The fawn. There was something strange with that fawn being there."

"Like what?"

Jason began pacing. "What if the ray *knew* how Monique would react when she saw it?"

"How could it possibly know th—"

"The mountain-lion cub in the bear trap. Darryl, it *was* up in the fog watching us yesterday. It saw Monique's reaction to that lion cub. So it called us to that exact spot with the equipment, it found the fawn, broke its leg, then waited for Monique to find it. When she did, it swooped down to draw us away, then kept going until we were so far removed that we couldn't get back to her."

Darryl swallowed sickly. It made horrifying sense. "Monique, did you hear all that?"

She hesitated over the hissing. "How could it possibly have broken the fawn's leg?"

Darryl felt like vomiting. He had no clue; he just knew it had happened. "Jason?"

Jason took the walkie-talkie, thinking it out. "It must have carried it in its mouth, Monique, then dropped it from the air. Is the fawn's fur sticky, like from saliva?"

MONIQUE HOLLIS swallowed nervously.

She didn't need to look. The tiny animal was covered with dried splotches of something. She'd been wondering what they were all along.

"Is its damn fur sticky?"

This was Darryl's voice again.

"Yeah, Darryl. It is." She calmly put the fawn down, grabbing her rifle off the soil.

She looked up. The forest was silent. No sign of the creature anywhere, just branches, tree trunks, and evergreen for as far as the eye could see. And still not a trace of fog.

"It's not here." Not yet anyway.

"You sure?"

She scanned everywhere. "Positive."

Although she had to admit . . . it was very, very quiet.

"STAY COOL," Darryl said, his face as tight as a guitar string. He reconsidered running back to her, but there wasn't enough time. He turned. "You buy that it's not there yet, Jason?"

Jason quickly ran some numbers in his head, quadruple-checking calculations he'd made earlier. Maybe the Demonray had flown slower than he'd anticipated, but he thought he'd estimated its speed conservatively. "If it's not, it should be *very soon*."

"Keep your eyes peeled, Monique."

But even as Darryl said the words, Jason feared she just wasn't seeing something.

MONIQUE TURNED, scanning everything, trunks, branches, patches of blue sky. There was nothing up there, nothing at all.

"It's not here."

"Are you sure?"

"Goddamn it; I'm positive!" She clutched her rifle tightly, still searching. "It must have gone somewhere else."

DARRYL TURNED to Jason. "Could it have gone somewhere else?"

Jason swallowed nervously. "I don't think so."

Darryl nodded. "Monique, it's gotta be there."

MONIQUE WALKED back in the direction they'd come from.

"Wait a second. . . ." Was it wrapped around a tree?

"What is it?"

She walked closer. . . . It was something a hundred feet up . . . something big and dark.

"Monique, what is it?"

She walked closer still.

No, just a discoloration in the bark.

"Nothing. There's nothing here, I really think you might have jumped the gun."

DARRYL looked to Jason for support but he shook his head firmly, eyes glaring. "It's up to something. It's there, I'm telling you; *it's got to be there.* Craig, do you remember anything special about that area when we set up the equipment? Anywhere it could be hiding?"

Craig frantically searched his brain. "Jesus, Jason . . . no."

"Are you sure?"

"Yeah, I don't remember a goddamn thing!"

"Something's up, Darryl." Jason shook his head. "It's hiding somehow. Get her out of there; get her out of there right now."

MONIQUE CONTINUED walking, still looking up.

"Monique, *just get out of there.*"

She walked faster, heading to the fallen tree they'd passed earlier. "Where is it?"

"Just get out of there! Run!"

She walked faster still. "Where is it, Darryl? I wanna know where it is."

"We don't know!"

She jogged, frantically scanning the skyline, spinning in circles. "Where is it? I just want to see it."

"Goddamn it, get out of there!"

She jogged faster, still looking up.

THE EYES were looking *up* at her.

Less than fifty feet away, the predator was flat on the soil, its colossal form gently rising and falling. It was in front of the fallen tree. The tree's dark coloring closely matched its own and made it very difficult to see, especially with the dark soil. The animal knew that if someone had been inclined to look up, and wasn't looking right at it, he or she wouldn't even notice it was there.

Still looking up, Monique ran straight for it. . . . Running and spinning, running and spinning.

The creature didn't move.

She saw the approaching mass in her periphery. She planned on climbing over it and simply ran closer.

The eyes shifted, no other body part moving.

She ran closer still, turning away from it.

Suddenly and silently, the great form rose up like a snake. Then it didn't move. It just held there, its front half in the air, standing slightly more than six feet tall.

As she started to turn, it rumbled.

Monique froze, dropping her walkie-talkie. The sound was astonishingly close.

Facing the wrong way, she turned slightly and saw the Demonray out of the corner of her eye, something huge and white, looming over her. She knew instantly that the creature must have been there all along. But it wasn't attacking. It was just standing there, coiled and watching her. She could actually feel its eyes.

Ever so slowly, she turned and looked up at it.

The deathly cold eyes looked right back at her.

She didn't move a muscle. She simply looked at it.

Then, never losing eye contact, she gently repositioned her fingers on the rifle.

Monique moved first. With lightning quickness, she slammed her back against the dirt and fired twice. Two small red holes appeared in the massive underside. The animal didn't seem to feel them. The head snapped downward with phenomenal quickness. A mouthful of the giant teeth rushed toward Monique, and she closed her eyes, firing three more times.

Suddenly the creature was gone.

Monique jumped to her feet, no idea where it was. Then she saw it flying away rapidly, just above the forest floor. She fired twice.

As if seeing the bullets, the pumping form suddenly darted straight up, climbing vertically along a redwood.

Monique sprinted to the base, aimed, and . . .

The creature smashed through the canopy above, disappearing into the sky.

Monique frantically scanned the patches of blue, catching little pieces of the Demonray, apparently on a towering trajectory above the trees. . . . She lost sight of it as it continued higher.

Then, a hundred yards away, something enormous and black plunged down like an elevator. Monique jerked her rifle down. The winged form knifed lower then banked violently above the soil, rocketing straight for her with the speed of a flying roller coaster.

She fired four times.

The body rose before the shots had even been taken. Every bullet missed.

She fired again. A bullet plunged into the creature's face, a few inches from the right eye. It had no effect. She fired again but missed badly. Her hands were shaking. She fired once more, but again, couldn't control her hands.

The great body roared closer, a hundred feet away . . . then fifty feet . . .

She fired three more times, but again her hands shook. She threw the rifle down, ripped the dagger from her pant leg, and sprinted toward it.

The creature let out a shattering roar.

Monique screamed back, her eyes filled with rage, raising the knife above her head with both hands.

The mouth rushed in, the great teeth rapidly growing larger.

She screamed again, running as hard as she could.

Suddenly her direction was violently reversed. Flying backward and shrieking in pain, she stabbed down on top of the head, four, five, six, seven times. Then the knife slipped from her hands, and she didn't know where she was. She wiped the blood from her face and wondered if she'd gotten free. She realized her eyes were closed. Why were her eyes closed? She opened them.

She was up to her chest in the creature's mouth, a doll in the jaws of a curious dog. Feeling down, she realized her legs were gone. Strangely, there was no pain. She looked up at the animal's eyes. They were so close now, less than a foot away, black, deathly calm, and staring right at her. Why wasn't it biting down? What was it waiting for?

The Demonray was flat on the soil; she could actually feel it breathing. It seemed to be playing with her, waiting to see if she'd try to escape.

But Monique didn't try to escape. She simply thought of her husband and the family they'd always wanted.

The creature bit down. Monique Hollis was gone.

THE BODY had been moved by the time the others arrived. All that remained were the walkie-talkie, rifle, and a pool of dark blood on the soil.

"Oh my God," Lisa said, weeping uncontrollably. She stepped back as Darryl walked closer. He was unable to hold back his tears.

Jason glanced at Craig, eyeing bloodstains with a look that could cut glass.

Then, out of the corner of his eye, Jason noticed the fawn, struggling to get up. He gently lifted it into his arms, eyeing its broken leg. This time he knew he'd have to splint it by himself.

CHAPTER 81

"**M**AYBE WE should end this—pack it in."

Jason's words hung in the air. They were seated around the living room. Out of respect for Monique Hollis, they'd done nothing at all for the past twenty-four hours. Darryl's mourning period had been powerful, intense, and was far from over. Seated on the hearth, he still looked numb, gazing down at the shiny wood floor. No one responded, and Jason nodded morosely. "I guess that's a yes."

Darryl turned to him, his eyes ice. "No, it's not."

"Darryl, we shouldn't make emotional decisions right now."

"Do I look emotional to you?"

A pause. "No, actually. You don't."

"Monique died for one reason: because that thing outsmarted us. Because we were stupid. Now we're gonna have to outsmart it. You mark my words, Jason. I'm still gonna kill that thing. So, no, I'm not packing anything in."

"Neither am I," Craig said.

Jason turned to him. The Hollises were Craig's best friends on the entire planet, people he'd literally waged war with. If Darryl wanted to fight, then so did Craig Summers. His eyes were steel. But then they turned quizzical. "Do *you* want to pack it in, Jason?"

"Monique was my friend, too, Craig." Even now, Jason's eyes were a little wet. "No, I don't."

Phil cleared his throat. "For what it's worth, neither do I."

On a couch next to Jason, Lisa was astounded by what she was hearing. "I don't believe this. *Darryl, your wife is dead.*"

"Thanks for the reminder."

"I'm sorry, it's just . . . you're not reacting to this the way I would. If we really want to kill this thing, let's call in the National Guard."

"That would be useless."

"What are you talking about? They're professional soldiers."

"You sure about that, Soccer Mom?"

"Well . . . yeah."

Craig shook his head. "They're not even close to professional soldiers, Lisa. More like accountants and auto mechanics who do weekend drills at the local armory. You get a bunch of those guys running around here . . . the deaths will really start piling up."

Darryl nodded. "Not to mention they don't know a goddamn thing about hunting."

"They can fire guns; they can help us. Right, Jason?"

Jason paused. "With all due respect, Lisa, I'll defer to Darryl and Craig's judgment on this. Just like I said I would. But from what little I know of the National Guard, I'm inclined to agree with them."

"Then forget the National Guard. What about the SEALs, the police, the FBI?"

"The FBI?" Craig was genuinely amused, "What are they gonna do? Flash their badges and tell that thing to come out with its hands up? And what makes you think the FBI or anybody else would even believe us, Lisa? Do you realize what we'd sound like? Even if the phones did work, if we made that call . . . forget the National Guard, they'd be more likely to send the *National Enquirer.*"

"We'd have to show it to them."

"How would we do that exactly?"

"Well . . . we'd have to take them out there."

"You think that thing's gonna pose for a picture?"

"Craig's right," Jason said. "No one would believe us, and with all of the back-and-forth explaining, it could take months to convince them."

"Which we don't have." Darryl eyed Lisa soberly. "That thing's out there *now*. If we wait just days, it could go anywhere."

Lisa stood, glaring at Jason. "Then stay and fight it. I've had enough." She walked out.

"IF YOU'RE leaving, so am I."

Alone on her bed, Lisa looked up. Jason was standing at the doorway. "Jason, I don't want you to leave. I know how important this is to you."

He entered. "If you're leaving, so am I."

"That's ridiculous, you've been waiting your whole life for something like this."

He got in her face, softly. "If you're leaving, so am I."

"You'd do that for me?"

"Uh-huh."

She exhaled. "Then I want to stay."

"You'd do that *for me?*"

"As long as you don't get us killed."

"*You and I will be fine.* Remember?"

She paused. "That's something I'll never forget."

He sat, and they hugged on the little bed.

"JASON, BRACE yourself. Phil might actually know how we can kill this thing."

Jason paused as he and Lisa entered the living room. Darryl was serious. "How?"

On the easy chair, Phil leaned forward. "We need to get it out of the forest, right?"

Jason eyed him hatefully. "That's Darryl's call."

Darryl nodded. "We do. Out of the forest, shooting it becomes a whole different ball game. Tell him your idea, Phil."

Phil turned. "How do you think this thing likes heat, Jason?"

"Heat? Physical heat?"

"Yes."

"It probably hates it. Cold as it is in the depths . . . It might not have evolved to deal with it." He paused, his revulsion for Phil Martino buried by his curiosity. "What's your idea?"

"To smoke it out. Literally."

"How would we do that?"

"With a prescribed burn. What the rangers were planning to do here anyway."

Jason's eyes narrowed. "Hmm. How would that work, exactly?"

CHAPTER 82

"First, I'll show you what a prescribed burn is. . . ." As Darryl, Jason, and Lisa watched, Phil removed the black mesh screen in front of the fireplace. "Now, all fires, whether they're in a fireplace, a forest, whatever, need what we call 'start-up fuel' to ignite."

He pointed to what was inside the fireplace, logs on top of kindling and crumpled newspaper. "Here, the start-up fuel is the newspaper and kindling. We burn the paper first, which in turn burns the kindling, which in turn burns the logs. All together, that gives us a big blaze. Simple, right? But what would happen if we *removed* the paper and kindling and just tried to light the logs directly? It would never burn, right? The match would burn out, and we wouldn't get anything close to a fire." He looked around the room. "Everybody follow?"

There were nods.

"Just like in a fireplace, forest fires start burning after the forest's version of kindling—dried grass, dead shrubs, fallen branches—burns first. *Then* the trees start burning. But. If that kindling's *already* been burned, then a major fire can't even get the chance to start. That's what a prescribed burn is, literally 'prescribing' a series of small fires so big, out-of-control ones don't burn later. To put this in perspective, a lot of national and state parks started doing prescribed burns after the big Yellowstone blazes in '88."

Lisa nodded. "Pretty cool."

Phil returned the mesh screen. "And pretty easy. They've been doing prescribed burns at this park for years, so they were prepped for another one anyway."

"How do you know that?" Jason asked.

"I found some of their old files. It's basically ready to go."

"You know how to oversee these burns?"

"I've done it before."

"We won't burn the entire forest down? You're *absolutely sure* of that?"

Craig cleared his throat. "Jason, it looks safe to me. According to their records, there's actually not that much fuel out there. Coincidentally, the part of the forest where this thing's been repeatedly returning to has fantastic natural fire barriers."

Phil pointed to a map. "Look. Ocean to the west, a double-lane paved road to the south, and the creek to the north and east. Basically, it's a prescribed burn's dream."

"You really think it's safe, Craig?" Jason asked tenuously.

A confident nod.

"And this makes sense to you, Darryl?"

"Perfect sense. We gotta get that thing outta the woods, and this seems like a great way to do that."

Jason reluctantly turned to Phil. "When would we do it?"

"First thing in the morning's best, when there's lots of cold air to help contain the fire."

Jason's eyes shifted, mindful of whom he was talking to. "What are the other risks?"

"We'll get some high, superficial flames from the rhododendrons, but nothing lasting, nothing really dangerous. We should be fine."

"We won't need to put it out somehow?"

"The beauty of these types of fires is that they pretty much burn themselves out. They just run out of fuel. We'll need to check for burning embers and things. . . ." Embers could burn for days if not properly extinguished. "But that's about it. Other than that, there shouldn't be any problems."

Jason turned to Darryl. "Say we do this. And say it actually works. If we drive that thing out of the trees, it could go anywhere, right?"

"We'd have to shepherd it."

"How would we do that?"

"With the helicopters. Craig and I already went over it. With all of the noise and electrical activity they generate they should scare the hell out of that thing. If it does pop out of the treetops, we'll have it."

"Where would we shepherd it to exactly?"

"Where it won't have anywhere to hide. Over the ocean."

Jason hesitated. "What if it decides to go for a swim?"

"Then it drowns. Its gills have long since dried out."

"That's right, they have. Hmm." Jason went over all of it in his head. At least on paper, it worked. He turned to Phil, despising him, distrusting him, and yet . . . "When do you want to do this?"

"Like I said, the air will be nice and cool first thing in the morning."

Jason nodded. "First thing in the morning, then."

CHAPTER 83

"IT'S EXACTLY where we thought it would be." Craig nodded confidently to Jason as a blinking dot shot across the radar sweep.

"Good." Jason stood. "I'll go see where Darryl is." Jason marched outside and reached the parking lot just as Darryl hopped out of the Vertol. "You set it up?"

Darryl nodded. "It's ready to go." He'd just removed the *Expedition*'s seldom-used deck-mounted harpoon gun, then anchored it to the floor of the mammoth Vertol. Jason peered in at the weapon. Though technically a harpoon gun, it looked like something off a battleship: a six-foot-tall piece of curved steel the size of a harp that fired harpoons with speeds just shy of guided missiles. Darryl would use it when the moment was right.

Jason pointed. "Looks like they're ready too."

Craig, Lisa, and Phil walked toward them, each carrying two "drip torches," devices with big black handles and long spouts that look like enormous metal coffee thermoses. They don't carry coffee. They are heavy-duty, fifteen-gauge aluminum canisters that transport a diesel/gasoline mixture that tiny igniters light to literally "drip" a fire. They are standard issue for fire rangers.

As the three walked closer, Phil eyed the man who refused to even look at him. "Jason, you'll come with me?" The plan was to drive to

different locations, then set multiple fires simultaneously and surround the creature with flames.

"No. I'll go with Darryl and Lisa. Craig will go with you."

"Oh, OK." Phil couldn't fight the quiet rage in Jason's eyes. He
checked his watch. "We'll light up in exactly . . . fifteen minutes."

Then they entered the SUVs and drove off.

"JASON AND Lisa are sure getting along, huh, Craig?"

Walking rapidly in the forest, Craig didn't answer Phil Martino. As
much as Phil seemed to be trying legitimately to help out now, his betrayal was repugnant and unforgivable. "Where do we set the first fire,
Phil?"

"You go to that dried-up fern patch over there." The area was the
size of a typical front lawn, waist height. "I'll start with these dead rhododendrons." It was a massive growth, all brown.

Drip torches in hand, they walked in separate directions, then began spilling fiery little drops of fuel. Small flames ignited and grew
shockingly fast, from a few inches, to one foot, to ten feet. Craig worried they were in the process of starting a wildfire, but Phil Martino
remained calm. He'd done it all a million times before—or a dozen
times anyway—and this was perfect. They moved quickly, lighting up
everything.

They didn't notice what was in the trees.

SEVERAL HUNDRED feet high, the creature watched them. On top of
a branch as big around as a boardroom table, its wings draping over
the sides, the Demonray suddenly smelled scents it never had before.
It felt something too, just the slightest tinge of it: heat.

The predator focused on Craig, trying to understand what he was
doing.

HEAD DOWN, Craig Summers continued to drop little fireballs everywhere. In minutes, he ignited 1,200 feet of terrain. The fire was already ferociously hot, many flames taller than three stories. Suddenly
Craig spotted movement out of the corner of his eye. Something big
and white near the treetops. A cloud of smoke? He didn't have time to

dawdle. They had to start the next fire. They sealed up the torches and hustled back to the SUV.

Nothing followed them. The creature was already somewhere else.

GLIDING BELOW the treetops in another part of the forest, the Demonray felt better. There was no hot air here, nor strange smells. Just redwoods, green foliage, and soil.

But then, as it continued, the predator detected the heat again. Only now, it was coming from another direction. In fact, the heat seemed to be coming from all sides.

MONITORING ANOTHER blaze from Redwood Inlet's embankment, Jason, Lisa, and Darryl watched the flames burn higher, already several stories up and hot as all hell.

Suddenly they noticed movement on the ground. Three dozen squirrels skittered out of the forest and down the embankment.

Jason's eyes narrowed, watching the rodents go. "This might actually work."

Lisa nodded. "It really might."

Darryl said nothing. But as Jason glanced at him, he saw he was watching the squirrels too. And he was smiling.

CHAPTER 84

"**Y**OU GUYS see anything over there, Craig?" At the controls of the huge Vertol, Darryl waited a moment when his headset crackled a response.

"Nothing at all here."

Darryl turned to Jason, next to him in the passenger seat. "They got nothing too."

Jason eyed the yellow Sikorsky, about a quarter of a mile away. "Should we spread out to cover more area?"

Darryl looked down at the massive plumes of black smoke wafting up from the treetops a thousand feet below. "We're fine here. That thing will come out sooner or later."

Jason suddenly jerked his head down. "Did you see that, Darryl?"

Darryl was stunned. "Yeah, I did."

Lisa jolted forward from the bench in back. "Where is it?"

Jason pointed. "Right there." It was the area between two of the tallest treetops, a few soccer fields apart and belching big puffs of black smoke. "It just popped up then zoomed right back in."

"Craig." Darryl adjusted his headset. "Did you guys see that over there?"

Craig and Phil were still leaning forward in their seats, staring at the same smoke-filled gap. "Do we go down after it or keep waiting?"

"Ask Phil how hot it is down there."

Craig relayed to his passenger. "How hot is it?"

Martino pulled some binoculars to his face. "Well . . . It looks like all the flames have burned themselves out by now, so it's probably just really cooking down there."

"What temperature?"

"A hundred fifty, maybe a hundred sixty degrees."

"Jesus Christ. Darryl, it could be as hot as a hundred and sixty degrees down there."

Darryl turned to Jason. "Up to a hundred and sixty degrees."

"Wow." Jason eyed the smoldering treetops. "I can't imagine it surviving that."

"Want to take a look and make sure?"

Jason looked down again. "Let's let it fry a little. If it doesn't come back out in thirty minutes, we'll go down after it."

THIRTY MINUTES later, the creature hadn't returned. There was just thick black smoke—everywhere, the clouds now so big that they were even larger than the trees.

Jason exhaled then turned to Darryl. "Let's get down there."

Darryl fingered a lever with his left hand and the jungle-green bird descended, dropping toward a gap in the trees the size of a college football stadium. Suddenly black smoke was swirling everywhere. It was impossible to see, but Darryl Hollis didn't blink. He descended through the blackness when the smoke abruptly cleared and they entered an eerie, charred world.

Seconds after the Vertol landed, Craig touched down in the Sikorsky. "Thanks a lot, Craig," Phil said happily.

Summers was stone. "No problem."

Phil yanked open the door, and suddenly the pilot felt like he might faint. He'd never felt such heat in his entire life. It was absolutely overwhelming. The door closed, and the Sikorsky immediately began rising. While the others searched the forest Craig would stand watch above. As he ascended back into the smoke his last sight was of the four of them sprinting into the superheated smoldering lair. He wondered what they'd find.

CHAPTER 85

EVERYTHING WAS black. The redwoods. The plants. The soil. Even the air. What had once been lively green ferns and big-leafed rhododendrons were now crumpled black skeletons and piles of soot. The redwoods were singed with forty-foot-high black streaks that smelled like charcoal.

And then there was the heat. The heat was fantastic, unlike anything any of them had ever experienced before, hotter than wearing a ski jacket in a sauna. The heat was just phenomenal.

Dripping sweat, Darryl ignored the temperature and ran right into the superheated gloom, his big bow slung over his shoulder.

"Form a circle."

They did, then slowly walked forward. The entire forest seemed to be smoldering.

At the rear of the circle, Jason saw there wasn't any fog at all in the treetops, just wispy black smoke and pieces of blue sky. His view leveled. If the predator was still alive, it would have no place to hide here. So where would it be? On the ground? Or up high, where it was cooler? He followed a massive black trunk into the air and realized the Demonray would blend in perfectly with the tree's new color. He saw nothing unusual. His gaze leveled, sweat pouring down with every step.

After fifteen minutes, they reached the base of a steep hill, its incline like that of a staircase. The hill was filled with more of the same—charcoal-streaked redwoods, twisted plant skeletons, and smoldering superheated black air. Darryl led them up. "Stay alert here."

Ten minutes later, they reached the top, and Jason felt like he was going to collapse. The heat was just stifling. But he knew as hot as it was for him, it was even hotter for the thick-skinned creature. He looked skyward, the cocktail of black smoke and streaky sunlight searing his eyes. The animal *had to be* up high. But he didn't see anything unusual, just more streaked trunks and dulled rays of blackened sunshine.

"Anybody notice anything different here?" Darryl asked.

Bathed in sweat and miserable, Lisa turned. "Like what?"

"Like a temperature change." Darryl studied the smoldering surroundings suspiciously. "It's a little cooler here. You feel it, Jason?"

"No."

"Phil?"

"No, but I saw in a file that this is one of the coolest spots in the forest."

"Is that right?"

Phil nodded. "Apparently there's a natural draft from the ocean."

Darryl eyed a distant pile of debris directly ahead. "Jason."

"Yeah."

"How well does this thing sense temperature gradients?"

"Possibly very well."

Darryl walked forward, stopping abruptly after a hundred feet. "Anybody smell something?"

Lisa wiped her forehead. "Like what?"

"Jesus. Like that." It was right on the blackened soil, a carpet of black skin the size of a pool cover, spread out in uneven folds.

Jason crouched to touch it. He couldn't believe it. He could barely lift it. It was thicker than his wrist, and it was only skin. And hot as hell, like burning rubber. He let go to avoid burning his hand.

"Shedding its skin like a goddamn snake." Darryl looked around. "Think it's still alive now, Jason?"

"I'm starting to wonder."

Darryl turned back to the massive pile he'd been eyeing earlier, still directly ahead. "Get back in the circle."

They walked forward, and Darryl just stared at the pile. There was something unusual about it. Since they'd been here, he'd seen hundreds of such piles, most just burned plant skeletons fallen on top of one another, a fern here, a rhododendron there, usually collapsed and strangely shaped.

But this pile was different. It didn't look like burned plants—not exactly. The top portion did, with bent and twisted forms that allowed Darryl to see the sun-dappled smoke rising on the other side of it. But the middle and lower portions looked *solid*. Was something else there? Darryl wasn't sure. He walked toward it.

THE HEAT was excruciating, unbearable, unfathomable. The predator couldn't take it anymore. And yet it had to. The prey was very close now. Like the rest of its body, its eyes were covered by the scorching pile of debris it had plunged into. It couldn't see them but it knew they were coming closer.

It remained perfectly still.

Then something moved. A tiny patch of black soot covering the predator's closed right eye had just fallen. The animal could see them now. It just had to open its eye.

MOVEMENT. DARRYL Hollis didn't know what had moved, but something. Walking closer, he stared at the spot. It was low on the pile, maybe two feet off the dirt. He thought a loose piece of debris had fallen, nothing else. But he stared at the spot anyway. And then he noticed it.

A reflection.

From a tiny pool of darkness.

He froze.

He was looking right into a large black eye.

BEFORE LISA knew what had happened, Darryl fired eight arrows straight into the pile. Instantaneously, the entire pile moved. Suddenly streams of black ash and twisted plants were flying everywhere, and a massive leathery white underbelly coiled upward. Darryl fired five times, the arrows plunging into the white like forks into a fillet. . . .

The animal didn't seem to feel them, bodily throwing itself into the air. Wings pumping frantically, it rose fast on the diagonal, away from Darryl.

He sprinted after it. It ascended immediately, climbing nearly straight up.

He fired four times. The arrows tore through the sun-dappled blackness like torpedoes, heading straight for it. All four plunged into its back. They had no effect. The pumping form rushed higher. And then Darryl realized where it was going. To the sky and then . . .

He reacted like lightning, sprinting back in the direction they'd just come from. "Come on! Come on! Come on. . . ."

Suddenly they were tearing through the smoldering landscape. They had to get into the air to help Craig.

If they didn't, the creature could fly anywhere. They ran as fast as they possibly could.

CHAPTER 86

CRAIG SUMMERS yawned in the Sikorsky. He'd been tensed up and ready to go earlier, but as time had dragged on, his adrenaline had waned. He was exhausted from looking at black smoke. The clouds had grown considerably bigger—thicker, too—and staring into them as much as he had, his eyes hurt. His yellow chopper was facing the ocean, positioned to physically block the creature from flying inland if it actually appeared. He drummed his fingers. Nobody had called to let him know what was going on. Where the hell were they?

Suddenly he saw something within the blackness. Deep within it. He leaned forward. He wasn't sure, but something appeared to be heading toward him. What is that? Then, very slowly, it came into shape. It was the size of a small airplane, but alive. A pumping vision. A monster.

"My God."

The smoke cleared, and the predator emerged fully into the blue. It was moving fantastically fast, a flying roller coaster heading straight for Craig.

Mesmerized, he froze, just staring at it.

He didn't realize it was flying away from the ocean.

"JESUS, *COME on!*"

Darryl pounded his fist against the Vertol's ceiling. Where the hell were they?! The chopper's propeller blades were already thumping but Darryl didn't see any sign of Jason, Lisa, and Phil in the smoldering forest. They had to get up to the sky *right now*. If they didn't, Craig would be all alone up the there, and the creature could escape. He pounded his fist again. "Jesus, Jason, where are you?!"

"GET UP, Phil! Please get up!"

Jason pulled frantically on Phil's sweaty arm, trying to yank him off the ground.

"I'm trying!" Phil had just fallen and was squirming in a massive pile of slippery black ash.

Jason suddenly saw that his bootlaces were undone. He spun to Lisa. "Go! Go right now!"

"Jason, I want to wait for—"

"We're gonna lose this damn thing! Get into the air with Darryl! Go!"

Lisa sprinted away, and Jason turned back—just as Phil rapidly tied his laces.

"WHERE ARE you, Darryl?" Craig drummed his fingers tensely, the creature rocketing straight toward his hovering bird, maybe four seconds from impact. He glanced down at the black clouds tensely, but there was no sign of the Vertol. He turned back as . . .

The predator rushed closer, the black eyes looking right at Craig through the window.

He swallowed nervously.

Then his eyes hardened. He looked right back at the creature. And didn't blink. "No way in hell are you getting past me."

He accelerated straight for the animal, picking up speed like a missile, a game of chicken in the air.

The predator didn't change direction. Neither did Craig. They were going to collide. . . .

LISA SPRINTED around a tree. Darryl was standing outside the Vertol now, torrents of black ash flying everywhere, frantically waving her forward. "Let's go! Let's go's! Let's—"

She covered her eyes and ran into the black. As she got into the Vertol, they immediately started rising. Very fast, like a fighter jet at take-off. Lisa felt like she might vomit and was suddenly blinded by black smoke. Then the smoke cleared, and they shot into the blue.

Darryl turned frantically. But where was Craig? Where was the creature? He didn't see them anywhere.

CRAIG SUMMERS opened his eyes. He didn't know what had happened. He was still airborne, but where was the Demonray? He frenetically searched everywhere—left, right, down, behind, above. Where was it? He looked straight ahead. The Demonray was flying away from him, toward the ocean. Suddenly the big Vertol shot past Craig's chopper and Darryl was in his headset. "We got it now, Craig, we got it. Go get Jason and Phil."

Darryl easily caught up with the creature, nosing just a few feet behind it, driving it toward the sea. The animal already looked tired, and Darryl told himself this wasn't going to be hard at all. Then he realized who he was flying with. Lisa Barton was still breathing heavily, her white skin reddened, her hair dotted with black ash. Until now, she'd performed fantastically—bravely, admirably. But now she had to take it up a level. Perhaps ten levels.

"Soccer Mom, you're gonna have to take this helicopter's controls soon."

"Yeah, right, Darryl."

Darryl turned to her, and he didn't wink. "I'm serious. We're ending this right here, and I can't shoot while I'm flying. Get ready. You're going to take the controls."

"COME ON! Come on! Come on!" Craig watched tensely as Jason and Phil rapidly climbed the ladder he'd just sent down. When they got in, he spun back. "Get the ladder up! Switch is over there!"

They started ascending, and Phil just pulled the ladder in bodily. When he finished he noticed Jason, clearly doing anything not to look at him. "Jason! I just want you to know how sorry I am!"

Hair blowing, in the swirling wind, Jason simply turned to him. He didn't say a word. It was all in the look.

Craig suddenly spun back to them. "Close the goddamn door!"

Phil tossed the ladder aside and slammed the door closed. Then they really started moving fast.

"DARRYL'S GOT it." In the passenger seat now, Jason saw it clearly as they screamed toward the ocean: the lumbering Vertol had driven the predator out to sea. A few hundred yards offshore, the Demonray was no longer flapping but gliding back and forth in uneven lines. It looked tired, like it didn't know what it was doing, the giant jungle-green bird blocking its path back to the land. The Sikorsky sped forward. It hovered to a stop next to the Vertol when Jason glanced over and saw who was at the controls. "Is that . . . Lisa?"

IN THE back of the Vertol, Darryl leaned up front. "You OK?"

At the controls, Lisa nodded, tense but composed. "You're right. Holding it steady's not that bad. Just make sure I don't have to move it, Darryl. We'll both die in a hurry."

Darryl pulled a headset to his ear. "Craig, you see who's at the controls over here?! If that thing goes anywhere, anywhere at all, you take care of it."

"Got that."

Darryl glanced outside. "We're gonna end this now anyway."

Lisa didn't doubt it. Mounted near the door was a truly frightening-looking piece of equipment. The "harpoon gun" was taller than she was, a heavy piece of steel with two elasticized cables as thick as baseball bats and an electric motor to pull the projectile back. Lisa thought the creature was in trouble.

The headset crackled. "Want anyone to shoot from my bird, Hoss?"

Darryl paused. His equipment alone would certainly be enough to kill the predator, but why take chances? "Tell Jason to shoot. Wait for me to fire first. Over and out, Craig." He tossed the headset and put his hand on the door. "You ready for this, Soccer Mom?"

Lisa's eyes hardened. "Go ahead."

As the wind rushed in, Darryl turned forward. "You still OK?!"

"Fine! Let's get going!"

Darryl didn't need to be told twice. He moved rapidly. On the far wall were two dozen extremely dangerous-looking projectiles. Technically they were harpoons, originally designed by a Japanese weapons manufacturer to shoot whales. The projectiles were eighty pounds each, six feet long, and had tips as sharp as broken glass. Darryl lifted one, loaded it, then pressed a button. In an instant, an electric pulley similar to a crossbow's pulled the spike back until the cables were taut.

Then he aimed at the predator gliding below.

"PLEASE HOLD on to that." Jason pointed to the unwound ladder at Phil's feet. "I don't want it blowing in the wind when I open the door."

Phil quickly shoved it under his seat.

"You got it?"

"Yeah."

"Here goes. . . ." Jason opened the door, and an explosion of wind blew in. He grabbed his rifle, then, over the wind, just watched the predator gliding back and forth, laboring mightily and visibly exhausted. Jason tried to see its eyes. He only caught glimpses but thought they weren't moving, like the creature wasn't thinking. Jason saw it plainly: the Demonray was physically weak, trapped, and vulnerable. He turned as Darryl aimed a truly horrifying piece of steel right at the animal. The sharpened stake looked like it could kill an elephant. Jason knew Darryl wouldn't miss. It's over, he thought. He removed the safety from his rifle, then aimed. He waited for Darryl to fire first.

CHAPTER 87

THE STEEL stake exploded away, rocketing toward the animal like a missile.

The predator made no attempt to evade it. In its weakened condition, it simply continued gliding, completely unaware. The stake plunged three feet deep into its right side and it suddenly began jerking in violent, spasmodic contortions.

In the other chopper, Jason didn't hesitate. He checked his aim carefully. Then fired eight times. Six bullets entered the head just above the eyes and the animal continued to contort.

In the Vertol, Darryl rapidly reloaded, then aimed again. *Voom!* On a line, another stake rocketed down. The projectile plunged into the Demonray's left side, and the predator suddenly contorted even more wildly, speared symmetrically, torrents of thick red blood gusting into the wind.

The wind blowing into his face, Darryl looked down cruelly. The animal that had killed his wife was about to die itself. He reached for the next spear, but it rolled away. . . .

In the other chopper, Jason suddenly felt a tinge of worry. He hadn't taken his eye off the creature and for some reason it abruptly seemed dramatically calmer. It was as if the animal had been startled by the first shots but had quickly gotten over it. It wasn't jerking spasmodically anymore. Incredibly, with two steel harpoons sticking out of it, it was gliding evenly. Watching it, Jason realized the harpoons were piercing the deepest part of its body but not its actual wings. The two projectiles really didn't seem to be bothering it.

Then the giant head moved, and Jason got a glimpse of its eyes. His stomach turned. The eyes were alive now—and looking down at the sea. Why's it looking *down there*? The animal seemed to be eyeing the surface, studying it even.

Craig spun around. "It can't breathe down there, right?!"

Jason shook his head over the wind. "I don't think so!"

"Then what the hell's it doing?!"

"I'd say looking for a way out!!"

The Demonray suddenly darted inland, toward the forest.

Like lightning, Craig jolted the chopper lower, cutting it off— and causing Phil to kick the ladder from under his seat. They watched it glide away . . . and didn't notice the ladder fly out the open door. . . .

In the Vertol, Darryl aimed once more. Completely focused on his target, he didn't notice the other helicopter's ladder, caught in a current of wind and speeding down toward the creature. Just as he released he saw it, heading to the same exact spot on the creature as his now-speeding projectile. . . .

"What the hell is that!" Craig screamed.

He'd just spotted the ladder himself. It was coming from *his* helicopter. If the harpoon caught the ladder and creature simultaneously . . . He turned the chopper up violently but too late. The stake knifed into the ladder, simultaneously plunged into the animal, and Craig instantly felt a pull on his machine. He spun around. "Unhook the goddamn ladder!!"

Phil jumped to the ladder hook, but it was impossibly tight. "It won't unhook!"

"Then cut it! Cut it right now!"

Phil looked around over the wind. "With what?!"

Craig ripped open a compartment and two red Swiss Army knives dropped out, sliding under the seats. They all reached down to find them . . . just as the predator began flapping, *flying straight up.*

Craig bolted up, holding the knives, shoving one to Jason, the other back to Phil. "Cut the damn ladder! *Cut it right now!*"

As Jason and Phil began cutting, Craig realized the creature was gone, the ladder now *above* the helicopter. If the ladder got caught in the speeding propeller blades . . . He gunned the machine higher, craning his head to see the animal. He couldn't see it. Where the hell was it?!

It was plunging straight down. Wings pulled tight, it was *behind* the chopper, dive-bombing toward the ocean.

Jason jerked his head violently. A black shape blurred past, moving with astonishing speed. But the helicopter was still ascending. . . .

"Craig! You're going the wrong way!"

"What!" Summers couldn't hear over the wind.

"The wrong way! *You're going the wrong way!*"

But even as he screamed the words, Jason knew it was too late. If they didn't change direction instantly, the ladder would tighten and then—

Suddenly the chopper jerked onto its side.

His seat belt off, Phil almost fell out the open door. The chopper jerked again, and Phil slid straight out. With both hands, Jason grabbed him, pulling him back in.

Craig frantically pulled the levers, trying to right the machine. It was too late. The chopper turned over and entered free fall.

"Bail out!" Craig screamed, "Bail out! Bail out! Bail out!"

From under the seats, he grabbed orange parachutes, shoving two to Jason and Phil.

Phil frantically put his on, but Jason couldn't get his hand through a strap.

"Bail out! Bail out! Bail out!"

The world started spinning . . . ocean and sky, ocean and sky . . .

"Bail out! Bail out! Bail out!"

Craig couldn't undo his seat belt. Phil lunged toward him, trying to help.

Jason got his hand through the strap then felt toward the open door. Trying to focus, he watched as Phil yanked frantically on Craig's seat belt. He couldn't undo it. Jason just watched. He didn't want to leave them.

"Bail out, Jason!" Phil screamed. Then he eyed him for a brief moment. "I'm sorry."

Jason flew out the door, instantaneously plunging toward the sea. He felt along his chest, trying to find the rip cord. It wasn't there. He frantically patted his chest. He found a little tab and pulled. He was sucked up into the air.

The chopper hurtled downward, Phil frantically tugging at the seat belt. "I can get it, Craig! I can get it!" But when the seat belt unclicked, Phil suddenly realized what Craig Summers already knew. It was too late for both of them. What had been a spinning kaleidoscope of ocean and sky suddenly became all ocean. The water rushed closer incredibly fast and . . .

THE CHOPPER didn't sink immediately. Like a drowning windmill, its rotors labored mightily against the sea. It floated for several seconds, then submerged.

Jason entered the sea feetfirst, the ocean's chill hitting his skin. He quickly removed the sopping-wet parachute and floated. It was suddenly very quiet, nothing but tiny breaking waves and light wind. He looked around nervously. The creature was still alive. Somehow, he knew it, he sensed it, even if its gills had dried out, it was still alive. And it was in the water with him. He looked up as the huge Vertol descended, Darryl at the helm now, Lisa looking down from the open door, weeping.

Jason suddenly sensed something behind him. There was a loud splash. He spun around and . . . A breaking wave. He felt sick. Craig Summers and Phil Martino were gone. Perhaps the creature was too. As the Vertol's blades started flattening the water around him, he realized if the Demonray *was* somehow dead—and still harpooned to the Sikorsky—its body would be dragged to bottom of the ocean. They'd never see it again, never know for sure what had happened. . . .

He dove, kicking as hard as he could. With sun-dappled water surging past his face, he quickly knifed lower. . . . Then he saw it far below him, something very large, descending slowly toward the depths. It was the helicopter, he could make out the bright yellow. He caught up to the machine, grabbing the trailing ladder. It pulled him lower, and he guessed the depth at a hundred feet. The water was darkening. Hand over hand, he climbed lower still, and forgot about the creature. He had to get Craig and Phil, their bodies. Barely able to breathe, he reached the passenger-side door and . . . There was nothing there, both men ripped out of their seats by the impact. Craig Summers and Phil Martino were gone.

Jason let go at a hundred and thirty feet and, strangely, didn't feel like he needed to breathe. He just floated in the half-light, watching as the machine descended toward the darkness. Then the end of the ladder was pulled down and past him. One of Darryl's harpoons was attached to it. But nothing else was. The creature was still alive.

He began swimming up. They had to find the Demonray fast, and he knew exactly how.

CHAPTER 88

"I'VE GOT to get my scuba gear!"

Sopping wet and hanging from the lifeline, Jason wasn't even inside the helicopter yet. "And harpoons!" He climbed in awkwardly, collapsing on the metal floor. "And I got to get them right now."

As Lisa slammed the door closed, Darryl's face was blank. He looked down at the smashed orange parachute in the sea below. "It's still alive?"

"I realized even if its gills did dry up, it might be able to get oxygen through its spiracle."

Darryl nodded. "I'm sorry about Phil."

Jason paused, looking up. "I'm very sorry about Craig, Darryl."

"At least it's out of the trees."

"It will be back. Unless we find it first, it will be back."

"Then let's get that equipment." The chopper sped back to the land.

"A HOMING beacon?"

As the Vertol shot out of the parking lot, Jason was surprised. In the tail of the slender harpoon Darryl had just handed him was a tiny transmitter the size of a quarter. "I didn't think these high-tech gizmos were your style, Darryl."

"They're not. Didn't even know we had them; they're Craig's."

Jason turned to Lisa. "If I can shoot it, we can use the homing beacon to locate it."

Lisa nodded. She was already holding the transmitter.

As they crossed the shoreline, Darryl glanced at the distant dark mountains looming over the sea. Moments later, he hovered to a stop at the exact location where the Sikorsky had gone down, then turned back. "Sure you don't want me to do this, Jason?"

Jason zipped up his wet suit. "Then who flies the helicopter?" He grabbed his harpoons and oxygen tank and clomped toward the door. When he put his hand on it, Lisa's was already there.

"Be careful."

He kissed her, then, seconds later, jumped into the flattened seas. From below, he gave her a final thumbs-up, then ducked under a wave and disappeared.

POOR VISIBILITY, Jason thought, diving lower. With broken rays of sunshine providing the only light, tons of particles were floating everywhere. Leveling off at a hundred and ten feet, he wished he'd brought a flashlight. Scanning in every direction, he saw no sign of the creature, no sign of anything. He swam north.

The ocean appeared empty, but with the poor visibility he couldn't be sure. After ten minutes he didn't see a single fish but came upon something considerably less exotic. Garbage, apparently from a construction crew: bloated cement bags, waterlogged cardboard boxes, and a punctured inner tube. What kind of people came out to the ocean to dump this stuff? As a cloud above blocked out the sunlight, he swam forward, clutching his harpoon gun tightly. Given the poor visibility, he could literally swim right into the creature if he wasn't careful—he suddenly stopped.

There it was. Just ten feet away. Huge and black, just floating there.

It didn't seem to be aware of him, perfectly still and not looking in his direction.

Ever so gently, he kicked backward, and it made no attempt to follow him.

He swam farther away, then stopped and watched it. It didn't budge. Was something wrong with it? Was it dead?

Minutes passed, and it still didn't move.

He swam toward it.

As he got closer, he realized: it wasn't the creature at all. It was a sheet of black plastic, another piece of floating garbage. He swam past it and saw something else behind it, also large and black. More of the same? He couldn't see it clearly, so he swam closer. . . .

It was thicker than plastic. He swam closer. Much thicker.

He froze.

It was the creature. This time he was sure of it. It was bleeding heavily, Darryl's harpoons no longer inside it, no doubt jarred loose by the violent plunge into the sea. The animal didn't seem to be aware of him. It didn't move or otherwise give any indication it knew he was near. Was it hunting him?

It suddenly jolted.

But then it didn't move. It had just repositioned itself.

Jason didn't understand. What was it doing? Why wasn't it swimming for the land?

The water lightened, and it turned right for him.

He didn't move, tried not even to breathe.

The Demonray held still—just twenty-five feet away.

Then the sun lightened further, and it swam toward him.

He kicked backward as hard as he could.

Like a bird in molasses, it just swam closer. Twenty feet away.

He positioned his harpoon, but it caught on his wet suit.

Fifteen feet.

He got it loose. . . .

Ten feet.

Aimed . . .

The creature suddenly froze.

He didn't fire. Breathing rapidly, he drifted lower and watched it, trying to understand. Why had it stopped? Was it afraid of the harpoon? Or were its sensory organs malfunctioning, perhaps in shock from the sudden environment change?

Watching it, Jason slowly glanced up and realized it was dark again, the sun gone.

Suddenly he understood. The animal was having problems with its vision. Its eyes hadn't readjusted to the seawater and it was using the sun to see.

The light returned. As if flipped by a switch, the creature swam straight for him.

He kicked hard, swimming back and down, getting out of its path. The creature made no attempt to follow him. Like a slow-moving children's ride, it continued straight ahead. And suddenly Jason saw what the Demonray was doing. It wasn't just using the sun to see, it was following it. It somehow knew the sun's position in the sky and was *following it to get back to the land.*

Jason drifted lower, raising the harpoon again. The creature was about to swim directly above him. . . .

It slowly did, wings pumping, engulfing him in shadows. He aimed at its heart, his finger easing down on the trigger. . . . *Whoosh!* The harpoon hurtled through the water and plunged right into the white underbelly.

There was no reaction. Literally none. The predator continued as if nothing had happened.

Jason watched in amazement as it faded into the watery distance and disappeared.

Very soon it would reach the land. Not if he could help it. He swam up rapidly. They had to get there first.

CHAPTER 89

"IT'S FOLLOWING the sun." Jason slammed the door closed. "It's following the sun to get back to the land."

Lisa raised a transmitter the size of a deck of cards, beeping slowly and steadily. "So I gather."

"Jason." Darryl pointed his finger at the sun. "If you're right, look what it's heading to." On a line, he lowered his finger . . . to the southern tip of the looming black mountains.

"So we just follow it?" Lisa asked, looking down at the rolling sea.

Jason eyed her beeping transmitter. "Follow it and listen."

THE CHOPPER inched forward at a snail's pace. Half an hour later, the beeping still slow and steady, the machine was just fifty feet away from the mountains, suddenly draped in their shadows. "It's gotta start coming up." Darryl turned back to Jason urgently. "Get ready."

Like magic, the beeping became faster.

Jason grabbed his rifle, opened the door, and looked down at the dark sea, trying to spot the creature.

The beeping grew faster still.

He aimed at the waves, trying to see it.

The beeping quickened again.

He swept his rifle across the waves, waiting.

The beeping quickened once more. Then stopped.

Jason paused, staring at the dark water. "Where is it? What happened?"

Lisa eyed the transmitter. "Is this thing still working?"

Darryl shook his head. "Let me see it." She handed it to him, and he carefully looked it over. "It's fine." He turned back to the ocean. What the hell had happened? He scanned the waves with eagle eyes. There was no sign of the predator anywhere.

"It was rising toward us, wasn't it?" Lisa eyed the mountains directly ahead. "That's solid rock, right?"

Darryl hesitated. "Wait a second. There might be caves in there." He'd forgotten, but Phil had mentioned it while going through the park's papers on prescribed burns. A vast network of caves had existed in the area for as long as the redwoods. Apparently they'd been made unstable during the California Gold Rush in the late 1840s and never become a tourist attraction for safety reasons. Then something else occurred to Darryl. "*A cave. That* could be the conduit it used to get to the land in the first place."

Jason suddenly felt sick. "And now it's trying to do it again. Darryl, we better get to the land side of these right now."

"Jesus, you're right. . . ." The big helicopter rose straight up, shot out of the shadows, and whipped over the mountains on the other side. They prayed they weren't too late.

CHAPTER 90

"I DON'T see it anywhere." The helicopter sped over the mountain range, peaks and valleys of black rock without any vegetation at all. Next to Darryl in the passenger seat, Lisa had binoculars to her face. "No sign of it at all. There sure are a lot of caves, though."

Darryl glanced down. "It's gotta be inside one. We're gonna have to go in after it."

Lisa swallowed nervously.

In the back and ignoring this conversation, Jason saw they were rapidly approaching a familiar cornfield.

"Look at how much bigger the caves are getting, Jason," Lisa advised from the front.

Jason peered out the other side. The caves were getting big indeed, some the size of one-car garages, others much larger. Regardless of size, the mountain was dotted with them.

Darryl sneered down. "That thing's here somewhere; I can smell it." He spotted a plateau the size of a soccer field and descended toward it.

Caves, Jason thought anew. Caves had no light at all and were the closest thing on land to the depths. As they touched down, he decided Darryl had to be right. The predator was here.

"No DAMN flares in this thing?" Stomping around in the back of the chopper, Darryl was frustrated. Their mission here was pointless if they couldn't see. He needed flares. He ripped open another compartment. Nothing.

Outside on the sunny black rock, Jason and Lisa searched the chopper's outer compartments, opening and closing one little door after another.

Lisa moved with particular speed. Nothing. Nothing. Nothing. "Oh, here we go."

Near the rear propeller, the compartment was the size of a car's trunk, holding half a dozen boxes of flares. Opening one, Lisa saw they were gold sticks the size of large hot dogs.

"Perfect." Darryl grabbed one from behind her. "These are long-burning ones, too." The standard safety flare burned bright red and lasted half an hour, but these burned gold and lasted for ninety minutes. Darryl grabbed a few boxes. He'd started to close the door when he noticed something else. Another box labeled NITROGLYCERIN-BASED DYNAMITE. He opened it. Inside were a dozen brick-size objects encased in black plastic. Darryl turned one over, and slid open a small compartment, revealing six tiny red switches, like a mini–fuse box.

"What do you have there?" Jason walked over.

"Explosives. Used the same type in the army. I think the loggers around here must use 'em to loosen up jams on the rivers." The explosives' active ingredient was ammonia gelatin dynamite, often used for blasts in quarries and mines. Ammonia gelatin has many beneficial features, like excellent water resistance and high blasting efficiency; also, unlike most nitroglycerin-based explosives, it can be detonated by remote control. But where were the remotes? Darryl quickly found them, two little silver things, each with a single red button that read USE ONLY WITH EXTREME CAUTION.

Jason shook his head. "Bad idea, Darryl."

"Why?"

"You said these caves are unstable."

"Exactly why these could be very useful." He eyed the surrounding bluffs, dotted with holes everywhere. "This mountain's one big piece of Swiss cheese, Jason. There could be tunnels everywhere in there."

"So?"

"So tunnels mean escape routes. That thing could go anywhere." He raised a black brick. "But with these, we can cut off every avenue. So it won't have a goddamn place to hide."

Jason turned to Lisa. This logic was hard to fight.

Darryl started grabbing things. "We gotta move before that thing finds its way out of there. . . ."

They quickly grabbed explosives, remotes, flares, and weapons. They'd started to walk when Darryl paused and looked around. "One way or another, this thing's gonna end here."

From a pocket, Lisa removed the once-beeping transmitter, now silent. "Which way do you want to start?"

Darryl gave the device a dirty look. Then he turned north. "The biggest caves were this way."

AT THE end of the plateau, they reached a towering sheer rock face that offered only one way to continue: through an extremely narrow crevice, barely the width of a human body. They squeezed in, leaving the hot sun, and became enshrouded in crisp, cool shadows. They began climbing an incline steeper than a San Francisco street. After several hundred feet, the terrain abruptly leveled, and they emerged into an open stretch of black rock, brightly lit by the sun, as long as a highway and dotted with caves.

They walked to the first cave, about three stories high and as wide as a one-car garage.

Darryl peered in suspiciously. "What do you think?"

Jason eyed the perimeter. "I think it couldn't fit."

"Maybe it's stuck, then."

"Let's see. . . ." Lisa raised the transmitter.

She waited for a moment.

The tiny device was silent.

Darryl ignored the little contraption and stared into the darkness. "I don't think it's here."

They continued. A dozen more caves in twenty minutes. All were too small or produced nothing from the transmitter.

As they walked to the next one, Jason again marveled at the redwood forest beyond the cornfield. What a view.

Then he felt the dank chill on his back. He turned. "Now, this is big enough." Jason couldn't believe the size of it. The hole was monstrous, eight or ten stories high and wider than a three-lane tunnel.

Lisa didn't know why, but the space made her nervous.

They walked toward it when the mountains above blocked out the sun, swallowing them in deep dark shadows.

Darryl just studied the space, saying nothing.

Lisa raised the transmitter.

The device was silent, no sound at all over the light wind. She shrugged at Jason. "Go to the next one?"

Jason nodded, and the two of them continued.

Darryl didn't budge. "It's here."

Lisa and Jason returned. She raised the transmitter again and again, it didn't make a sound. But then she took a single step forward, and it beeped. One time. Then went silent again.

Darryl turned to it curiously. "How do ya like that."

Jason eyed the darkened space nervously. How do you like that indeed.

"I'LL GO."

Jason shook his head at Darryl. "No, we all go."

"We can't all go."

"Why not?"

"It's putting all our eggs in one basket. You see how many tunnels there are here, so there could be fifty ways out of this rock. If all of us go in here and it comes out somewhere else . . ." Darryl shook his head. "And even if this is the only way out, if it gets past whoever goes in . . . Someone's gotta stay out here to guard against that. I nominate you two. Unless you want to go in instead of me."

Jason and Lisa suddenly looked pale.

"Didn't think so."

Jason cleared his throat. "Darryl, if you go in by yourself, and it really does get past you, we're supposed to stop it with *this*?" He raised his rifle.

"No." Darryl raised a black brick. "With this."

Jason eyed him skeptically. "What do you mean?"

"If these caves are as unstable as they say . . ." Darryl studied the ceiling and walls. "A few of these will take this tunnel right down. Here, I'll set 'em up. . . ." Darryl put his bow on the rock and trotted right in, removing five black bricks. He flipped a series of switches, then carefully placed them in strategic locations: on jagged shelves in the walls and two in the middle of the rock floor. Then he trotted back out and handed the remote to Lisa. "Just press the red button."

Jason shook his head. "Some plan."

"It's a backup, and we won't have to use it. On Monique and Craig's lives, that thing's not coming outta here." Darryl eyed the remote in Lisa's hand. "And if you press that button, neither will I."

Lisa swallowed, then flipped a cover over the button and carefully pocketed the remote.

Darryl started to walk in. "OK, I'll see ya—" He stopped, noticing the walkie-talkie in Jason's hand. "Let me borrow that. I'll call you when it's done."

Jason handed it to him, and Lisa raised the transmitter. "Want this, too?"

Darryl gave the device a dirty look. He rarely discussed it, but he was superstitious. The transmitter had beeped a moment before and he was worried it was a sign. "All right, give it to me." He grabbed it angrily, felt for the arrows in the rear pouch of his hunting vest, then slowly entered the dark space. "See ya soon."

Watching him go, neither said it, but Jason and Lisa both wondered if they'd ever see Darryl Hollis again.

CHAPTER 91

THE LIGHT disappeared and so did the wind. In less than a minute, Darryl Hollis was enshrouded in a silent, blackened void. Walking forward, he strained his eyes, trying to see something, *anything*. But the darkness was absolute. He wondered what his own senses would have been like if *he* had evolved in a place like this. Would he be able to see now? Could anything? Could the creature?

He removed a flare. A brief snapping sound echoed everywhere. And then there was light. The flare shot out a long stream of sparkling yellow, and Darryl held it in front of him, astonished at how long the tunnel was. He couldn't see the end of it. He glanced up, barely able to see the dirt-brown ceiling, the same ugly rock as the walls. It wasn't a romantic place to die, was it? He tossed the flare on the rock and saw that it created a small halo. Maybe I'm an angel, Darryl thought cruelly.

He walked forward, snapped another flare, and dropped it. He repeated this every hundred feet. He walked for nearly a quarter mile when the transmitter beeped again. Not a single pulse, but a series of them, slow and steady, separated by three-second gaps.

He paused, looking around. He saw nothing unusual. Without

snapping another flare, he walked forward, and the darkness slowly returned. He continued for a hundred feet when the air abruptly cooled and the pulses' echoes changed. He knew he'd entered a larger space. He snapped the next flare.

"My God."

The cavern was gargantuan, the size of a football stadium. Darryl squinted in the dim light, wondering if his eyes were fooling him. But no. He whipped a flare straight up. Gold sparks flying, the flare toppled end over end. It rose a hundred feet, not even close to the ceiling, before falling back down. He snapped a dozen more flares and whipped them in every direction.

With more light, he studied the space anew. The cavern was an enormous circle, lined with twenty other tunnel mouths, all apparently identical to the one he'd just entered through. He dropped five flares at his feet, a marker to find the right tunnel on the way out.

His awe of the vast arena evaporated. The beeping continued. The Demonray was close. He walked to the nearest tunnel, to his left left, and peered in. The tunnel was long, dark, and cavernous. He considered smashing the transmitter in his hand. Instead, he raised it to the tunnel and listened. The beeping didn't change. One pulse, three seconds of silence, a small echo, then the next pulse. He walked to the next tunnel, and again, the beeping continued as before. Five more tunnels responded identically.

But at the tunnel directly across from where he'd first entered, the beeping picked up by a half second. He gazed into the void. "Fee, fi, fo, fum."

Then, feeling for his bow, he entered it.

LIKE THE others, this tunnel was dark, dank, and seemingly endless. Dropping one flare after another, Darryl descended deeper and deeper, the beeping maintaining its slow, steady pace. He wondered if this very passage was where the creature had first entered from the sea. He froze. Or was it *that one*? He stood at the mouth of yet another tunnel, an offshoot. He raised the transmitter, and the beeping was unchanged, slow and steady. He ignored the offshoot and walked on, faster now, dropping flares every hundred feet. Then he reached a fork, and the tunnel split in two.

He went to the left side, and the beeping increased ever so slightly. He eyed the looming dark void. This was where the predator was hiding.

He walked to the right side and the beeping slowed. Then he heard another sound. The ocean, ever so faintly. This side was an escape route. Not if Darryl could help it. He removed several explosives and carefully positioned them in the walls and floor. He checked and rechecked that they were properly set, then trotted away and removed the remote.

He eyed the little red button for a moment, then pressed it.

The explosion was like an earthquake. The ground literally shook, and suddenly boulders the size of swimming pools were falling everywhere, from the walls, the ceiling . . . In seconds, there was silence except for the faint trickling of falling pebbles.

Darryl lifted himself off the rock floor. Through thick plumes of dust he saw it, the passageway, completely caved in now, the sounds of the sea gone. He returned to the left fork, and again, the transmitter picked up its pace, the beeps now a second and a half apart. He removed two more explosives and placed them on the center of the floor. Another precaution, just in case. He snapped the next flare and walked forward.

Ten flares later, the beeping increased.

He stopped, studying the tunnel, looking for any sign of the creature.

There was nothing, just a long dank hole.

He continued walking, faster now.

The beeping increased again, markedly so.

He still didn't see the predator.

He walked even faster.

The beeping increased further.

He looked around, twisting in every direction. He didn't see the animal anywhere.

He walked faster still.

The beeping increased further, the pulses separated by milliseconds.

He jogged.

Suddenly he froze. It was directly in front of him, something huge and looming.

He couldn't make it out entirely. He threw a flare at it.

The flare bounced backward.

He loaded an arrow and walked forward, the beeping almost droning.

And then, amid a burst of sparkling gold light, it came into view. A solid rock wall. The end of the tunnel.

He noticed something in front of it. In the far-right corner, just lying there. He stepped toward it and the beeping became a steady drone.

It wasn't the creature.

It was a bloodied harpoon with a homing beacon inside it. Somehow the animal had pulled it out.

"Son of a bitch!"

Darryl hurled the transmitter to the floor, smashing it to pieces.

In an instant, there was pure silence—almost. The only sound was from the softly hissing flares, illuminating the tunnel behind him like streetlamps on a foggy road.

Then there was a second sound. Off in the distance. Flapping.

It was so far away, Darryl couldn't even see it yet. But he knew. The predator was coming for him.

He breathed, calmly, evenly. A war was about to start. Darryl Hollis was ready for it.

CHAPTER 92

THE POWER of the roar was extraordinary. It erupted without warning, shattering the silence and echoing everywhere.

Darryl didn't flinch. He couldn't see the Demonray yet—it was just a faint outline in the distance—but hearing its roar only made him want to kill it more. He marched forward. "Come on, you ugly mother."

Surging forward, the animal gradually became visible, gliding higher than Darryl had expected, halfway between the floor and ceiling. He halted and fired. Eight times. In rapid succession, the arrows exploded away at different heights.

The creature veered down sharply. Three arrows missed, but five were direct hits to the face. They had no effect. The predator continued, ten feet high, neither slowing down nor speeding up, simply maintaining its pace.

Darryl paused. He'd hit it, he was sure of it, numerous times, but the animal hadn't roared, shuddered, slowed down, or sped up. Nothing. It simply hadn't reacted. He didn't care. He could almost make out the blacks of its eyes.

He strode forward and fired again. Ten times.

All ten were direct hits, plunging nearly a foot deep into the head and body.

The Demonray continued gliding.

Reaching back for the next arrow, Darryl noticed the flares, moving ever so slightly, apparently tossed by gusts of wind. The predator was no longer gliding. It flapped its wings, suddenly moving faster.

Darryl strode forward and fired six times.

They all missed. The flapping form suddenly climbed to the very top of the hundred-foot ceiling then plunged down, rocketing just above the floor. The increase in speed was fantastic. Moving with tremendous momentum, it hurtled straight for Darryl. . . .

He fired twice more. On a line, two projectiles penetrated the creature's face.

The Demonray sped closer, three hundred feet away, two hundred . . .

Darryl reached for something in his breast pocket.

The creature rushed in, one hundred feet, fifty feet . . .

Darryl didn't budge. He just removed whatever was in his pocket. . . .

The creature rocketed in, thirty feet, ten feet, the mouth opening, the teeth zooming in. . . .

Suddenly Darryl dove to the rock, simultaneously thrusting a knife up with both hands. As the enormous body hurtled overhead, he dug a ten-foot, gaping slash into the white canopy. A powerful stabbing pain shot through his upper arm. As the body surged over him, he saw his shirt was suddenly soaked through with blood, his left shoulder almost gone.

The predator glided unevenly toward the dead-end wall, a small river of blood gushing from its underside. It suddenly veered away from the wall, then banked and landed with a loud, thwacking thud.

Darryl just looked at it, perfectly still, three dozen arrows blanketing its body like a pincushion. Its eyes were still open, looking right back at him over the sparkling golden light. Then he heard it, wheezing, struggling to breathe.

Darryl had to finish it. He painfully raised his arm to get the next arrow. He walked toward it, halted, then . . . *Voom!* He fired a speeding projectile into its face, just below the left eye.

The Demonray didn't move. Didn't flinch.

"My God." Darryl couldn't believe it. It was like it hadn't felt it, like the animal *literally hadn't felt the arrow enter its body.* Jason had said its brain had a minuscule pain center but this . . . Darryl reached back for the next arrow. There weren't any.

He painfully raised his knife. "I'm gonna carve you up good." Feeling the blade's heft, he marched toward it, praying it didn't have anything left.

As he got closer, it didn't move.

He jogged

It still didn't move.

He sprinted.

Suddenly the predator lifted its front half into the air and let out a shattering roar.

Darryl froze, just watching it, the taut muscles on the bloody white underside, the huge head, the teeth flickering in the dim light.

Then the mouth snapped shut like a trap, and there was perfect silence. The great body just stood there, slightly more than six feet high.

Then, very slowly, the head turned, and the black eyes, as cold and rational as ever, focused on Darryl anew.

"Jesus." Darryl stepped backward. The animal still had something left. It still had a lot left.

He eyed the tiny knife in his hand. He had to get away; he had to get away immediately. He turned and sprinted.

The creature threw itself into the air. And landed on the rock. Its wings weren't working. The eyes shifted, barely able to see Darryl now. Then they slowly closed.

Sprinting awkwardly, his shoulder in agony, Darryl glanced back. He thought the predator had just closed its eyes, but he didn't care. He'd blow the explosives he'd left on the tunnel's floor and trap it. He ran as hard as he could. He was halfway there.

The body flinched. Then the eyes blinked and opened, focusing on Darryl anew. They could see him now. The animal coiled its front half off the rock, pushed off, and, like a wobbly airplane, rose on the diagonal.

Darryl turned back. The creature was flying again. Out of control, but flying. Clutching his knife, he ran as hard as he could. The explosives were a few hundred feet away. He could make it.

The predator veered back and forth, its rippling muscles out of sync. Then it smacked into a wall and seemed to right itself. It flew straight. It pumped its wings and suddenly surged ahead.

Darryl turned back and couldn't believe it. The predator was really moving now.

He turned forward. The explosives were less than a hundred feet away. He could make it; he knew he could make it.

The animal flew faster, closing rapidly.

Darryl ran for dear life, chest heaving, arms pumping. The knife slipped from his hand. He just ran. The explosives were fifty feet away. Then forty, thirty, ten . . .

He ran past them and stopped at the fork.

The Demonray hurtled closer, ripping over the halos of light, seconds from the bombs.

Darryl reached for the remote.

It wasn't there.

He frantically patted his pockets.

He found a lump, removed it, and positioned his finger over the button.

The speeding animal looked right at him and let out a deafening roar.

Darryl stared right back at it. "Yell all ya want. You're done." He pressed the button.

Nothing happened.

He pressed the button frantically. Nothing.

The predator sped forward, refocusing on its prey.

Darryl sprinted away. As he rounded a corner, he focused on the offshoot tunnel he'd ignored earlier, praying it had a place to hide. He ran in. . . .

Banking around the corner like a fighter jet, the animal focused on the offshoot tunnel. . . .

Darryl ran hard, looking for someplace, anyplace. He froze. It was another dead end, a solid rock wall. He turned back as the creature rocketed in. . . .

Darryl scanned the wall frantically. There had to be an opening, a crevice, something. There was nothing, just solid rock.

The predator rushed closer, dipping slightly, eyes locked, mouth opening.

Darryl backed against the wall.

The animal sped closer, dipping, a few feet above the rock.

Darryl braced himself.

The predator dipped farther, inches above the floor, a hundred feet away.

Darryl raised his fists.

The Demonray dipped again, suddenly *on* the rock, sliding very fast, like a train on ice. It skidded for a hundred feet and stopped a yard from Darryl's boots.

His back against the wall, Darryl just stared at it.

The predator didn't budge. It just lay there, eyes open, looking right at him.

He slid off the wall.

It didn't move.

He held his breath and listened to it. There wasn't a sound. The body wasn't rising and falling anymore. He noticed the eyes again. They were still looking straight at the wall.

He stepped toward it.

It didn't move.

He stepped again.

It still didn't move.

He kicked it in the head.

No movement of any kind. The Demonray was dead.

Darryl fell hard to the floor and laughed his head off. "Just like I planned it."

CHAPTER 93

"YOU TWO still awake out there?"

Lisa and Jason shared a stunned look. Darryl Hollis's voice had just crackled from the little walkie-talkie, glinting slightly in the late-afternoon sun.

Jason fumbled to grab it off the rock. "Darryl?"

"Better get in here fast."

"Why?"

"You wanna see this thing before rigor mortis sets in?"

Jason couldn't believe it. "My God, you killed it? You *actually* killed it?"

"I thought you could trust people now."

A smile. "How do we find you?"

"Just follow the light."

I MUST have banged my damn knee somehow, Darryl thought, staggering into the central cavern. With the burning flares lighting the way, he lumbered into the middle of the giant space and lay down, wondering how much blood he'd lost. He was tired. He'd lost his wife, his best friend; he was so very tired.

Minutes later, he heard Jason's stunned voice.

"My God, look at the size of this place."

Lisa looked around, marveling. "Wow."

"Impressive, huh?"

They turned, trying to see him in the flickering space. Darryl Hollis was invisible.

"Where are you?" Jason called out.

"Over here. In the middle."

Lisa pointed. "There."

They trotted over to him.

Jason looked down at him and smiled. "You did it. My God, you really did it."

Darryl nodded sadly on the floor. "Monique and Craig deserved it. So did Phil."

"They all deserved it."

Lisa noticed Darryl's soaked shirt and crouched. "Are you OK?"

He leaned back painfully on the rock. "Fine, Soccer Mom."

She moved in to examine him. "Holy cow, your shoulder. We better get you a doctor."

"Did Monique get a doctor?" Darryl turned to Jason. "Better start calling you Charlie Darwin from now on, huh?"

Jason shook his head, noticing a pair of explosives and a remote on the rock. "Leftovers?"

"Souvenirs. Take 'em."

Jason did, then looked around the vast cavern. "So you really killed it?"

"Body's over there. Just follow the flares."

Jason paused. "Will you be all right?"

"Go. You too, Lisa."

She looked uncomfortable, even sick. "Darryl, I really think you need to see a—"

"I'll see one later, OK? I just need some rest now." He exhaled painfully and lay back.

Lisa nodded to Jason, and they followed the flares. Into one tunnel, then the offshoot.

From a distance, they saw it in front of the dead-end wall, something huge and dark, facing away from them. It didn't move, but as they walked closer, in the sparkling golden light, Lisa wondered if somehow it was still alive. She stopped walking, but Jason continued until he was just a few feet away. He saw the animal wasn't breathing. It had to be dead, and yet . . . He reached down to poke it. Then jolted back.

"Jesus!" Lisa jolted, too. "What's wrong?"

"Its skin's still warm."

Lisa stepped backward. "What's that mean?"

Jason paused. "Nothing. Its blood's still settling." Of course. Darryl had just killed it.

Jason poked it again. It didn't more. He walked to the predator's front. The eyes were wide open, as cold and black as ever but somehow devoid of life now. He surveyed the rest of it. Darryl's arrows were sticking out from *everywhere*—left wing, right wing, the middle, the head, the horns, the face. "You want to see it?"

Lisa looked around in the sputtering light. "No."

Jason turned back to it and started thinking like a scientist again. Darryl was right. Rigor mortis *would* set in. He had to do an autopsy, fast—within the next twenty-four hours. Which meant they had to get the body into a lab and . . . "How are we going to get it out of here?"

"What?"

"How are we going to move this thing?"

"I have no idea. For Christ's sake, Jason, let's get Darryl to a doctor first."

"You think he'll be OK?"

"I don't know, but his health's a little more important than doing a damn autopsy. I'm going to check on him. . . ." She walked away angrily, and Jason followed. She was exactly right. The autopsy could wait.

"My God, Darryl, are you really OK?"

Lisa stood over him again, eyeing the blood-soaked shirt over his missing shoulder.

He looked up at her sadly. There were tears in his eyes, and he tried to smile through them. "I'll be fine, Soccer Mom."

Tears formed in Lisa's eyes too. Darryl Hollis was anything but fine, and she knew it had nothing to do with his shoulder. "I'm so very sorry, Darryl."

He nodded sadly when . . . "Can we get a truck up here somehow?!"

Darryl chuckled. "Doesn't waste any time, does he?"

Lisa shook her head. "No, he doesn't."

"You guys are gonna make a great couple, Lisa."

"Oh, be quiet."

"He's in love with you."

She hesitated. "Did he tell you that?"

"Didn't need to. Just like you didn't. The Big Dog sees all, Soccer Mom."

"We'd have to airlift it up, wouldn't we?!"

Genuinely amused, Darryl turned. "Airlift what up?!"

"The truck to carry that thing out of here!"

Darryl closed his eyes. "You're gonna have a lot of fun with him."

Lisa stomped toward Jason like an angry, chiding mother. "Will you take it easy, for Christ's sake?"

"What, I want to—"

"You're anxious—I get that—but can we just bask in the glory of this for like five seconds?"

"I'm a little . . . overeager?"

"Maybe just a smidge."

He looked around. "This place really is incredible, isn't it?" He picked a flare off the rock and peered into another tunnel.

Lisa looked around herself. "Honestly, Jason . . . it creeps me out a little. If you don't mind, I'd like to get out of here. . . ." Then she realized he hadn't heard her. He was in the tunnel.

"Lisa, come over here! Look at this!"

"What is it?"

He walked in farther. "I'll show you!"

She reluctantly followed. "What?"

He pointed. "Look at that."

It was dark and not easy to see, something on the middle of the floor, it looked almost like . . . "What is that?"

Jason walked closer, illuminating it with the flare: a human skeleton, bent at impossible angles, like a marionette tossed aside. "This must be where it was feeding."

Lisa suddenly felt like she was going to lose her lunch. "Jason, I want to go *right now*."

"Wait." He walked farther in. "Look at that."

It was near the wall on the right side. Another skeleton, eight feet long with a large triangular head. Jason recognized the type of animal it belonged to right away. Not long ago, they'd seen a much smaller version. "I think that's a bear."

Standing alone and growing increasingly nervous, Lisa walked forward, joining him.

Jason raised the flare, scanning the rest of the dimly lit space. "Look, there are more, looks like a couple dozen."

Lisa swallowed nervously. "Please, Jason. I really want to go now. Come on. . . ." She started to walk away, but he grabbed her hand tightly.

"What the hell is that?"

It was near one of the bear skeletons. Something small. Something moving.

Jason moved his flare toward it. It went perfectly still, trying not to be seen.

But Jason saw it. He saw it very clearly. He suddenly couldn't speak.

"What is it?" Lisa tried to see it, but he'd lowered his flare.

"Jason?" She put a hand on his shoulder. "Jesus, you're shaking. What the hell is it?"

Numb, he raised the flare.

It was larger than a seagull, probably twenty pounds. A living animal. A newborn. Perhaps the first of its kind to have been born on land. A small stealth-shaped ray. Lying on the rock near the bear skeleton, it had been teething on the bone. It was perfectly frozen now, apparently frightened.

Lisa just stared at it, trying to understand. "So that thing . . . had a baby?"

Jason looked around nervously. "It couldn't have."

"Why?"

"I just checked. The one Darryl killed was a male."

"Then that means—"

"There's a female around here."

"How could that be?"

Jason's head shifted rapidly, looking everywhere. "A pregnant female must have followed the first one out of the water. And if there's one, there should be a bunch. From everything we know, this order of animal spawns in large groups, so—" His head froze. "Jesus." Five more of the tiny animals were lying near the far wall. He looked around nervously. "We better get out of here. We better get out of here *right now.*"

They turned and sprinted out.

CHAPTER 94

THEY HALTED at the rim of the main cavern, looking for any sign of movement. They scanned walls, tunnel mouths, the towering ceiling, everything.

Lisa thought it looked perfectly safe. "I don't see anything."

Jason nodded. "Me neither. Let's get Darryl and get out of here."

"OK."

But neither of them moved. They just turned to Darryl, in the middle of the cavern a few hundred feet away.

"Darryl," Jason said in a loud voice.

He didn't move.

"Darryl!"

He didn't flinch.

Lisa squinted, trying to see him in the dim light. "I think he might be asleep."

Jason scanned the vast space again, but all he saw was lifeless dark rock. "Let's get him and go. . . ." He started toward the center of the cavern when Lisa grabbed his elbow.

"Jason, look."

He turned as another creature, slightly larger than the one Darryl had killed, glided silently out of a tunnel, then landed on the rock floor.

He dropped his flare, staring at it.

Then a second creature emerged.

Then a third. And a fourth.

From another tunnel, one more emerged. From yet another, two more. Suddenly they were flying out of *every* tunnel, one enormous winged body after another, gliding silently and settling on the rock floor. Four dozen in total, the creatures had surrounded Darryl, still asleep and completely unaware.

But the Demonrays were ignoring Darryl Hollis, focused somewhere else. Lisa could feel them, she could actually feel their eyes watching her and Jason. Then one of them rumbled, a deep reverberating sound. The rumble continued for moment, then ceased. Then Lisa thought she saw Darryl stir, ever so slightly.

Darryl Hollis had been dreaming. For the first time in days, his subconscious had been in another place, a peaceful one. He'd been at home with Monique and their two kids, barbecuing on a nice summer day with Craig Summers. But then a sound had disturbed him. A strange sound. A dangerous sound. A sound he thought he'd never hear again his entire life. His eyes snapped open. Five of the creatures were staring right at him. They were twenty feet away.

"Jesus Christ." One side of his face flat against the dank rock, Darryl didn't move a muscle.

Another predator rumbled. Then they all rumbled, the sounds echoing like a symphony of church organs. Then, one after another, they lifted their front halves off the rock, pushed off, and flew. Within seconds, they were darting everywhere below the towering ceiling.

Darryl didn't move. His free eye shifted, just watching them and wondering how he could escape.

Seeing this, Lisa squeezed Jason's hand so tight the fingertips turned white. But Jason felt nothing. He just stared at Darryl, the Demonrays looking down at him. He'd be the first to go.

But Darryl Hollis told himself he could escape, he knew he could, he just had to make it to the nearest tunnel. A predator suddenly roared, and Darryl sat bolt upright. Then he noticed Jason and Lisa, their backs pressed against a wall on the perimeter. They were staring at him pitifully and Lisa was crying.

THE CREATURE roared again, and Darryl jolted to his feet, immediately running, awkwardly, painfully.

The predator swooped down toward him, eyes locked.

Frantic, Darryl ran hard, focused on the approaching tunnel. He could make it; he knew he could make it. He just had to—

Something was in front of the tunnel. Another creature.

He froze, looking for another way out. There wasn't one. He looked up. The horrific form hurtled down toward him. Strangely, in the instant that followed, Darryl Hollis breathed easier. The certainty of it actually calmed him. He was about to see his wife and best friend again, much sooner than he'd expected. His face hardened to stone. He wouldn't die like a coward.

The animal sped down, the open mouth rapidly growing larger. . . .

Darryl didn't flinch. His torso was pierced then slammed violently to the rock floor and devoured, just like any animal killed in the wild.

"Oh my God." Jason turned away, unable to watch.

Lisa wanted to look away but couldn't. She watched with shockingly cold eyes. There was no point in grieving for Darryl Hollis. They were next. A drop of saliva the size of a water balloon splashed in front of them, and she barely reacted. She simply exhaled.

"Jason . . . I don't want to die like Darryl did."

"What do you mean?"

She turned. "The explosives he gave you."

He looked at her. She was serious. "You sure?"

"If you're OK with it."

He swallowed nervously. Then grabbed a flare. He started to remove two black bricks from a pocket when he paused and looked at her, the sparks reflecting in her eyes. "I love you, Lisa."

She ignored everything around them. Every single thing. "I love you, too."

The predators rumbled, now jockeying for position in the air, fighting over which got first dibs.

Jason tossed the flare away and removed the explosives, holding them with both hands. "Take the remote out of my right pocket."

Lisa did and placed it on top of the bombs.

He stared into her eyes. *"You're sure?"*

The rumbles grew louder, and she swallowed. "Yes."

Suddenly three predators plunged down.

Lisa's hands started to shake, but Jason held firm, positioning a finger over the button.

The creatures hurtled closer, suddenly roaring with deafening volume. . . .

Lisa continued to shake, crying now, closing her eyes.

Out of the corner of his eye, Jason noticed a creature on the ground, jerking away from a flare, apparently afraid of it. Just like the dead one had been afraid of fire.

The creatures zoomed closer, roaring, mouths open, teeth growing larger. . . .

But then nothing happened. Lisa opened her eyes. The explosives and remote were gone, the creatures flown off. Jason was just standing there with a flare in his hand. "They're afraid of these."

Lisa didn't have time to respond.

Jason grabbed three more flares off the rock, handed her two, then yanked her toward the entrance tunnel, and they sprinted for dear life.

Lisa didn't look up. She just ran as hard as she could.

One flare in each hand, Jason couldn't believe it. The creatures weren't attacking. Gliding above, they seemed to be letting them go. The tunnel rapidly came closer, a hundred feet away, eighty feet, sixty, thirty . . .

They ran right in. The Demonrays didn't follow.

They ran and ran and ran. Jason turned back. All he saw was dark air. Nothing was following.

Lisa ran as hard as she could, legs kicking, arms pumping. She was very fast and got ahead of him.

Jason looked back again, slowing considerably. This was too easy. Something wasn't right. He looked up. Were they hanging from the ceiling? The walls? He didn't see them anywhere.

He turned forward. Lisa was much farther ahead now. Beyond her, he saw a small dot of light in the distance. The outside. He turned back. There was still nothing near, just silent, dark passageway.

Lisa ran hard. The dot of light was no dot now, but something much larger, only half a football field away. Almost there. She ran hard. She passed the explosives Darryl had put down earlier, then turned back. Without taking her eyes off Jason, she removed the remote and walked backward to the entrance.

Gasping for breath, Jason told himself he was going to make it. He turned back a final time. There was just an empty dark void. He started to turn forward. . . .

As a dozen creatures rocketed out of the darkness.

"Jesus." Lisa stepped back. They'd appeared so suddenly, filling the entire space, like water gushing into a pipe.

Jason immediately knew the animals were moving much too fast. He wasn't going to make it. Lisa had to blow the tunnel; she had to blow it *right now.*

She saw the creatures were almost on top of him. She stepped back, her finger on the button, not pressing down. Jason was so close, almost there, almost past the explosives. . . . She backed completely out of the darkness and into the light, not taking her eyes off him.

He looked back at her, and his eyes said it. I love you. *And don't wait.*

She pressed the button.

Like an earthquake, the entire mountain shook. Lisa was thrown hard to the rock as the great space fell on top of itself, massive boulders plunging with violent, loud crashes. As the rocks settled, nothing flew out of the space. Nothing walked out either.

Then she couldn't see. Thick clouds of black dust rose up. Lisa ran into them, looking everywhere. Jason was leaning against a boulder the size of an SUV. She extended a hand and they entered the clean air.

She hugged him. "It's over, my God, Jason. It's finally over."

Over the twinkling of falling pebbles, he eyed the distant sea. "You think?"

She broke the hug. "You don't?"

He eyed her cryptically. "Lisa, I think this was just the beginning."

EPILOGUE

BEYOND THE clanging glasses and chatter, Jason Aldridge and Lisa Barton stood alone on the balcony, admiring the distant sunset over the Pacific Ocean. They hadn't enjoyed a sunset in a while. After the San Diego funerals of Darryl and Monique Hollis, Craig Summers, and Phil Martino, Jason and Lisa had done nothing but prepare for this moment. And now it was finally here. Their "coming-out party." A dinner/news conference presenting them and the new order of Demonray to the entire world. A roomful of tables, each with white linen tablecloths and patterned Spode china set for ten awaited. While guests dined on rack of lamb and seared tuna, Jason and Lisa would make a full slide-show presentation. Notes, pictures, charts, and detailed commentary from Bandar Vishakeratne of Princeton and Mike Cohen of UC Berkeley would also be highlighted. Publicists had tirelessly promoted the event to every major TV station and newspaper around and, in the words of one, "hyped it to the moon." Besides the media, the guest list of 250 was a virtual who's who of the most respected ichthyologists, oceanographers, and evolutionary biologists alive. They'd come from far and wide to this tasteful oceanside reception hall in Laguna Beach, an hour south of Los Angeles. Soon they would make Jason Aldridge and Lisa Barton household names.

"Hors d'oeuvre, sir?" In a tuxedo and white gloves, an enormous eighteen-year-old, probably a football player from the local high school, held out a tray filled with tasty little morsels.

Jason peered down. "What are those?"

"Carmelized onions on crostini with Gorgonzola cheese, sir."

Jason gave the kid a look. "Pretty fancy. You pick those out?"

The kid smiled. "The catering manager, sir."

"I'm fine, thanks."

"Ma'am?"

"Oh, thank you." Lisa took one. "Mmm, delicious."

The kid went back inside, and Jason shook his head at all of it. "Swanky affair, huh?"

Lisa nodded sadly. "Craig and Darryl would have loved it."

"Yeah." Jason exhaled, sadder than he could say. Then he kissed Lisa's hand. "Look at my beautiful fiancée."

She smiled at her new one-carat diamond engagement ring. A celebrity would have laughed at its size, but Lisa Barton absolutely loved her ring. She loved the man who'd given it to her even more. "Thank you, Jason. For everything."

"Want a drink?"

"Sure."

They entered the reception area, heading toward a tiny crowded bar when—

"Excuse me. Jason, Lisa?"

They turned. And so did their stomachs. It was Harry Ackerman, as cold-eyed and even-tempered as ever. "How are you two doing?"

With several reporters in earshot, the couple just stared at him.

"What do you want?" Jason said in a loud voice meant to be over-heard.

Ackerman's pleasant demeanor evaporated. "Everything here is my property. Every last thing."

"It was nice seeing you at Darryl and Monique's funeral, Harry." This was also very loud.

Ackerman blinked. "Oh. Yes, I heard about that. I couldn't make it."

"But you didn't send chocolates either."

Ackerman started looking self-conscious. Jason was staring at him with palpable rage. He was the evening's star attraction, and several reporters were beginning to take notice.

"You also didn't make it to Craig and Phil's funerals."

Ackerman looked away, saying nothing.

"You remember Phil Martino, don't you, Harry?" Again, more volume.

The eyes remained calm. "This is my news conference."

"I said you remember Phil Martino, don't you?" The entire room was watching them now.

"Yes, I remember him." People Ackerman didn't know were starting to give him angry looks. "Everything related to the discoveries you made while working for me is my property. It's in the contracts, and I want all of it."

"You terminated the contracts and voided your rights. My attorney assured me of that."

Ackerman paused. "I didn't think attorneys were your style, Jason."

"They weren't." He glanced at Lisa. "My technical adviser suggested I get one. Take us to court if you don't like it."

"You son of a bitch. I will."

Jason almost smiled. "Will you? Because I heard you had to declare bankruptcy and are under investigation by the IRS, too. You sure you have the financial resources for a lawsuit?"

Ackerman couldn't retort. It was all true. One of his companies had defaulted on several loans he was personally liable for. To cover it, the banks had already acquired his stock and bond portfolios and were in the process of taking possession of his massive La Jolla home.

Jason thrust out a powerful hand, daring the man to shake it. "But thanks for coming by to congratulate us."

Ackerman just eyed the hand nervously. And Lisa laughed hard in his face. Others didn't know what was so funny, but they smiled. Humiliated, Ackerman stormed off.

Before Jason could put his hand down, someone else strode up and shook it. "Jason, it's great to see you." Bandar Vishakeratne looked excited. "I just flew in, but I must say these bloody appetizers are the best I've ever had." He raised a tiny plate. "This one right here, I swear to Buddha, is called 'miniature poppy-seed-and-chive

buttermilk blini with onion.' It tastes fantastic *and* it's vegetarian."
He glanced at Lisa. "Do you believe it? Even at Princeton, they don't
serve appetizers like these."

Jason and Lisa laughed heartily. Then Veesh leaned into Jason and
whispered, "All joking aside, my sincerest congratulations to you.
From the bottom of my heart, you deserve this, all of it, and I'm hon-
ored to participate."

Jason shook the hand warmly. "Thank you very much, Veesh. By
the way, have you met my colleague and fiancée, Lisa Barton?"

"Fiancée?" Veesh smiled. "It's a pleasure to meet you, Lisa. You
know, I'm sure you're very accomplished; but I must say, I think
you've landed a good one here."

Lisa chuckled. Then Veesh excused himself and the pair returned
to the balcony. It was so quiet out here, the sunset even more beautiful than it had been a moment ago.

Lisa turned to her husband-to-be. "Did I tell you how proud I am
of you?"

"Lisa, we both—we *all* did this."

"But you were our leader. You guided us. You even trusted us. You
wanted this more than anyone, and . . . I mean it: I'm proud of you."

"Thank you very much." No one had said these words to him in his
entire life.

He looked up at the sky. "Want to get liquored up after all this?"

She laughed hard. "Definitely."

He studied the horizon. The creatures in the caves were long since
dead. Hundreds of National Guard troops had descended upon the
mountains north of Redwood National Park, then dynamited every
passageway above and below the waterline. One dead specimen had
been transported to Laguna Beach for the presentation tonight. Near
the slide projector inside, the great body was covered by a nylon tarp
and being guarded by four men with neat haircuts and concealed
weapons.

As Jason stared up at the heavens, he saw none of their beauty. Despite his excitement over his and Lisa's budding fame, he'd been trou-
bled for months, speculating over what Craig Summers had once said
that night in the cabin: What if a million Demonrays made their way
to the land? Or just a few thousand? Or even ten or twenty?

"You OK?"

He turned to Lisa. "Fine."

"What's with the spooky look in your eye?"

"Nothing."

"Really opening up to your fiancée, huh?"

He didn't smile. "I'm worried, Lisa. I'm still really worried."

They'd discussed this before. "About more of them coming to land?"

"Maybe a lot more."

"You don't know that's going to happen, Jason. No one knows that's going to happen." She poked him playfully. "We're about to give the most important presentation of our lives and then we're getting married. Why don't we think happy thoughts for a little while?"

He chuckled. Happy thoughts indeed. His life was so much better than it had ever been. "I'll try to relax."

She looked at him. " You OK?"

"I'm great. I mean it. The best I've ever been."

He seemed to mean that. She checked her watch. "We better get started."

He looked up at the sky, black now, and he noticed the moon. "After you."

They walked in. And the moon watched them go. Just as it had watched them come. Unblinking, the moon was still watching. Them, every one, every thing. It was watching a seagull hundreds of miles up the California coast. In the last moments of twilight, the bird circled the rolling seas below, looking for its final meal of the day. It spotted movement and dove down. But as it plunged in, it found nothing other than a strand of kelp that it had mistaken for a fish. The gull returned to the surface and floated lazily, staring at the place where the sunset had just faded into the oblivion. Then it pushed off and flew toward the shore.

As the gull disappeared, it had no idea it had just saved its own life. Through the shimmering watery plane, the newborn Demonrays were watching it. Born to the sea, their food had disappeared again, and they were in the midst of another migration. This time their destination wasn't at sea, but on land, a place where they'd already detected massive amounts of prey. Only not seagulls and not bears, either. For the moment, they remained hungry. And perfectly still. So still they seemed like they weren't even there. And maybe, one day, they wouldn't be. Maybe nothing would. Maybe there would only be what there always had been. The rolling ocean, the blowing wind, and the moon. The moon from a never-ending sea of pure and absolute darkness, it was still watching.

ACKNOWLEDGMENTS

Thank you very much to Bob Miller, Will Schwalbe, Marly Rusoff, Leslie Wells, Jeff and Marian Freedman, Steve and Judy Katcher, and David Groff. I am truly grateful to all of you for helping make *Natural Selection* a reality. I'd also like to thank Sarah Schaffer and her colleagues in sales for their enthusiastic response to the book and for really getting behind it. Along the same lines, I am also indebted to Corinna Harmon, Jane Comins, Katie Wainwright, Jill Sansone, and Phil Rose. In particular, I'd like to thank Ellen Archer, who believed in this project from day one right through to publication.